Gasolina

CREATED BY SEAN MACKIEWICZ & NIKO WALTER

SEAN MACKIEWICZ
CREATOR, WRITER

NIKO WALTER
CREATOR, ARTIST

MAT LOPES
COLORIST

RUS WOOTON
LETTERER

ARIELLE BASICH
EDITOR

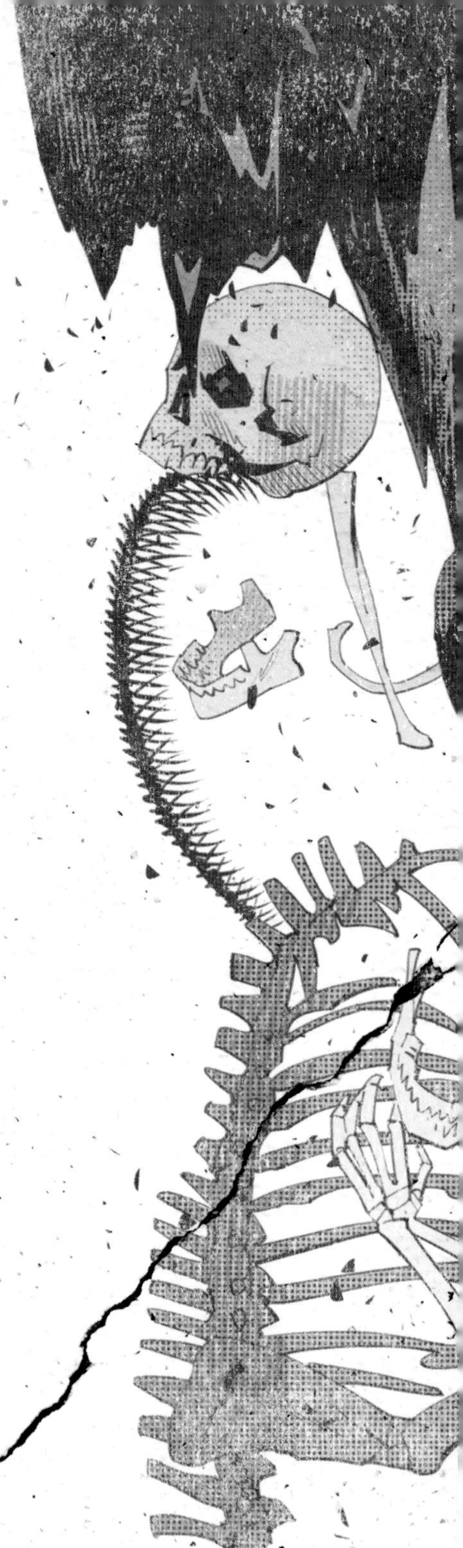

FOR SKYBOUND ENTERTAINMENT

Robert Kirkman *Chairman*
David Alpert *CEO*
Sean Mackiewicz *SVP, Editor-in-Chief*
Shawn Kirkham *SVP, Business Development*
Brian Huntington *VP, Online Content*
June Alian *Publicity Director*
Andres Juarez *Art Director*
Jon Moisan *Editor*
Arielle Basich *Associate Editor*
Carina Taylor *Production Artist*
Paul Shin *Business Development Coordinator*
Johnny O'Dell *Social Media Manager*
Sally Jacka *Skybound Retailer Relations*
Dan Petersen *Sr. Director of Operations & Events*

International Inquiries: ag@sequentialrights.com
Licensing Inquiries: contact@skybound.com

WWW.SKYBOUND.COM

IMAGE COMICS, INC.
Robert Kirkman *Chief Operating Officer*
Erik Larsen *Chief Financial Officer*
Todd McFarlane *President*
Marc Silvestri *Chief Executive Officer*
Jim Valentino *Vice-President*

Eric Stephenson *Publisher / Chief Creative Officer*
Corey Hart *Director of Sales*
Jeff Boison *Director of Publishing Planning & Book Trade Sales*
Chris Ross *Director of Digital Sales*
Jeff Stang *Director of Specialty Sales*
Kat Salazar *Director of PR & Marketing*
Drew Gill *Art Director*
Heather Doornink *Production Director*
Branwyn Bigglestone *Controller*

WWW.IMAGECOMICS.COM

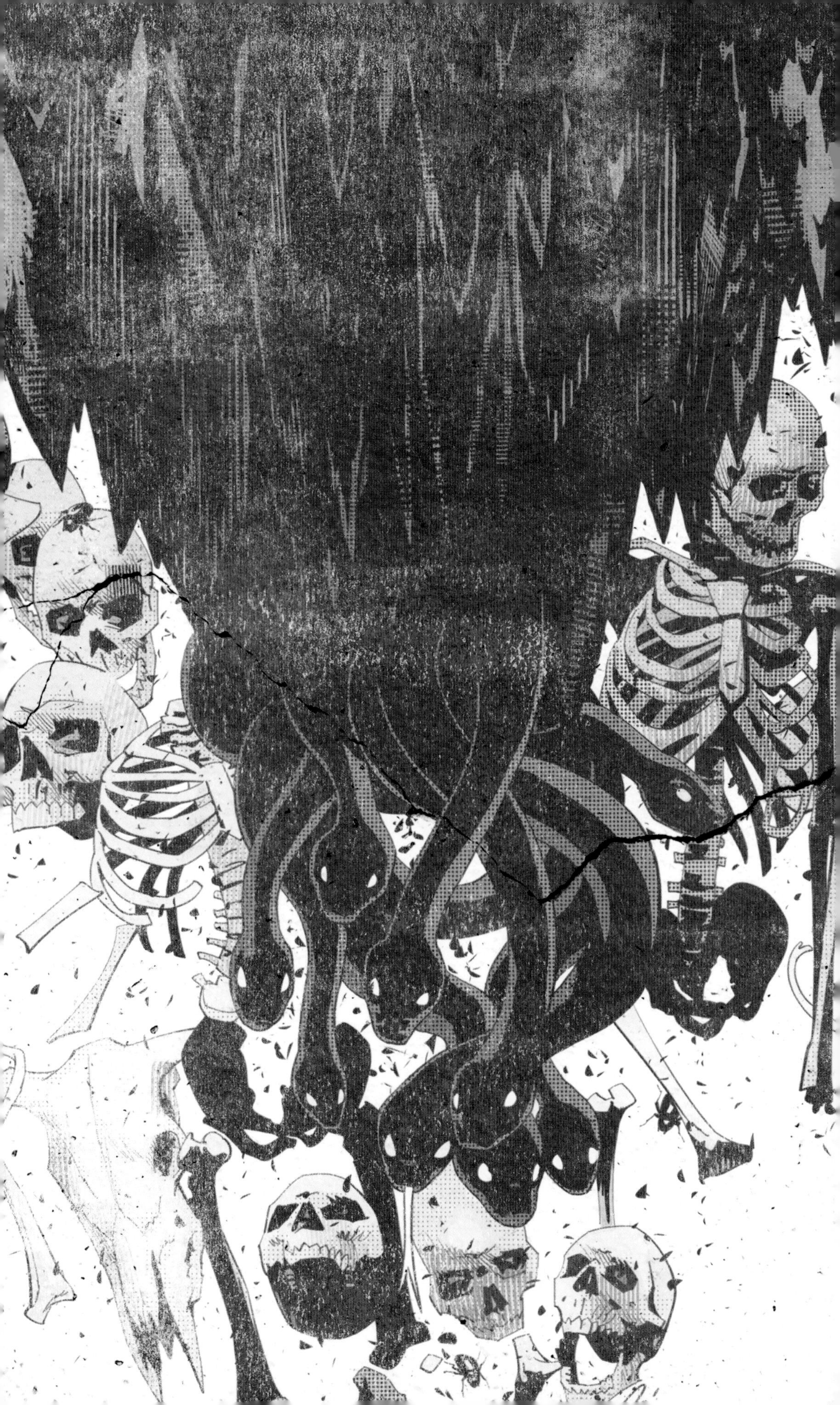

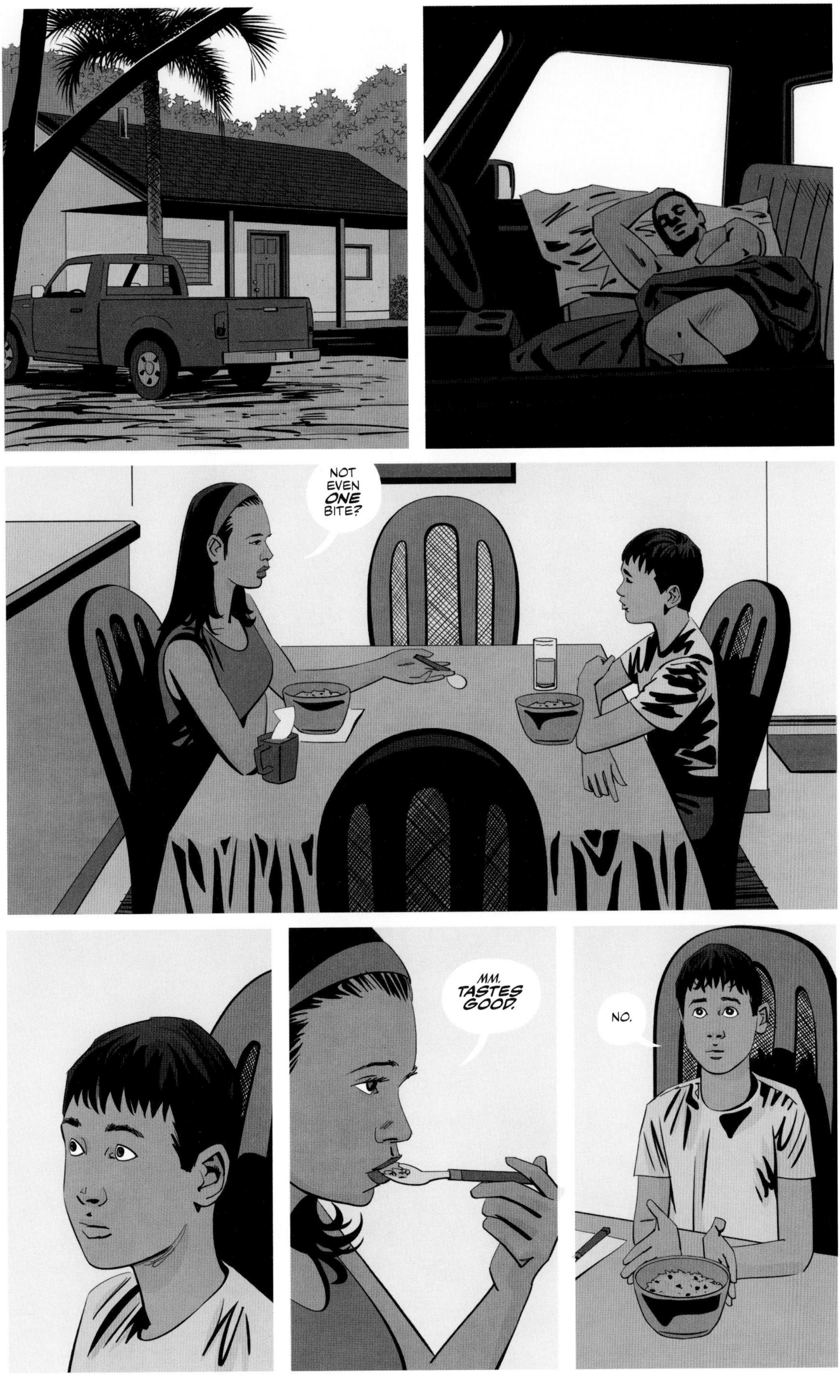
NOT EVEN ONE BITE?
MM. TASTES GOOD.
NO.

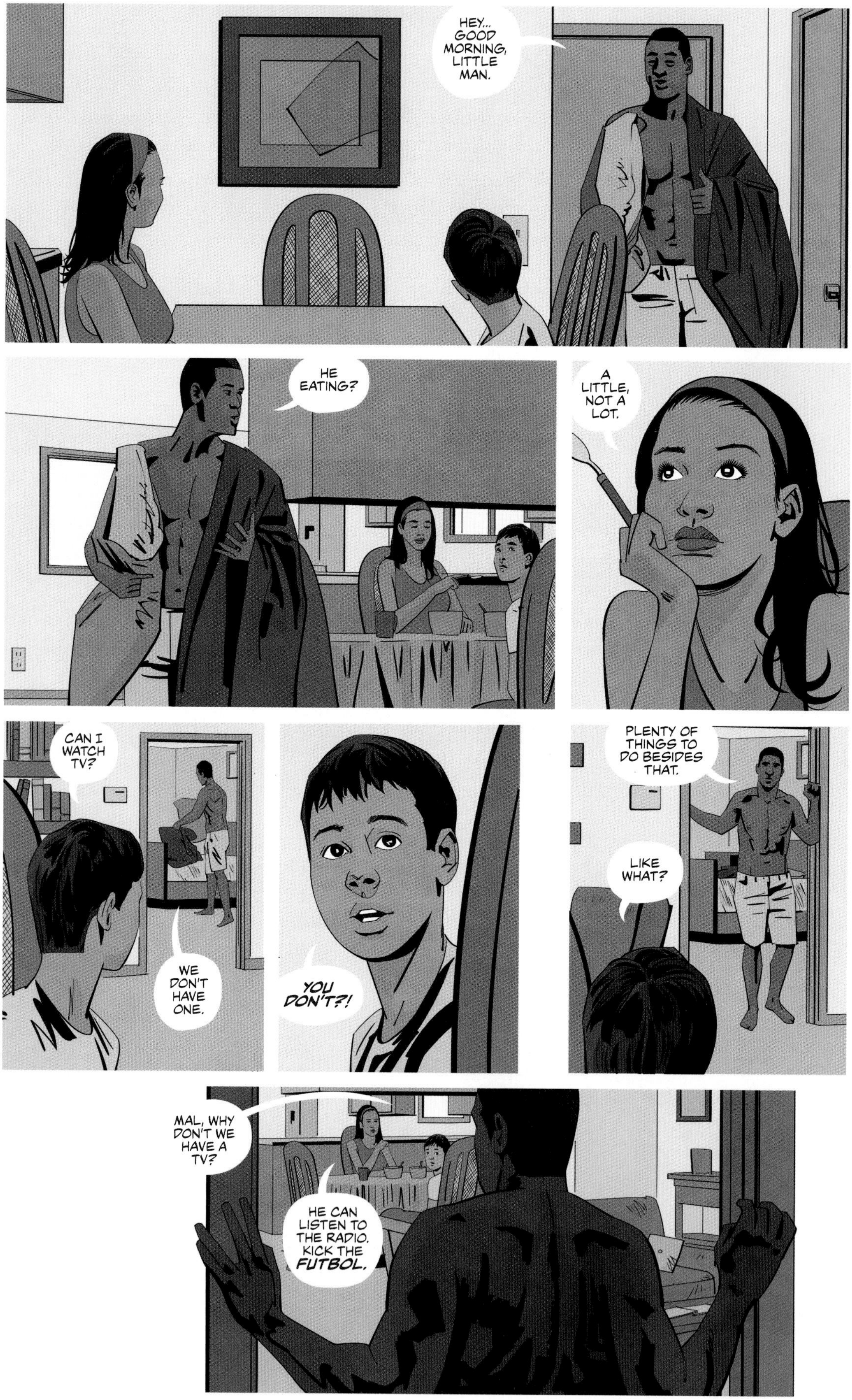
HEY... GOOD MORNING, LITTLE MAN.
HE EATING?
A LITTLE, NOT A LOT.
CAN I WATCH TV?
WE DON'T HAVE ONE.
YOU DON'T?!
PLENTY OF THINGS TO DO BESIDES THAT.
LIKE WHAT?
MAL, WHY DON'T WE HAVE A TV?
HE CAN LISTEN TO THE RADIO. KICK THE FUTBOL.

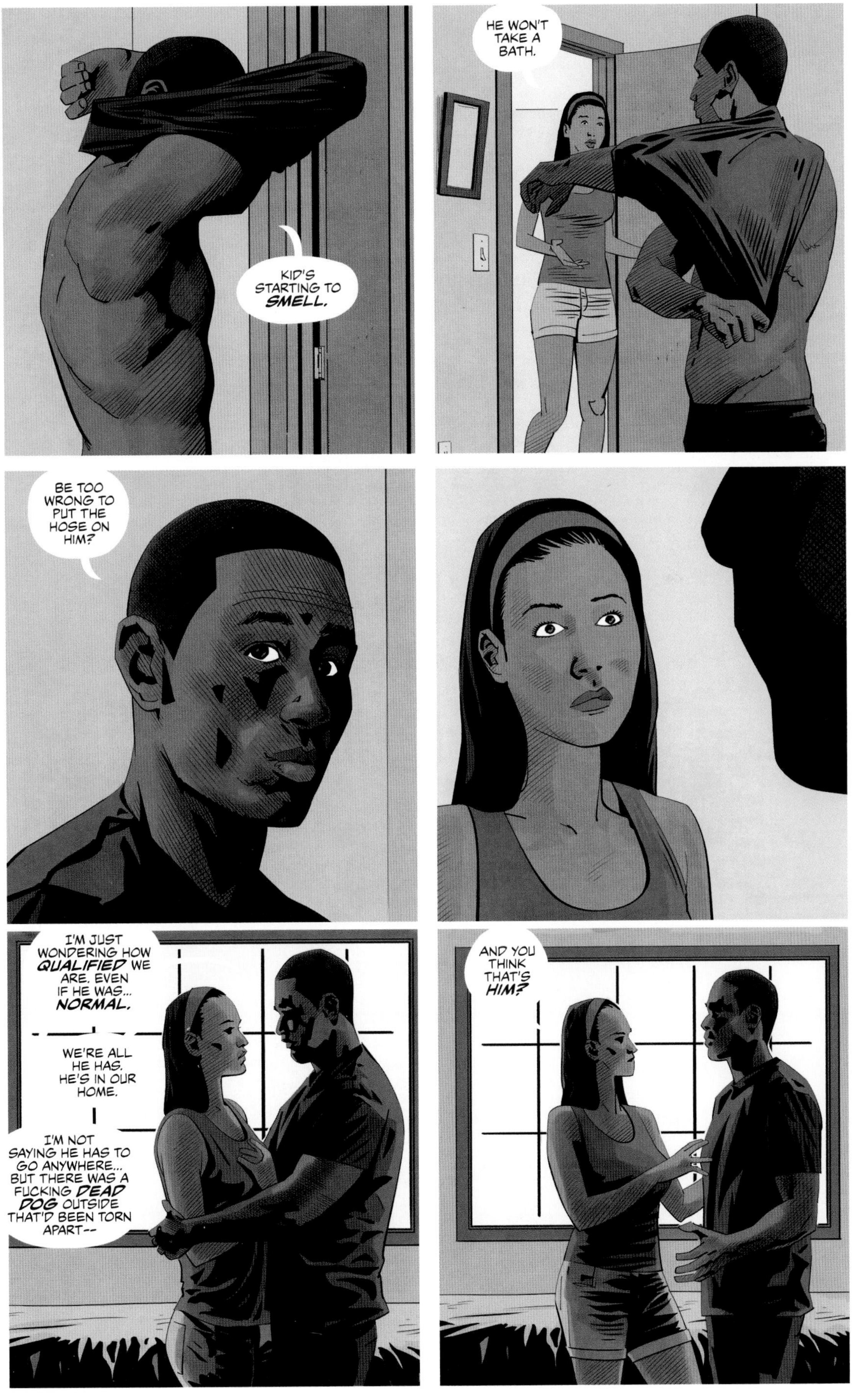
KID'S STARTING TO SMELL.
HE WON'T TAKE A BATH.
BE TOO WRONG TO PUT THE HOSE ON HIM?
I'M JUST WONDERING HOW QUALIFIED WE ARE. EVEN IF HE WAS... NORMAL.
WE'RE ALL HE HAS. HE'S IN OUR HOME.
I'M NOT SAYING HE HAS TO GO ANYWHERE... BUT THERE WAS A FUCKING DEAD DOG OUTSIDE THAT'D BEEN TORN APART--
AND YOU THINK THAT'S HIM?

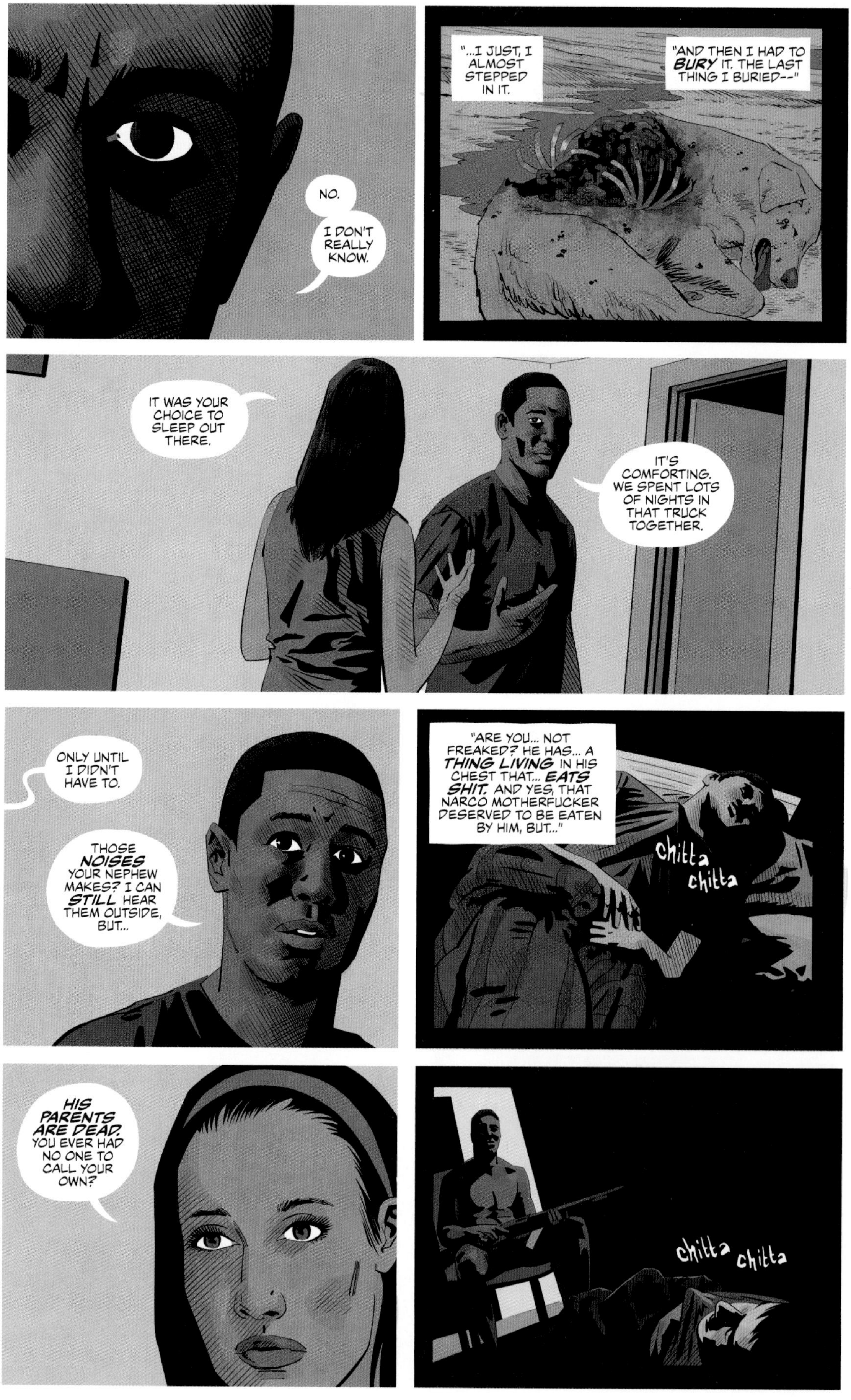
NO.
I DON'T REALLY KNOW.
"...I JUST, I ALMOST STEPPED IN IT.
"AND THEN I HAD TO BURY IT. THE LAST THING I BURIED--"
IT WAS YOUR CHOICE TO SLEEP OUT THERE.
IT'S COMFORTING. WE SPENT LOTS OF NIGHTS IN THAT TRUCK TOGETHER.
ONLY UNTIL I DIDN'T HAVE TO.
THOSE NOISES YOUR NEPHEW MAKES? I CAN STILL HEAR THEM OUTSIDE, BUT...
"ARE YOU... NOT FREAKED? HE HAS... A THING LIVING IN HIS CHEST THAT... EATS SHIT. AND YES, THAT NARCO MOTHERFUCKER DESERVED TO BE EATEN BY HIM, BUT..."
chitta chitta
HIS PARENTS ARE DEAD. YOU EVER HAD NO ONE TO CALL YOUR OWN?
chitta chitta

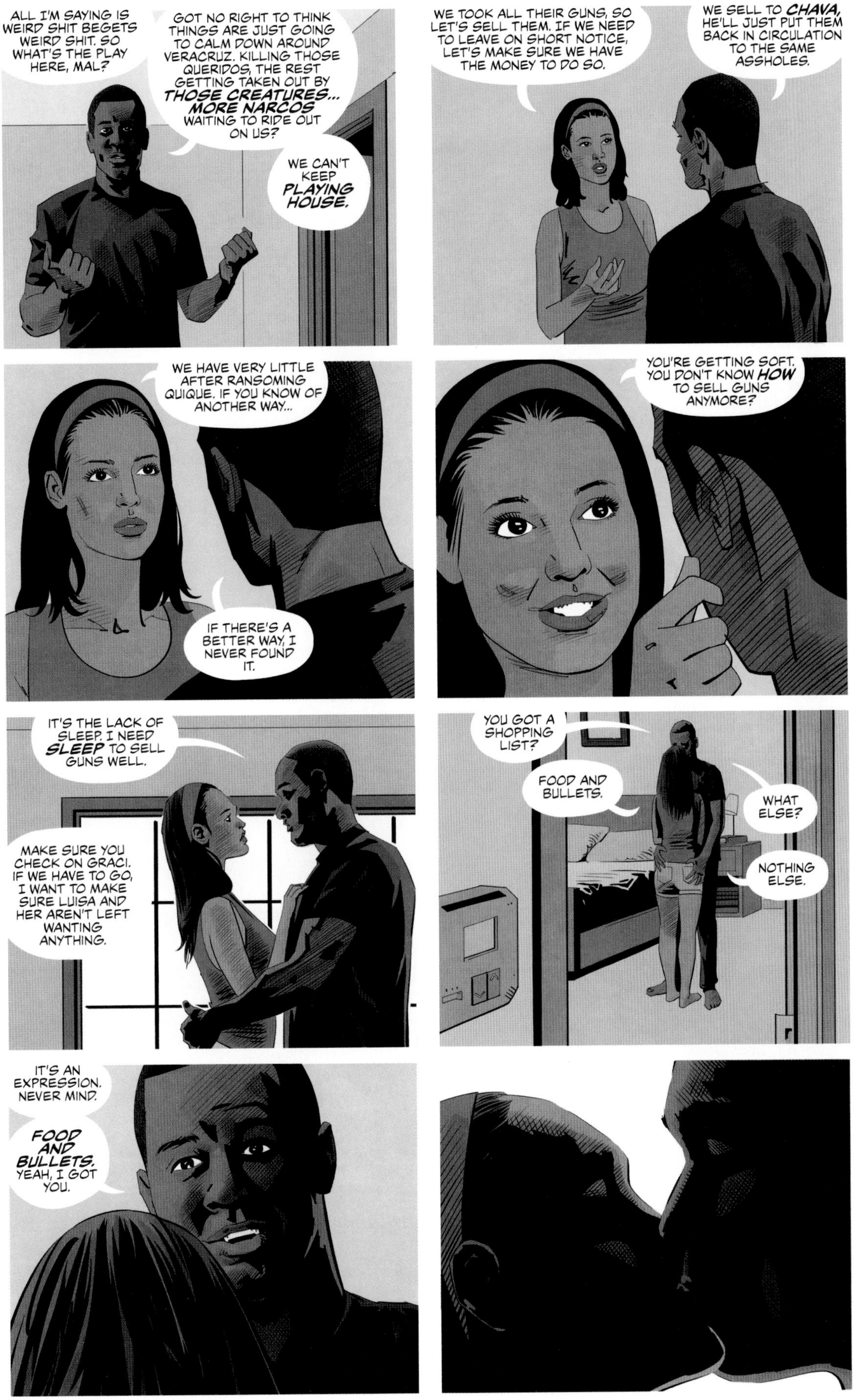
ALL I'M SAYING IS WEIRD SHIT BEGETS WEIRD SHIT. SO WHAT'S THE PLAY HERE, MAL?
GOT NO RIGHT TO THINK THINGS ARE JUST GOING TO CALM DOWN AROUND VERACRUZ. KILLING THOSE QUERIDOS, THE REST GETTING TAKEN OUT BY THOSE CREATURES... MORE NARCOS WAITING TO RIDE OUT ON US?
WE CAN'T KEEP PLAYING HOUSE.
WE TOOK ALL THEIR GUNS, SO LET'S SELL THEM. IF WE NEED TO LEAVE ON SHORT NOTICE, LET'S MAKE SURE WE HAVE THE MONEY TO DO SO.
WE SELL TO CHAVA, HE'LL JUST PUT THEM BACK IN CIRCULATION TO THE SAME ASSHOLES.
WE HAVE VERY LITTLE AFTER RANSOMING QUIQUE. IF YOU KNOW OF ANOTHER WAY...
IF THERE'S A BETTER WAY, I NEVER FOUND IT.
YOU'RE GETTING SOFT. YOU DON'T KNOW HOW TO SELL GUNS ANYMORE?
IT'S THE LACK OF SLEEP. I NEED SLEEP TO SELL GUNS WELL.
MAKE SURE YOU CHECK ON GRACI. IF WE HAVE TO GO, I WANT TO MAKE SURE LUISA AND HER AREN'T LEFT WANTING ANYTHING.
YOU GOT A SHOPPING LIST?
FOOD AND BULLETS.
WHAT ELSE?
NOTHING ELSE.
IT'S AN EXPRESSION. NEVER MIND.
FOOD AND BULLETS. YEAH, I GOT YOU.

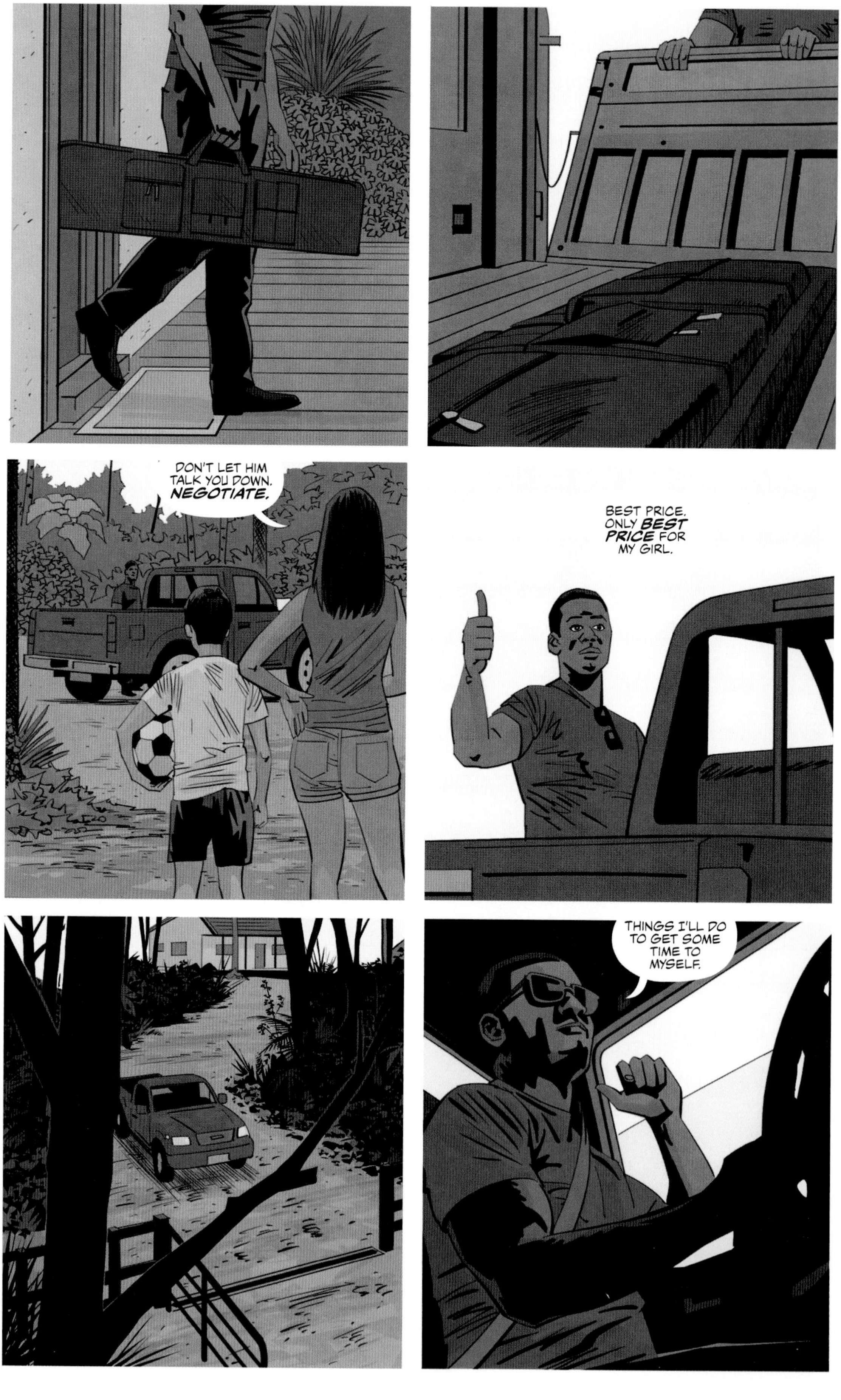
DON'T LET HIM TALK YOU DOWN. NEGOTIATE.
BEST PRICE. ONLY BEST PRICE FOR MY GIRL.
THINGS I'LL DO TO GET SOME TIME TO MYSELF.

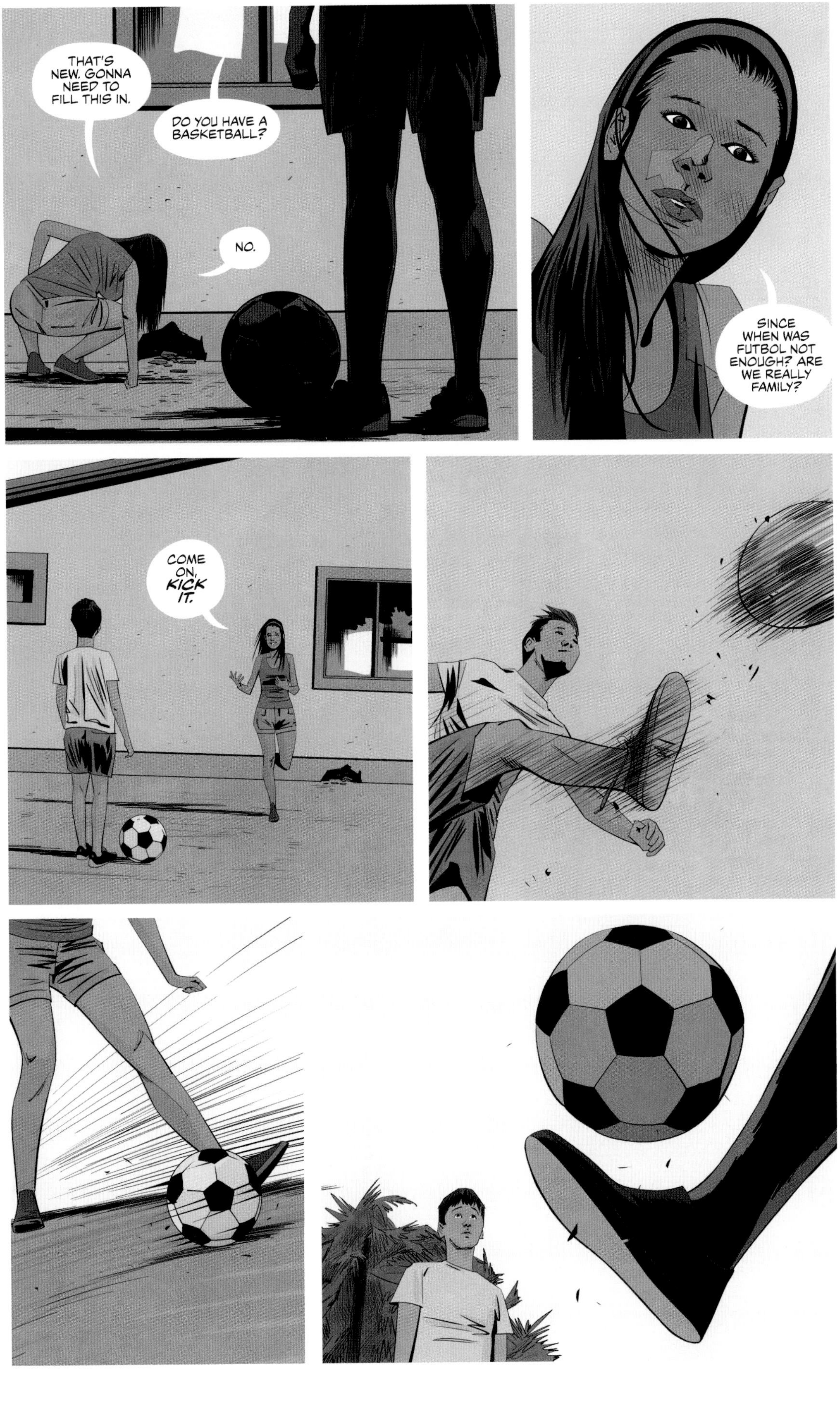
THAT'S NEW. GONNA NEED TO FILL THIS IN.
DO YOU HAVE A BASKETBALL?
NO.
SINCE WHEN WAS FUTBOL NOT ENOUGH? ARE WE REALLY FAMILY?
COME ON, KICK IT.

SURPRISED?

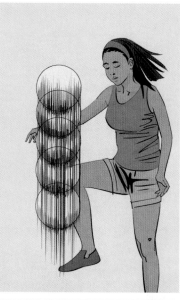

SsSSQooSHh

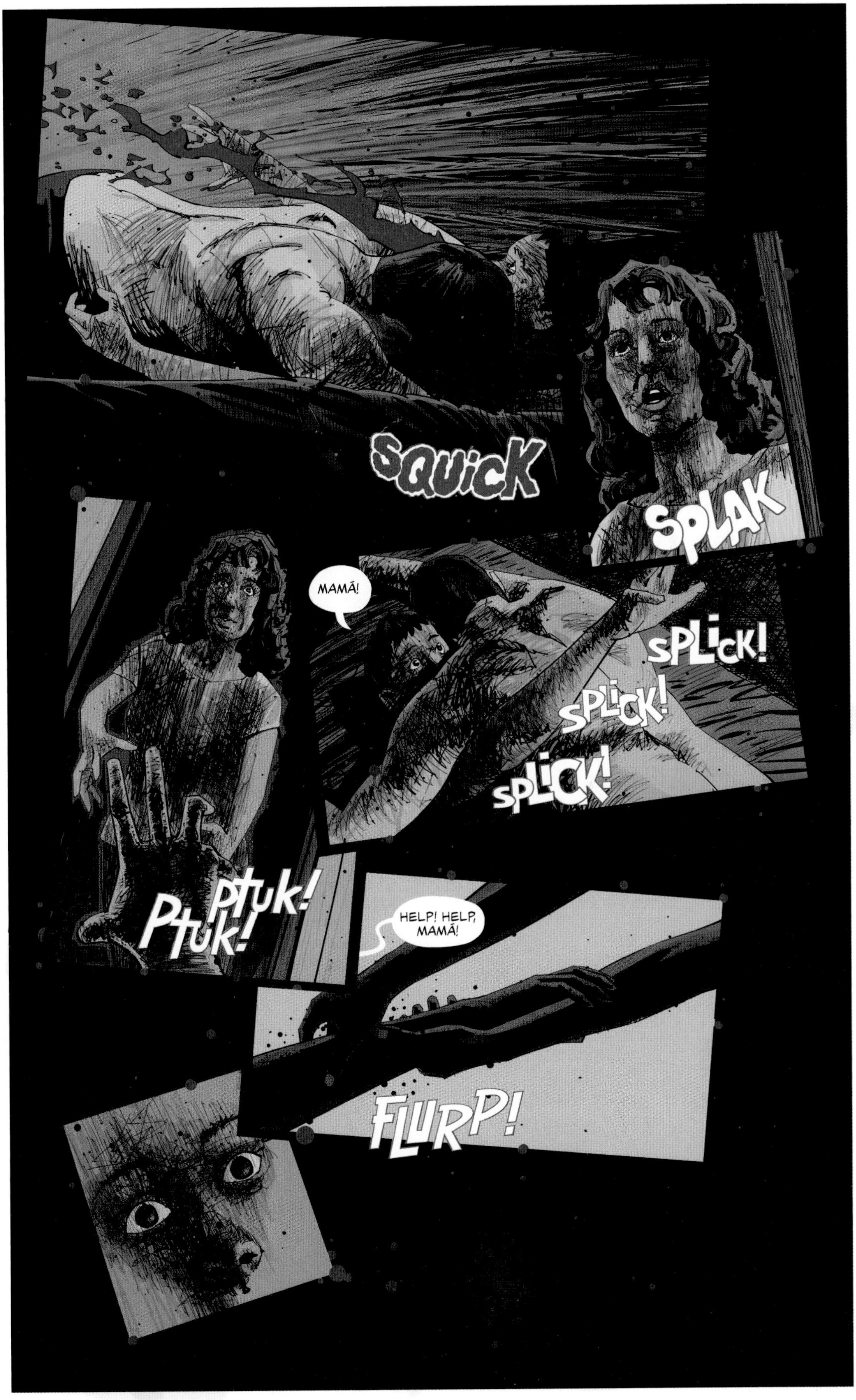
SQUICK
SPLAK
MAMÃ!
SPLICK!
SPLICK!
SPLICK!
PTUK!
PTUK!
HELP! HELP, MAMÃ!
FLURP!

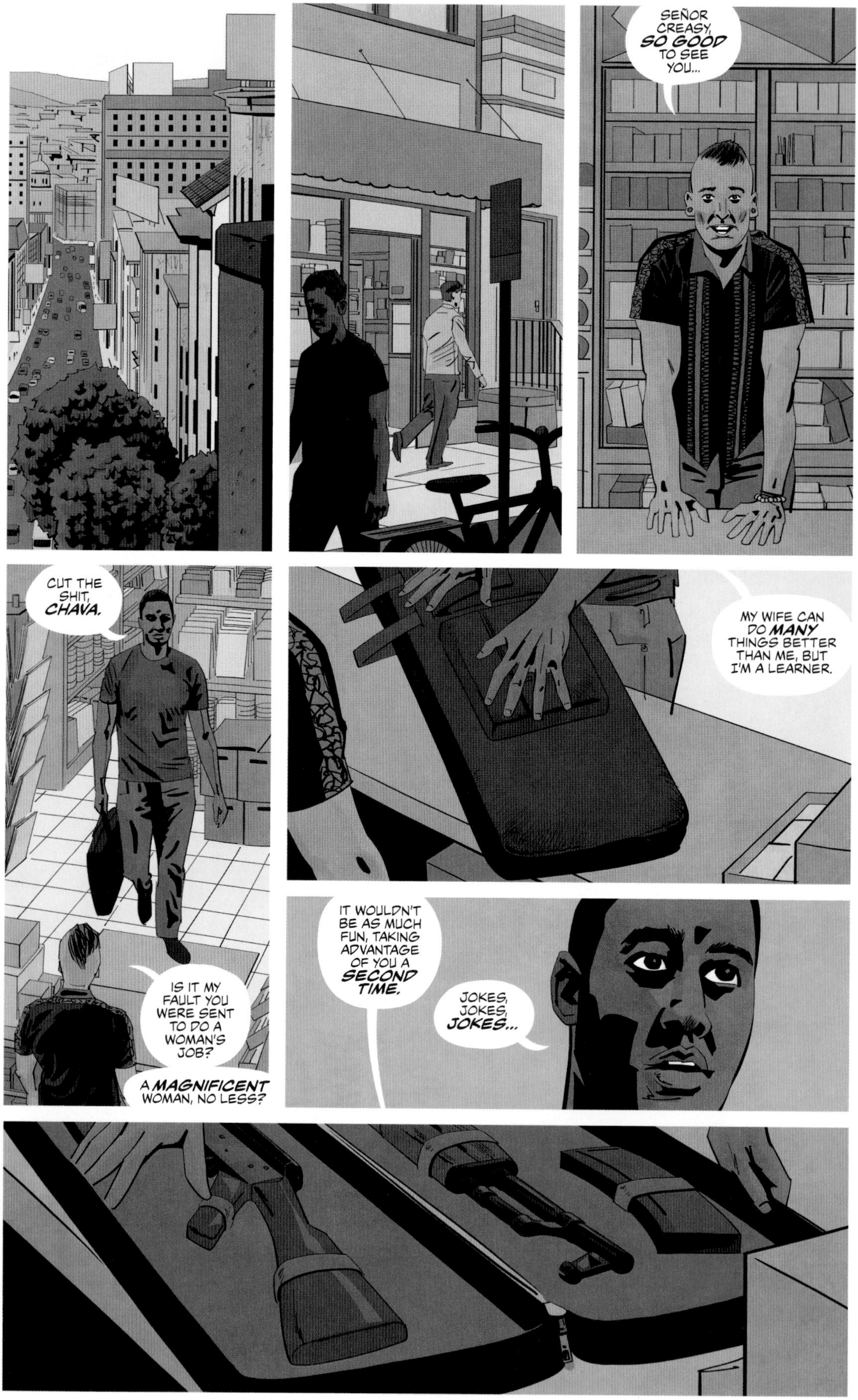
SEÑOR CREASY, SO GOOD TO SEE YOU...
CUT THE SHIT, CHAVA.
MY WIFE CAN DO MANY THINGS BETTER THAN ME, BUT I'M A LEARNER.
IS IT MY FAULT YOU WERE SENT TO DO A WOMAN'S JOB?
A MAGNIFICENT WOMAN, NO LESS?
IT WOULDN'T BE AS MUCH FUN, TAKING ADVANTAGE OF YOU A SECOND TIME.
JOKES, JOKES, JOKES...

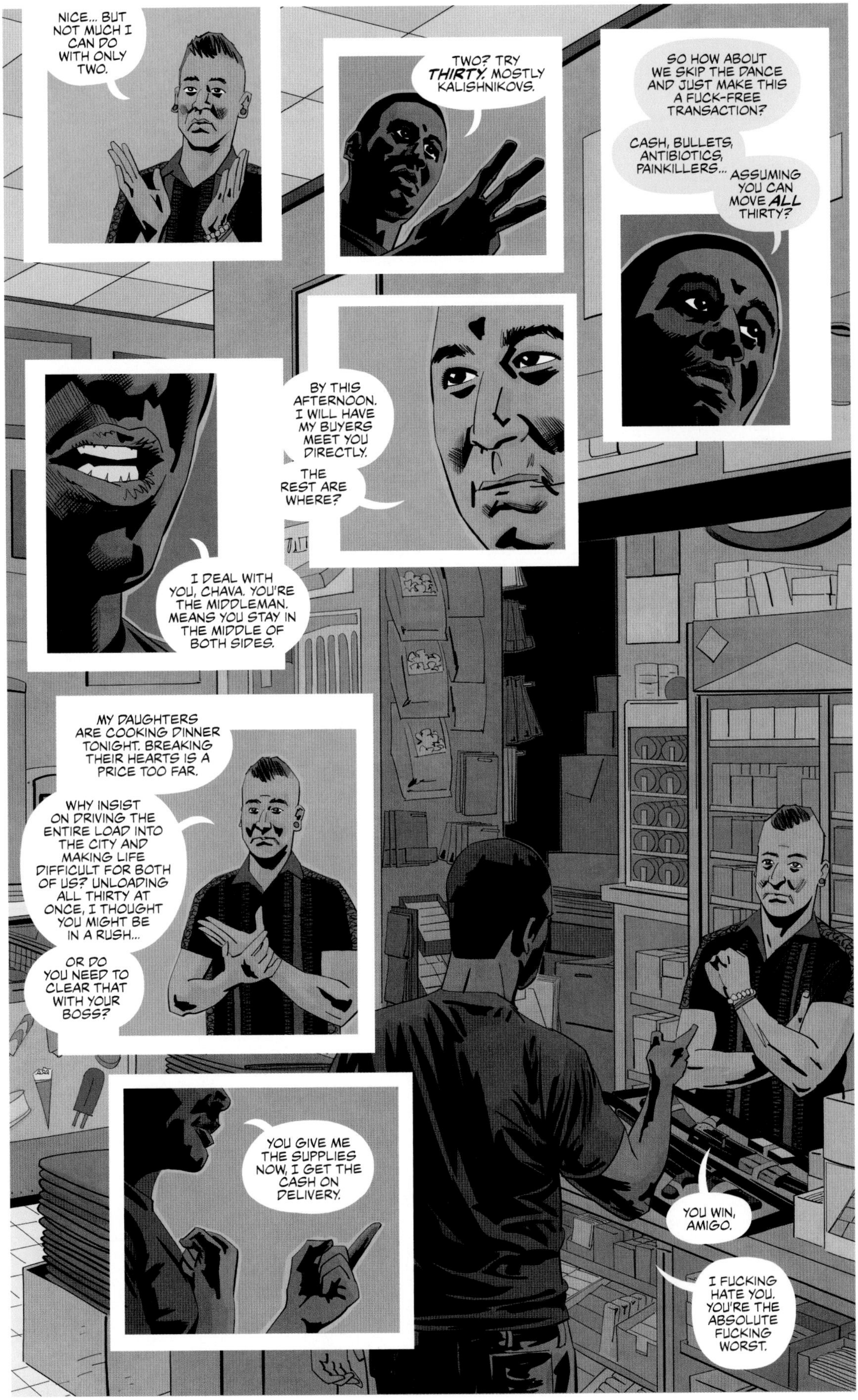
NICE... BUT NOT MUCH I CAN DO WITH ONLY TWO.
TWO? TRY THIRTY. MOSTLY KALISHNIKOVS.
SO HOW ABOUT WE SKIP THE DANCE AND JUST MAKE THIS A FUCK-FREE TRANSACTION?
CASH, BULLETS, ANTIBIOTICS, PAINKILLERS... ASSUMING YOU CAN MOVE ALL THIRTY?
BY THIS AFTERNOON. I WILL HAVE MY BUYERS MEET YOU DIRECTLY.
THE REST ARE WHERE?
I DEAL WITH YOU, CHAVA. YOU'RE THE MIDDLEMAN. MEANS YOU STAY IN THE MIDDLE OF BOTH SIDES.
MY DAUGHTERS ARE COOKING DINNER TONIGHT. BREAKING THEIR HEARTS IS A PRICE TOO FAR.
WHY INSIST ON DRIVING THE ENTIRE LOAD INTO THE CITY AND MAKING LIFE DIFFICULT FOR BOTH OF US? UNLOADING ALL THIRTY AT ONCE, I THOUGHT YOU MIGHT BE IN A RUSH...
OR DO YOU NEED TO CLEAR THAT WITH YOUR BOSS?
YOU GIVE ME THE SUPPLIES NOW, I GET THE CASH ON DELIVERY.
YOU WIN, AMIGO.
I FUCKING HATE YOU. YOU'RE THE ABSOLUTE FUCKING WORST.

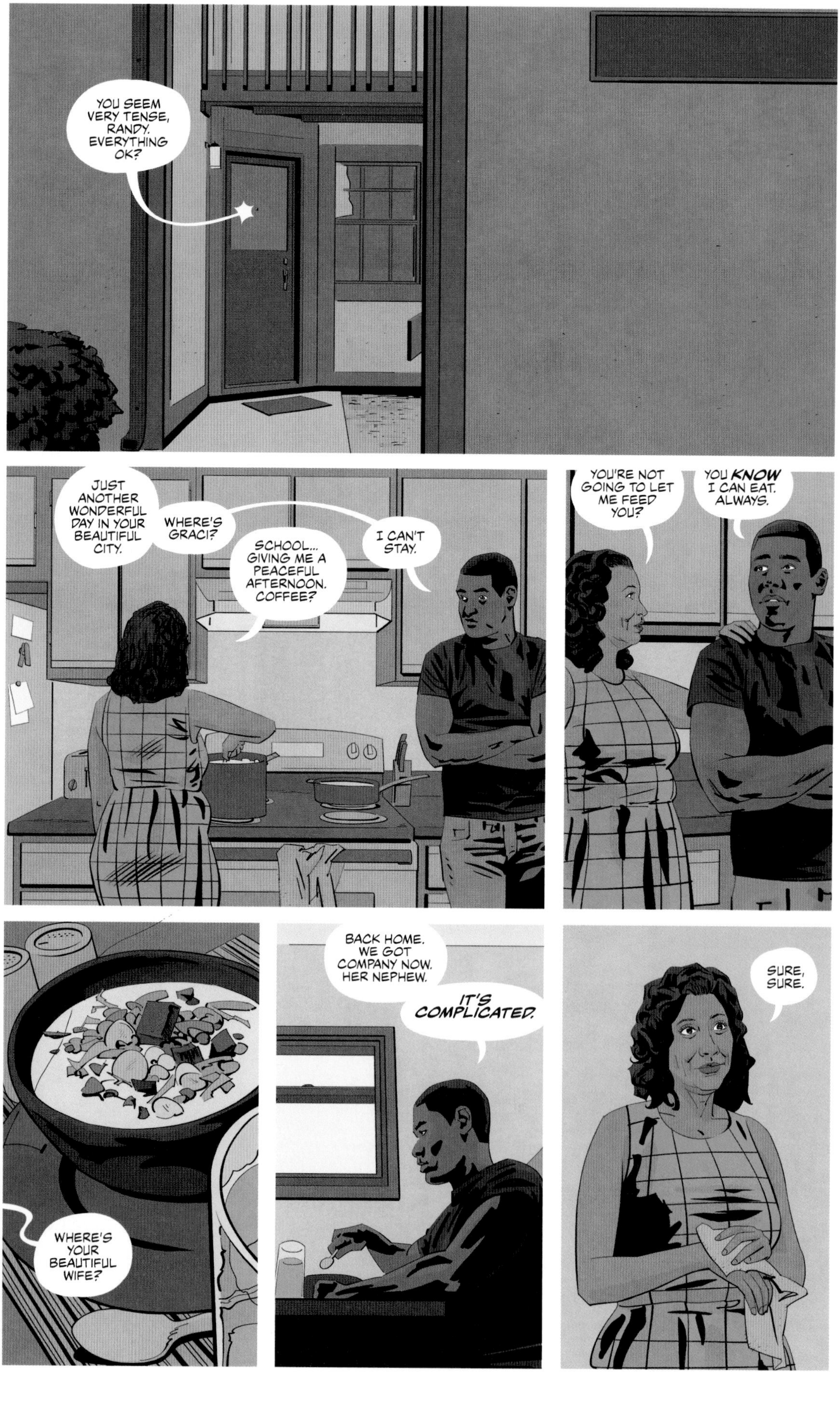
YOU SEEM VERY TENSE, RANDY. EVERYTHING OK?
JUST ANOTHER WONDERFUL DAY IN YOUR BEAUTIFUL CITY.
WHERE'S GRACI?
I CAN'T STAY.
SCHOOL... GIVING ME A PEACEFUL AFTERNOON. COFFEE?
YOU'RE NOT GOING TO LET ME FEED YOU?
YOU KNOW I CAN EAT. ALWAYS.
WHERE'S YOUR BEAUTIFUL WIFE?
BACK HOME. WE GOT COMPANY NOW. HER NEPHEW.
IT'S COMPLICATED.
SURE, SURE.

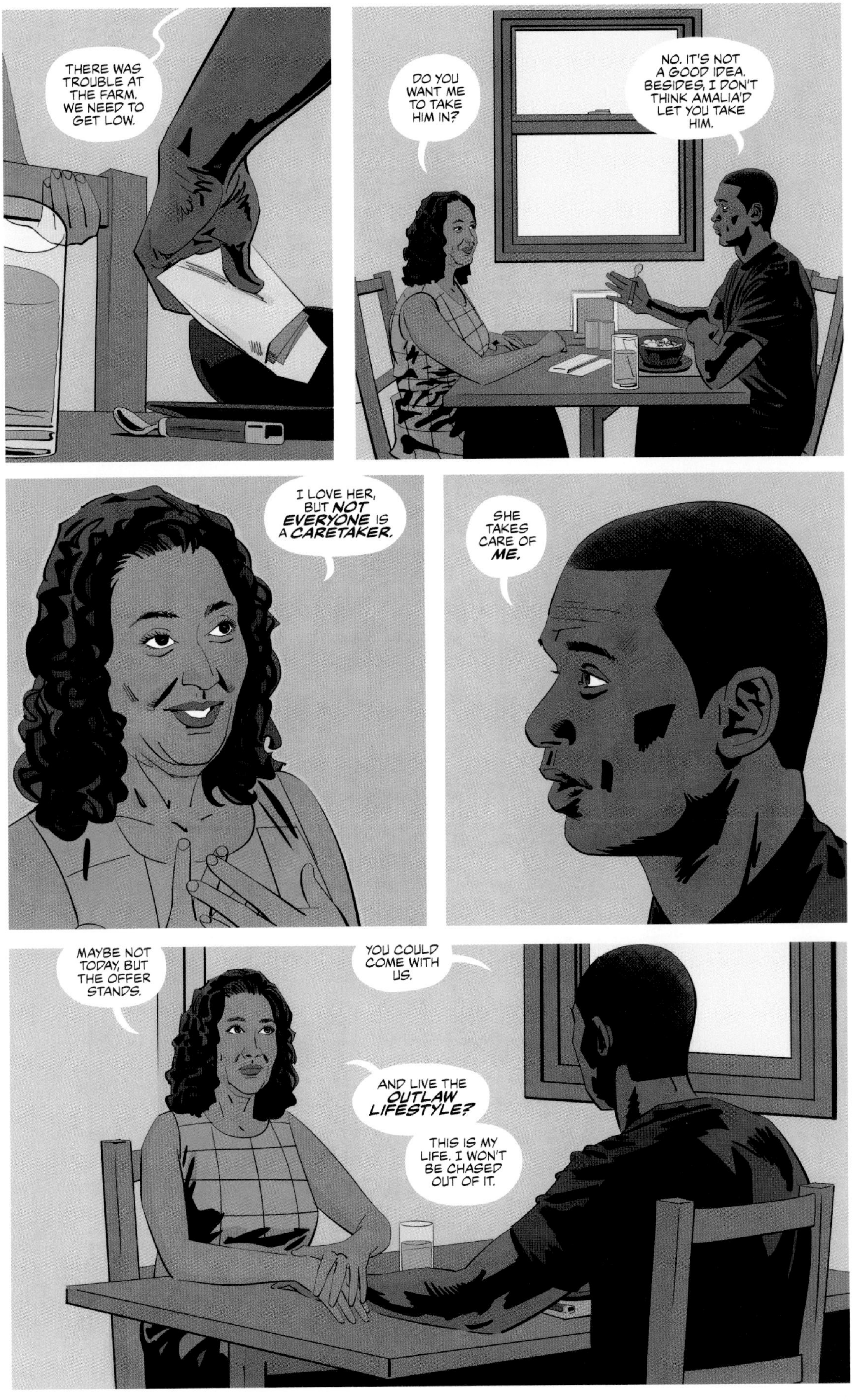
THERE WAS TROUBLE AT THE FARM. WE NEED TO GET LOW.
DO YOU WANT ME TO TAKE HIM IN?
NO. IT'S NOT A GOOD IDEA. BESIDES, I DON'T THINK AMALIA'D LET YOU TAKE HIM.
I LOVE HER, BUT NOT EVERYONE IS A CARETAKER.
SHE TAKES CARE OF ME.
MAYBE NOT TODAY, BUT THE OFFER STANDS.
YOU COULD COME WITH US.
AND LIVE THE OUTLAW LIFESTYLE?
THIS IS MY LIFE. I WON'T BE CHASED OUT OF IT.

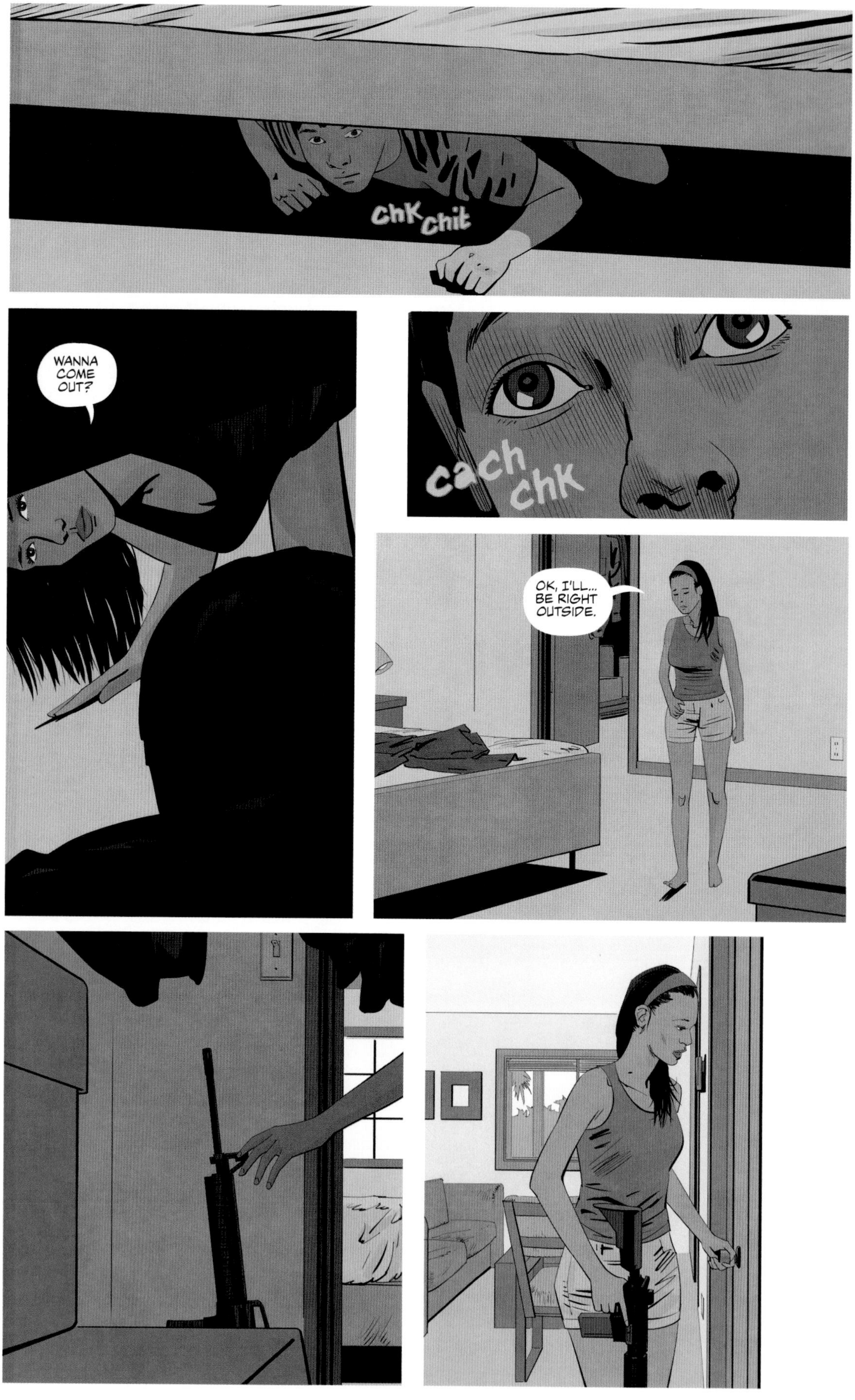

ChK
Chit
WANNA COME OUT?
cach
chK
OK, I'LL... BE RIGHT OUTSIDE.

thnk!

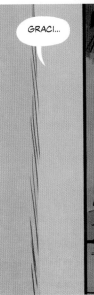

GRACI...

WHERE DID YOU GET *THIS?!*

IT WAS ON THE FRONT STEPS WHEN I GOT HOME.

AND WHY DIDN'T YOU TELL ME?!

...I LIKE IT.

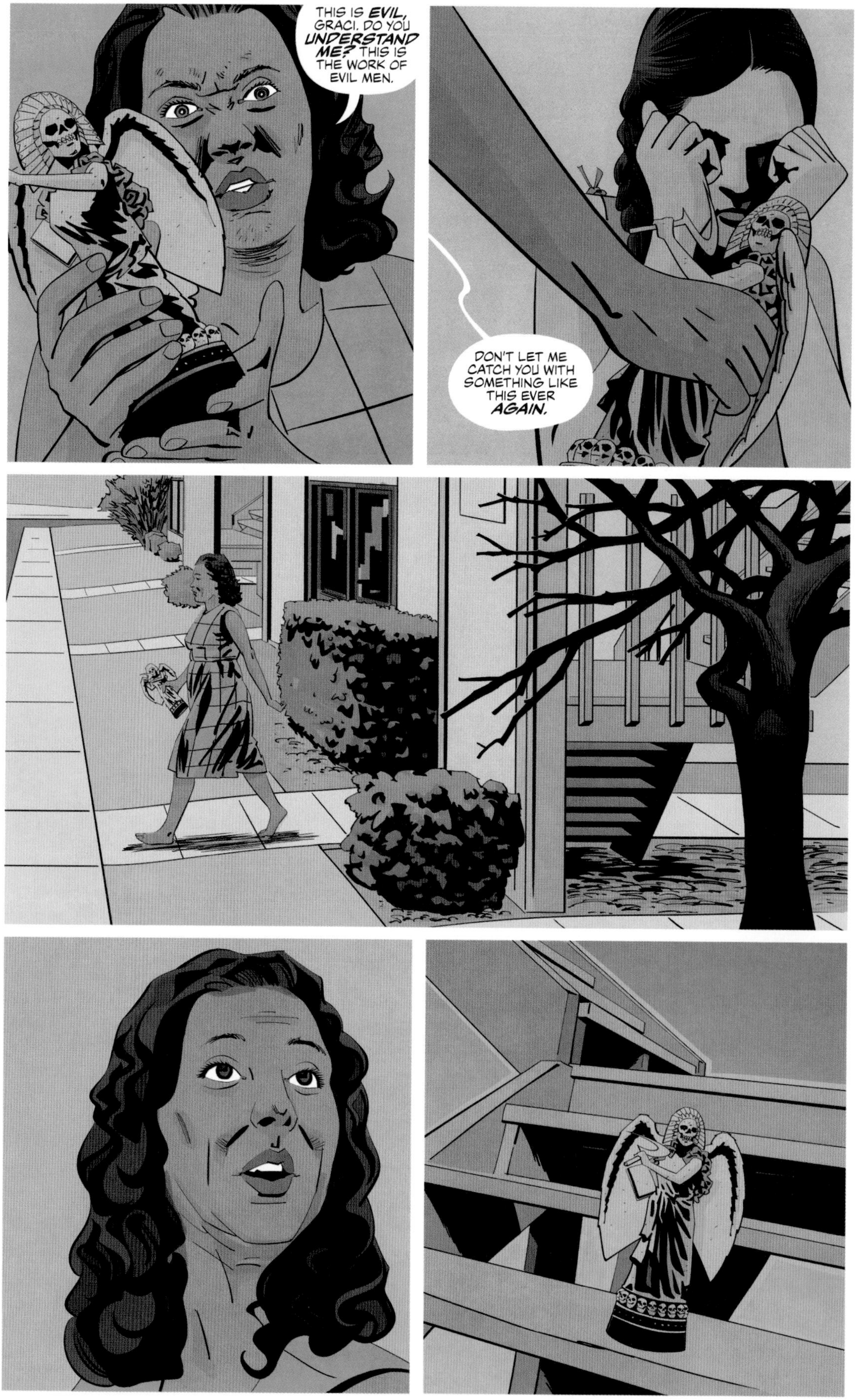
THIS IS EVIL, GRACI. DO YOU UNDERSTAND ME? THIS IS THE WORK OF EVIL MEN.
DON'T LET ME CATCH YOU WITH SOMETHING LIKE THIS EVER AGAIN.

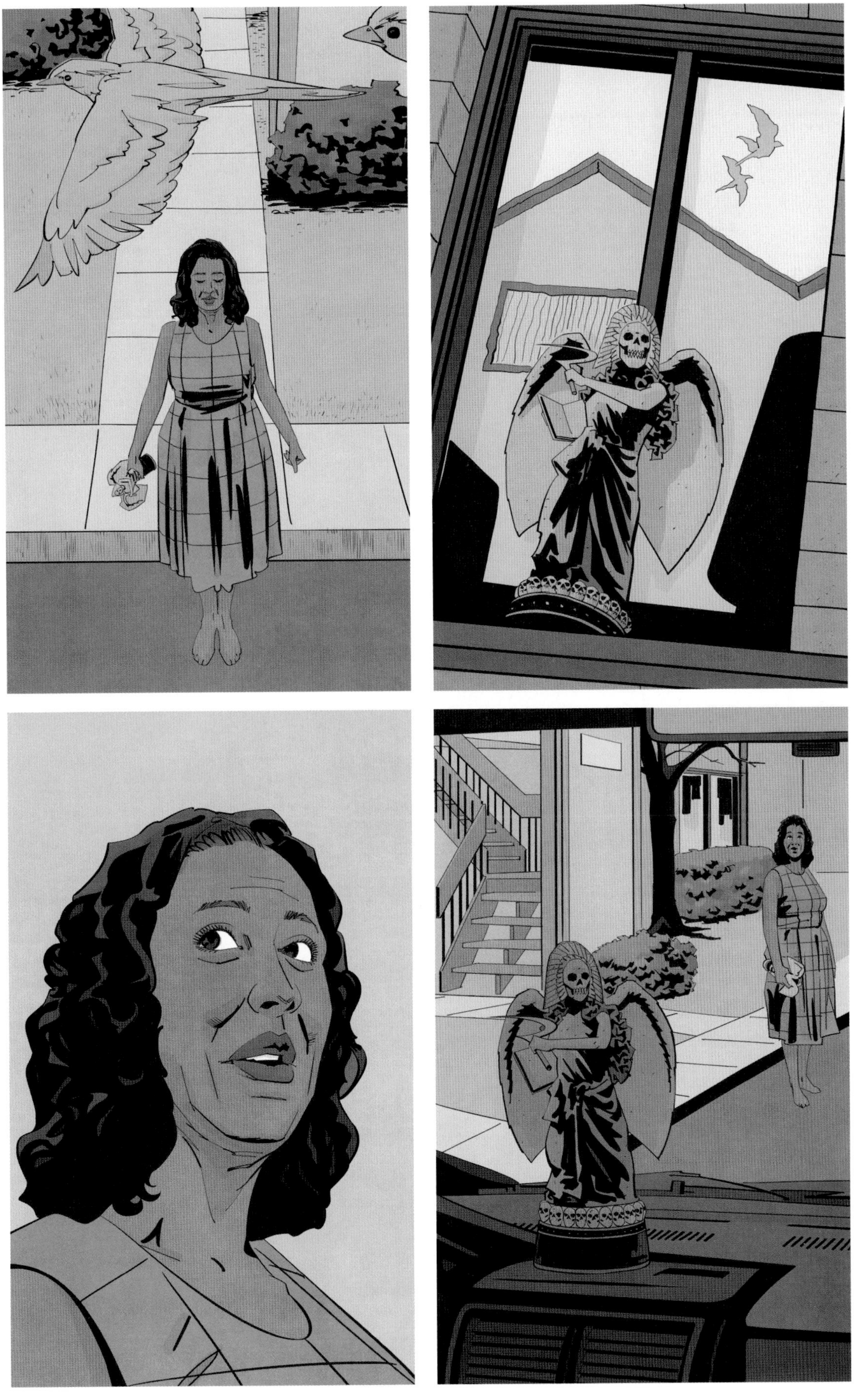

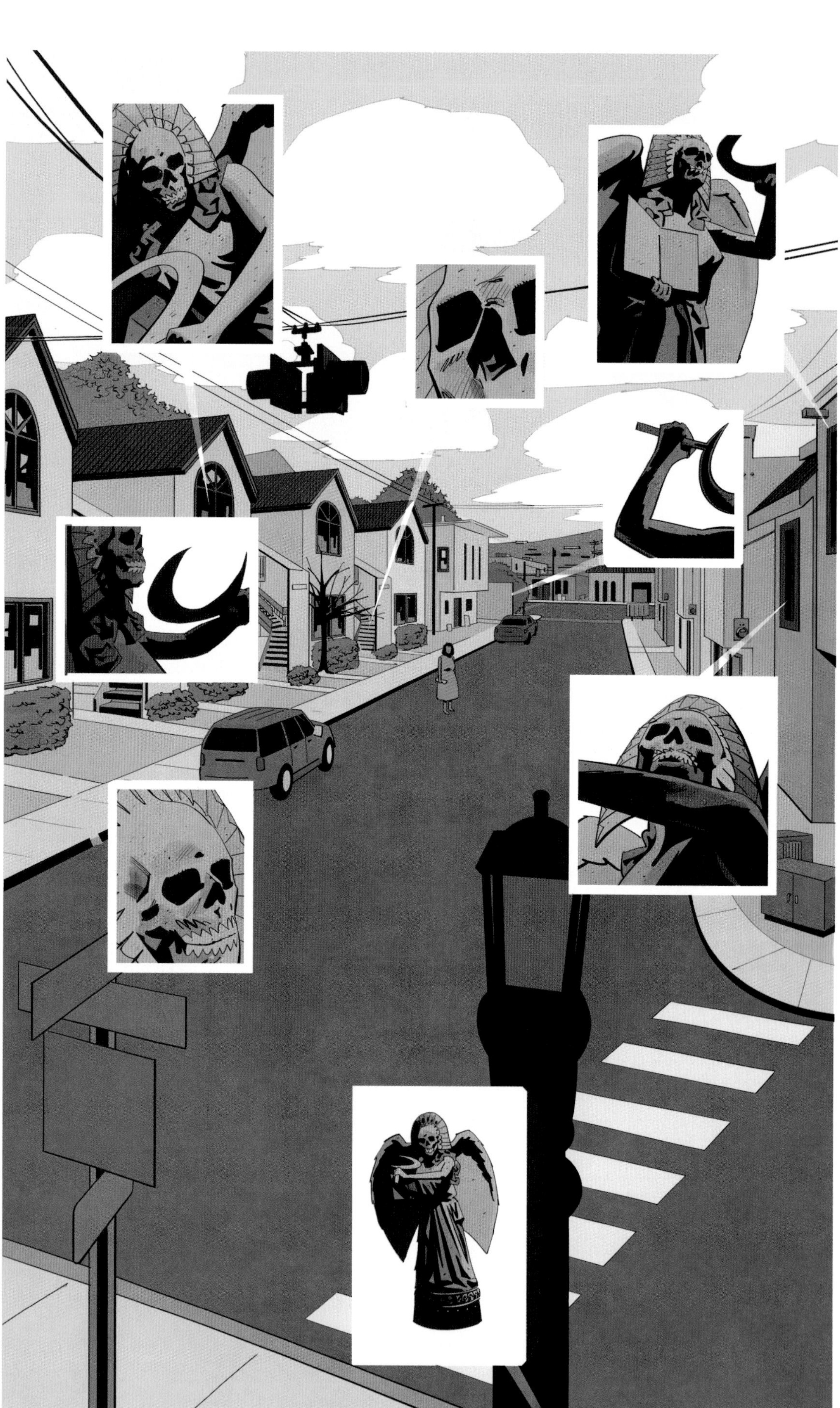

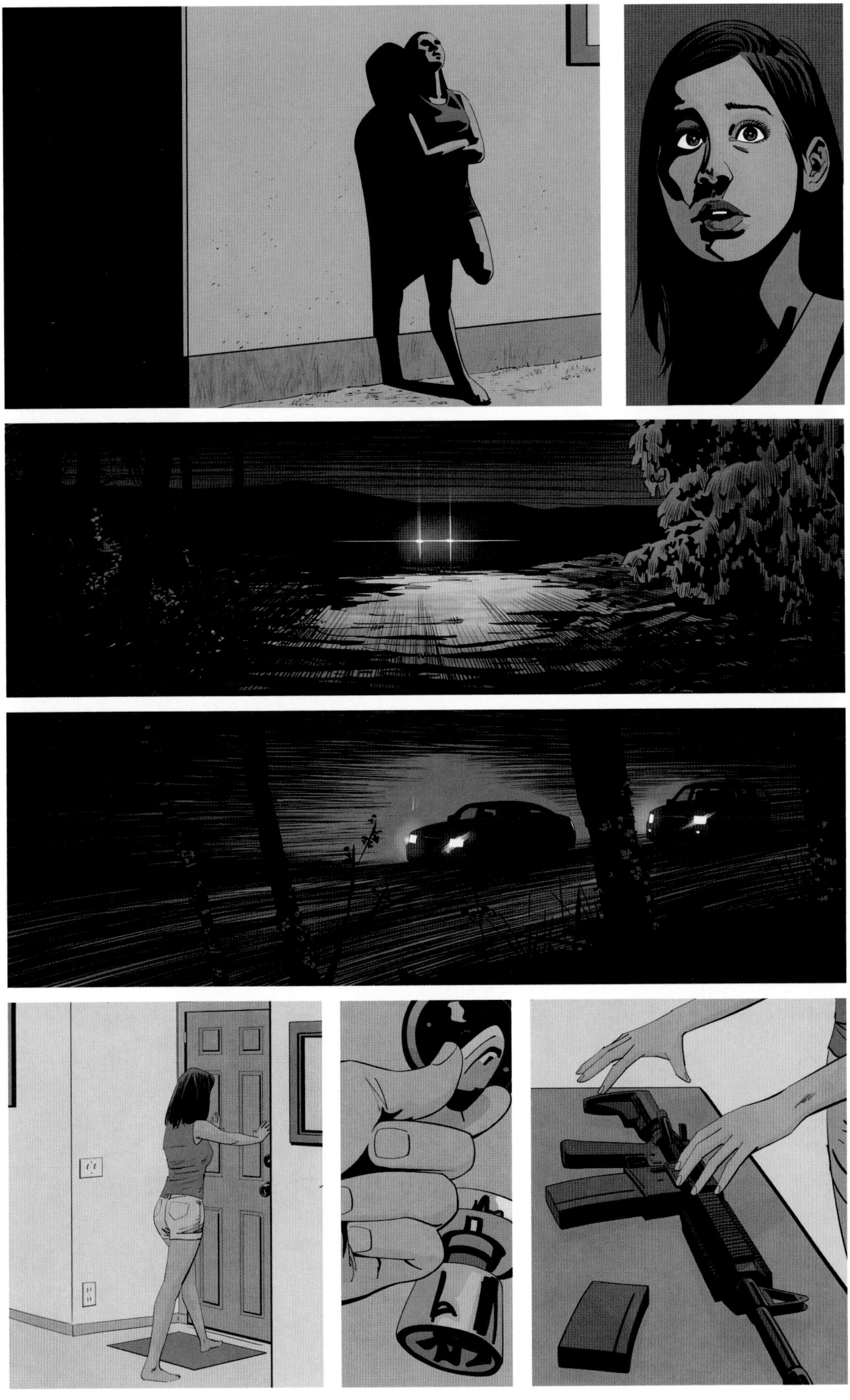

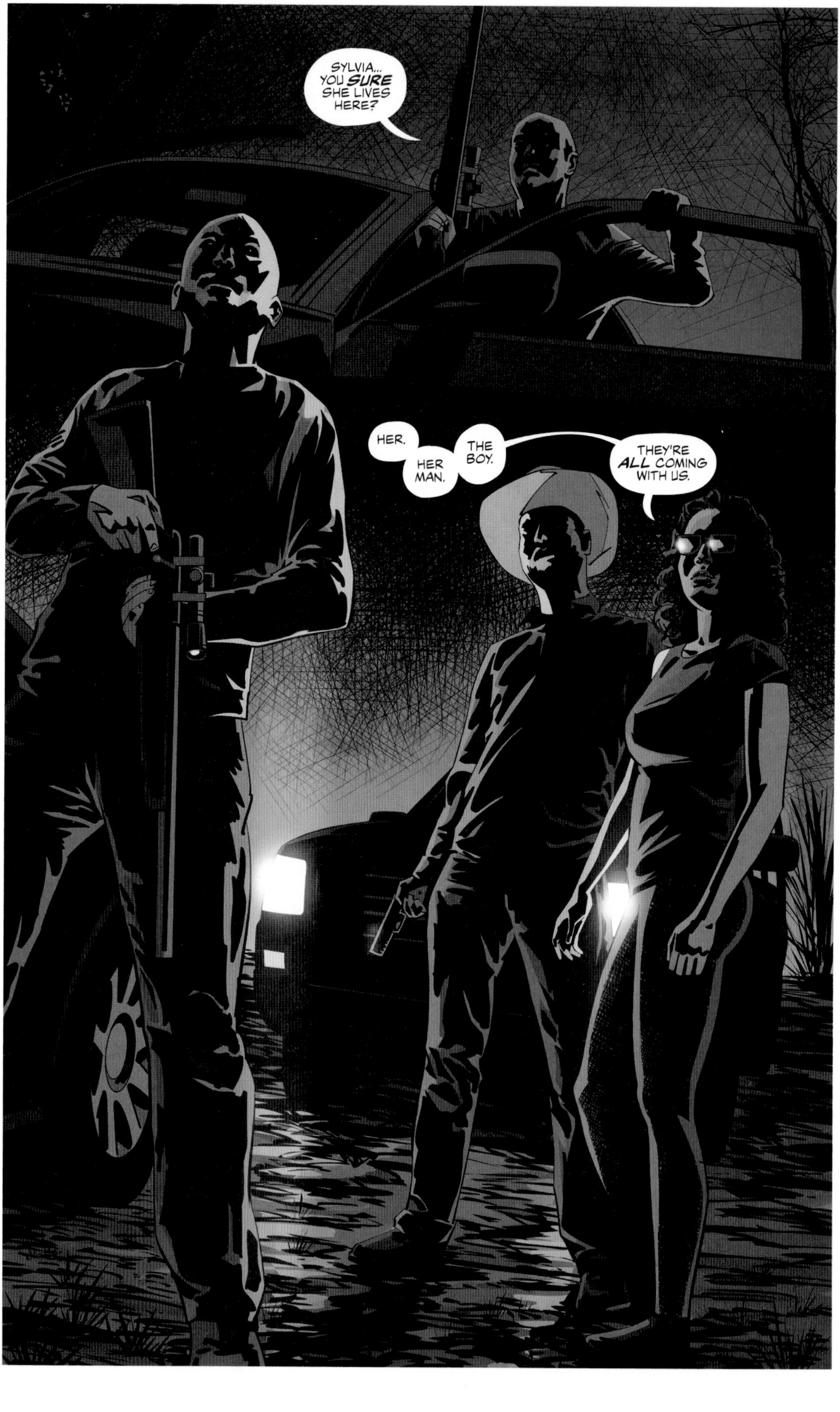
SYLVIA... YOU **SURE** SHE LIVES HERE?
HER.
HER MAN.
THE BOY.
THEY'RE **ALL** COMING WITH US.

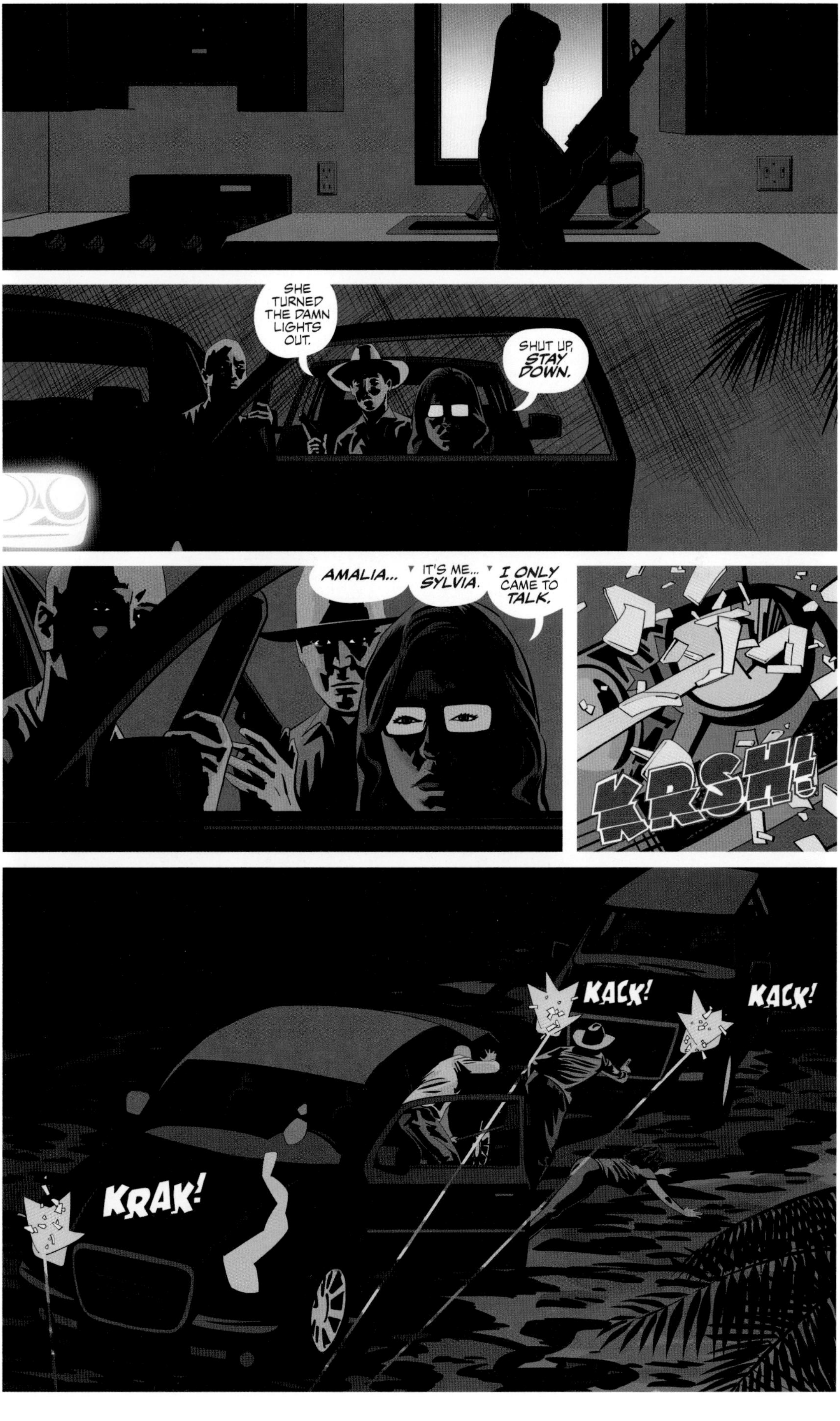

SHE TURNED THE DAMN LIGHTS OUT.
SHUT UP, STAY DOWN.
AMALIA...
IT'S ME... SYLVIA.
I ONLY CAME TO TALK.
KRSH!
KACK!
KACK!
KRAK!

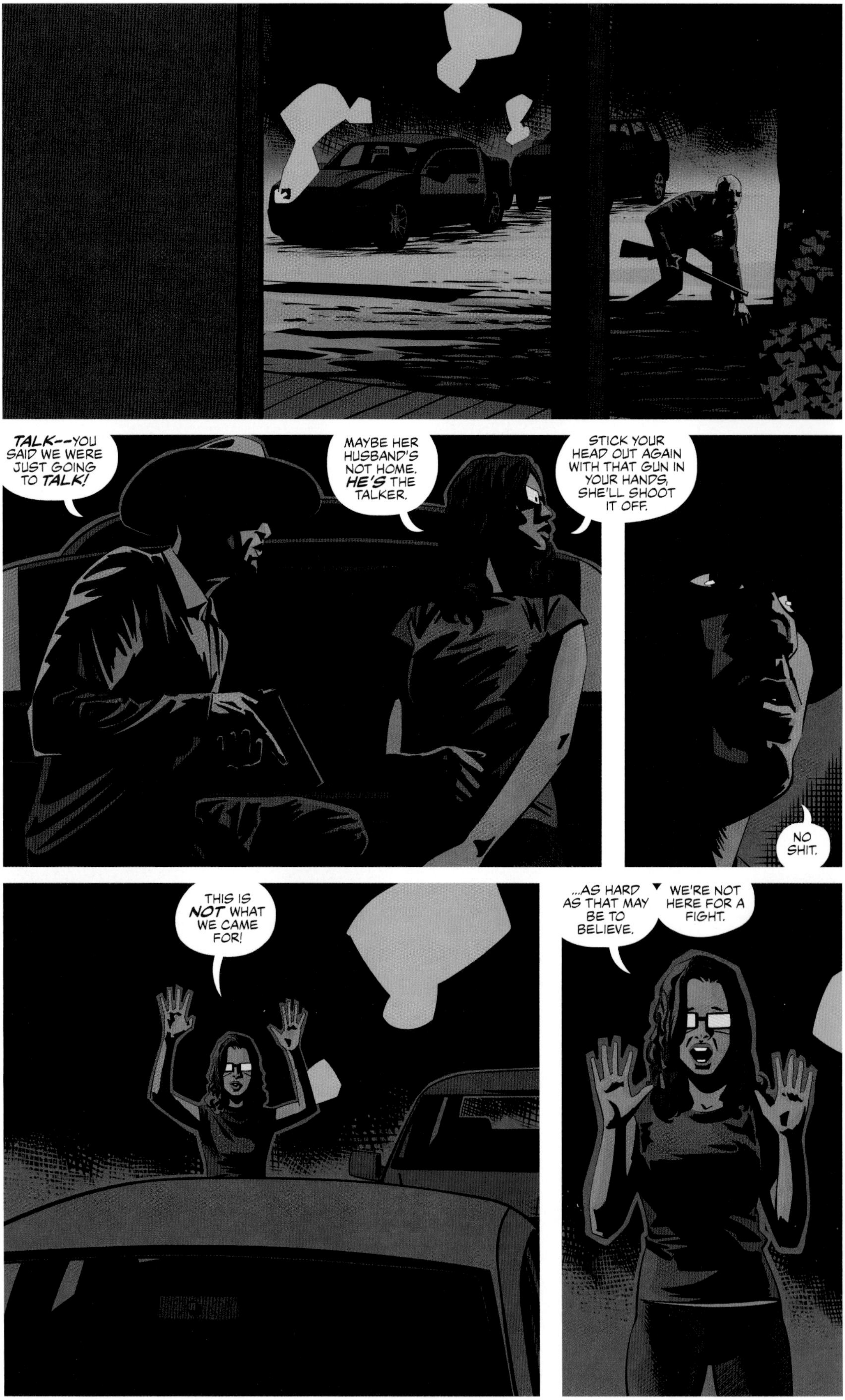
TALK--YOU SAID WE WERE JUST GOING TO TALK!
MAYBE HER HUSBAND'S NOT HOME. HE'S THE TALKER.
STICK YOUR HEAD OUT AGAIN WITH THAT GUN IN YOUR HANDS, SHE'LL SHOOT IT OFF.
NO SHIT.
THIS IS NOT WHAT WE CAME FOR!
WE'RE NOT HERE FOR A FIGHT.
...AS HARD AS THAT MAY BE TO BELIEVE.

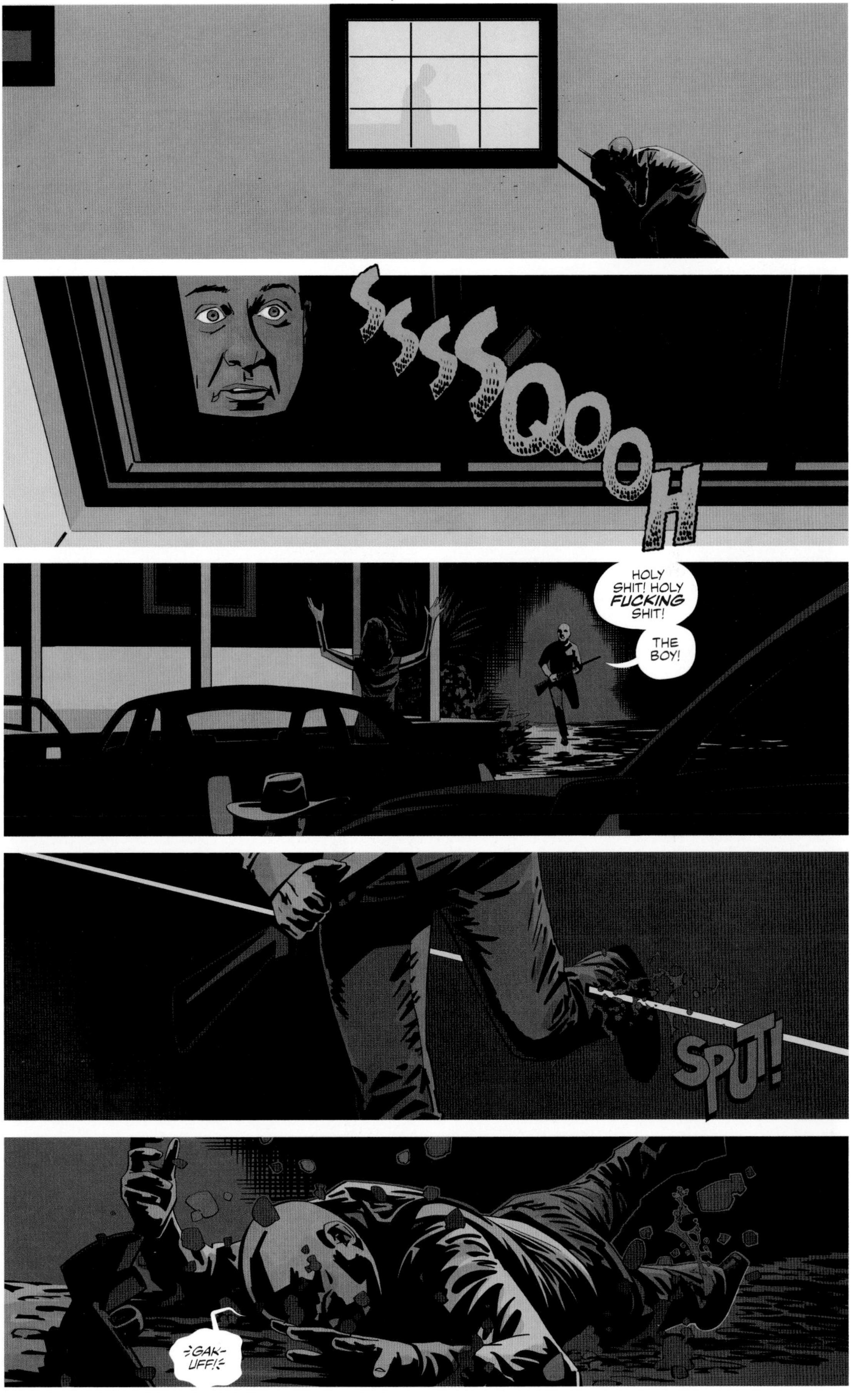
SSSSQOOOH
HOLY SHIT! HOLY FUCKING SHIT!
THE BOY!
SPUT!
GAK-UFF!

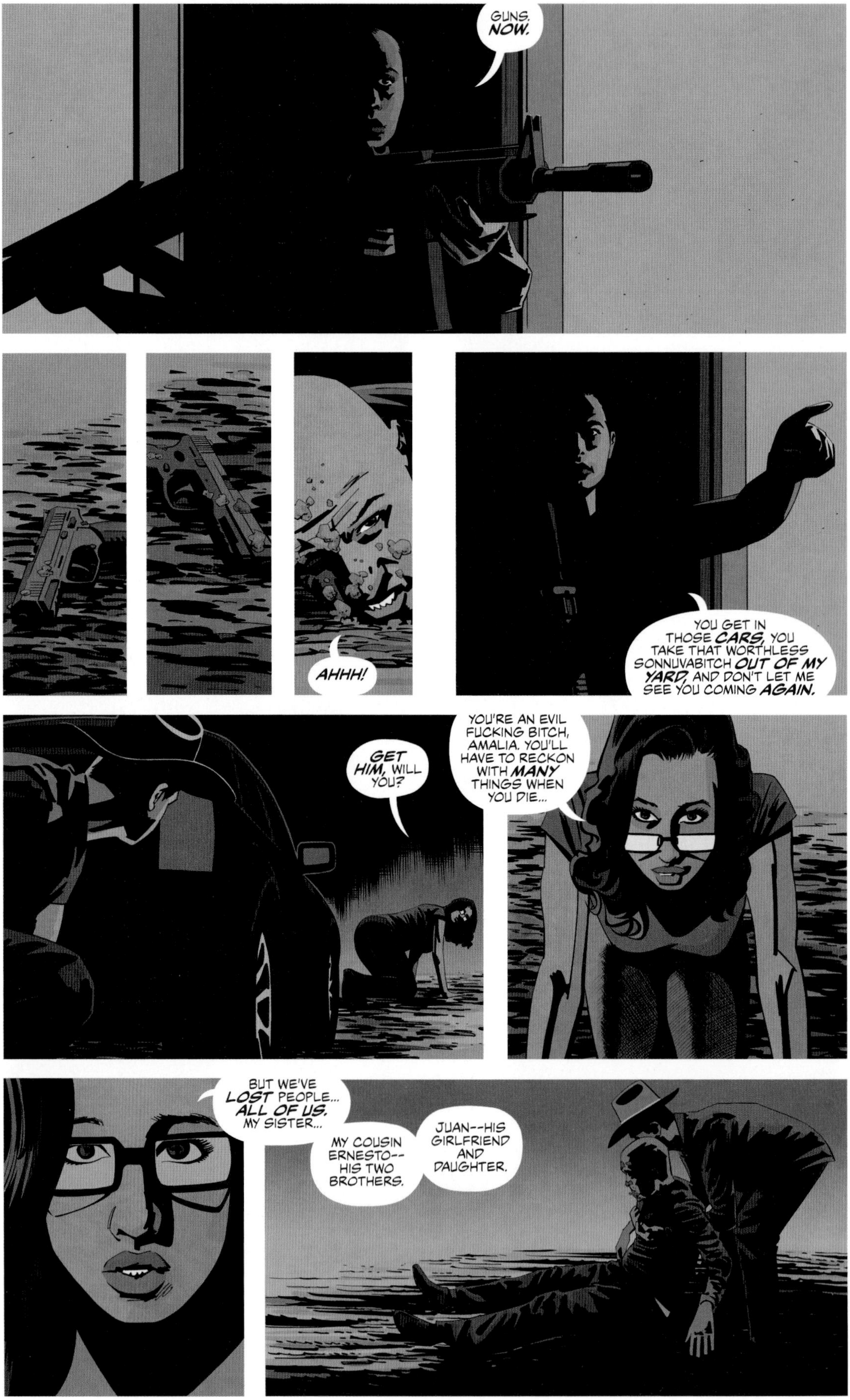
GUNS. *NOW.*
AHHH!
YOU GET IN THOSE *CARS,* YOU TAKE THAT WORTHLESS SONNUVABITCH *OUT OF MY YARD,* AND DON'T LET ME SEE YOU COMING *AGAIN.*
GET HIM, WILL YOU?
YOU'RE AN EVIL FUCKING BITCH, AMALIA. YOU'LL HAVE TO RECKON WITH *MANY* THINGS WHEN YOU DIE...
BUT WE'VE *LOST* PEOPLE... *ALL OF US.* MY SISTER...
MY COUSIN ERNESTO--HIS TWO BROTHERS.
JUAN--HIS GIRLFRIEND AND DAUGHTER.

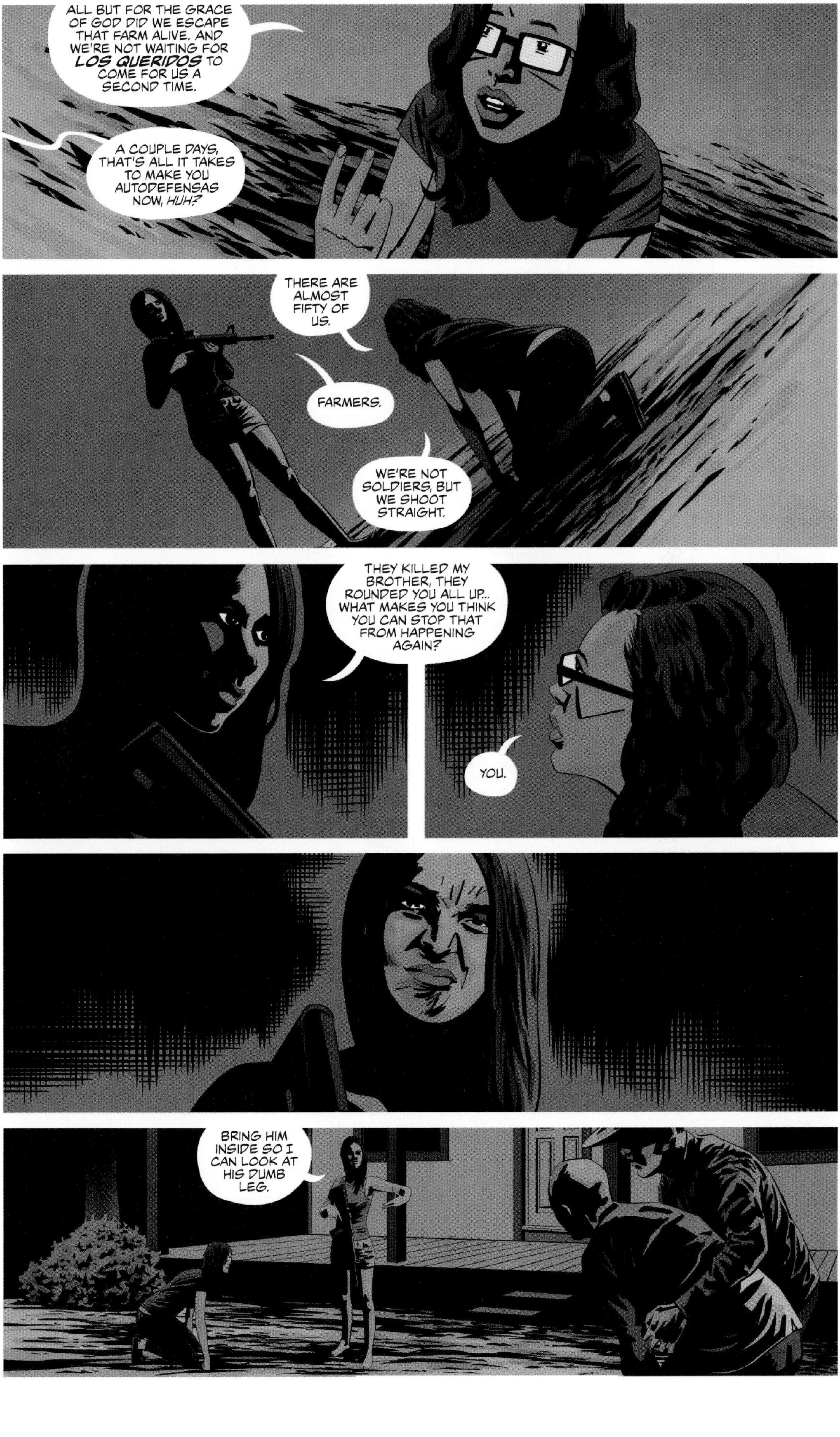
ALL BUT FOR THE GRACE OF GOD DID WE ESCAPE THAT FARM ALIVE. AND WE'RE NOT WAITING FOR LOS QUERIDOS TO COME FOR US A SECOND TIME.
A COUPLE DAYS, THAT'S ALL IT TAKES TO MAKE YOU AUTODEFENSAS NOW, HUH?
THERE ARE ALMOST FIFTY OF US.
FARMERS.
WE'RE NOT SOLDIERS, BUT WE SHOOT STRAIGHT.
THEY KILLED MY BROTHER, THEY ROUNDED YOU ALL UP... WHAT MAKES YOU THINK YOU CAN STOP THAT FROM HAPPENING AGAIN?
YOU.
BRING HIM INSIDE SO I CAN LOOK AT HIS DUMB LEG.

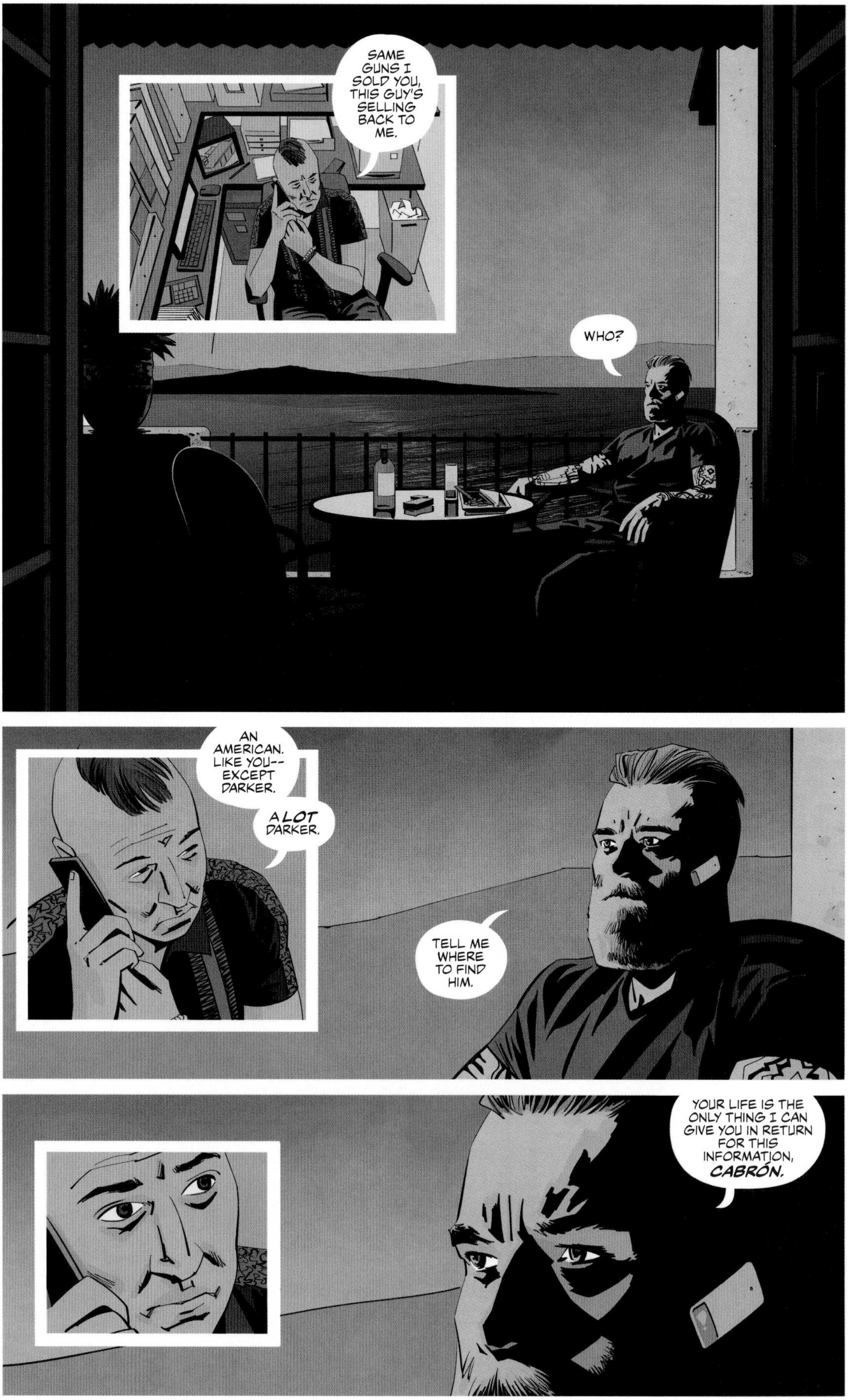
SAME GUNS I SOLD YOU, THIS GUY'S SELLING BACK TO ME.
WHO?
AN AMERICAN. LIKE YOU-- EXCEPT DARKER.
A *LOT* DARKER.
TELL ME WHERE TO FIND HIM.
YOUR LIFE IS THE ONLY THING I CAN GIVE YOU IN RETURN FOR THIS INFORMATION, ***CABRÓN.***

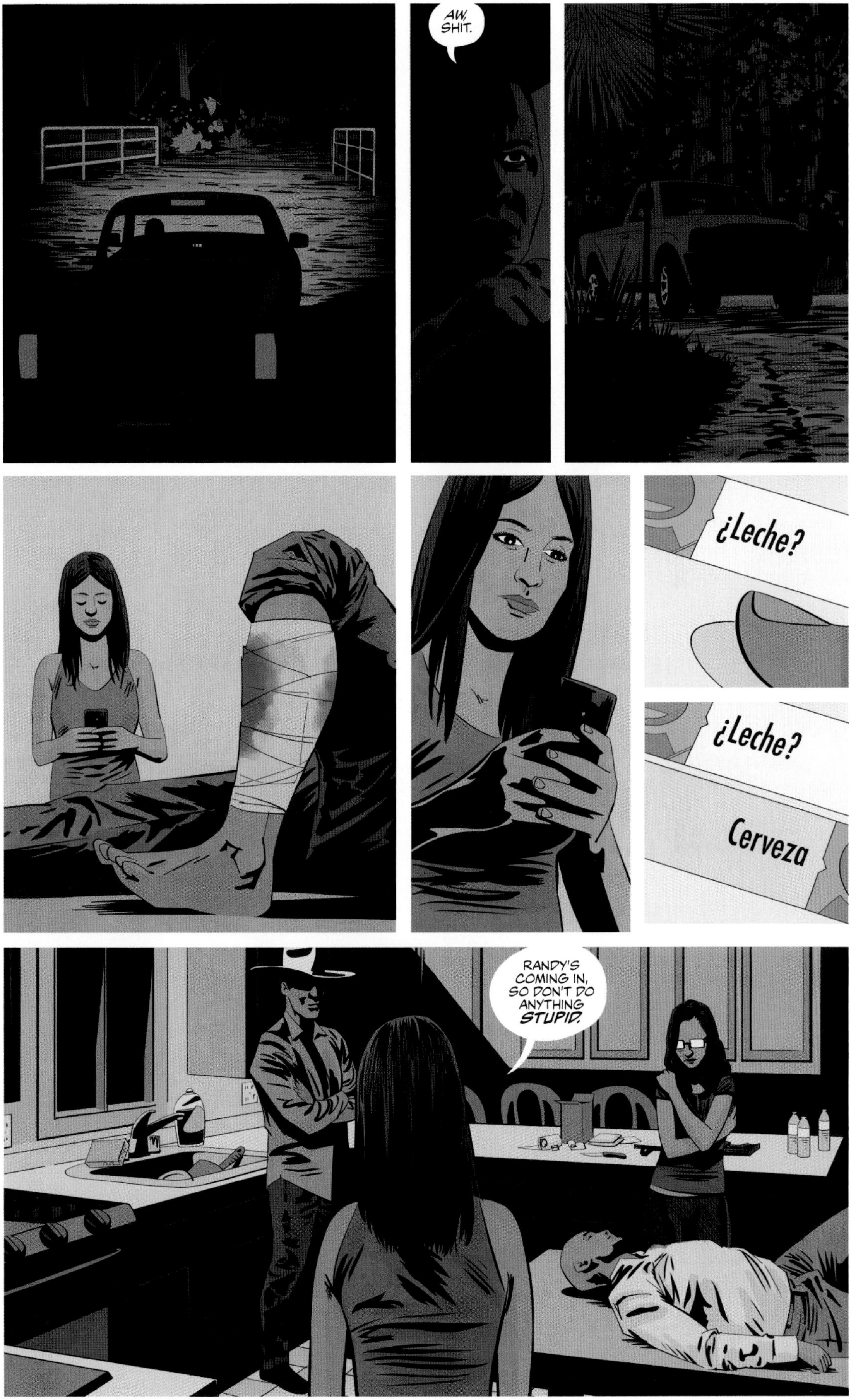
AW, SHIT.
¿Leche?
¿Leche?
Cerveza
RANDY'S COMING IN, SO DON'T DO ANYTHING STUPID.

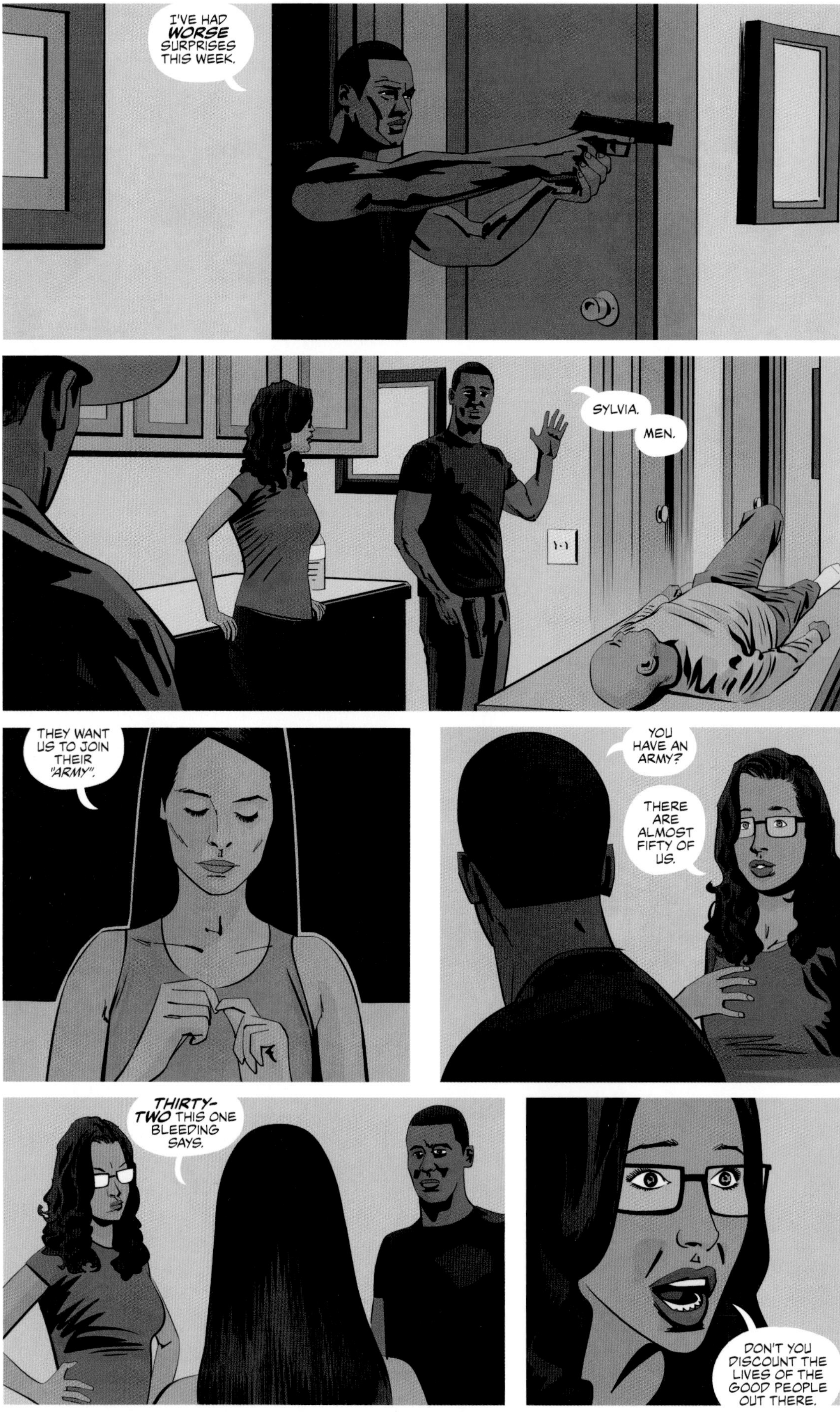

I'VE HAD *WORSE* SURPRISES THIS WEEK.
SYLVIA.
MEN.
THEY WANT US TO JOIN THEIR *"ARMY"*.
YOU HAVE AN ARMY?
THERE ARE ALMOST FIFTY OF US.
THIRTY-TWO THIS ONE BLEEDING SAYS.
DON'T YOU DISCOUNT THE LIVES OF THE GOOD PEOPLE OUT THERE.

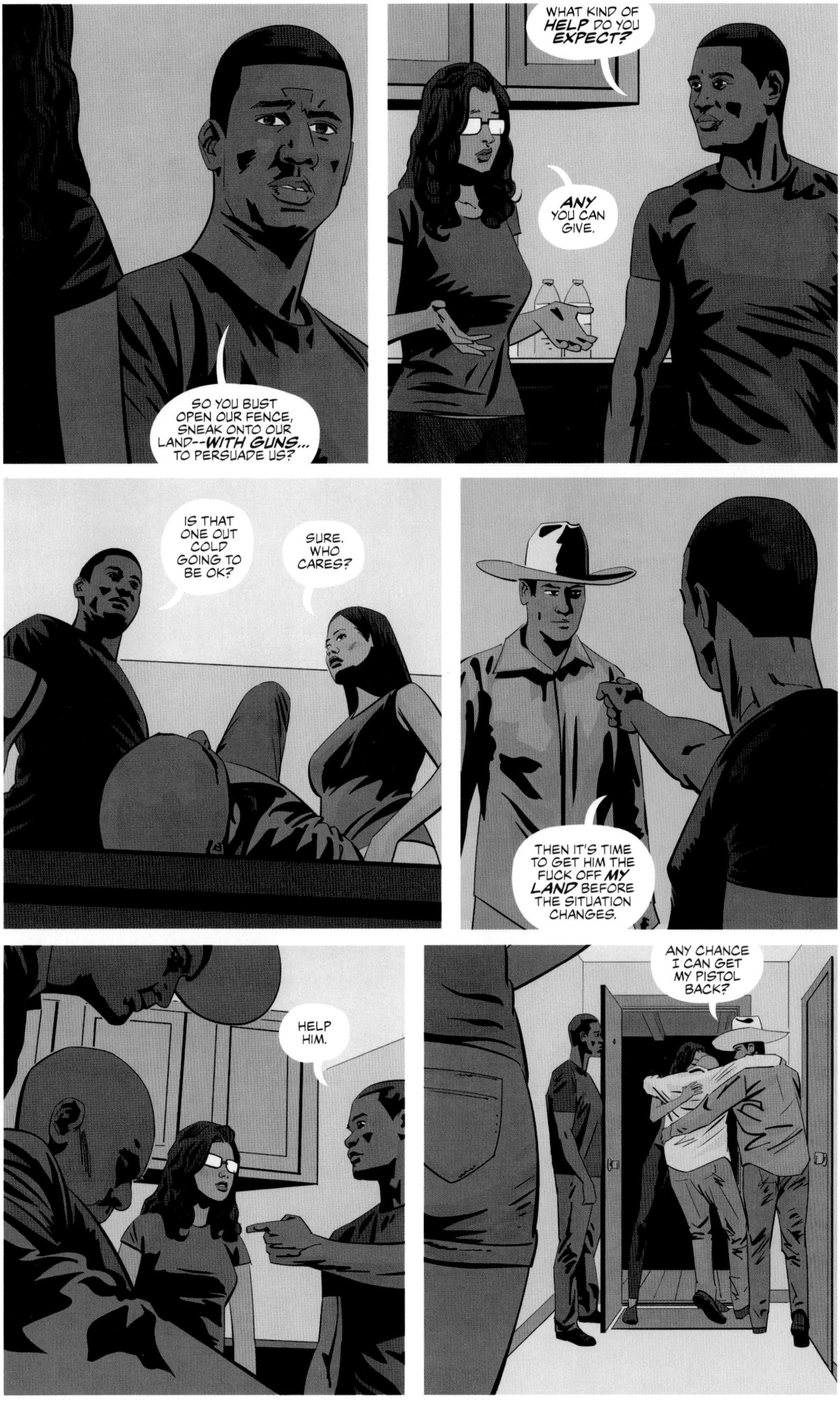
SO YOU BUST OPEN OUR FENCE, SNEAK ONTO OUR LAND--WITH GUNS... TO PERSUADE US?
WHAT KIND OF HELP DO YOU EXPECT?
ANY YOU CAN GIVE.
IS THAT ONE OUT COLD GOING TO BE OK?
SURE. WHO CARES?
THEN IT'S TIME TO GET HIM THE FUCK OFF MY LAND BEFORE THE SITUATION CHANGES.
HELP HIM.
ANY CHANCE I CAN GET MY PISTOL BACK?

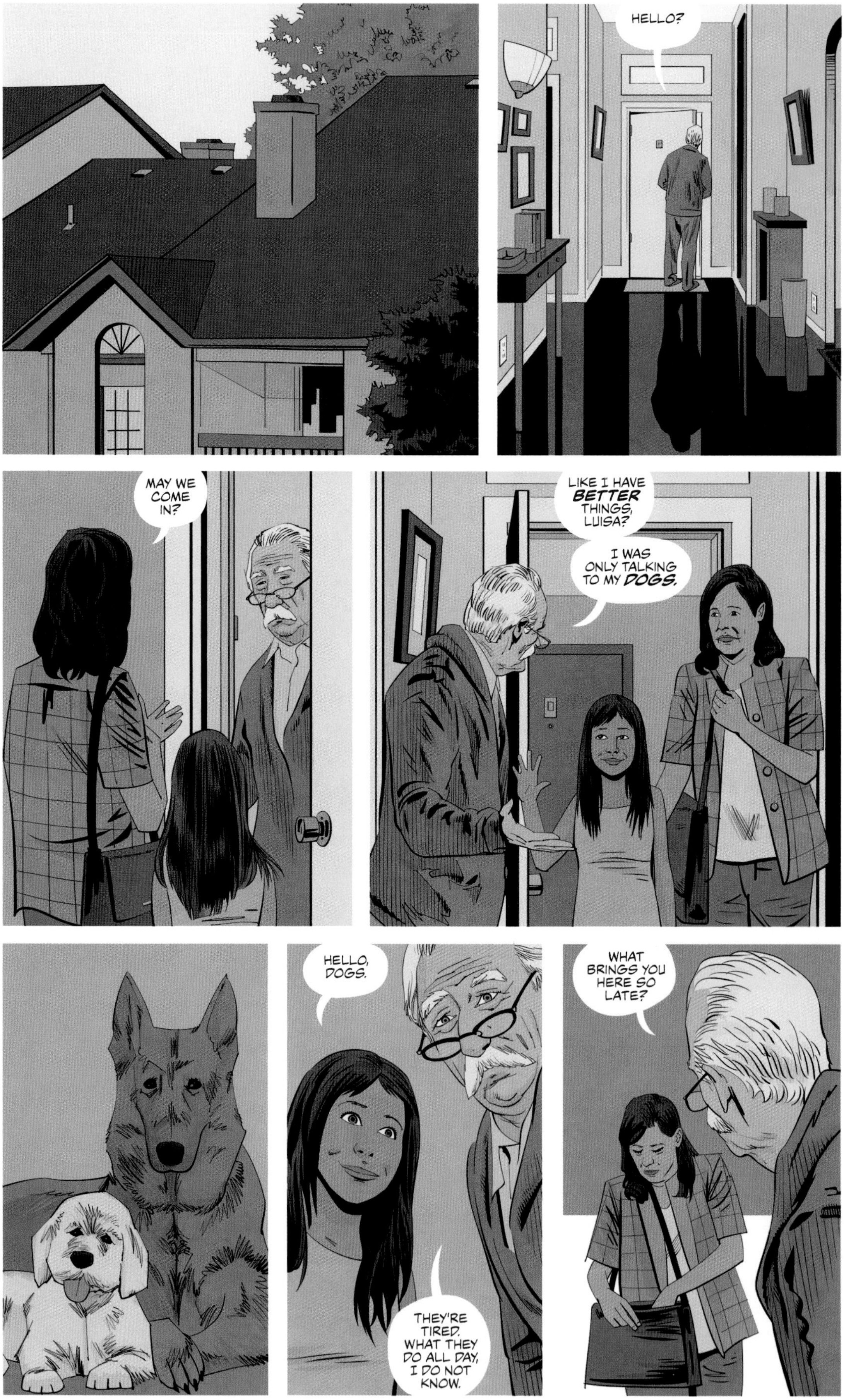
HELLO?
MAY WE COME IN?
LIKE I HAVE BETTER THINGS, LUISA?
I WAS ONLY TALKING TO MY DOGS.
HELLO, DOGS.
THEY'RE TIRED. WHAT THEY DO ALL DAY, I DO NOT KNOW.
WHAT BRINGS YOU HERE SO LATE?

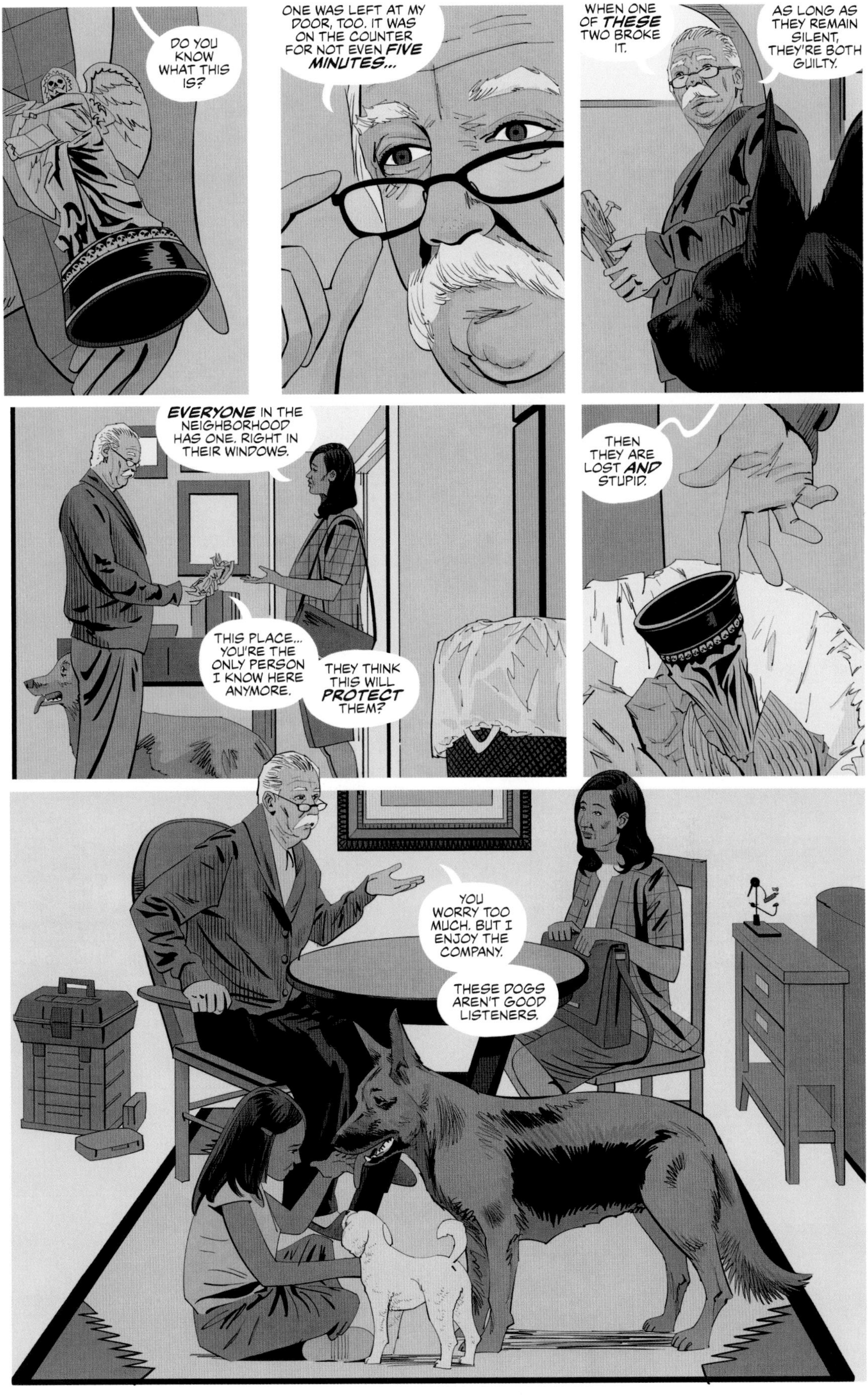

DO YOU KNOW WHAT THIS IS?
ONE WAS LEFT AT MY DOOR, TOO. IT WAS ON THE COUNTER FOR NOT EVEN FIVE MINUTES...
WHEN ONE OF THESE TWO BROKE IT.
AS LONG AS THEY REMAIN SILENT, THEY'RE BOTH GUILTY.
EVERYONE IN THE NEIGHBORHOOD HAS ONE. RIGHT IN THEIR WINDOWS.
THIS PLACE... YOU'RE THE ONLY PERSON I KNOW HERE ANYMORE.
THEY THINK THIS WILL PROTECT THEM?
THEN THEY ARE LOST AND STUPID.
YOU WORRY TOO MUCH. BUT I ENJOY THE COMPANY.
THESE DOGS AREN'T GOOD LISTENERS.

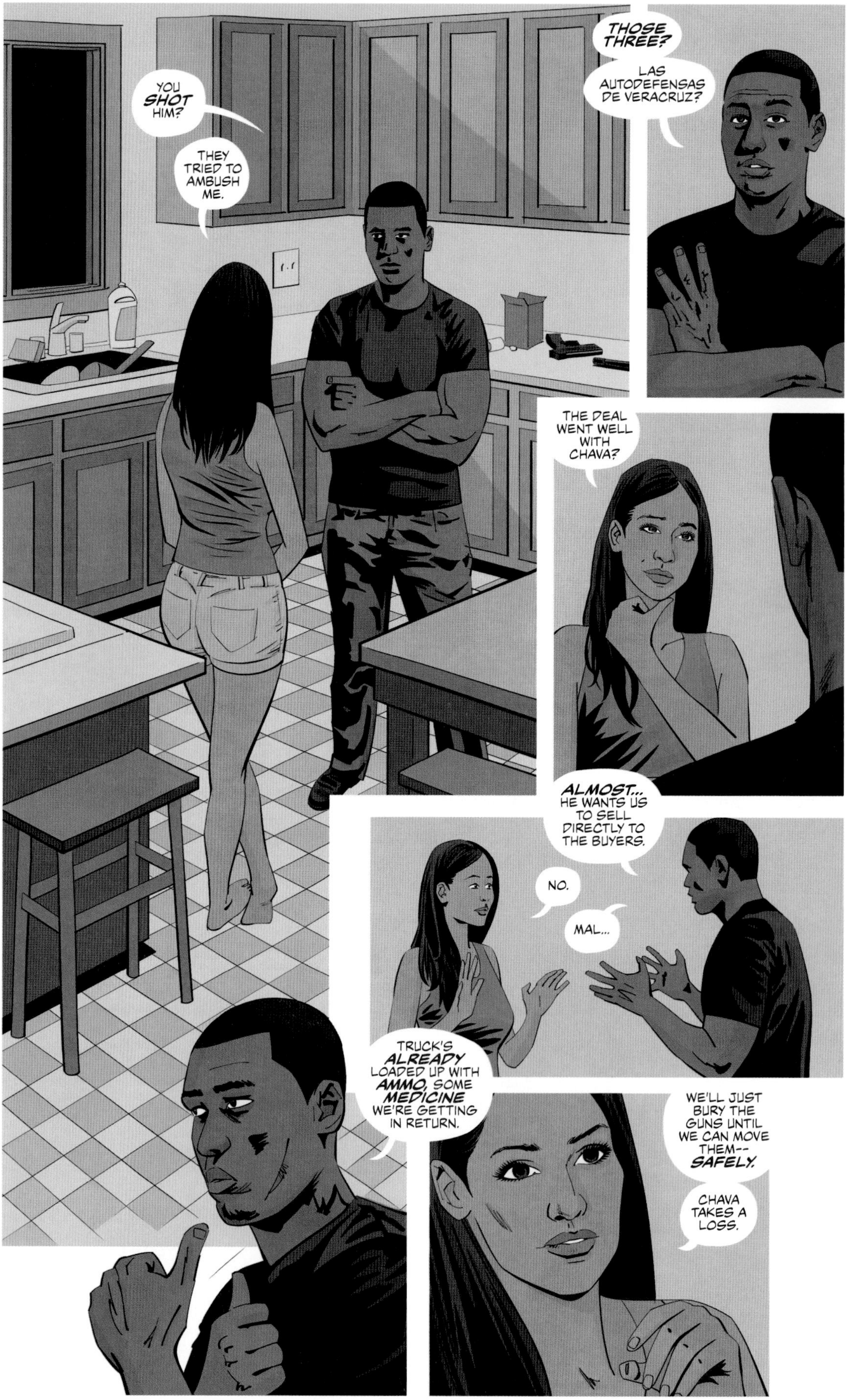

YOU SHOT HIM?
THEY TRIED TO AMBUSH ME.
THOSE THREE?
LAS AUTODEFENSAS DE VERACRUZ?
THE DEAL WENT WELL WITH CHAVA?
ALMOST... HE WANTS US TO SELL DIRECTLY TO THE BUYERS.
NO.
MAL...
TRUCK'S ALREADY LOADED UP WITH AMMO, SOME MEDICINE WE'RE GETTING IN RETURN.
WE'LL JUST BURY THE GUNS UNTIL WE CAN MOVE THEM-- SAFELY.
CHAVA TAKES A LOSS.

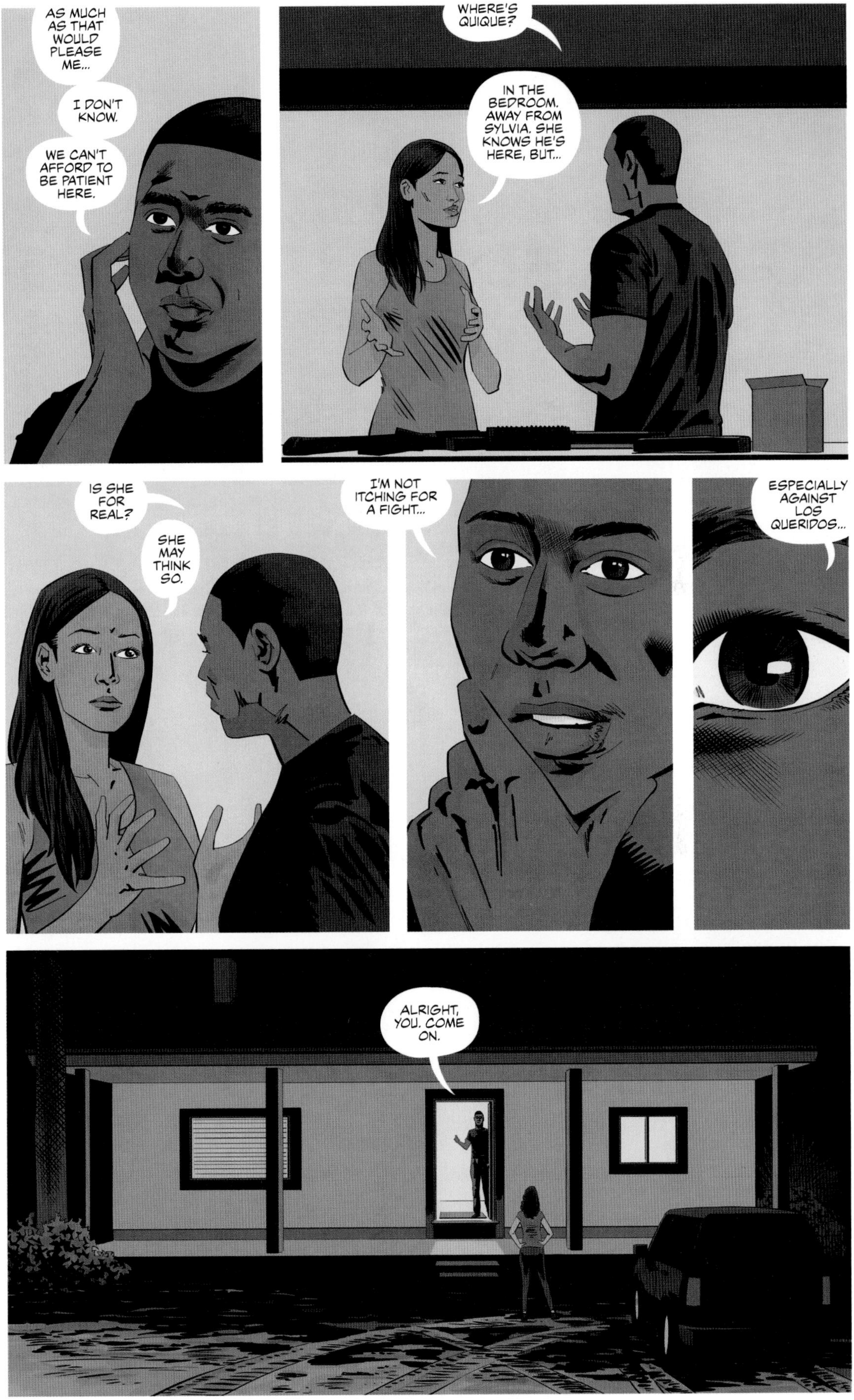
AS MUCH AS THAT WOULD PLEASE ME...
I DON'T KNOW.
WE CAN'T AFFORD TO BE PATIENT HERE.
WHERE'S QUIQUE?
IN THE BEDROOM. AWAY FROM SYLVIA. SHE KNOWS HE'S HERE, BUT...
IS SHE FOR REAL?
SHE MAY THINK SO.
I'M NOT ITCHING FOR A FIGHT...
ESPECIALLY AGAINST LOS QUERIDOS...
ALRIGHT, YOU. COME ON.

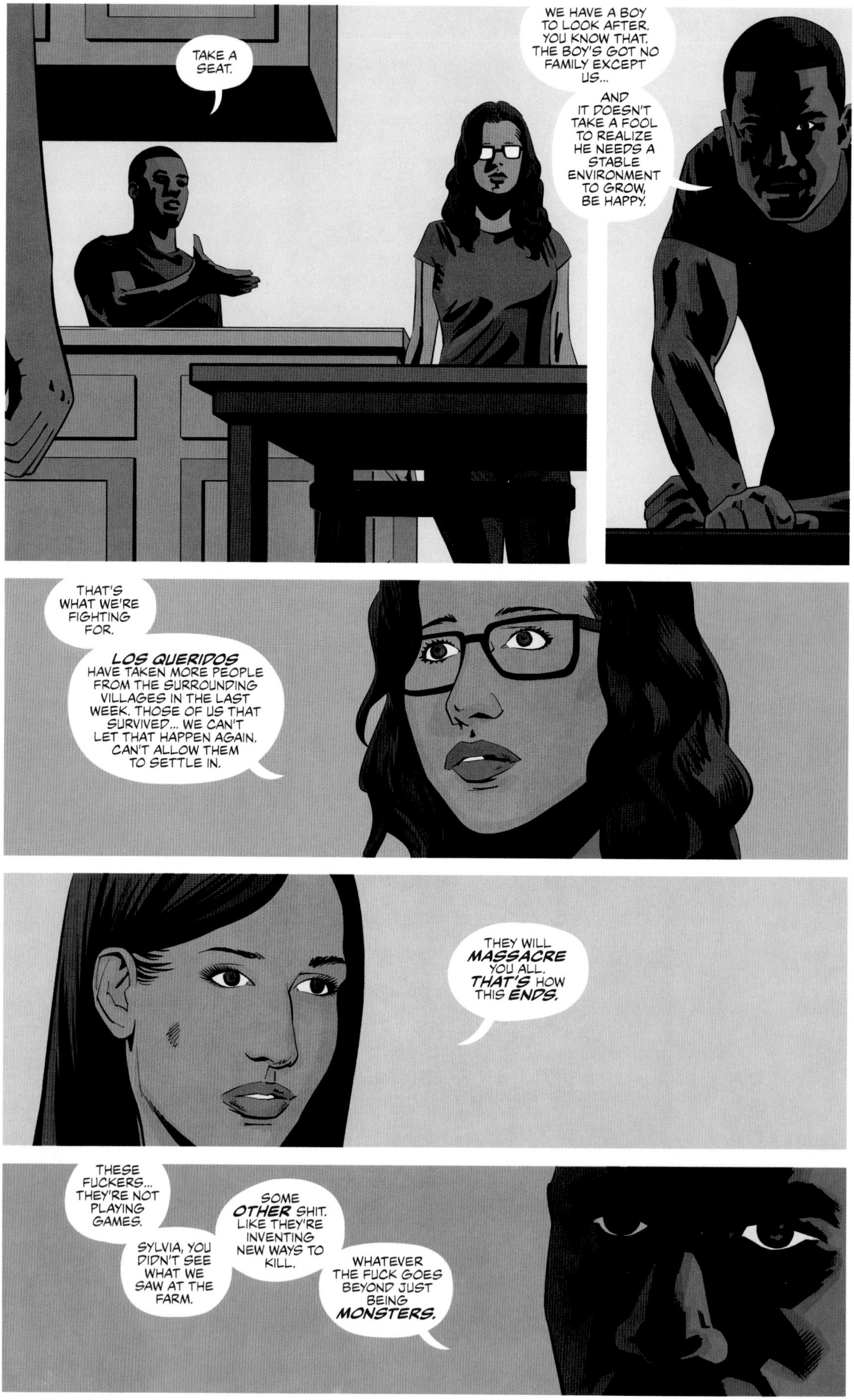
TAKE A SEAT.
WE HAVE A BOY TO LOOK AFTER. YOU KNOW THAT. THE BOY'S GOT NO FAMILY EXCEPT US...
AND IT DOESN'T TAKE A FOOL TO REALIZE HE NEEDS A STABLE ENVIRONMENT TO GROW, BE HAPPY.
THAT'S WHAT WE'RE FIGHTING FOR.
LOS QUERIDOS HAVE TAKEN MORE PEOPLE FROM THE SURROUNDING VILLAGES IN THE LAST WEEK. THOSE OF US THAT SURVIVED... WE CAN'T LET THAT HAPPEN AGAIN. CAN'T ALLOW THEM TO SETTLE IN.
THEY WILL MASSACRE YOU ALL. THAT'S HOW THIS ENDS.
THESE FUCKERS... THEY'RE NOT PLAYING GAMES.
SYLVIA, YOU DIDN'T SEE WHAT WE SAW AT THE FARM.
SOME OTHER SHIT. LIKE THEY'RE INVENTING NEW WAYS TO KILL.
WHATEVER THE FUCK GOES BEYOND JUST BEING MONSTERS.

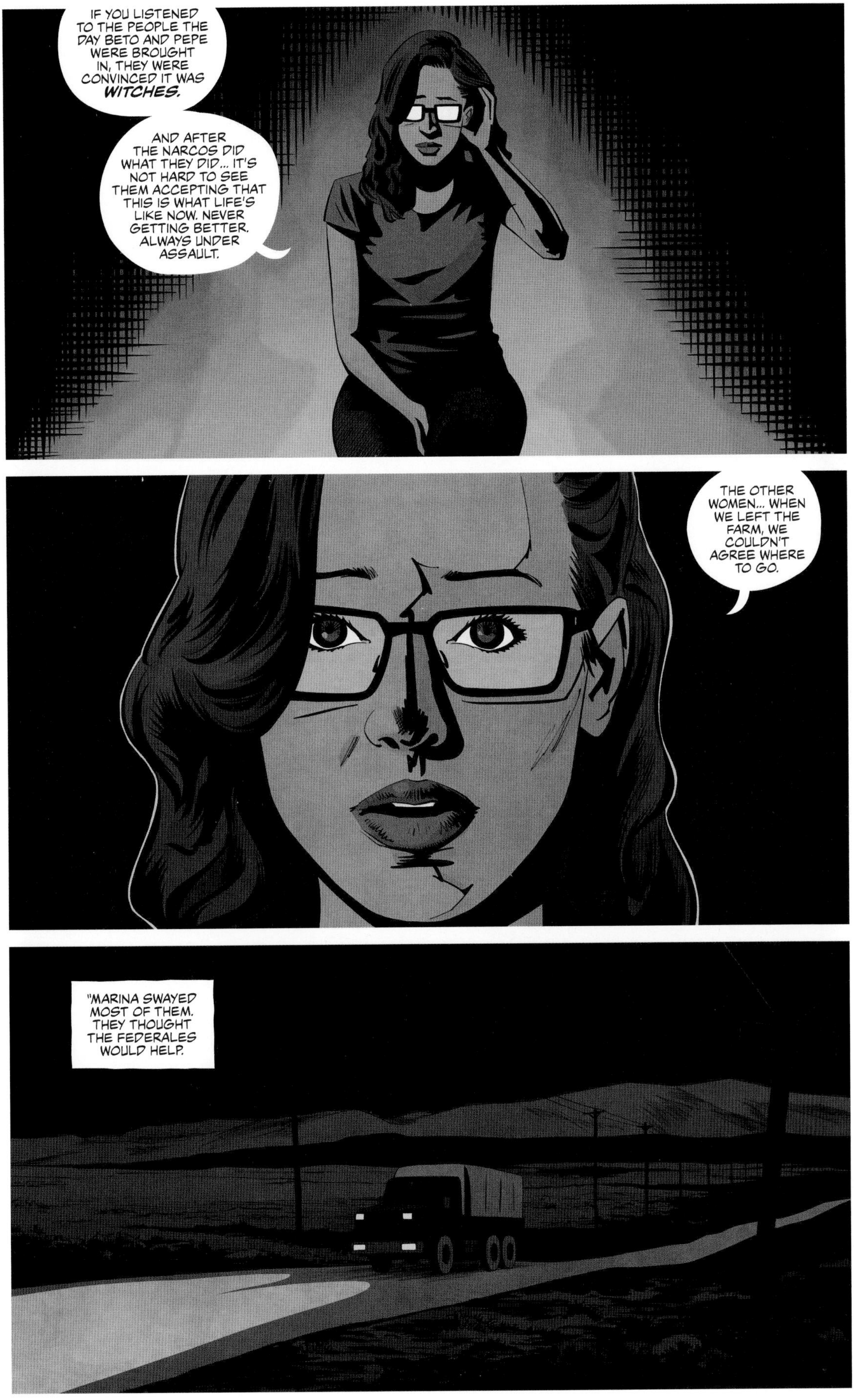
IF YOU LISTENED TO THE PEOPLE THE DAY BETO AND PEPE WERE BROUGHT IN, THEY WERE CONVINCED IT WAS *WITCHES.*
AND AFTER THE NARCOS DID WHAT THEY DID... IT'S NOT HARD TO SEE THEM ACCEPTING THAT THIS IS WHAT LIFE'S LIKE NOW. NEVER GETTING BETTER. ALWAYS UNDER ASSAULT.
THE OTHER WOMEN... WHEN WE LEFT THE FARM, WE COULDN'T AGREE WHERE TO GO.
"MARINA SWAYED MOST OF THEM. THEY THOUGHT THE FEDERALES WOULD HELP.

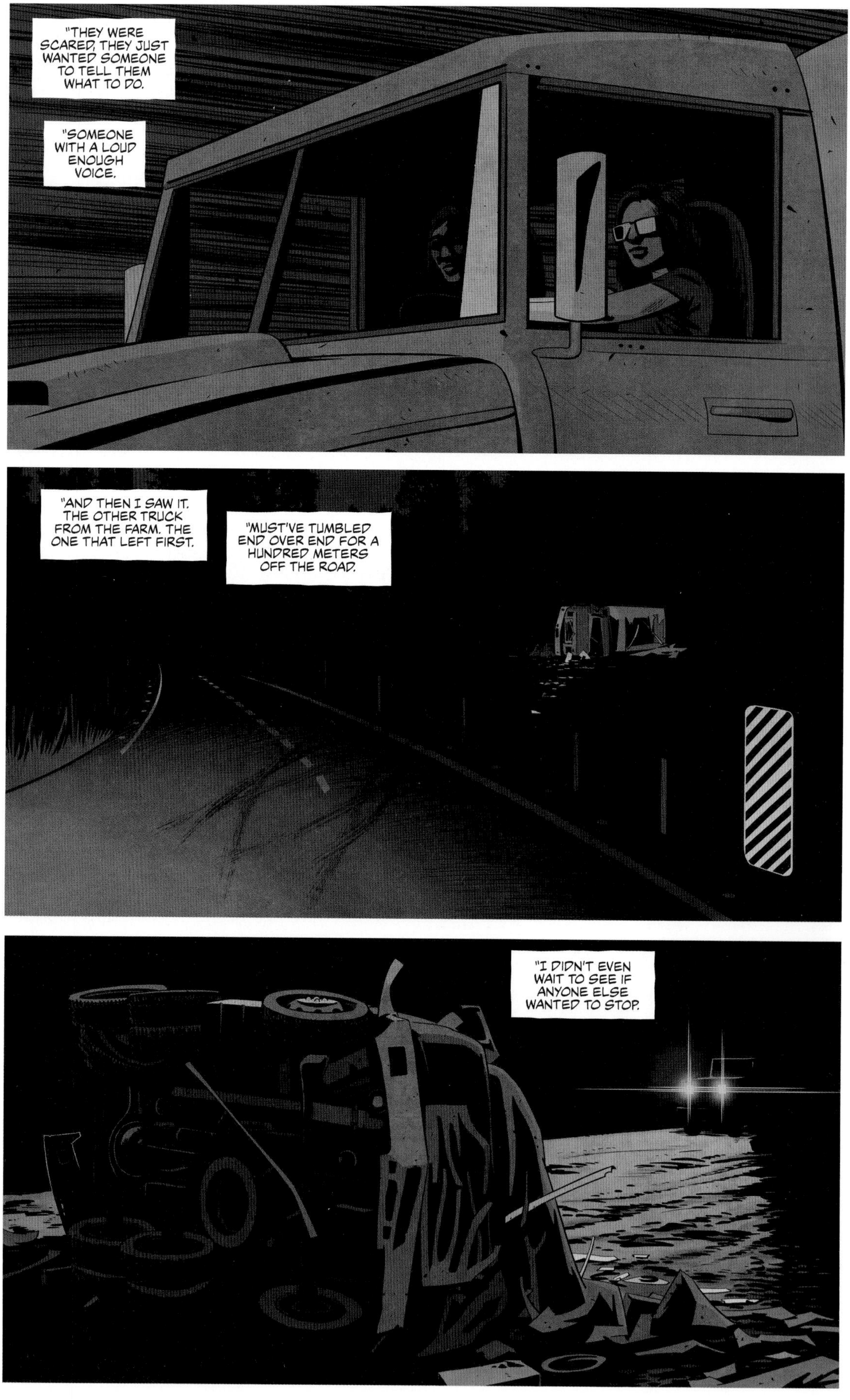
"THEY WERE SCARED, THEY JUST WANTED SOMEONE TO TELL THEM WHAT TO DO.
"SOMEONE WITH A LOUD ENOUGH VOICE.
"AND THEN I SAW IT. THE OTHER TRUCK FROM THE FARM. THE ONE THAT LEFT FIRST.
"MUST'VE TUMBLED END OVER END FOR A HUNDRED METERS OFF THE ROAD.
"I DIDN'T EVEN WAIT TO SEE IF ANYONE ELSE WANTED TO STOP.

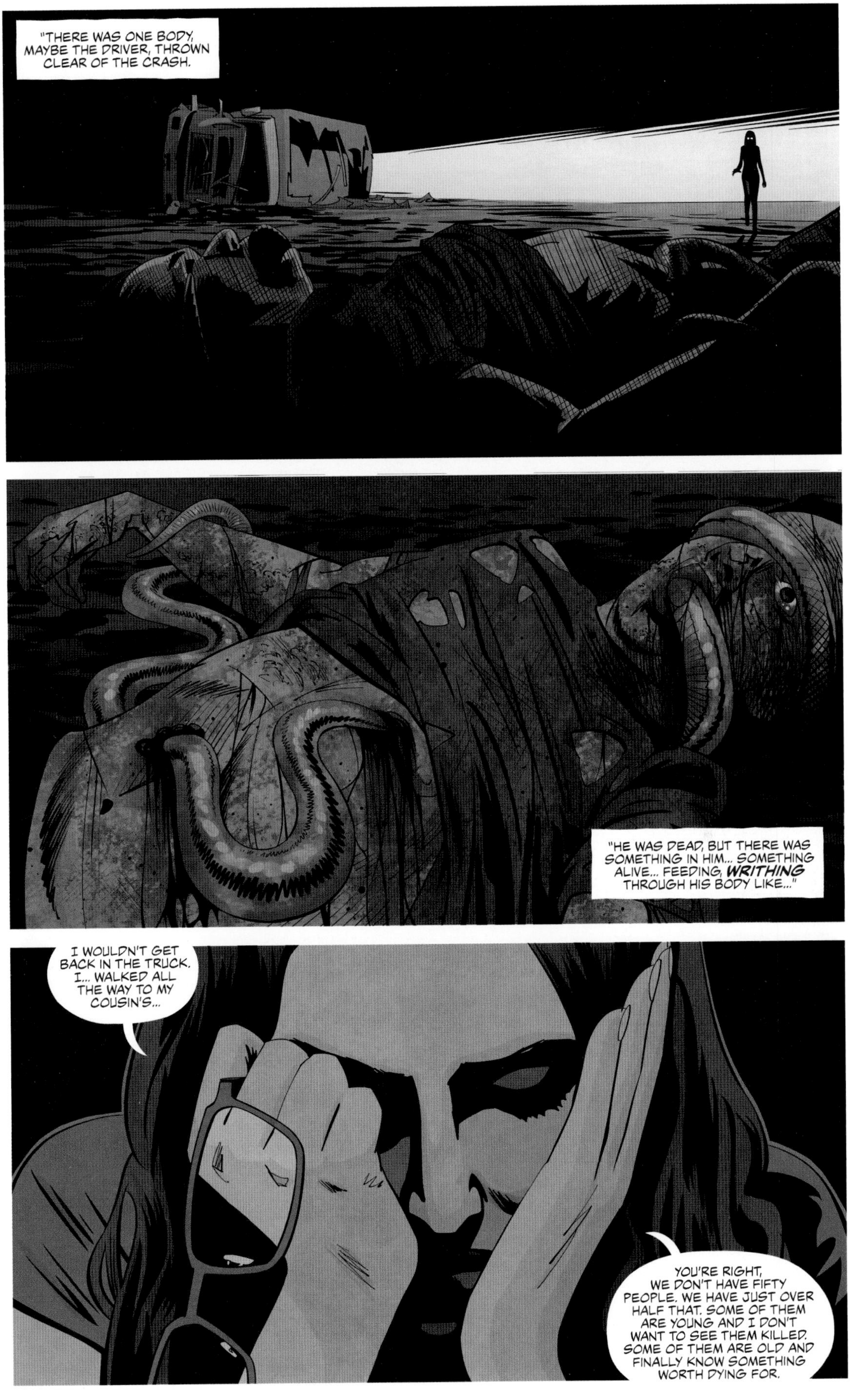
"THERE WAS ONE BODY, MAYBE THE DRIVER, THROWN CLEAR OF THE CRASH.
"HE WAS DEAD, BUT THERE WAS SOMETHING IN HIM... SOMETHING ALIVE... FEEDING, WRITHING THROUGH HIS BODY LIKE..."
I WOULDN'T GET BACK IN THE TRUCK. I... WALKED ALL THE WAY TO MY COUSIN'S...
YOU'RE RIGHT, WE DON'T HAVE FIFTY PEOPLE. WE HAVE JUST OVER HALF THAT. SOME OF THEM ARE YOUNG AND I DON'T WANT TO SEE THEM KILLED. SOME OF THEM ARE OLD AND FINALLY KNOW SOMETHING WORTH DYING FOR.

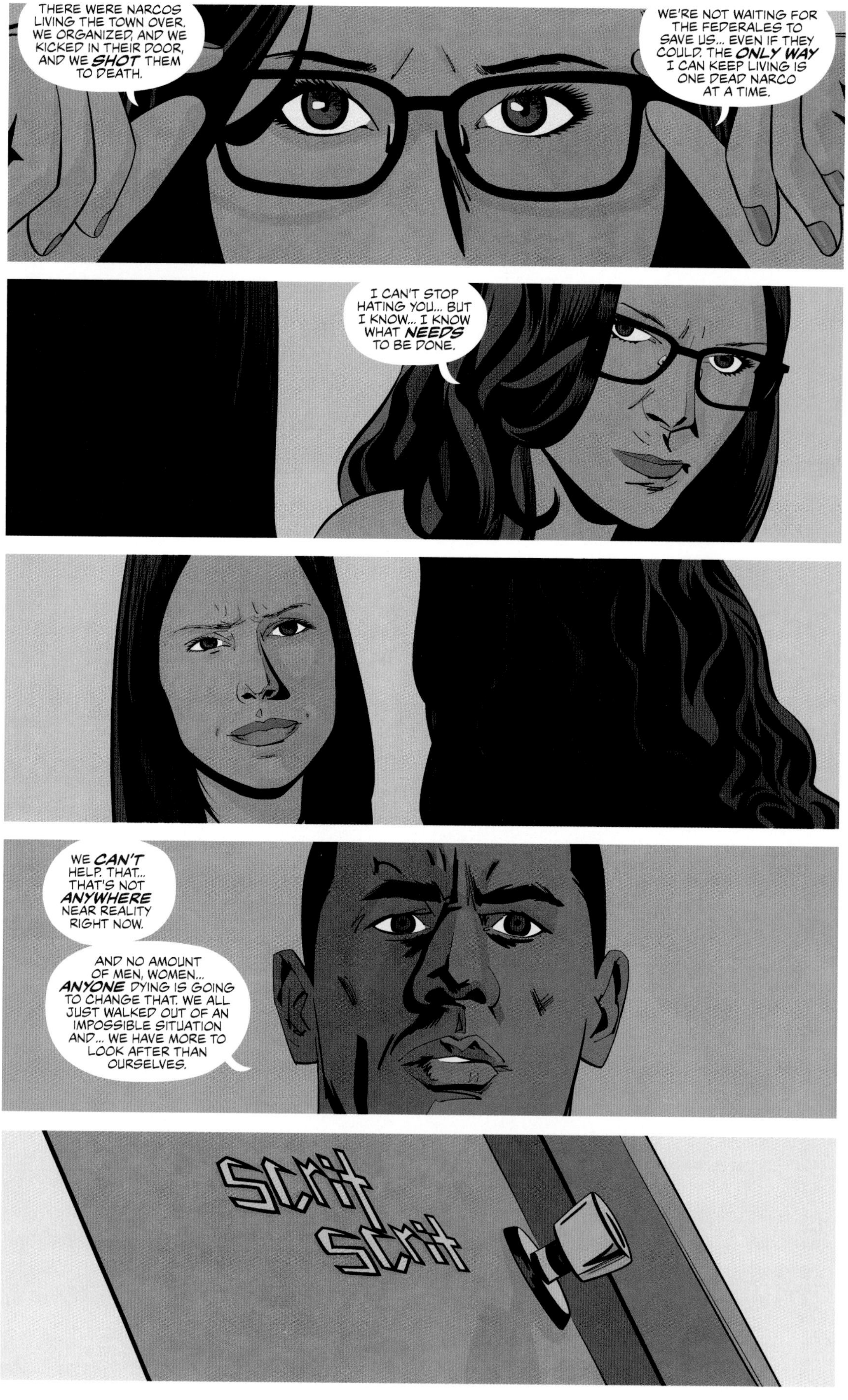
THERE WERE NARCOS LIVING THE TOWN OVER. WE ORGANIZED, AND WE KICKED IN THEIR DOOR, AND WE SHOT THEM TO DEATH.
WE'RE NOT WAITING FOR THE FEDERALES TO SAVE US... EVEN IF THEY COULD. THE ONLY WAY I CAN KEEP LIVING IS ONE DEAD NARCO AT A TIME.
I CAN'T STOP HATING YOU... BUT I KNOW... I KNOW WHAT NEEDS TO BE DONE.
WE CAN'T HELP. THAT... THAT'S NOT ANYWHERE NEAR REALITY RIGHT NOW.
AND NO AMOUNT OF MEN, WOMEN... ANYONE DYING IS GOING TO CHANGE THAT. WE ALL JUST WALKED OUT OF AN IMPOSSIBLE SITUATION AND... WE HAVE MORE TO LOOK AFTER THAN OURSELVES.
SCRIT
SCRIT

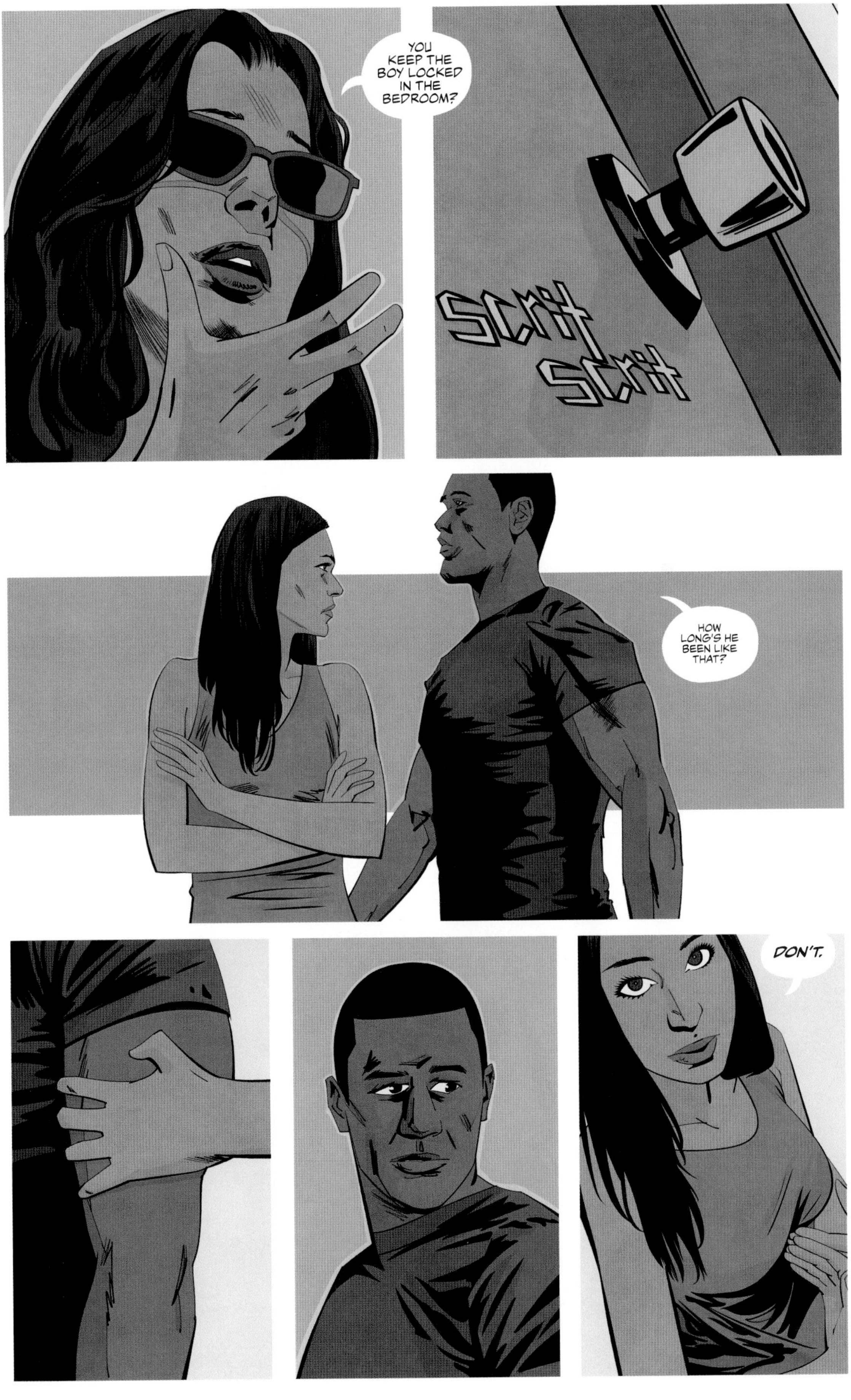
YOU KEEP THE BOY LOCKED IN THE BEDROOM?
SCRIT
SCRIT
HOW LONG'S HE BEEN LIKE THAT?
DON'T.

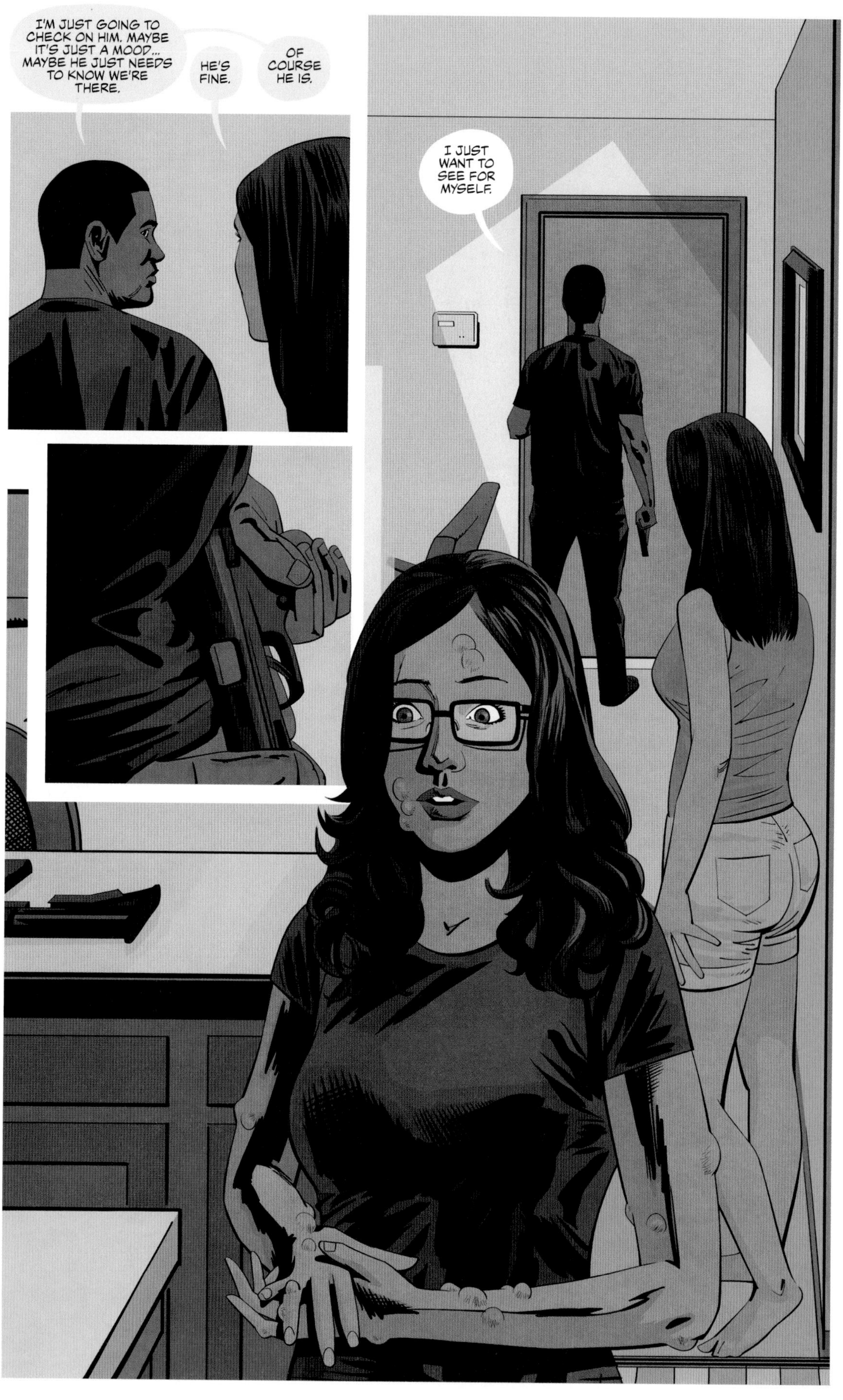
I'M JUST GOING TO CHECK ON HIM. MAYBE IT'S JUST A MOOD... MAYBE HE JUST NEEDS TO KNOW WE'RE THERE.
HE'S FINE.
OF COURSE HE IS.
I JUST WANT TO SEE FOR MYSELF.

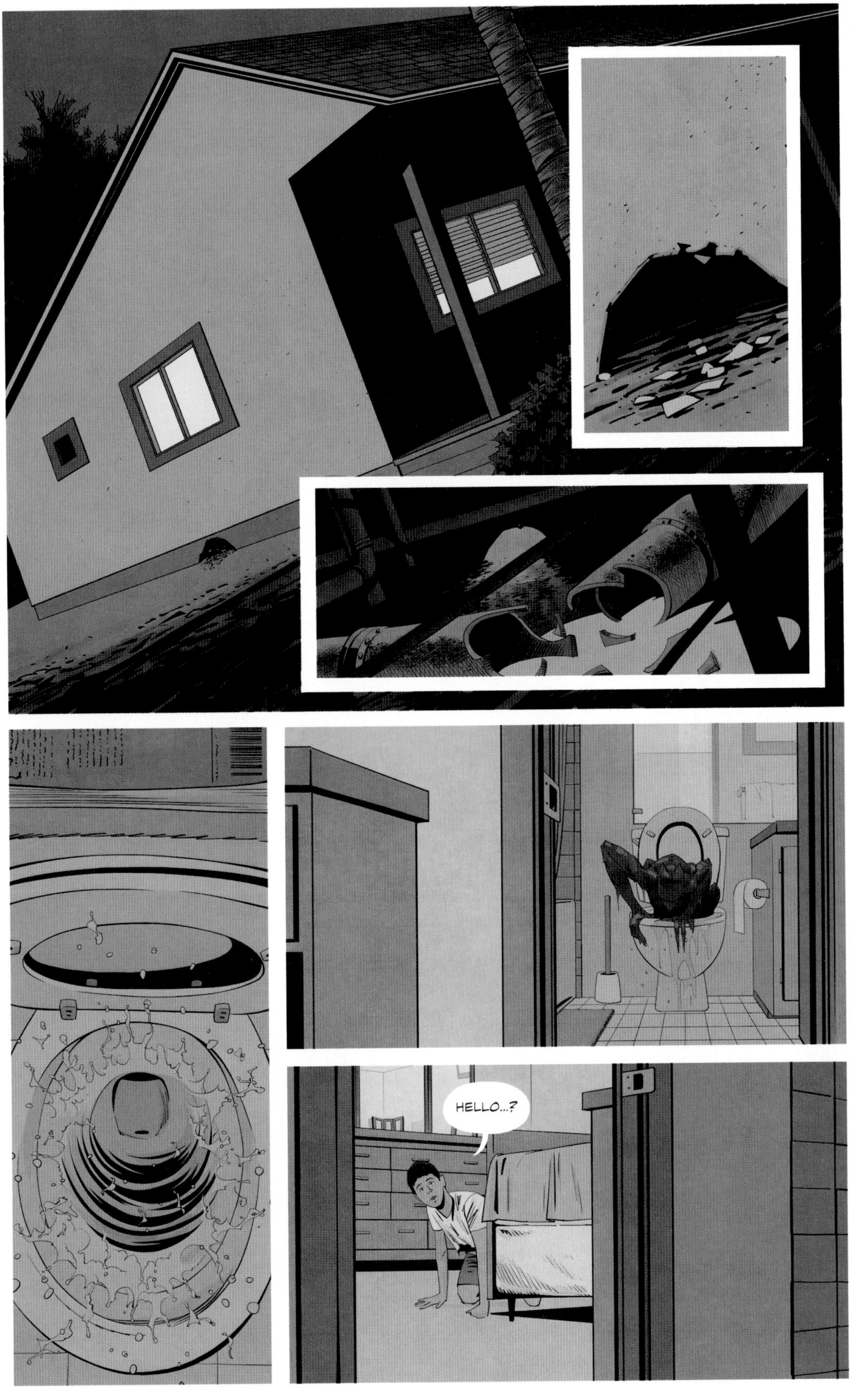
HELLO...?

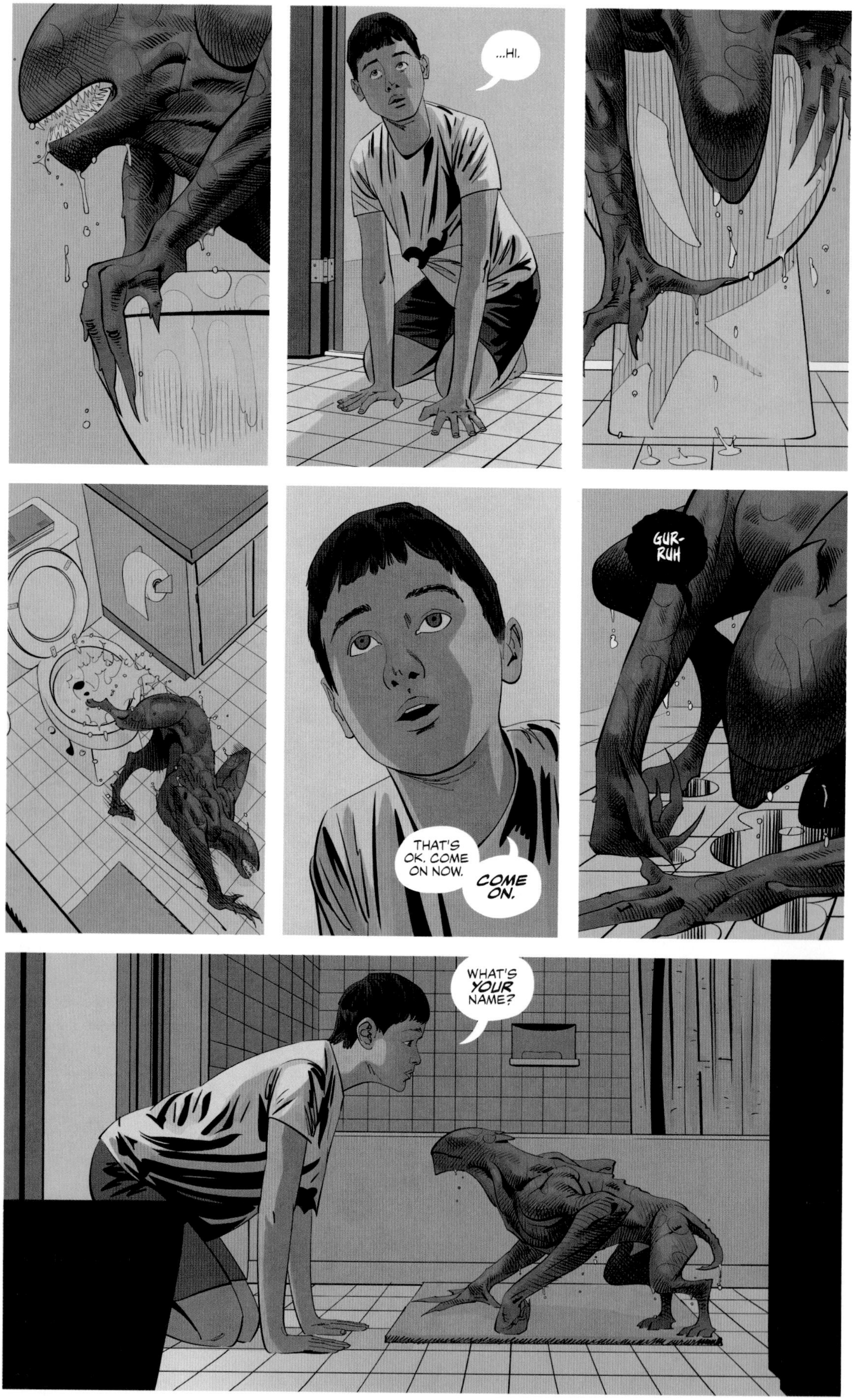

...HI.
THAT'S OK. COME ON NOW.
COME ON.
GUR-RUH
WHAT'S YOUR NAME?

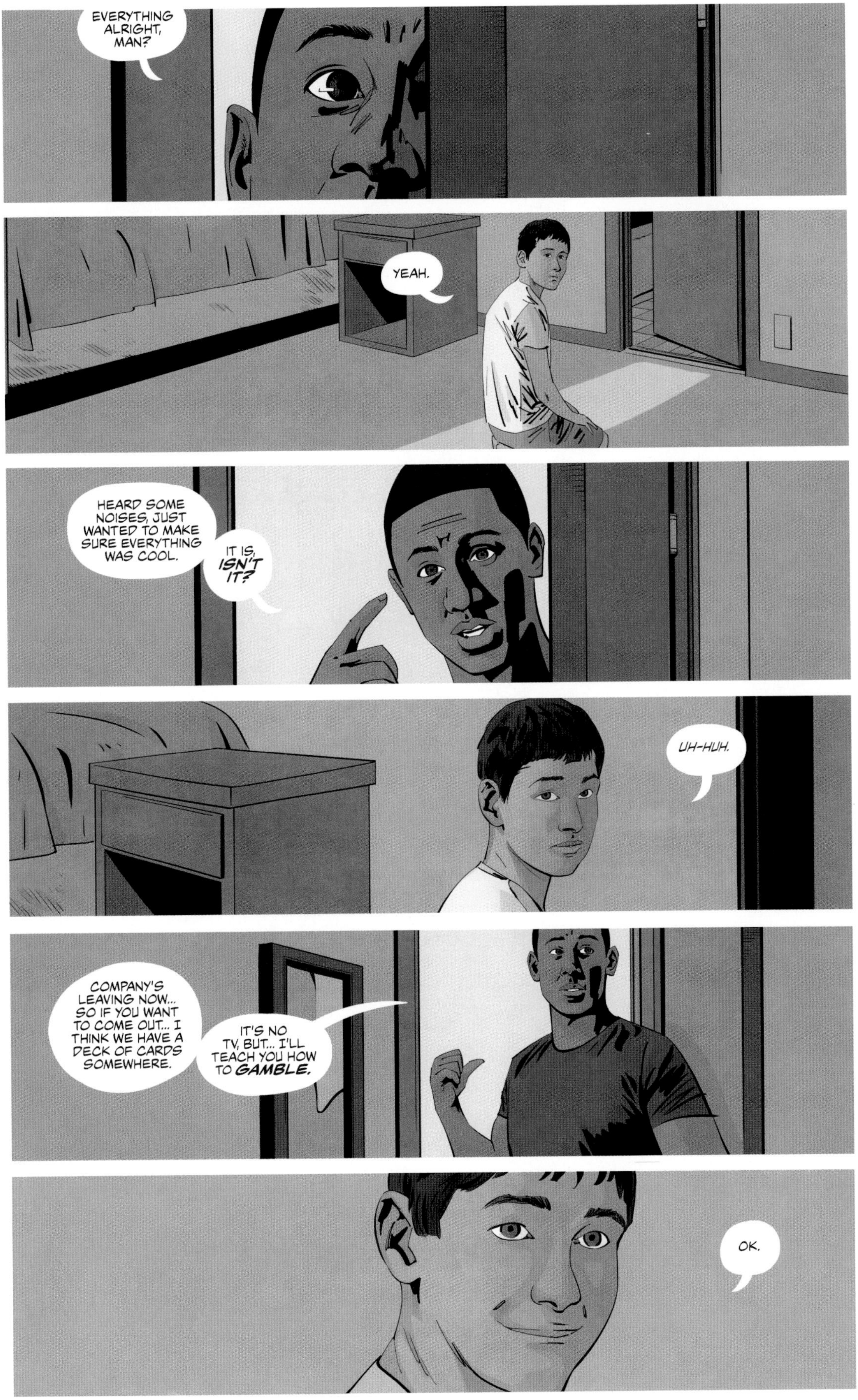
EVERYTHING ALRIGHT, MAN?
YEAH.
HEARD SOME NOISES, JUST WANTED TO MAKE SURE EVERYTHING WAS COOL.
IT IS, *ISN'T IT?*
UH-HUH.
COMPANY'S LEAVING NOW... SO IF YOU WANT TO COME OUT... I THINK WE HAVE A DECK OF CARDS SOMEWHERE.
IT'S NO TV, BUT... I'LL TEACH YOU HOW TO **GAMBLE.**
OK.

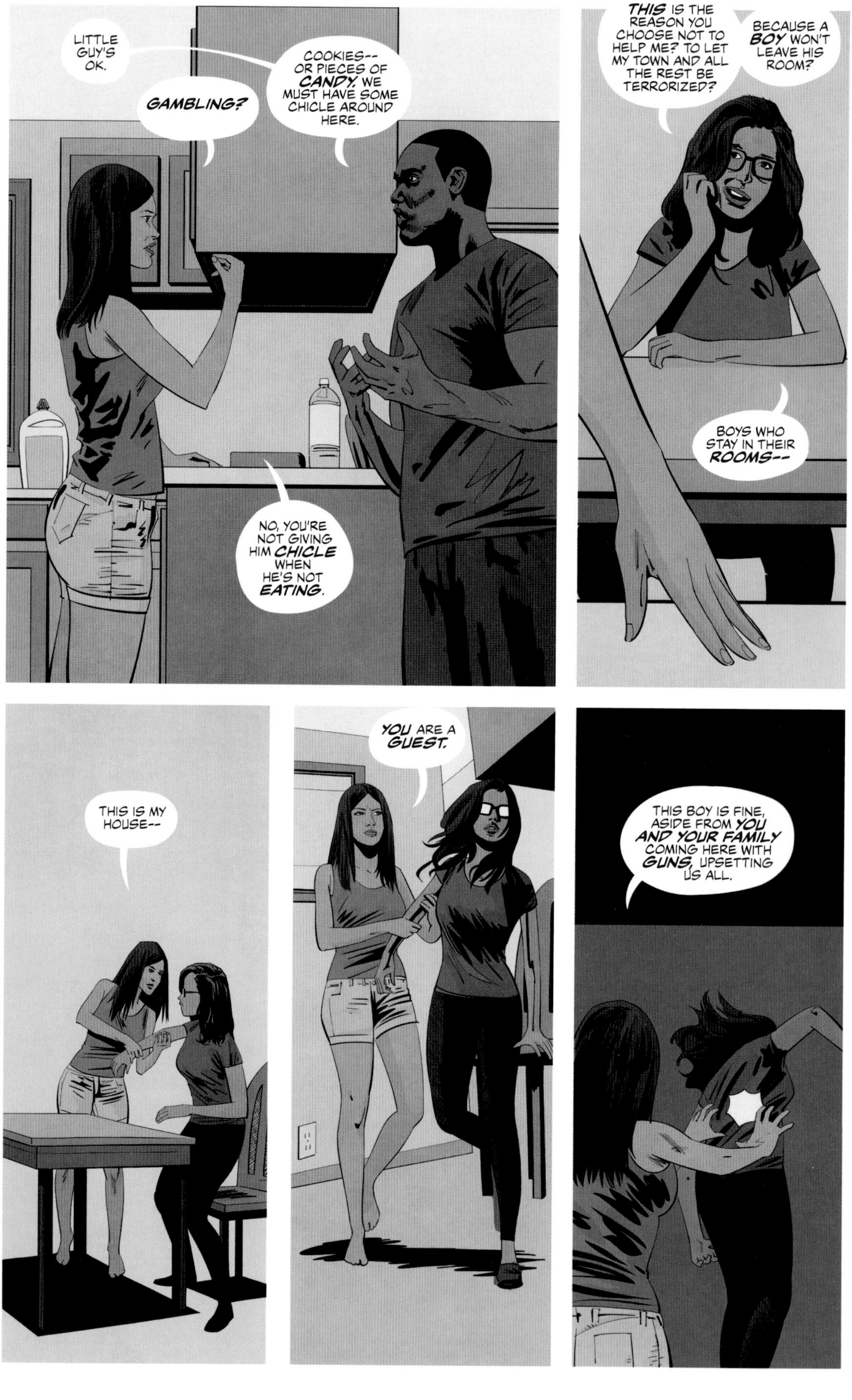

LITTLE GUY'S OK.
GAMBLING?
COOKIES-- OR PIECES OF CANDY. WE MUST HAVE SOME CHICLE AROUND HERE.
NO, YOU'RE NOT GIVING HIM CHICLE WHEN HE'S NOT EATING.
THIS IS THE REASON YOU CHOOSE NOT TO HELP ME? TO LET MY TOWN AND ALL THE REST BE TERRORIZED?
BECAUSE A BOY WON'T LEAVE HIS ROOM?
BOYS WHO STAY IN THEIR ROOMS--
THIS IS MY HOUSE--
YOU ARE A GUEST.
THIS BOY IS FINE, ASIDE FROM YOU AND YOUR FAMILY COMING HERE WITH GUNS, UPSETTING US ALL.

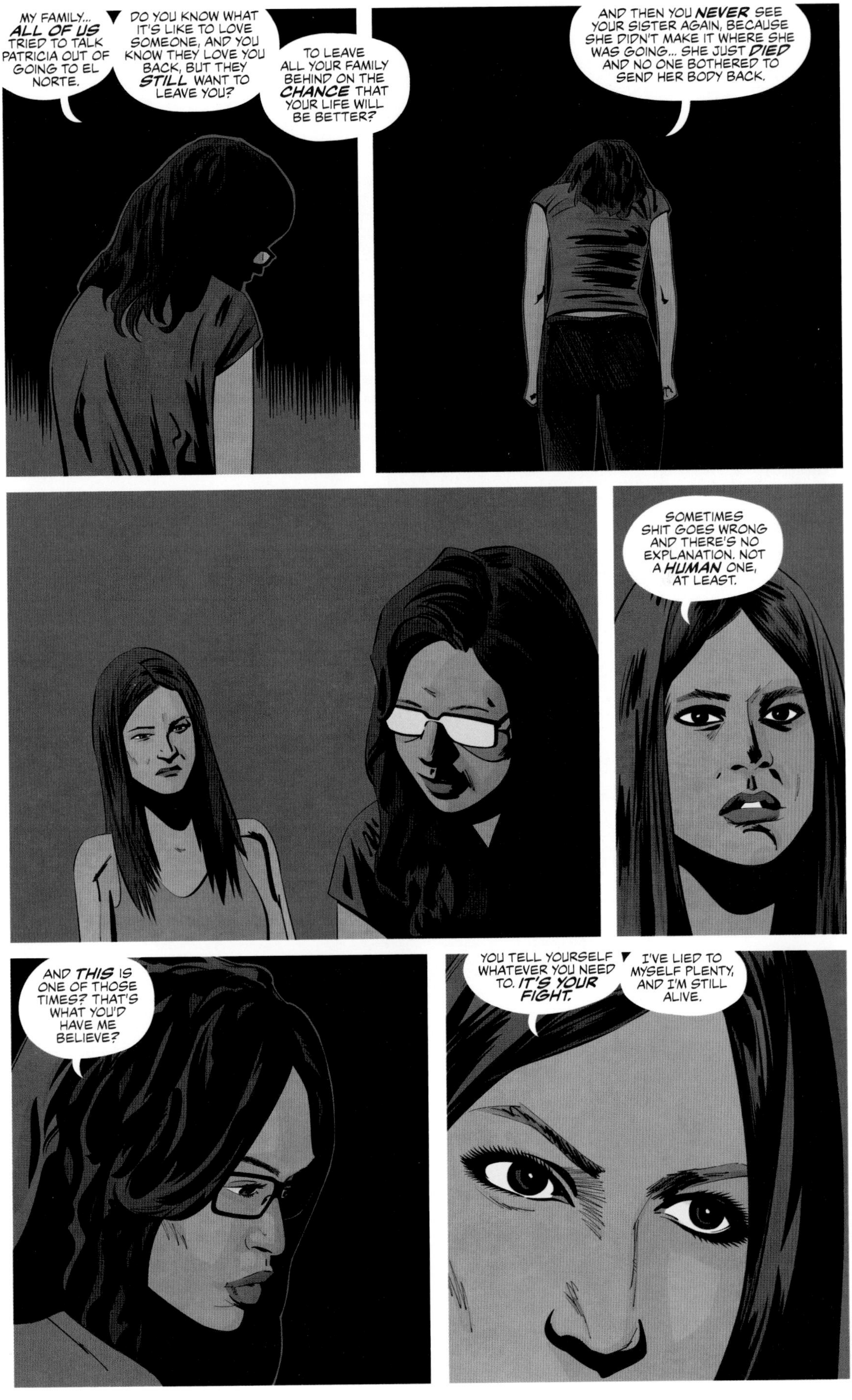
MY FAMILY... ALL OF US TRIED TO TALK PATRICIA OUT OF GOING TO EL NORTE.
DO YOU KNOW WHAT IT'S LIKE TO LOVE SOMEONE, AND YOU KNOW THEY LOVE YOU BACK, BUT THEY STILL WANT TO LEAVE YOU?
TO LEAVE ALL YOUR FAMILY BEHIND ON THE CHANCE THAT YOUR LIFE WILL BE BETTER?
AND THEN YOU NEVER SEE YOUR SISTER AGAIN, BECAUSE SHE DIDN'T MAKE IT WHERE SHE WAS GOING... SHE JUST DIED AND NO ONE BOTHERED TO SEND HER BODY BACK.
SOMETIMES SHIT GOES WRONG AND THERE'S NO EXPLANATION. NOT A HUMAN ONE, AT LEAST.
AND THIS IS ONE OF THOSE TIMES? THAT'S WHAT YOU'D HAVE ME BELIEVE?
YOU TELL YOURSELF WHATEVER YOU NEED TO. IT'S YOUR FIGHT.
I'VE LIED TO MYSELF PLENTY, AND I'M STILL ALIVE.

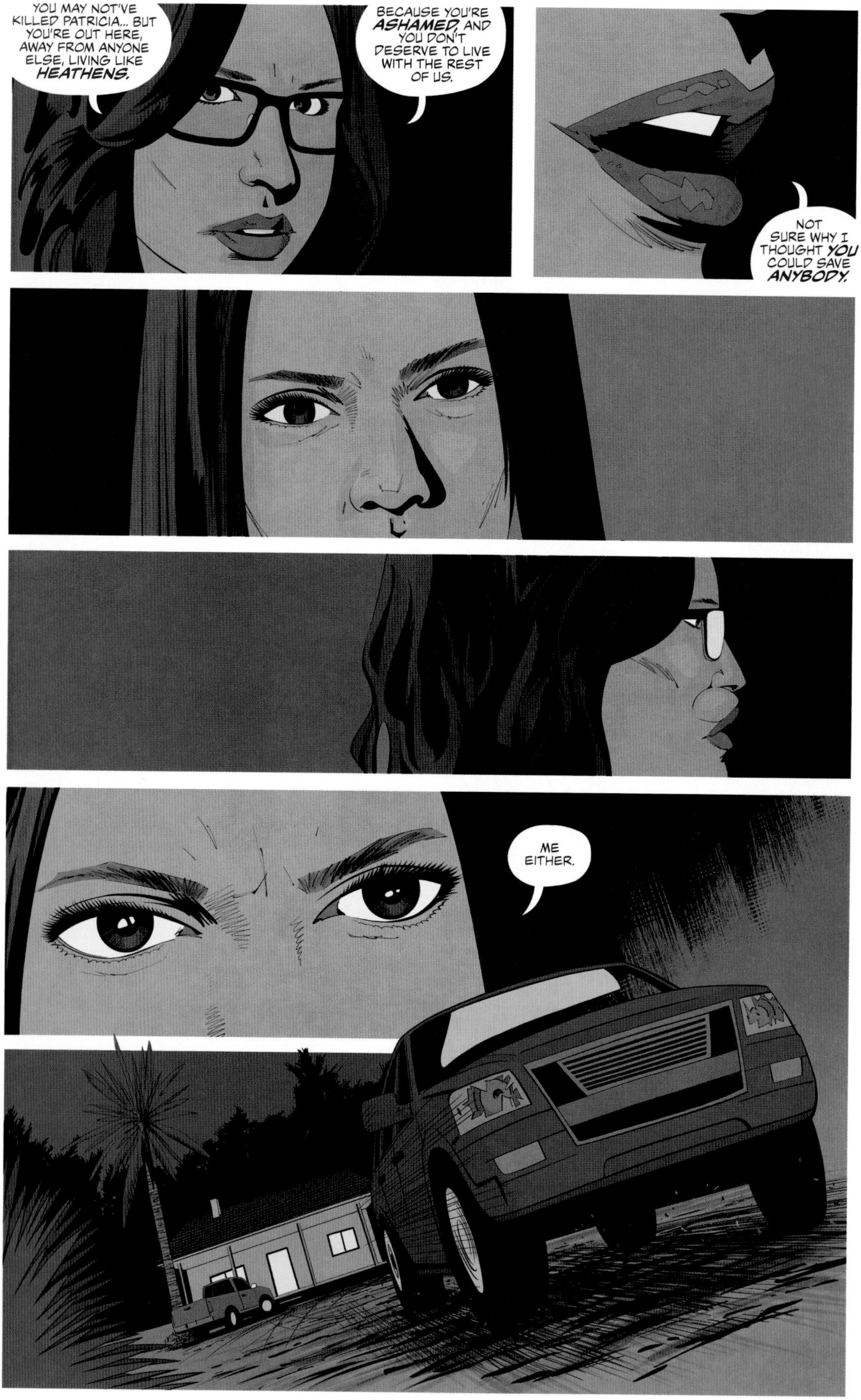
YOU MAY NOT'VE KILLED PATRICIA... BUT YOU'RE OUT HERE, AWAY FROM ANYONE ELSE, LIVING LIKE HEATHENS.
BECAUSE YOU'RE ASHAMED, AND YOU DON'T DESERVE TO LIVE WITH THE REST OF US.
NOT SURE WHY I THOUGHT YOU COULD SAVE ANYBODY.
ME EITHER.

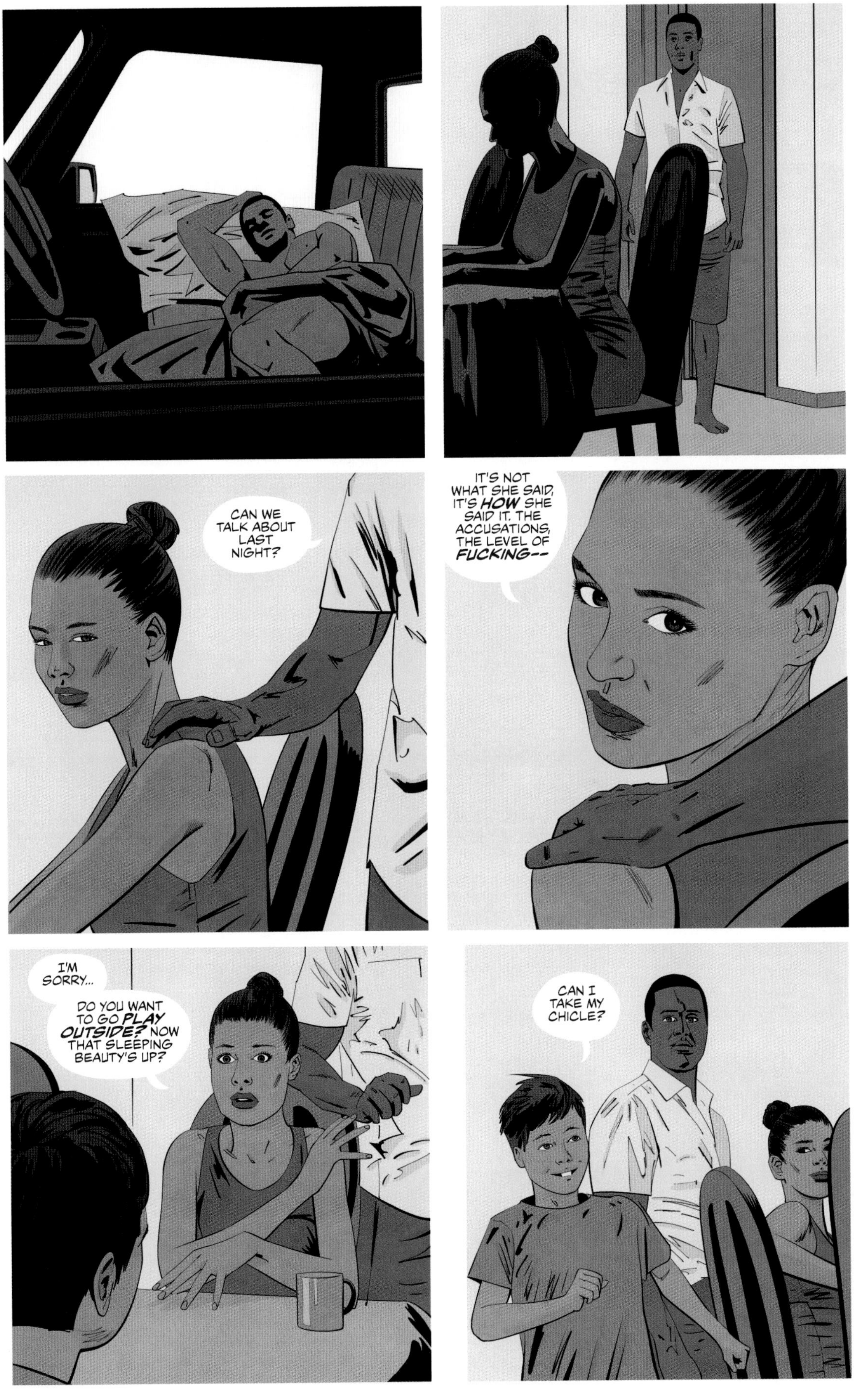
CAN WE TALK ABOUT LAST NIGHT?
IT'S NOT WHAT SHE SAID, IT'S HOW SHE SAID IT. THE ACCUSATIONS, THE LEVEL OF FUCKING--
I'M SORRY...
DO YOU WANT TO GO PLAY OUTSIDE? NOW THAT SLEEPING BEAUTY'S UP?
CAN I TAKE MY CHICLE?

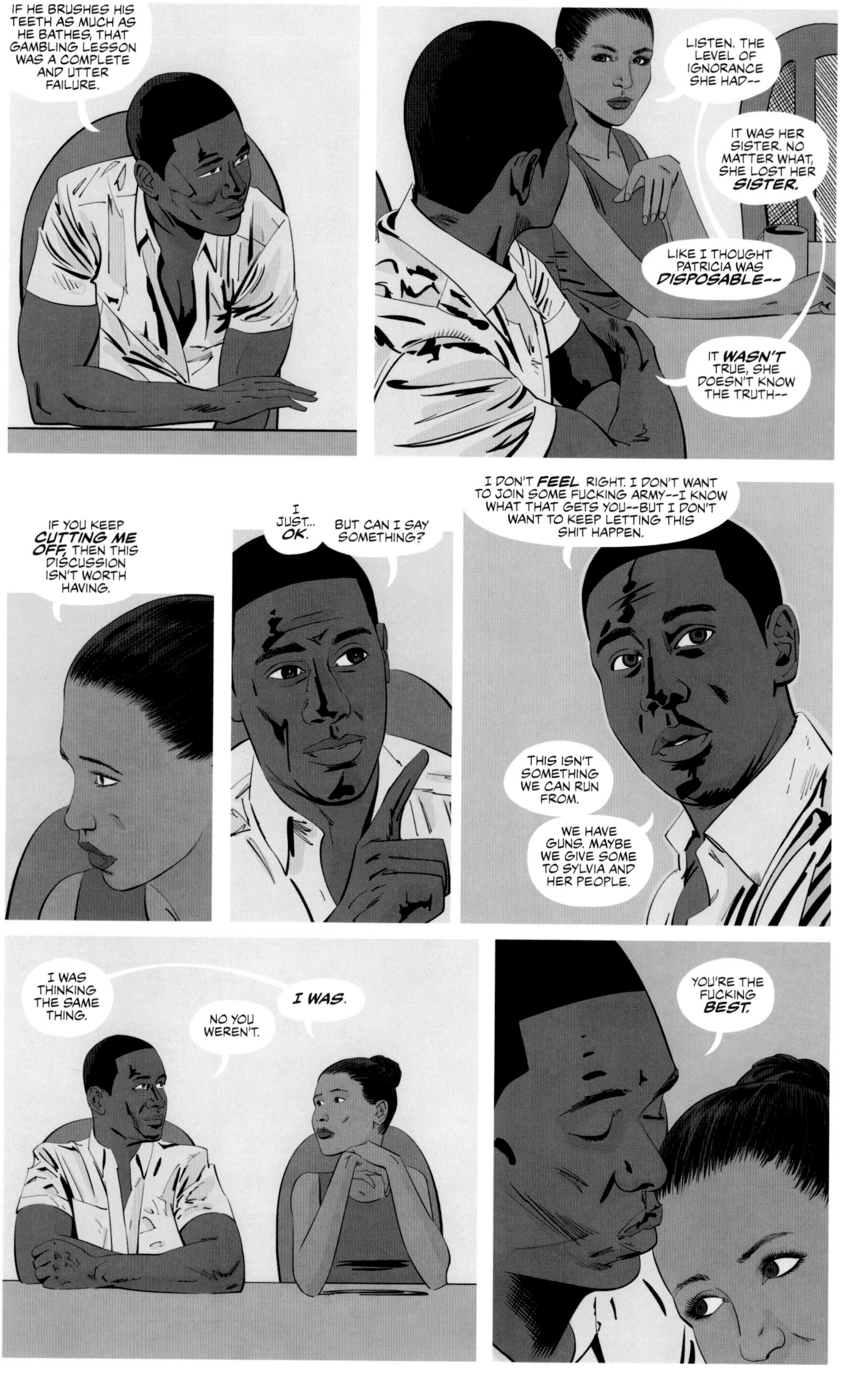
IF HE BRUSHES HIS TEETH AS MUCH AS HE BATHES, THAT GAMBLING LESSON WAS A COMPLETE AND UTTER FAILURE.
LISTEN. THE LEVEL OF IGNORANCE SHE HAD--
IT WAS HER SISTER. NO MATTER WHAT, SHE LOST HER SISTER.
LIKE I THOUGHT PATRICIA WAS DISPOSABLE--
IT WASN'T TRUE, SHE DOESN'T KNOW THE TRUTH--
IF YOU KEEP CUTTING ME OFF, THEN THIS DISCUSSION ISN'T WORTH HAVING.
I JUST... OK.
BUT CAN I SAY SOMETHING?
I DON'T FEEL RIGHT. I DON'T WANT TO JOIN SOME FUCKING ARMY--I KNOW WHAT THAT GETS YOU--BUT I DON'T WANT TO KEEP LETTING THIS SHIT HAPPEN.
THIS ISN'T SOMETHING WE CAN RUN FROM.
WE HAVE GUNS. MAYBE WE GIVE SOME TO SYLVIA AND HER PEOPLE.
I WAS THINKING THE SAME THING.
NO YOU WEREN'T.
I WAS.
YOU'RE THE FUCKING BEST.

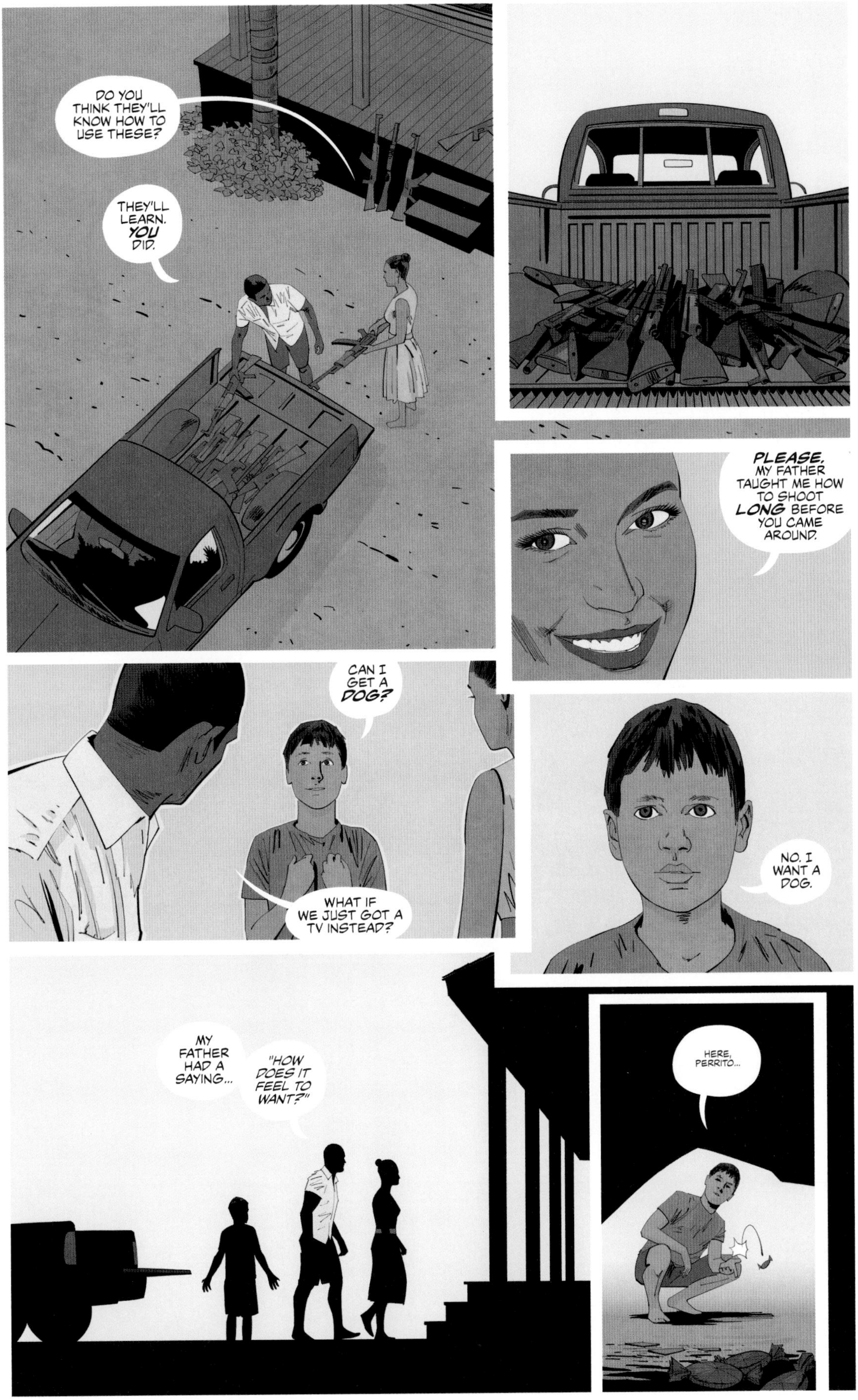
DO YOU THINK THEY'LL KNOW HOW TO USE THESE?
THEY'LL LEARN. YOU DID.
PLEASE. MY FATHER TAUGHT ME HOW TO SHOOT LONG BEFORE YOU CAME AROUND.
CAN I GET A DOG?
WHAT IF WE JUST GOT A TV INSTEAD?
NO. I WANT A DOG.
MY FATHER HAD A SAYING...
"HOW DOES IT FEEL TO WANT?"
HERE, PERRITO...

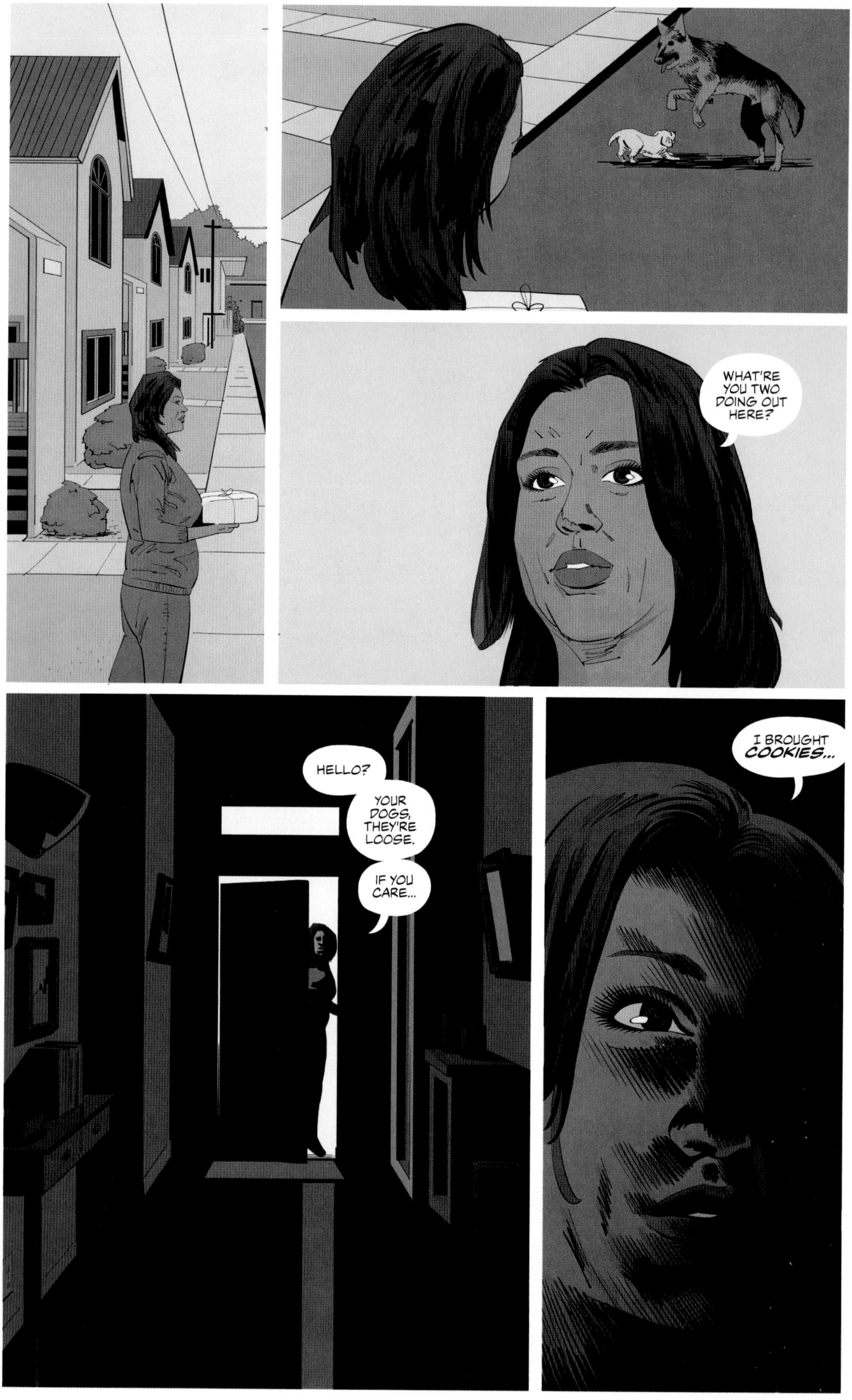
WHAT'RE YOU TWO DOING OUT HERE?
HELLO?
YOUR DOGS, THEY'RE LOOSE.
IF YOU CARE...
I BROUGHT COOKIES...

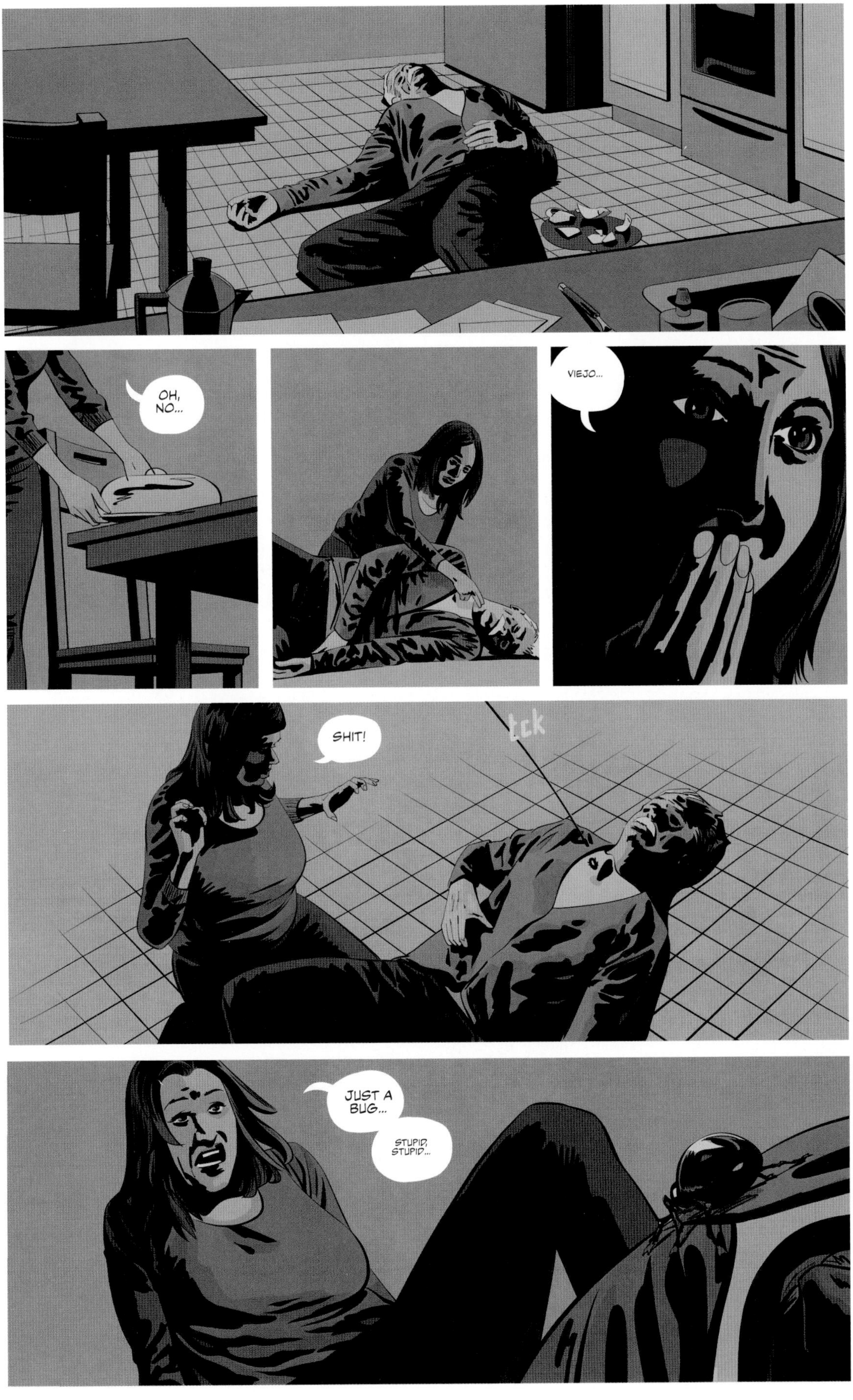
OH, NO...
VIEJO...
SHIT!
tck
JUST A BUG...
STUPID, STUPID...

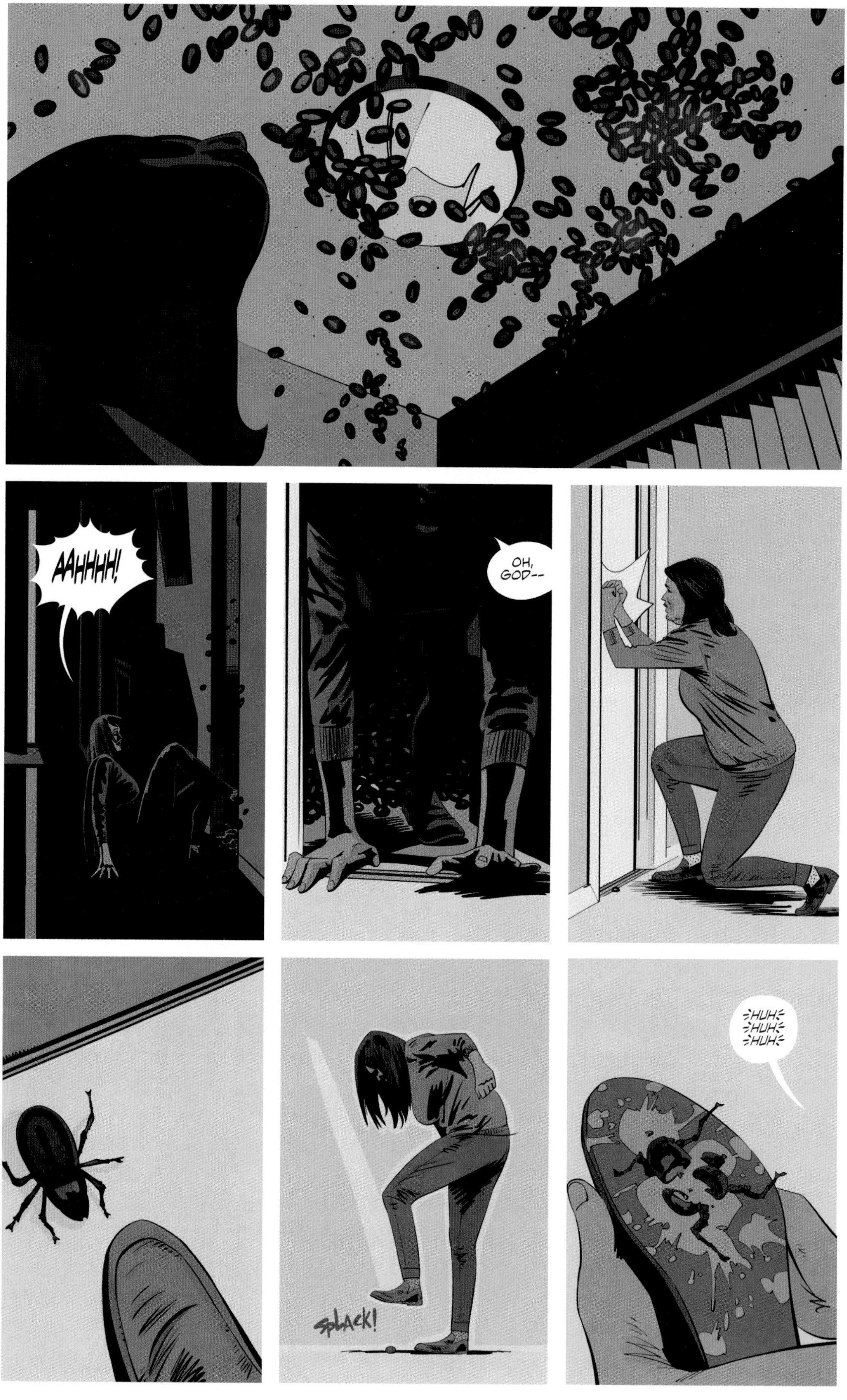
AAHHHH!
OH, GOD--
HUH HUH HUH
SPLACK!

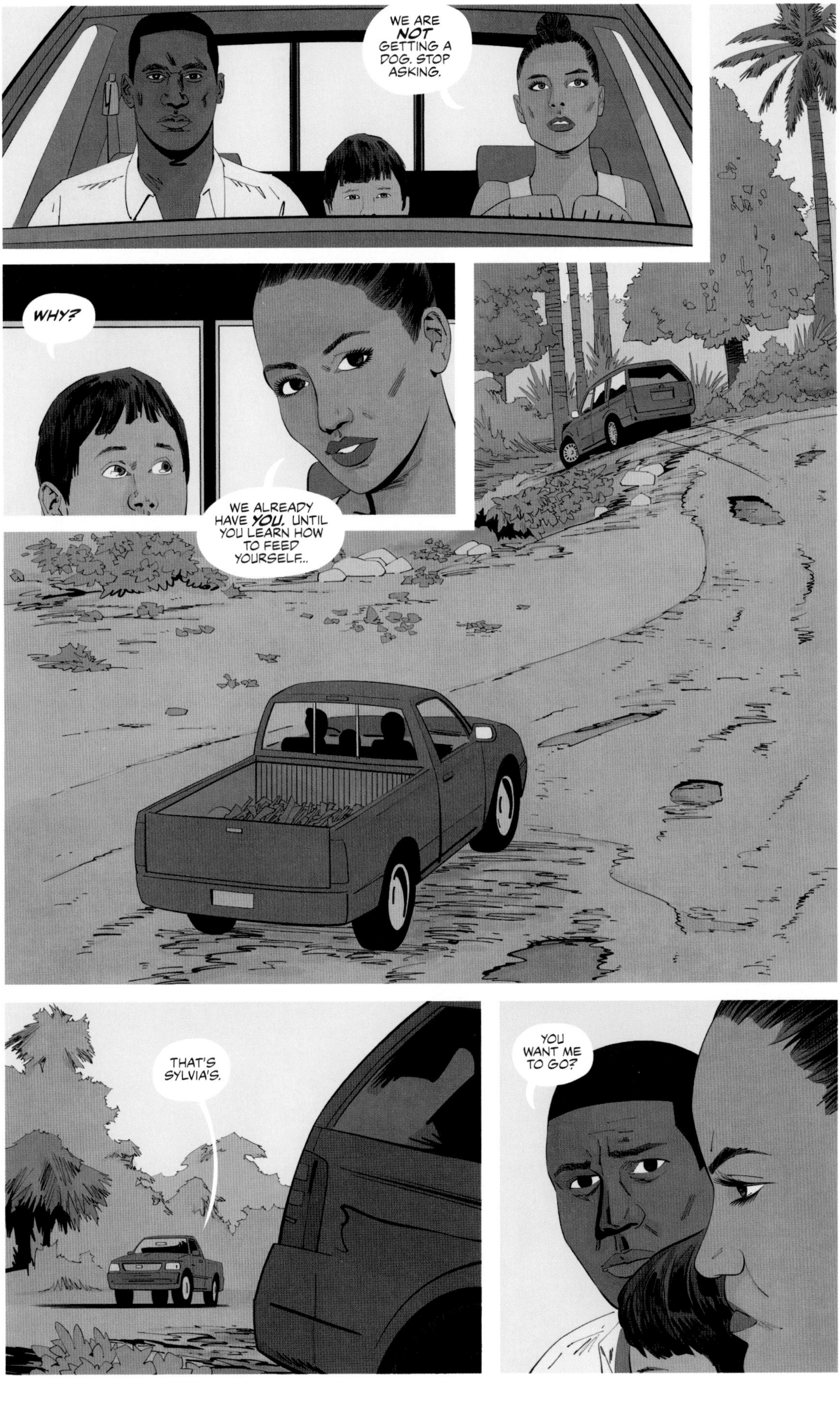
WE ARE NOT GETTING A DOG. STOP ASKING.
WHY?
WE ALREADY HAVE YOU. UNTIL YOU LEARN HOW TO FEED YOURSELF...
THAT'S SYLVIA'S.
YOU WANT ME TO GO?

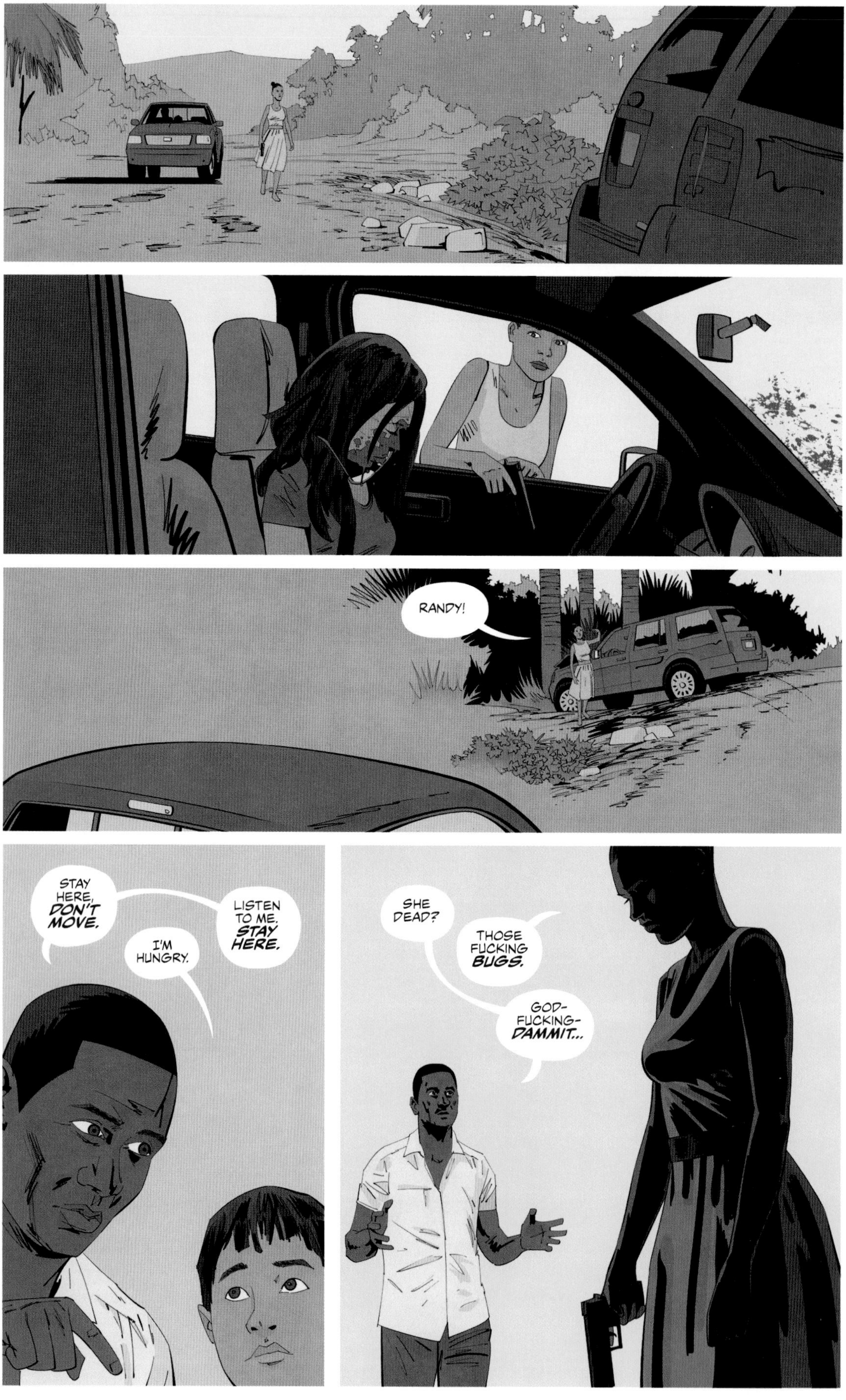
RANDY!
STAY HERE, DON'T MOVE.
LISTEN TO ME. STAY HERE.
I'M HUNGRY.
SHE DEAD?
THOSE FUCKING BUGS.
GOD-FUCKING-DAMMIT...

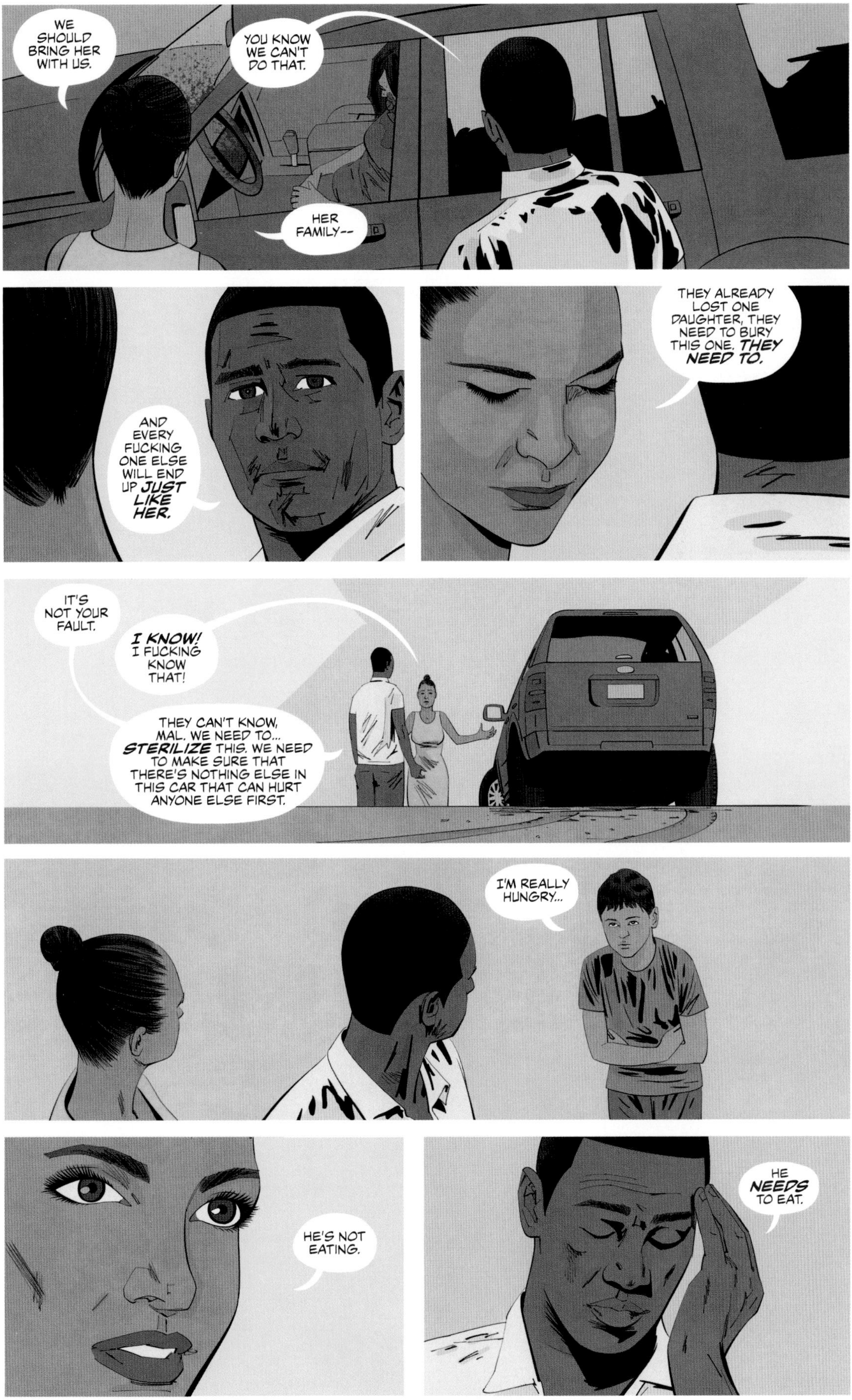

WE SHOULD BRING HER WITH US.
YOU KNOW WE CAN'T DO THAT.
HER FAMILY--
AND EVERY FUCKING ONE ELSE WILL END UP JUST LIKE HER.
THEY ALREADY LOST ONE DAUGHTER, THEY NEED TO BURY THIS ONE. THEY NEED TO.
IT'S NOT YOUR FAULT.
I KNOW! I FUCKING KNOW THAT!
THEY CAN'T KNOW, MAL. WE NEED TO... STERILIZE THIS. WE NEED TO MAKE SURE THAT THERE'S NOTHING ELSE IN THIS CAR THAT CAN HURT ANYONE ELSE FIRST.
I'M REALLY HUNGRY...
HE'S NOT EATING.
HE NEEDS TO EAT.

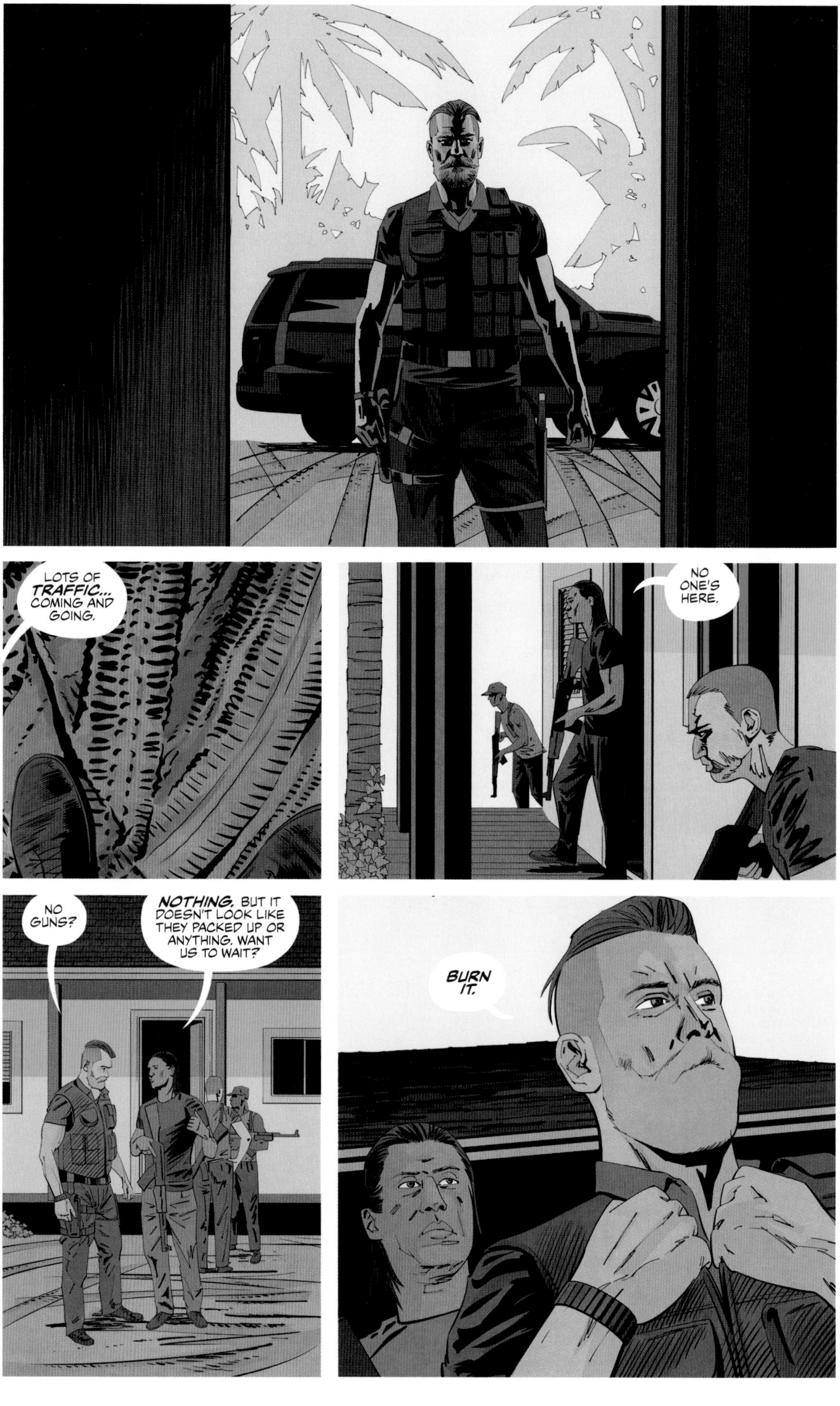
LOTS OF *TRAFFIC...* COMING AND GOING.
NO ONE'S HERE.
NO GUNS?
NOTHING. BUT IT DOESN'T LOOK LIKE THEY PACKED UP OR ANYTHING. WANT US TO WAIT?
BURN IT.

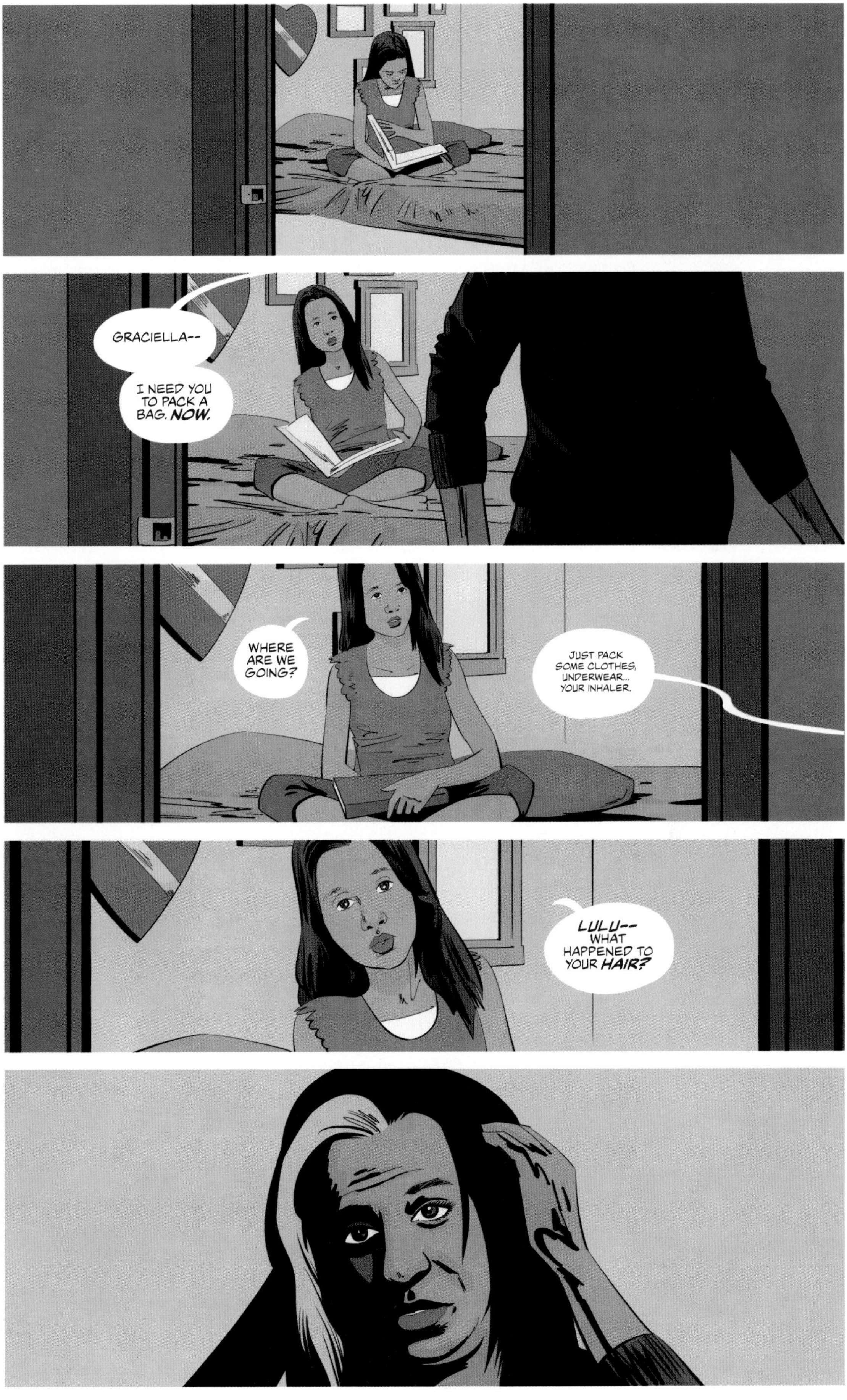
GRACIELLA--
I NEED YOU TO PACK A BAG. ***NOW.***
WHERE ARE WE GOING?
JUST PACK SOME CLOTHES, UNDERWEAR... YOUR INHALER.
LULU-- WHAT HAPPENED TO YOUR ***HAIR?***

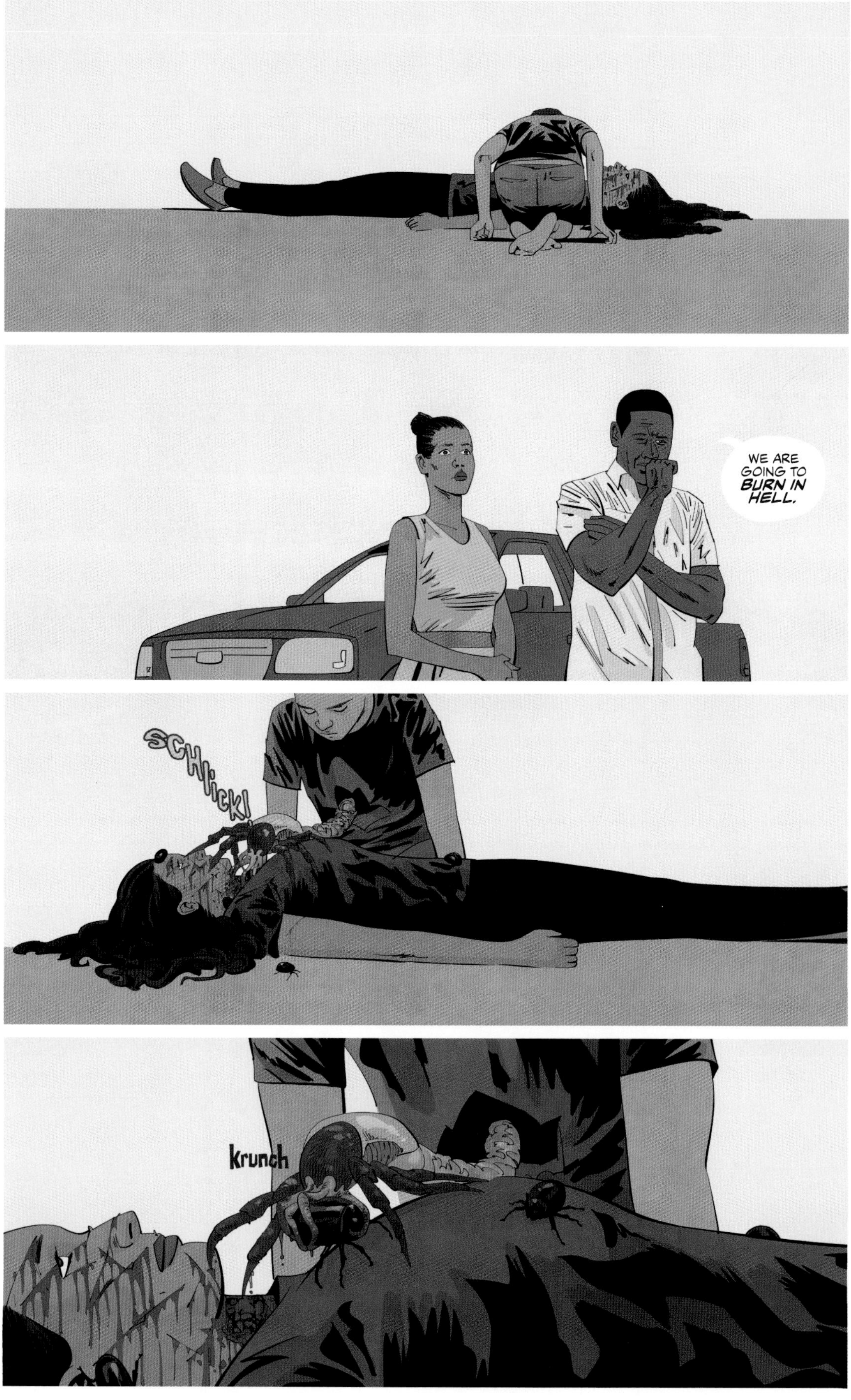
WE ARE GOING TO BURN IN HELL.
SCHLICK!
krunch

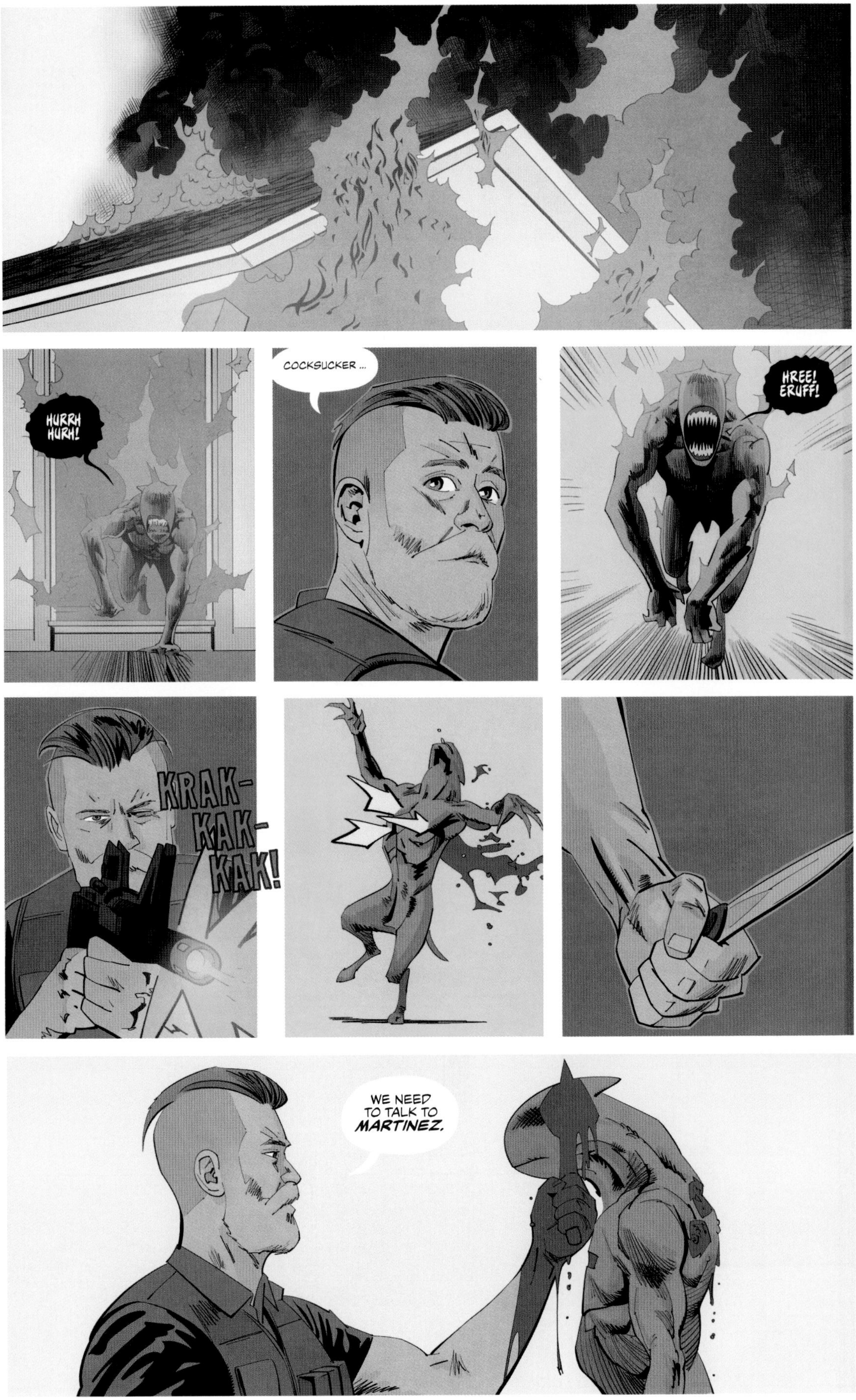
HURRH HURH!
COCKSUCKER ...
HREE! ERUFF!
KRAK-KAK-KAK!
WE NEED TO TALK TO *MARTINEZ.*

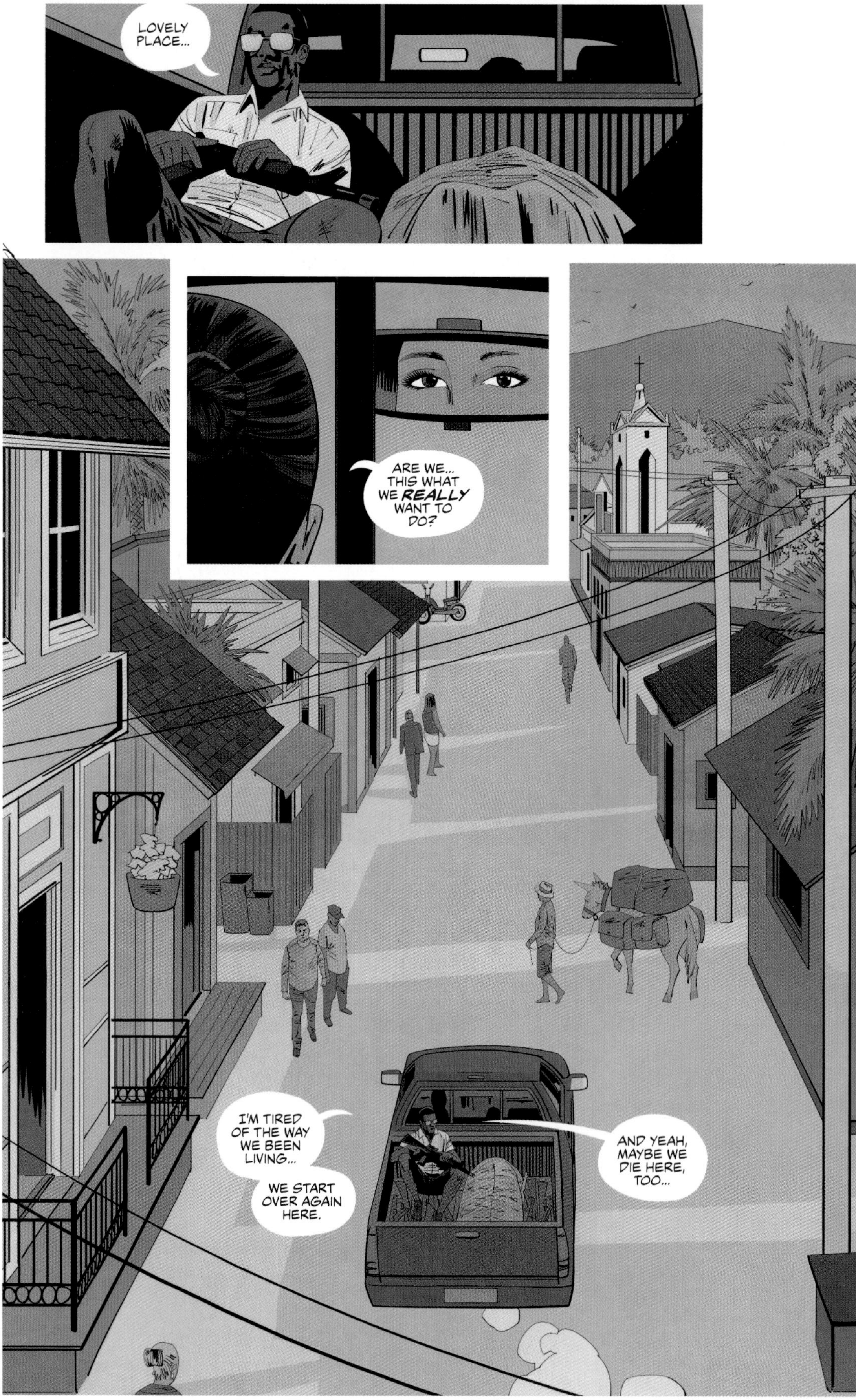
LOVELY PLACE...
ARE WE... THIS WHAT WE *REALLY* WANT TO DO?
I'M TIRED OF THE WAY WE BEEN LIVING...
WE START OVER AGAIN HERE.
AND YEAH, MAYBE WE DIE HERE, TOO...

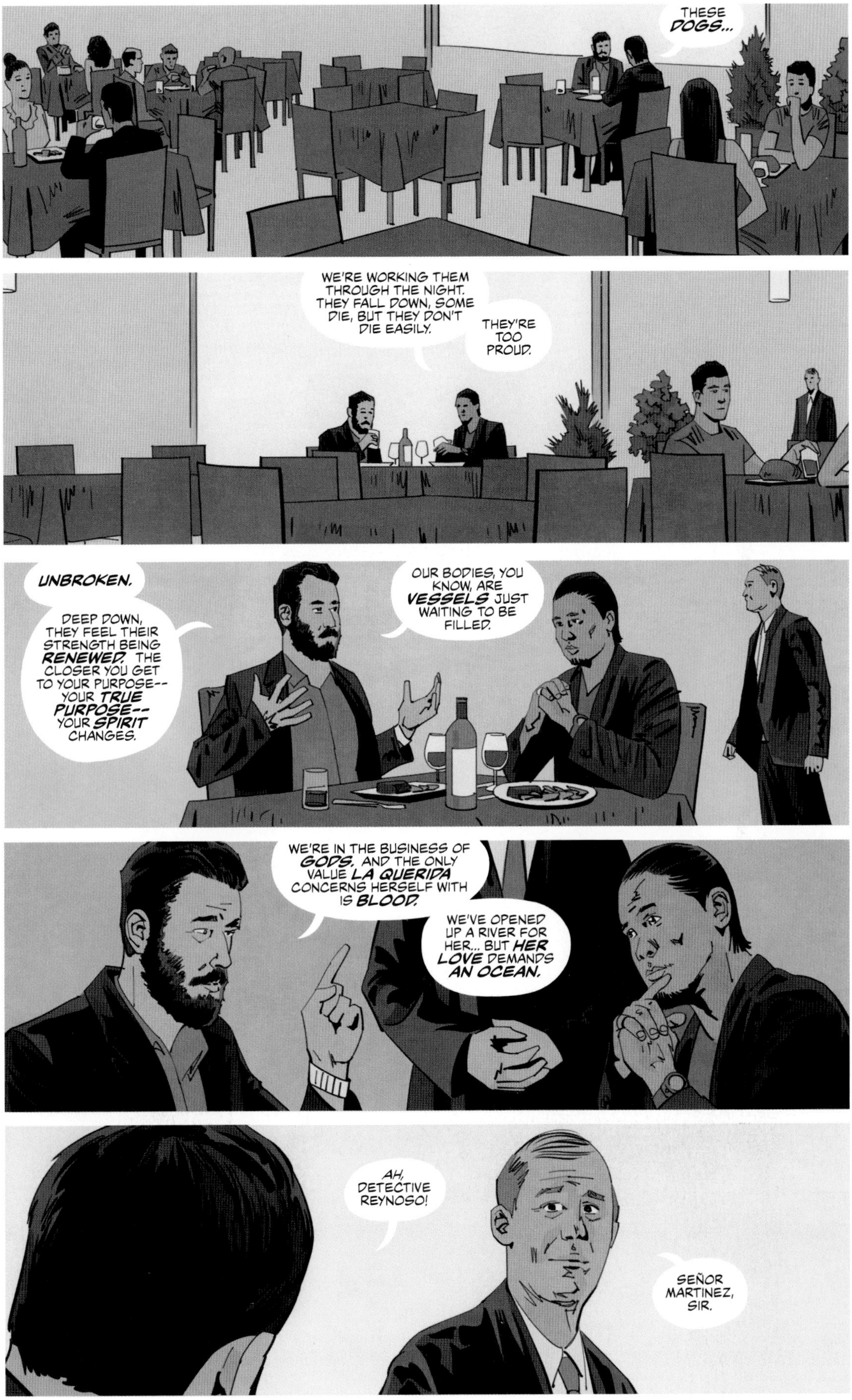

THESE DOGS...
WE'RE WORKING THEM THROUGH THE NIGHT. THEY FALL DOWN, SOME DIE, BUT THEY DON'T DIE EASILY.
THEY'RE TOO PROUD.
UNBROKEN.
DEEP DOWN, THEY FEEL THEIR STRENGTH BEING RENEWED. THE CLOSER YOU GET TO YOUR PURPOSE-- YOUR TRUE PURPOSE-- YOUR SPIRIT CHANGES.
OUR BODIES, YOU KNOW, ARE VESSELS JUST WAITING TO BE FILLED.
WE'RE IN THE BUSINESS OF GODS, AND THE ONLY VALUE LA QUERIDA CONCERNS HERSELF WITH IS BLOOD.
WE'VE OPENED UP A RIVER FOR HER... BUT HER LOVE DEMANDS AN OCEAN.
AH, DETECTIVE REYNOSO!
SEÑOR MARTINEZ, SIR.

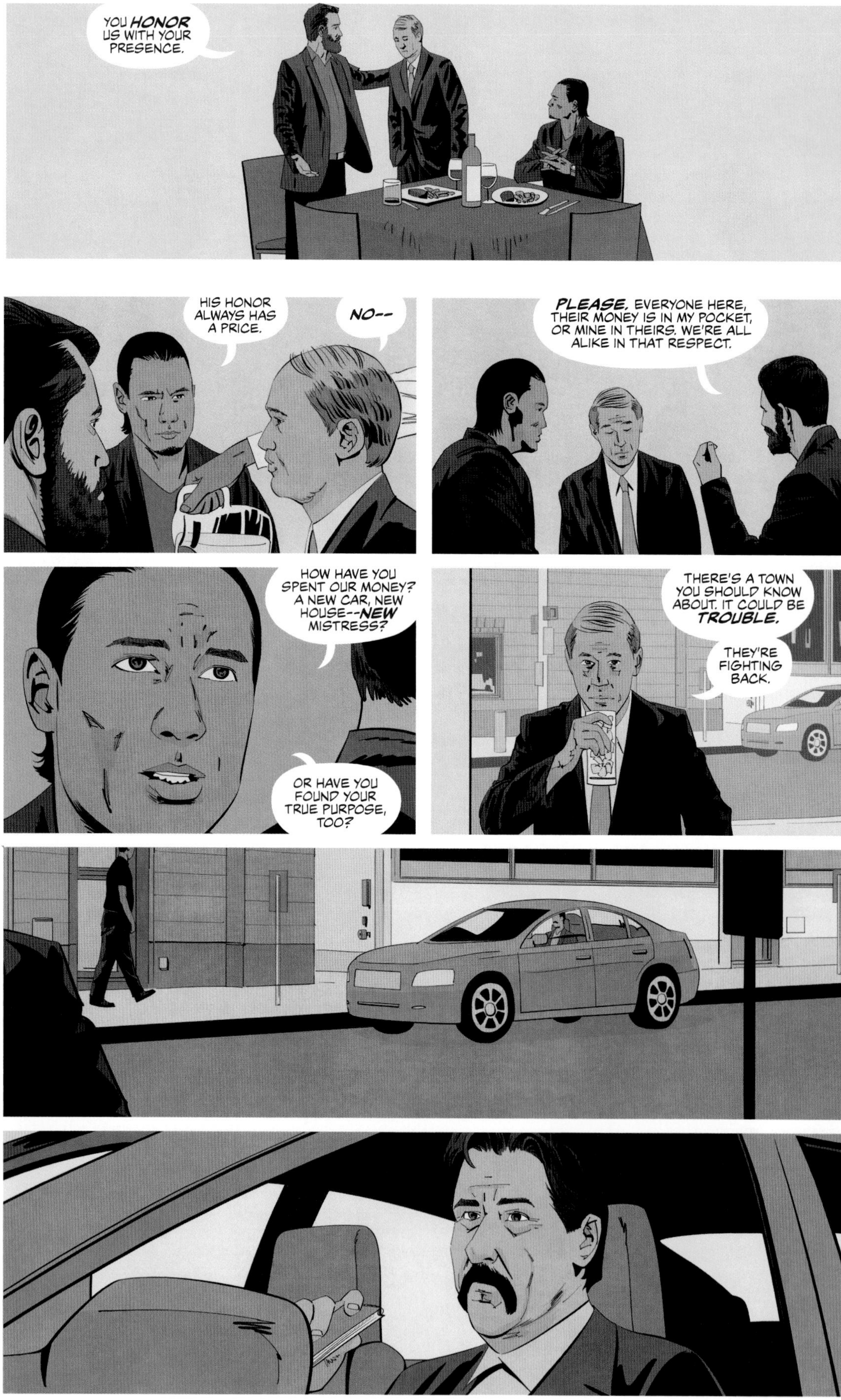
YOU HONOR US WITH YOUR PRESENCE.
HIS HONOR ALWAYS HAS A PRICE.
NO--
PLEASE. EVERYONE HERE, THEIR MONEY IS IN MY POCKET, OR MINE IN THEIRS. WE'RE ALL ALIKE IN THAT RESPECT.
HOW HAVE YOU SPENT OUR MONEY? A NEW CAR, NEW HOUSE--NEW MISTRESS?
OR HAVE YOU FOUND YOUR TRUE PURPOSE, TOO?
THERE'S A TOWN YOU SHOULD KNOW ABOUT. IT COULD BE TROUBLE.
THEY'RE FIGHTING BACK.

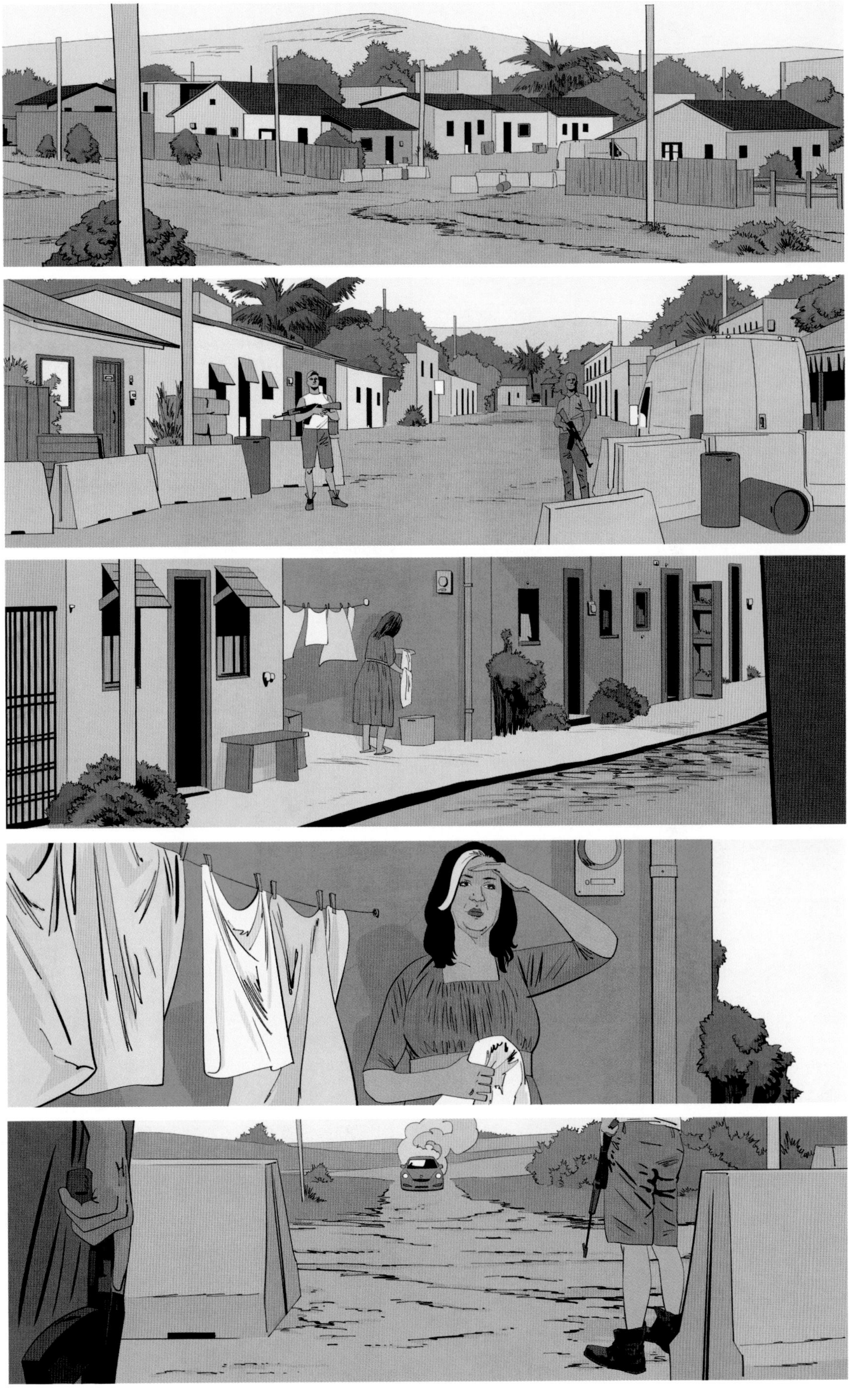

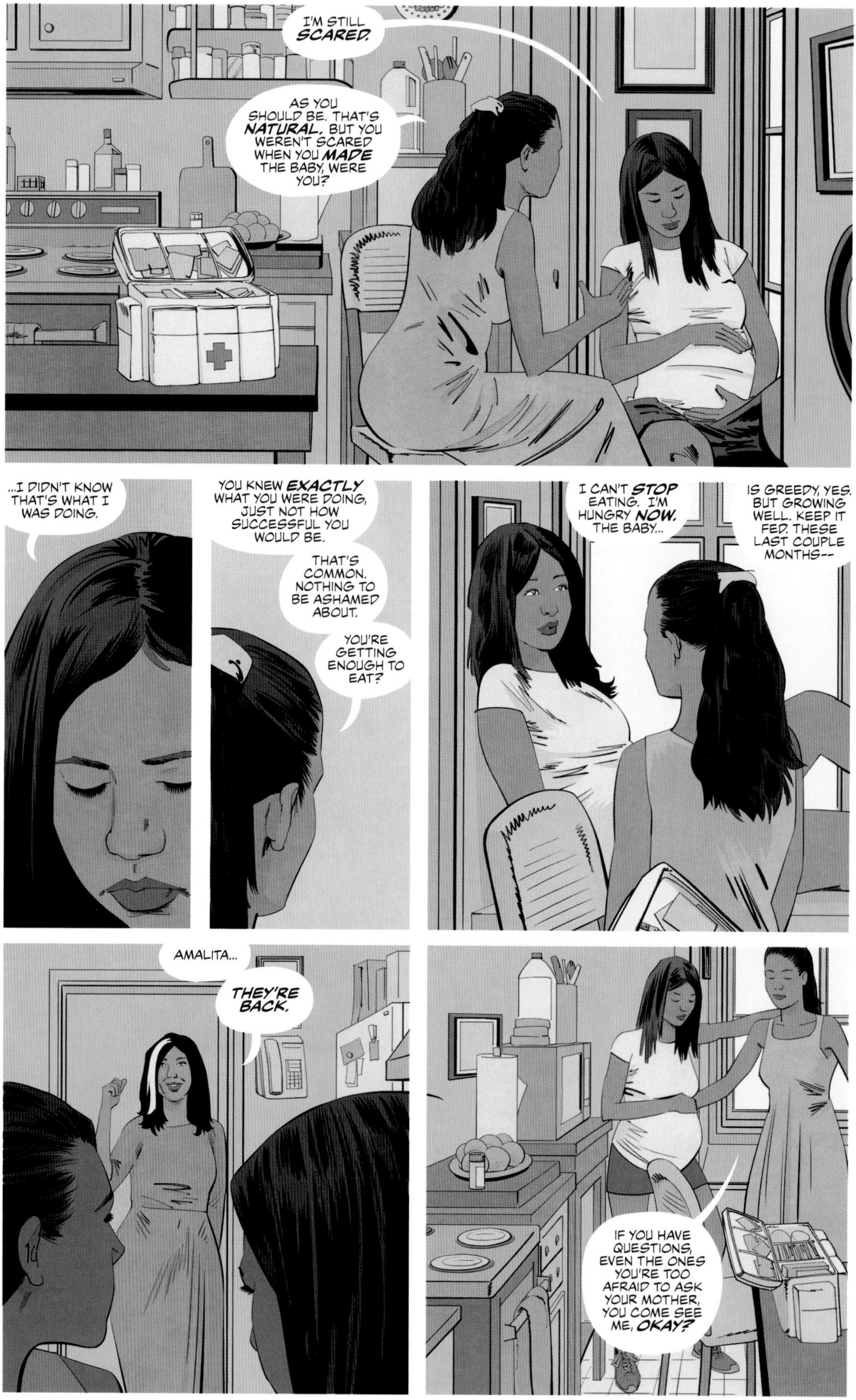
I'M STILL SCARED.
AS YOU SHOULD BE. THAT'S NATURAL. BUT YOU WEREN'T SCARED WHEN YOU MADE THE BABY, WERE YOU?
...I DIDN'T KNOW THAT'S WHAT I WAS DOING.
YOU KNEW EXACTLY WHAT YOU WERE DOING, JUST NOT HOW SUCCESSFUL YOU WOULD BE.
THAT'S COMMON. NOTHING TO BE ASHAMED ABOUT.
YOU'RE GETTING ENOUGH TO EAT?
I CAN'T STOP EATING. I'M HUNGRY NOW. THE BABY...
IS GREEDY, YES. BUT GROWING WELL. KEEP IT FED. THESE LAST COUPLE MONTHS--
AMALITA...
THEY'RE BACK.
IF YOU HAVE QUESTIONS, EVEN THE ONES YOU'RE TOO AFRAID TO ASK YOUR MOTHER, YOU COME SEE ME, OKAY?

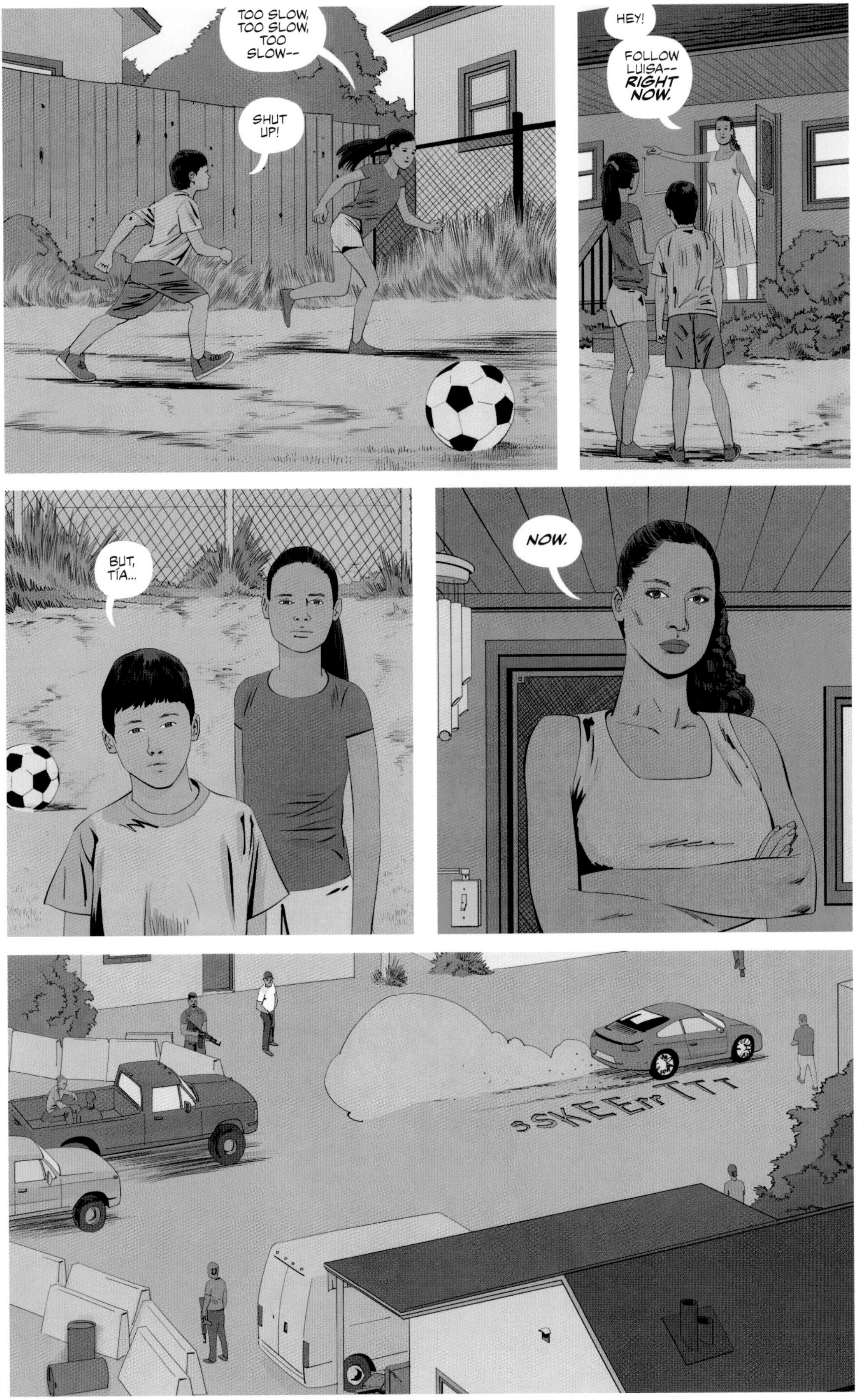

TOO SLOW, TOO SLOW, TOO SLOW--
SHUT UP!
HEY!
FOLLOW LUISA-- RIGHT NOW.
BUT, TÍA...
NOW.
SSKEErrTTT

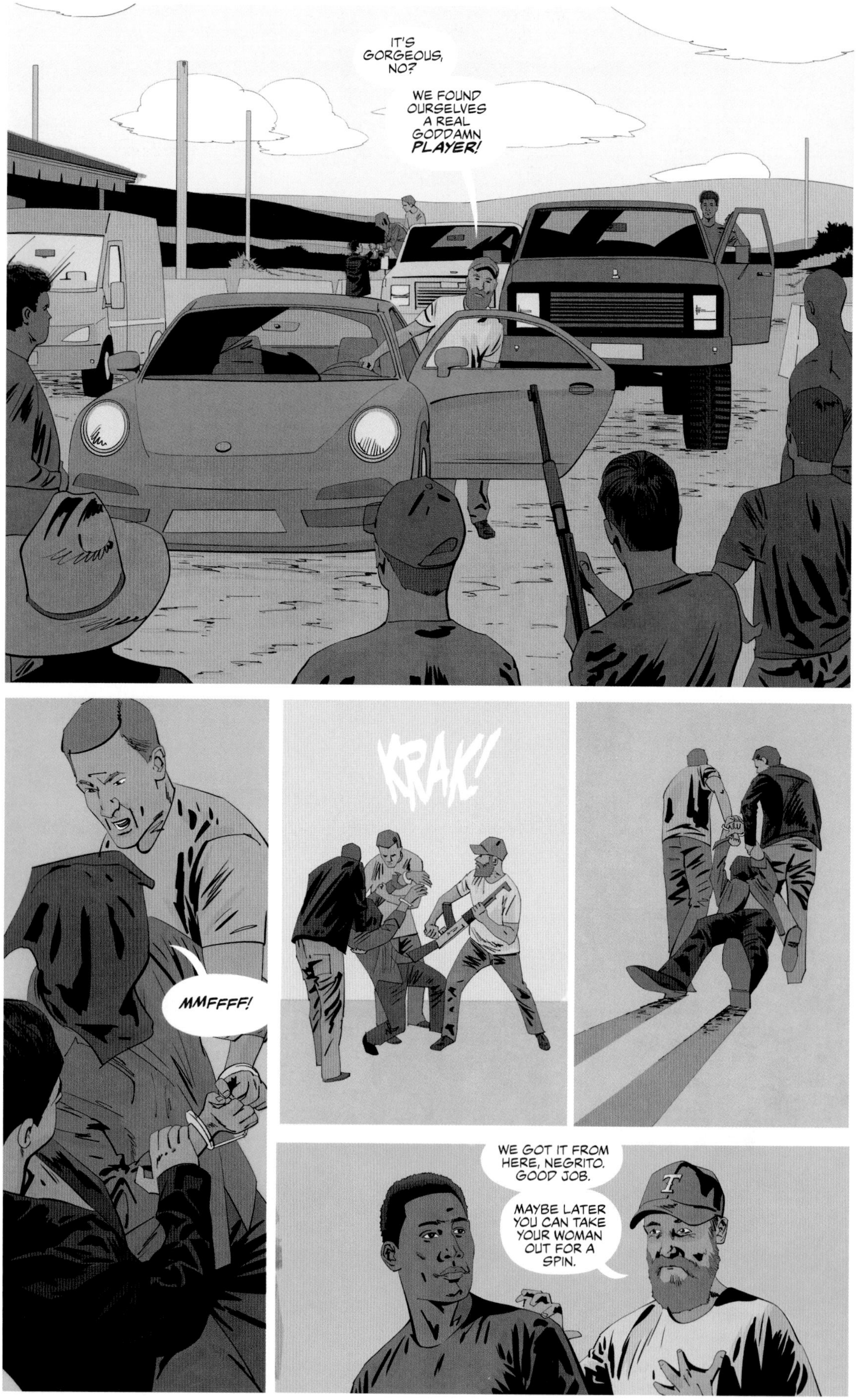
IT'S GORGEOUS, NO?
WE FOUND OURSELVES A REAL GODDAMN *PLAYER!*
MMFFFF!
KRAK!
WE GOT IT FROM HERE, NEGRITO. GOOD JOB.
MAYBE LATER YOU CAN TAKE YOUR WOMAN OUT FOR A SPIN.

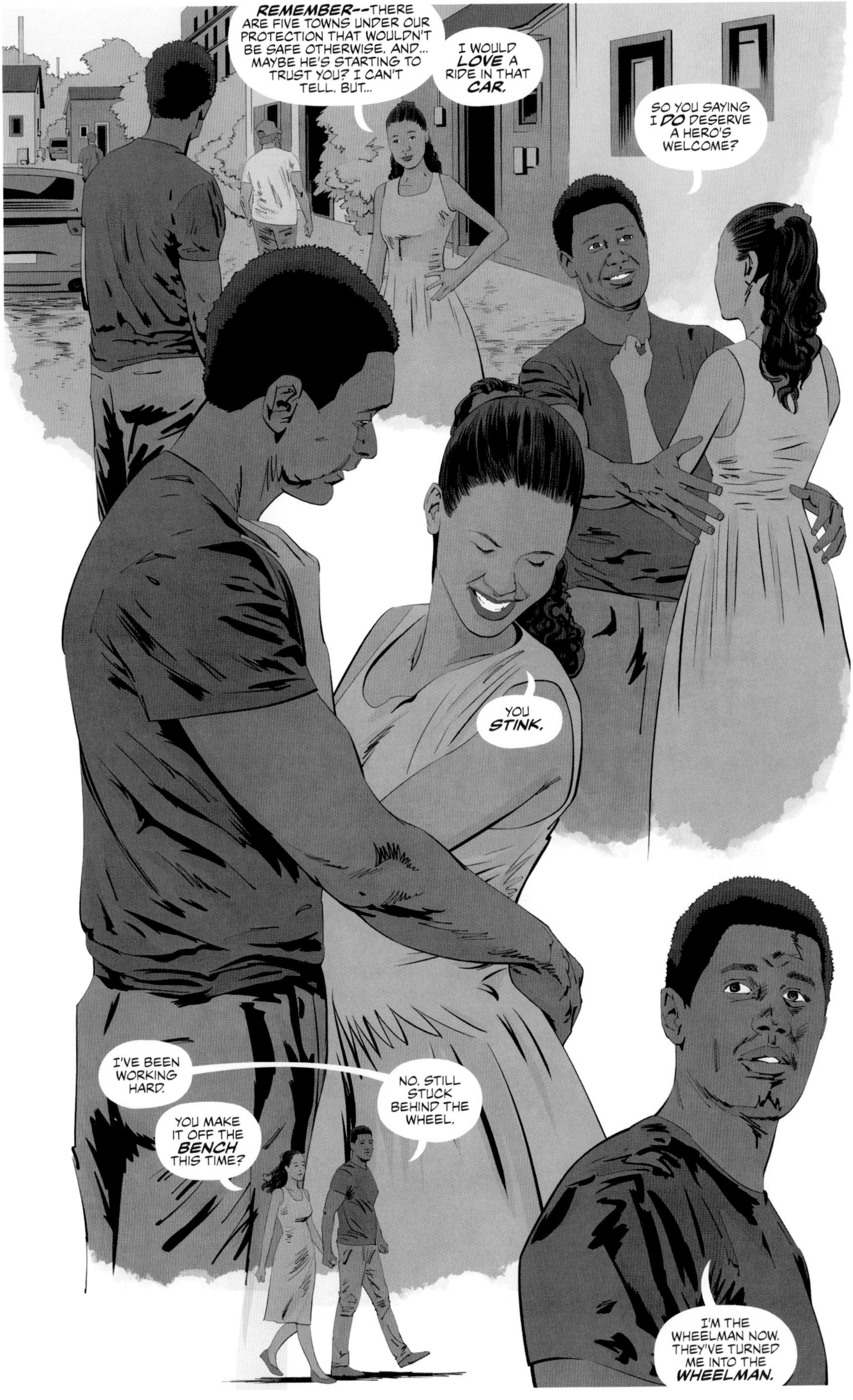
REMEMBER--THERE ARE FIVE TOWNS UNDER OUR PROTECTION THAT WOULDN'T BE SAFE OTHERWISE. AND... MAYBE HE'S STARTING TO TRUST YOU? I CAN'T TELL. BUT...
I WOULD LOVE A RIDE IN THAT CAR.
SO YOU SAYING I DO DESERVE A HERO'S WELCOME?
YOU STINK.
I'VE BEEN WORKING HARD.
YOU MAKE IT OFF THE BENCH THIS TIME?
NO. STILL STUCK BEHIND THE WHEEL.
I'M THE WHEELMAN NOW. THEY'VE TURNED ME INTO THE WHEELMAN.

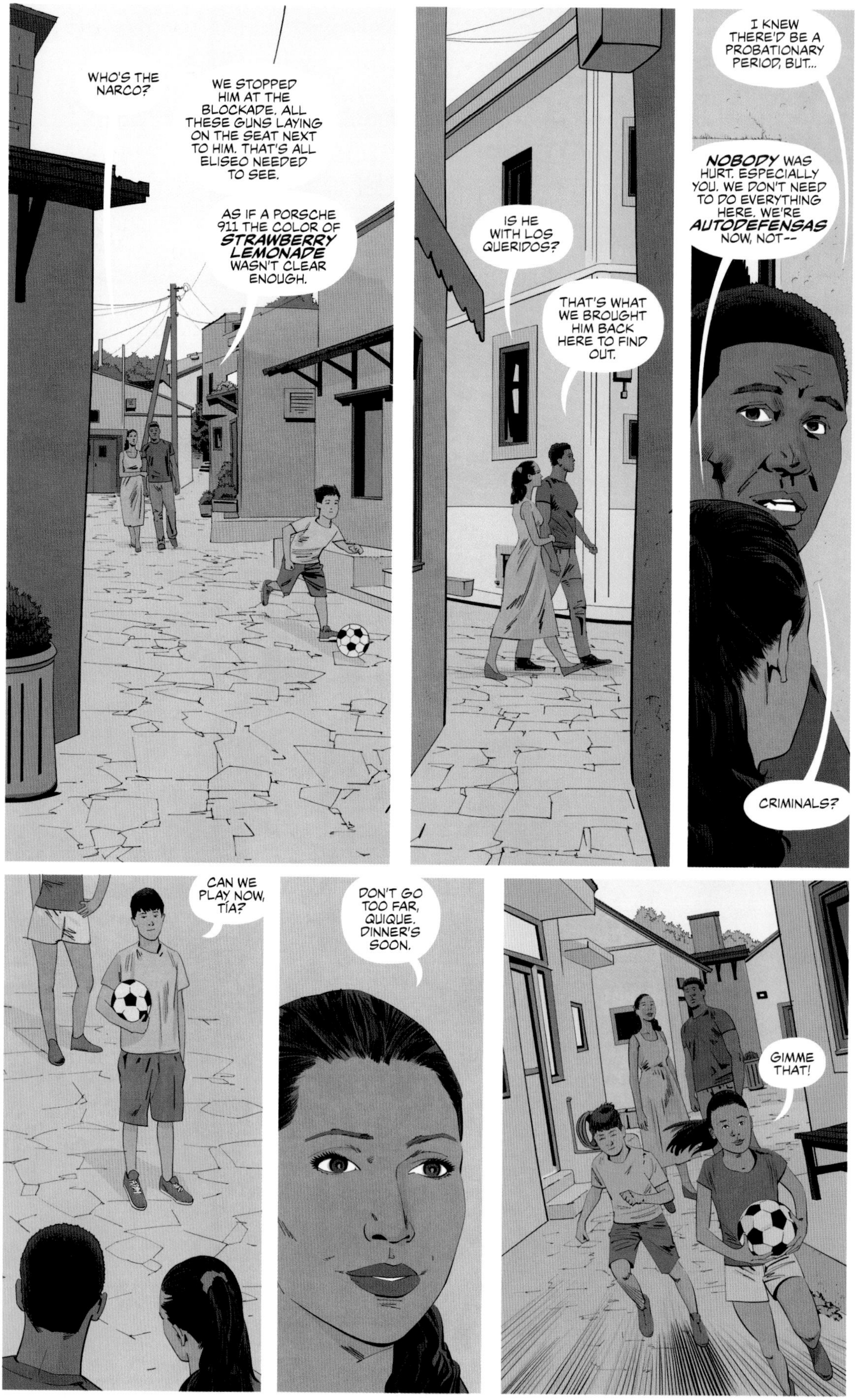
WHO'S THE NARCO?
WE STOPPED HIM AT THE BLOCKADE. ALL THESE GUNS LAYING ON THE SEAT NEXT TO HIM. THAT'S ALL ELISEO NEEDED TO SEE.
AS IF A PORSCHE 911 THE COLOR OF STRAWBERRY LEMONADE WASN'T CLEAR ENOUGH.
IS HE WITH LOS QUERIDOS?
THAT'S WHAT WE BROUGHT HIM BACK HERE TO FIND OUT.
I KNEW THERE'D BE A PROBATIONARY PERIOD, BUT...
NOBODY WAS HURT. ESPECIALLY YOU. WE DON'T NEED TO DO EVERYTHING HERE. WE'RE AUTODEFENSAS NOW, NOT--
CRIMINALS?
CAN WE PLAY NOW, TÍA?
DON'T GO TOO FAR, QUIQUE. DINNER'S SOON.
GIMME THAT!

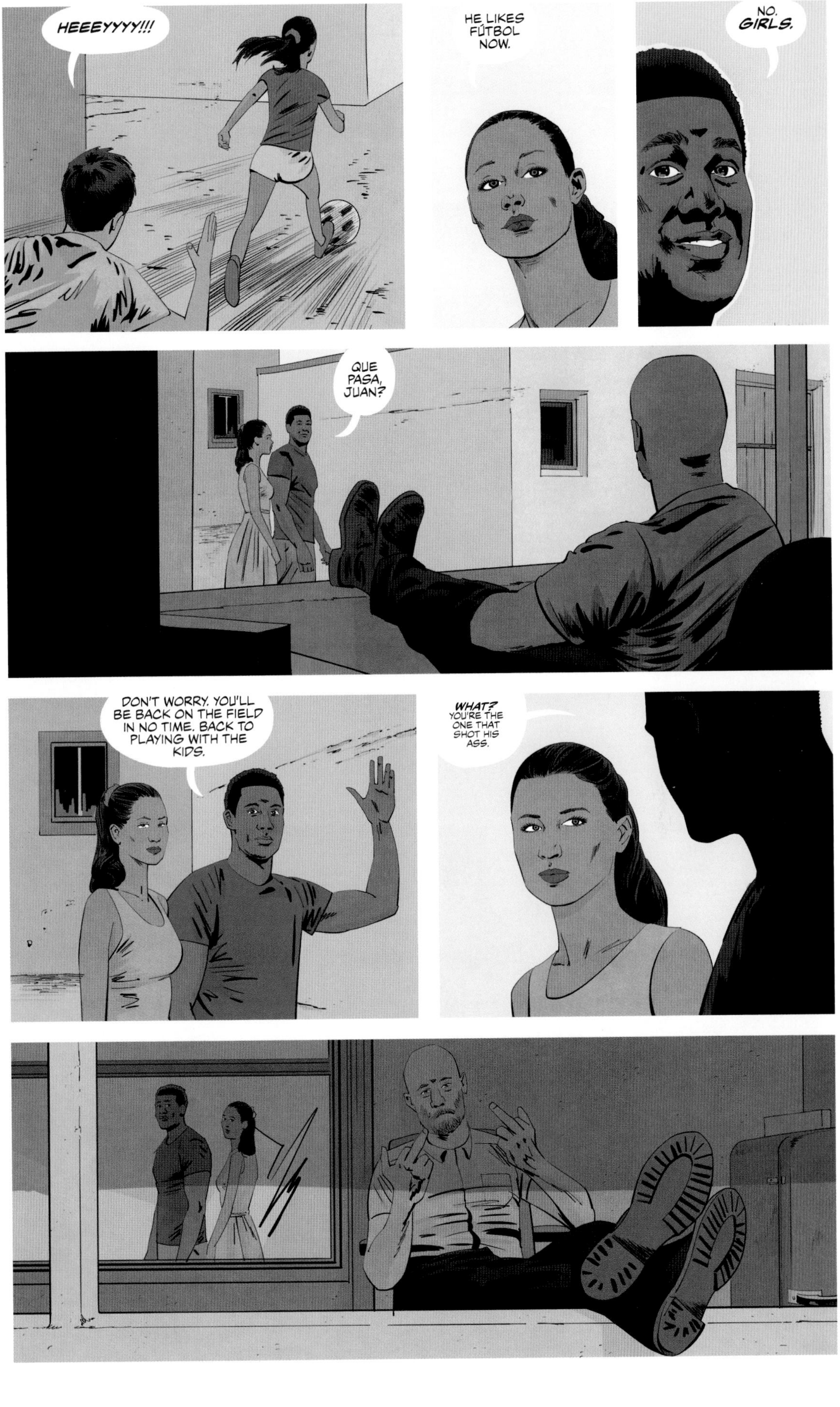
HEEEYYYY!!!
HE LIKES FÚTBOL NOW.
NO. GIRLS.
QUE PASA, JUAN?
DON'T WORRY. YOU'LL BE BACK ON THE FIELD IN NO TIME. BACK TO PLAYING WITH THE KIDS.
WHAT? YOU'RE THE ONE THAT SHOT HIS ASS.

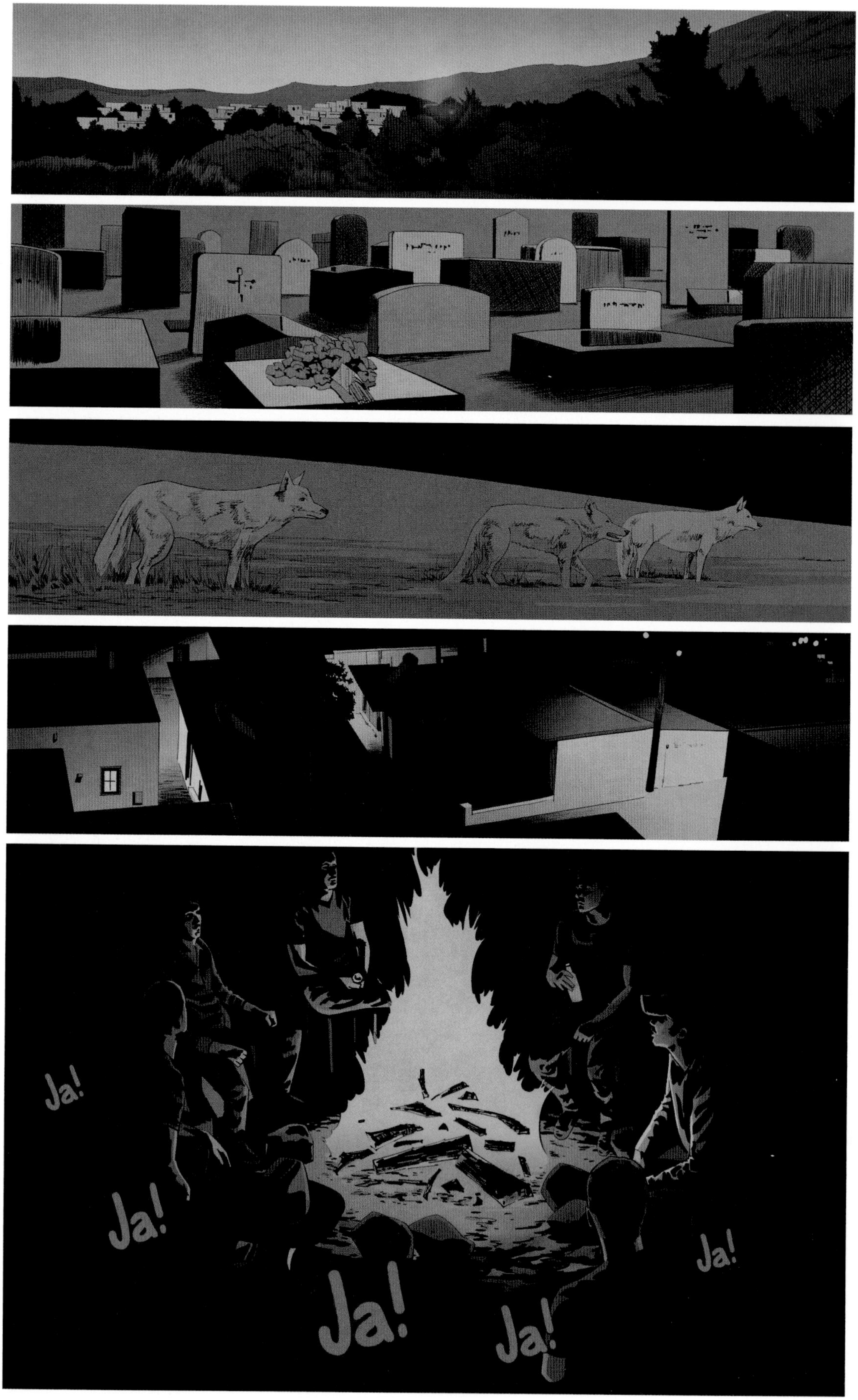
Ja!
Ja!
Ja!
Ja!
Ja!

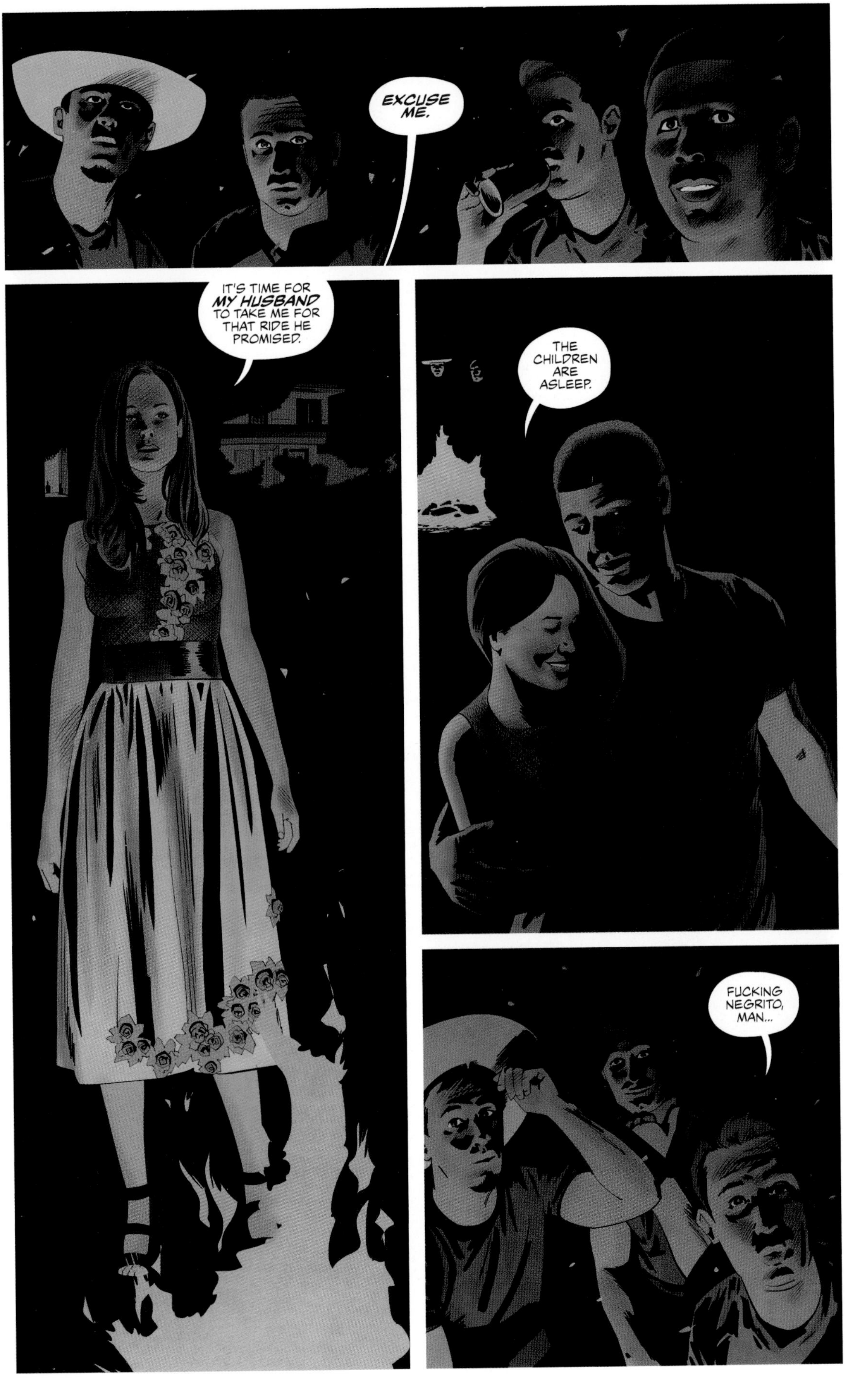
EXCUSE ME.
IT'S TIME FOR MY HUSBAND TO TAKE ME FOR THAT RIDE HE PROMISED.
THE CHILDREN ARE ASLEEP.
FUCKING NEGRITO, MAN...

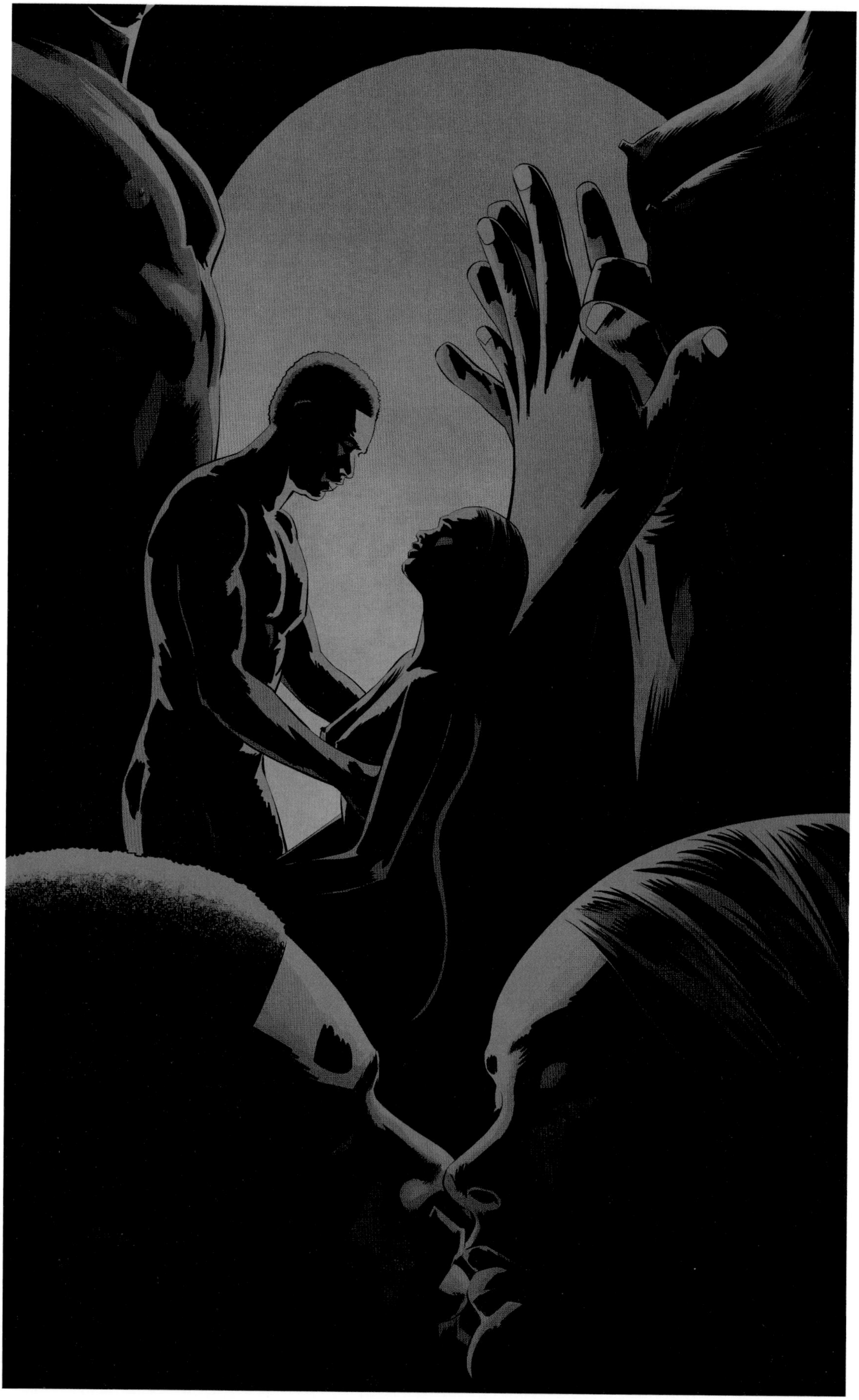

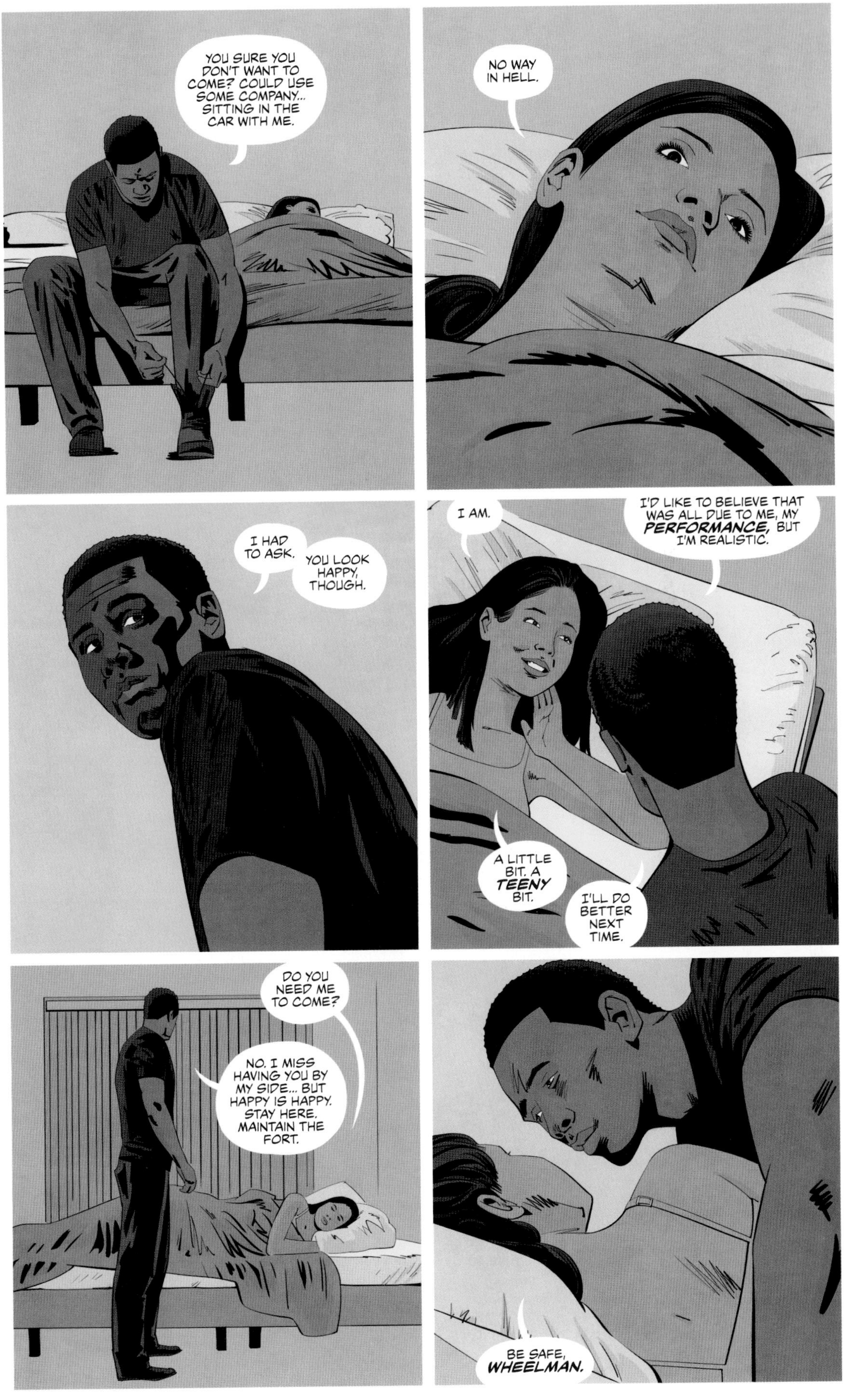
YOU SURE YOU DON'T WANT TO COME? COULD USE SOME COMPANY... SITTING IN THE CAR WITH ME.
NO WAY IN HELL.
I HAD TO ASK.
YOU LOOK HAPPY, THOUGH.
I AM.
I'D LIKE TO BELIEVE THAT WAS ALL DUE TO ME, MY PERFORMANCE, BUT I'M REALISTIC.
A LITTLE BIT. A TEENY BIT.
I'LL DO BETTER NEXT TIME.
DO YOU NEED ME TO COME?
NO. I MISS HAVING YOU BY MY SIDE... BUT HAPPY IS HAPPY. STAY HERE. MAINTAIN THE FORT.
BE SAFE, WHEELMAN.

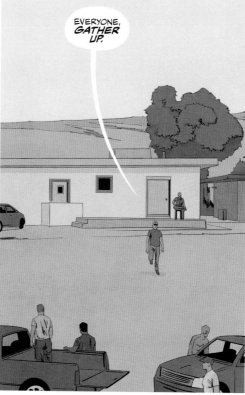

EVERYONE, *GATHER UP.*

THE COWARD FUCK HAS BROKEN.

JUST SO THESE NARCO RAPISTS CAN MOVE *WOMEN* AND *DRUGS* AND CONTINUE TO WORK OUR *BROTHERS* TO *DEATH!*

LOS QUERIDOS HAVE TAKEN A CASERÍO SOUTHWEST OF US.

THEY THINK WE ARE SO COWED THAT TWO MEN ARE ENOUGH TO KEEP US AWAY.

THERE'S A DOZEN MORE *RANCHERÍAS* IN THIS STATE THAT THEY'VE OCCUPIED. NOT TO ESCAPE DETECTION, BUT TO *TERRORIZE.* IF WE SHUT THIS ONE DOWN, WE START TO CUT THEM OFF. WE TIGHTEN *OUR* GRIP.

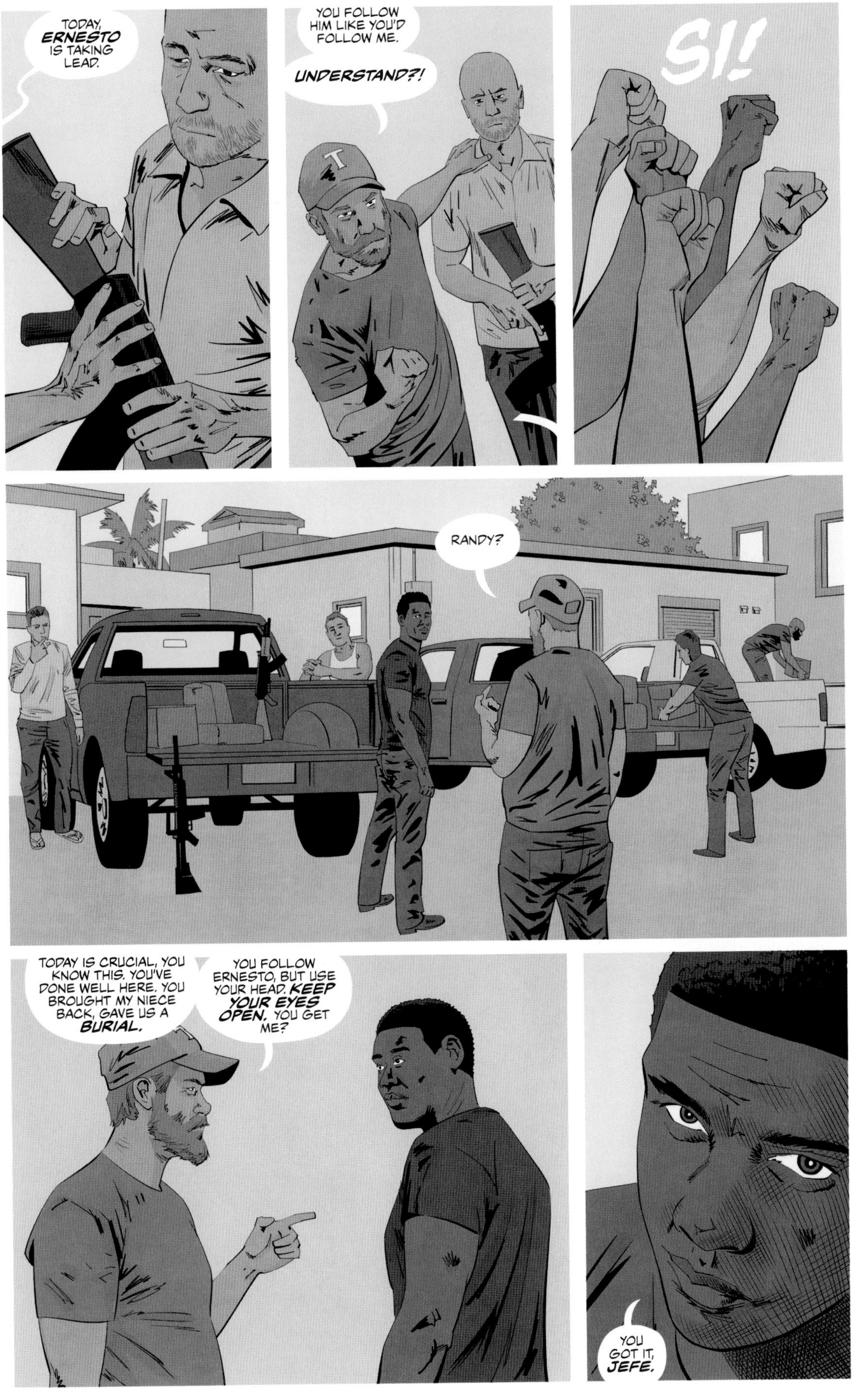
TODAY, ERNESTO IS TAKING LEAD.
YOU FOLLOW HIM LIKE YOU'D FOLLOW ME.
UNDERSTAND?!
SI!
RANDY?
TODAY IS CRUCIAL, YOU KNOW THIS. YOU'VE DONE WELL HERE. YOU BROUGHT MY NIECE BACK, GAVE US A BURIAL.
YOU FOLLOW ERNESTO, BUT USE YOUR HEAD. KEEP YOUR EYES OPEN. YOU GET ME?
YOU GOT IT, JEFE.

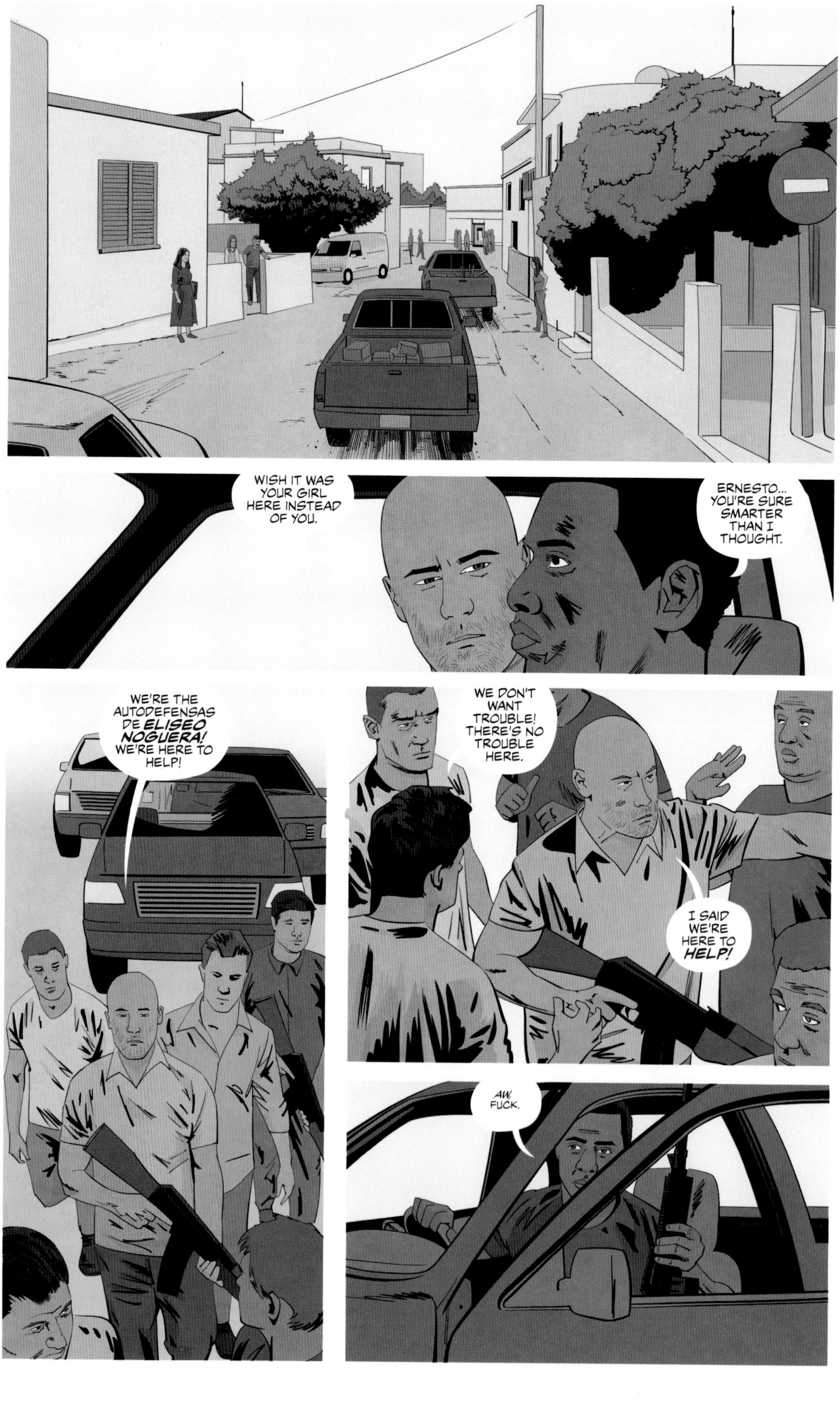
WISH IT WAS YOUR GIRL HERE INSTEAD OF YOU.
ERNESTO... YOU'RE SURE SMARTER THAN I THOUGHT.
WE'RE THE AUTODEFENSAS DE **ELISEO NOGUERA!** WE'RE HERE TO HELP!
WE DON'T WANT TROUBLE! THERE'S NO TROUBLE HERE.
I SAID WE'RE HERE TO **HELP!**
AW, FUCK.

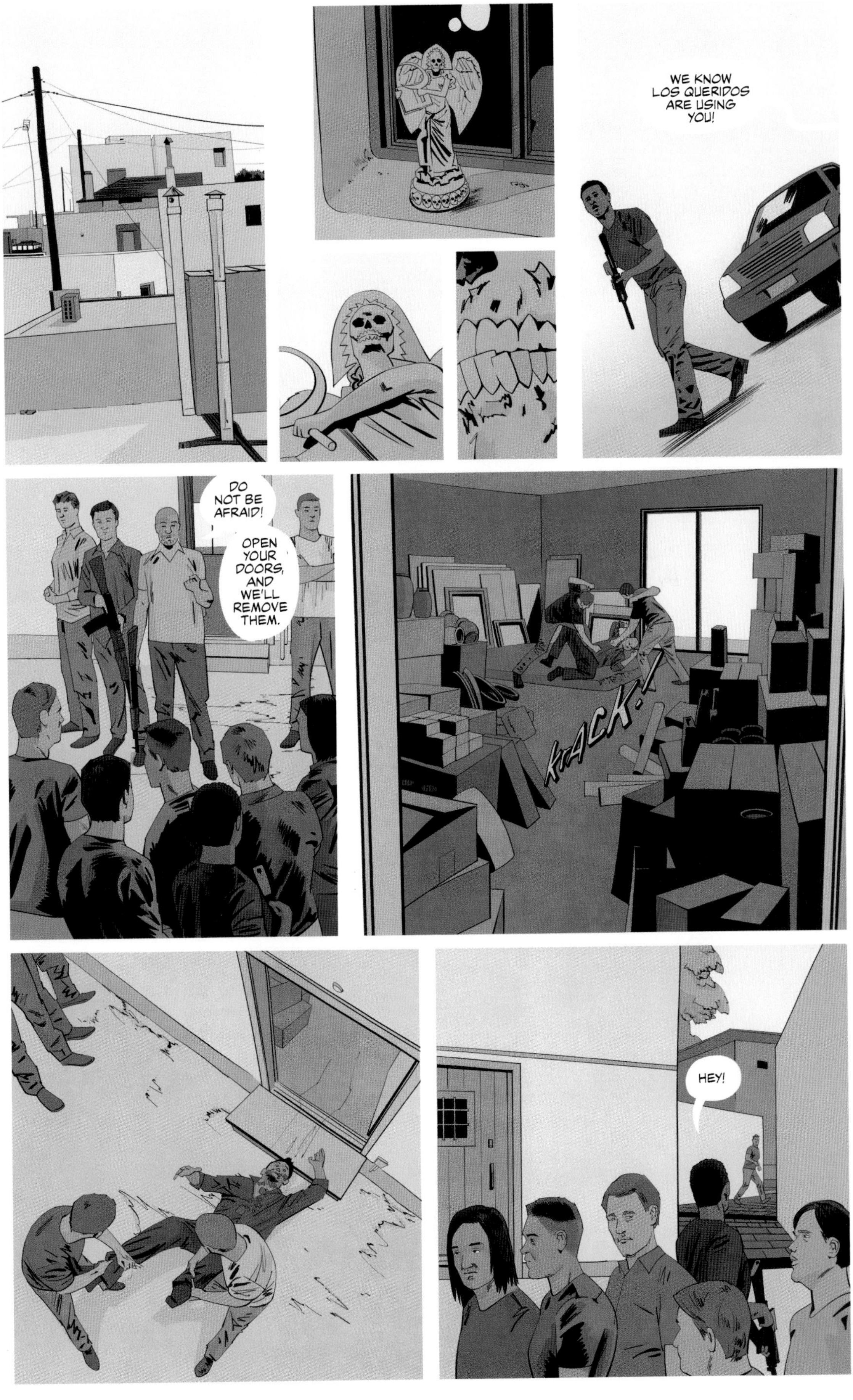
WE KNOW LOS QUERIDOS ARE USING YOU!
DO NOT BE AFRAID!
OPEN YOUR DOORS, AND WE'LL REMOVE THEM.
KRACK!
HEY!

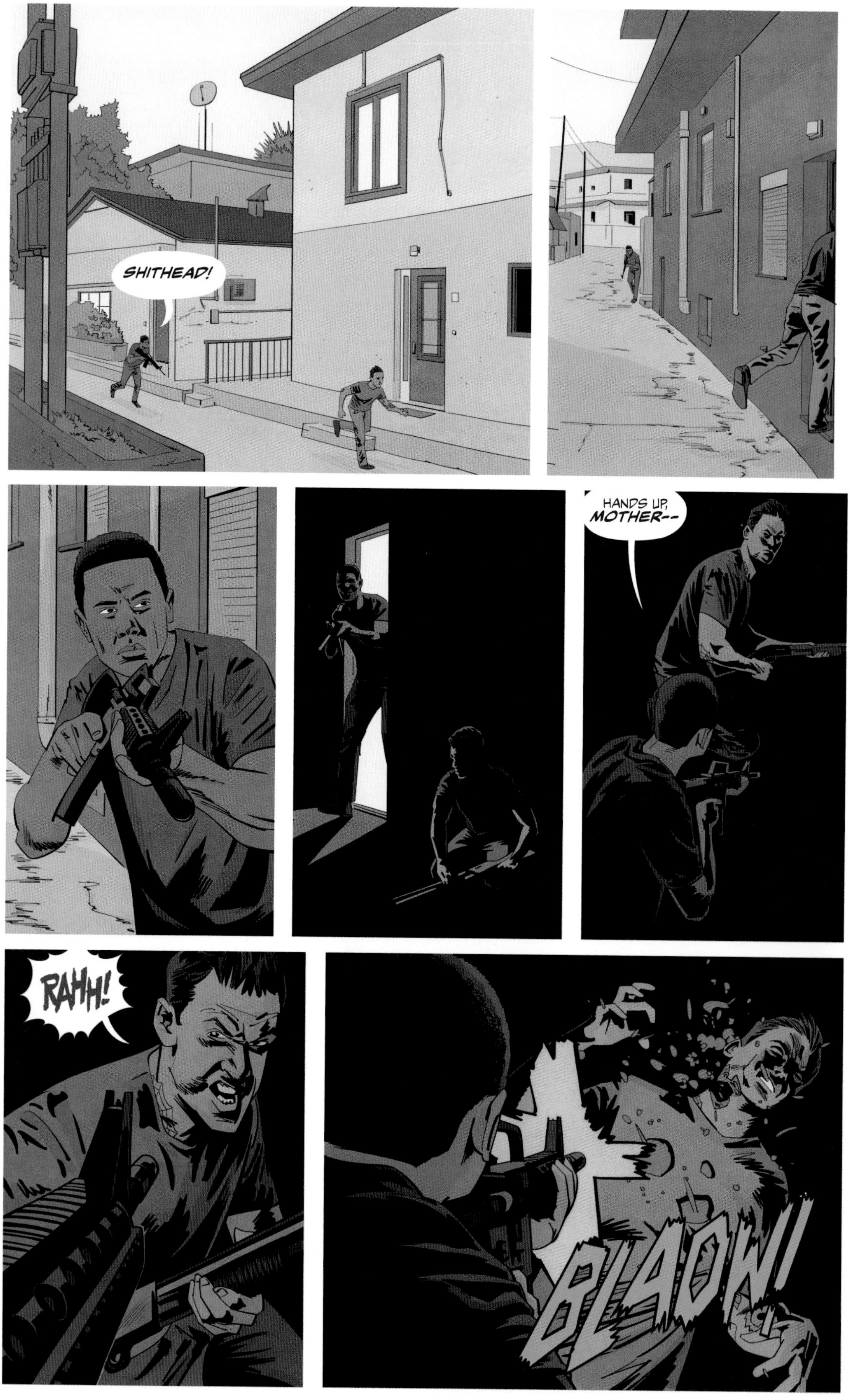
SHITHEAD!
HANDS UP,
MOTHER--
RAHH!
BLAOW!

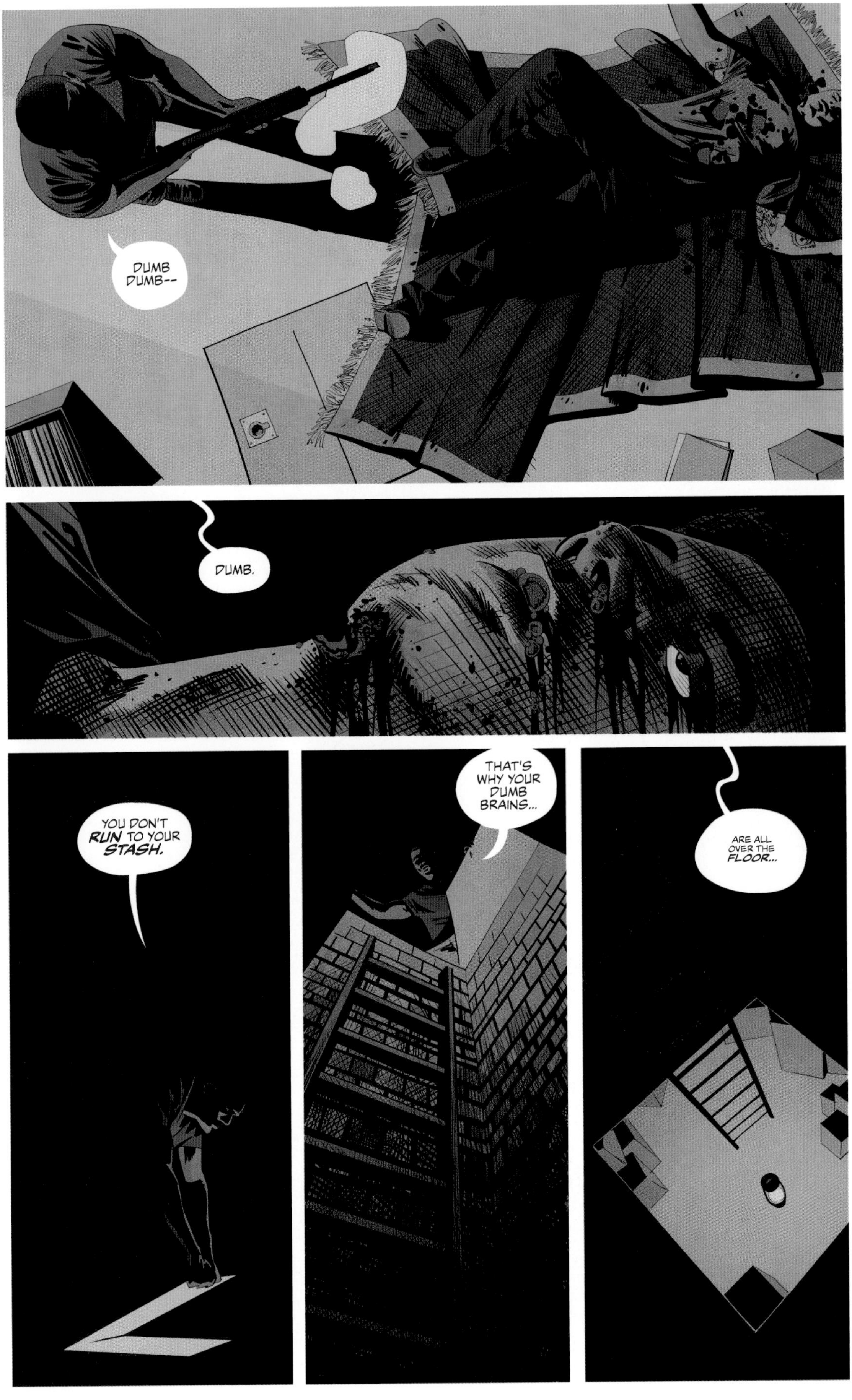
DUMB DUMB--
DUMB.
YOU DON'T RUN TO YOUR STASH.
THAT'S WHY YOUR DUMB BRAINS...
ARE ALL OVER THE FLOOR...

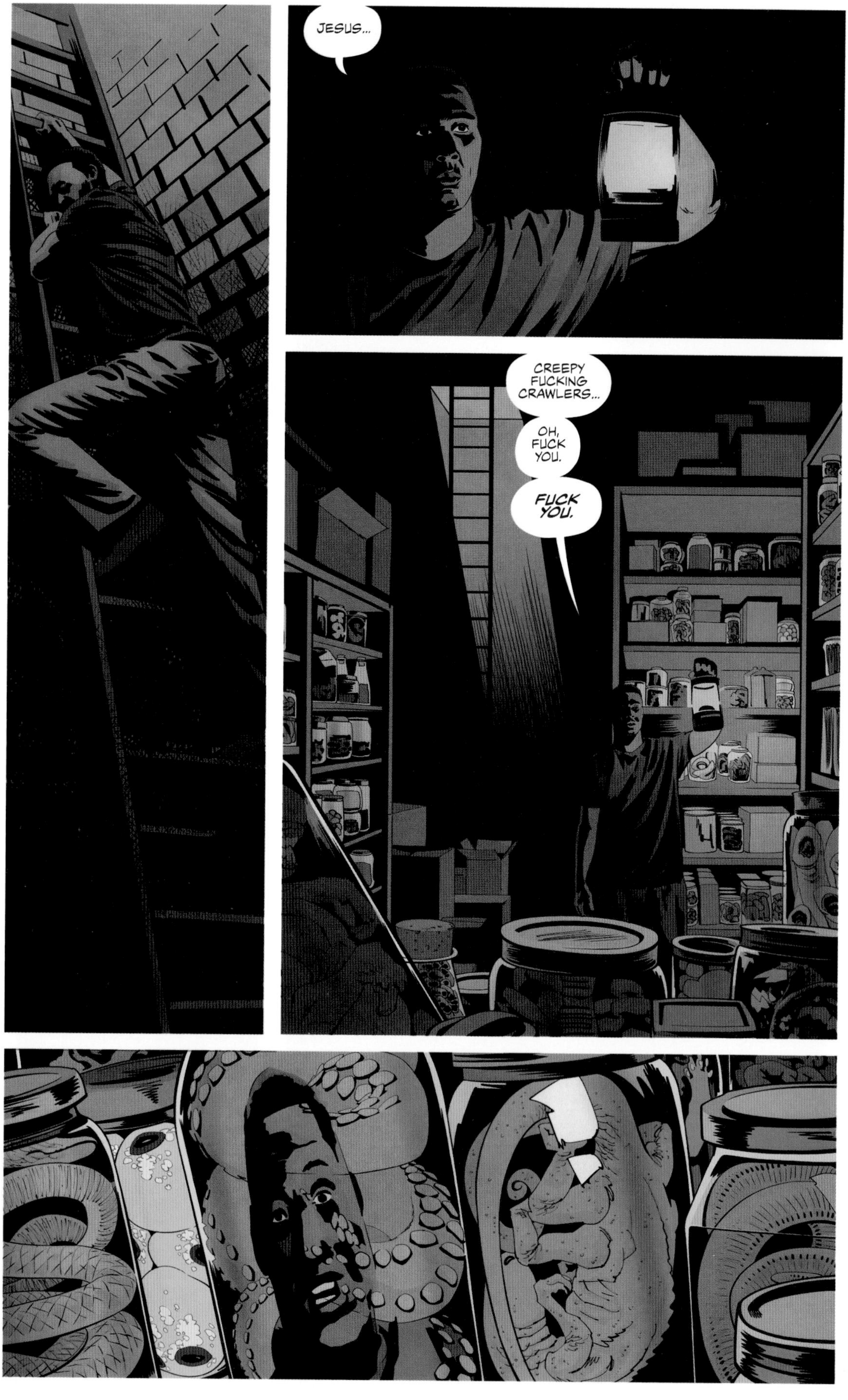
JESUS...
CREEPY FUCKING CRAWLERS...
OH, FUCK YOU.
FUCK YOU.

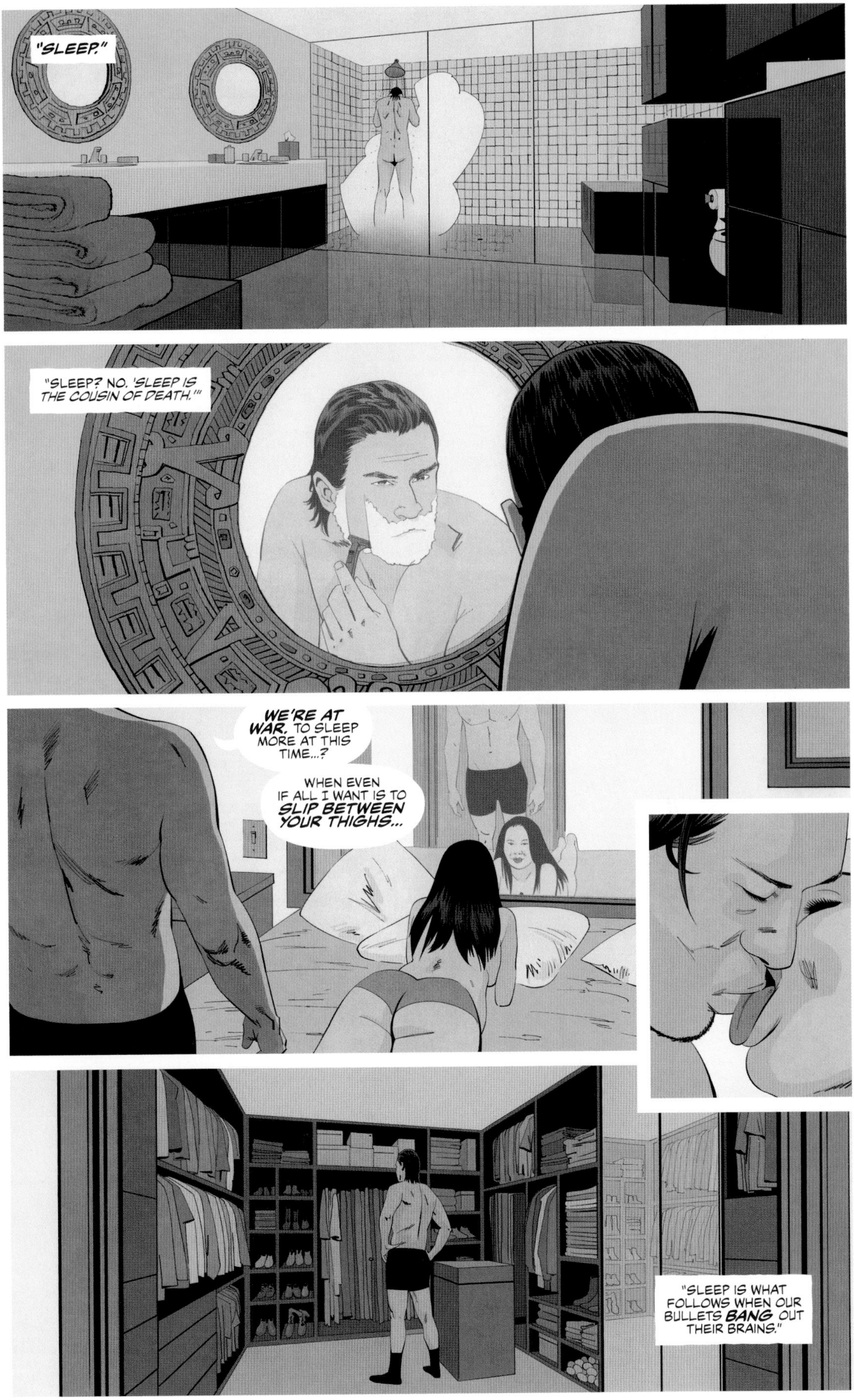

"SLEEP."
"SLEEP? NO. 'SLEEP IS THE COUSIN OF DEATH.'"
WE'RE AT WAR. TO SLEEP MORE AT THIS TIME...?
WHEN EVEN IF ALL I WANT IS TO SLIP BETWEEN YOUR THIGHS...
"SLEEP IS WHAT FOLLOWS WHEN OUR BULLETS BANG OUT THEIR BRAINS."

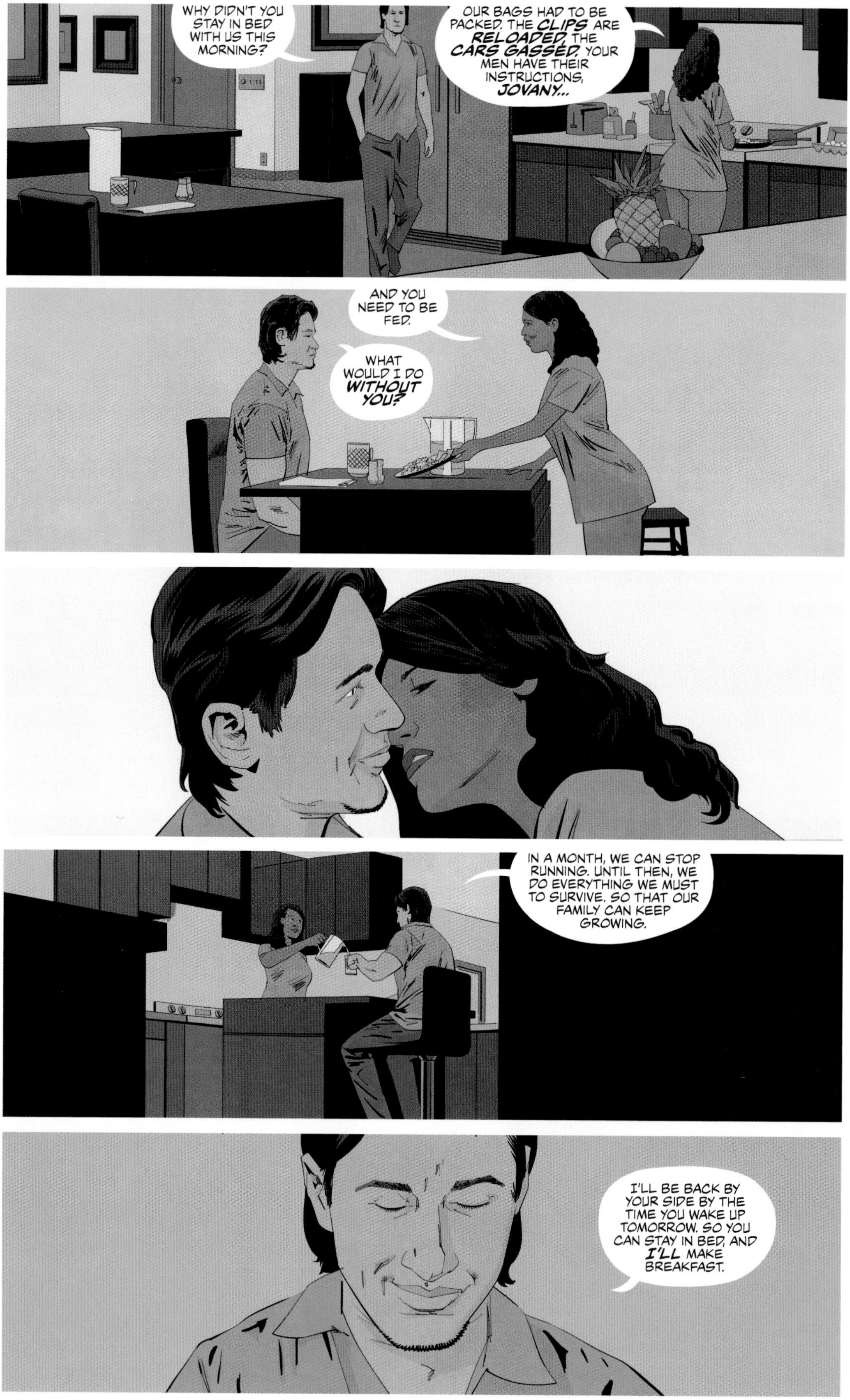
WHY DIDN'T YOU STAY IN BED WITH US THIS MORNING?
OUR BAGS HAD TO BE PACKED. THE CLIPS ARE RELOADED, THE CARS GASSED. YOUR MEN HAVE THEIR INSTRUCTIONS, JOVANY...
AND YOU NEED TO BE FED.
WHAT WOULD I DO WITHOUT YOU?
IN A MONTH, WE CAN STOP RUNNING. UNTIL THEN, WE DO EVERYTHING WE MUST TO SURVIVE. SO THAT OUR FAMILY CAN KEEP GROWING.
I'LL BE BACK BY YOUR SIDE BY THE TIME YOU WAKE UP TOMORROW. SO YOU CAN STAY IN BED, AND I'LL MAKE BREAKFAST.

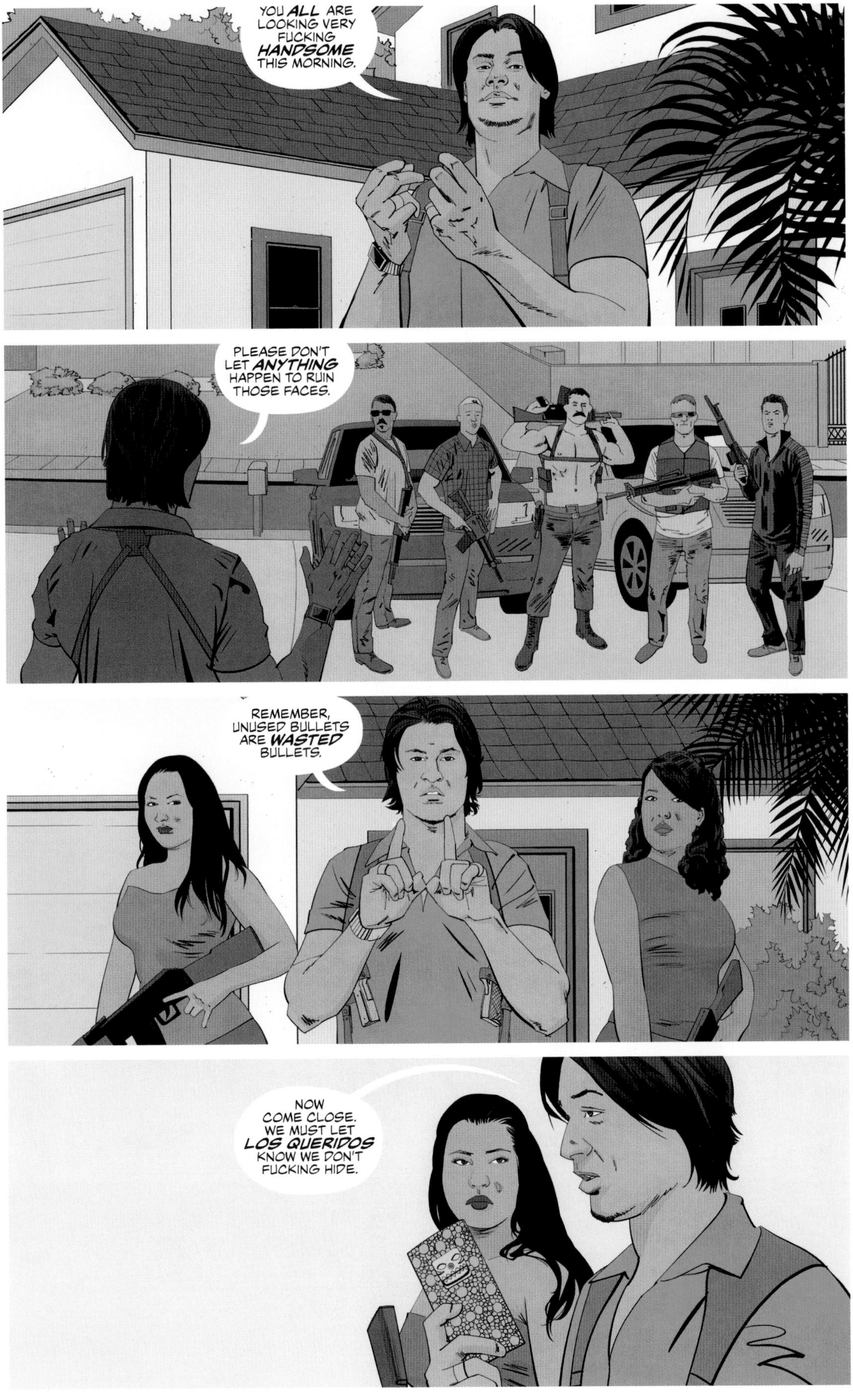
YOU ALL ARE LOOKING VERY FUCKING HANDSOME THIS MORNING.
PLEASE DON'T LET ANYTHING HAPPEN TO RUIN THOSE FACES.
REMEMBER, UNUSED BULLETS ARE WASTED BULLETS.
NOW COME CLOSE. WE MUST LET LOS QUERIDOS KNOW WE DON'T FUCKING HIDE.

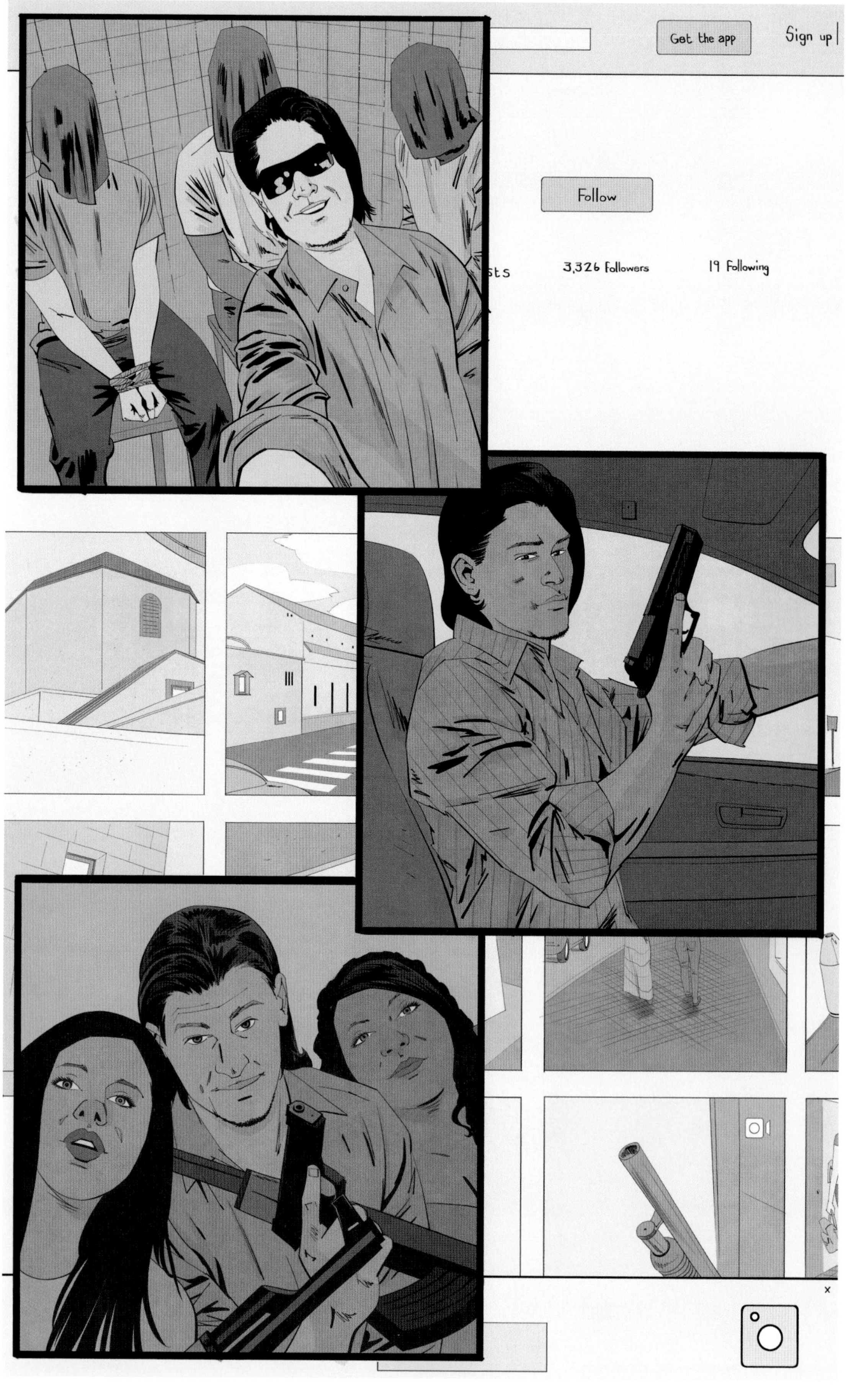

Get the app
Sign up
Follow
sts
3,326 followers
19 Following

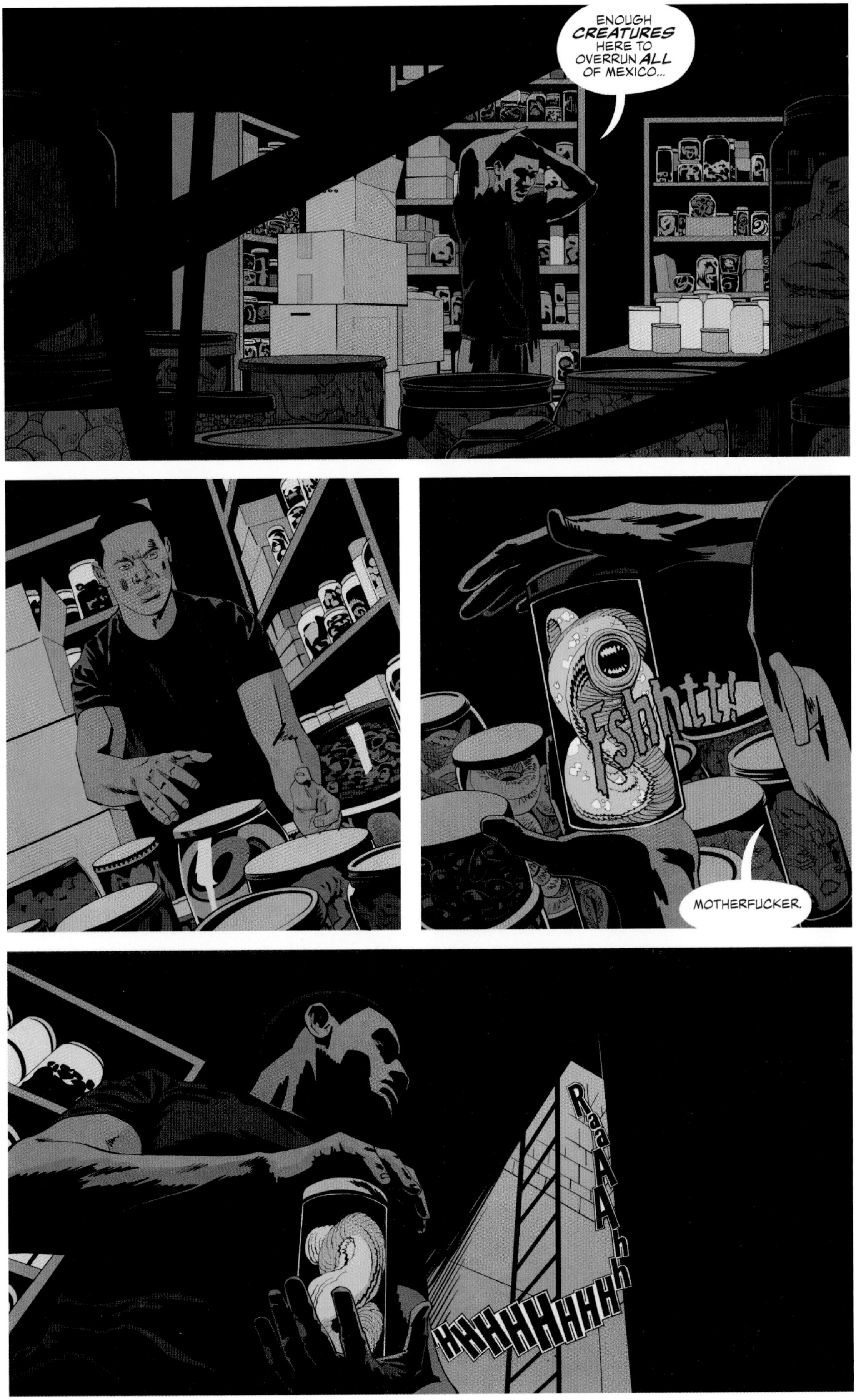
ENOUGH CREATURES HERE TO OVERRUN ALL OF MEXICO...
Fshhttt
MOTHERFUCKER.
RaaaAAAhhhHHHHHHHHH

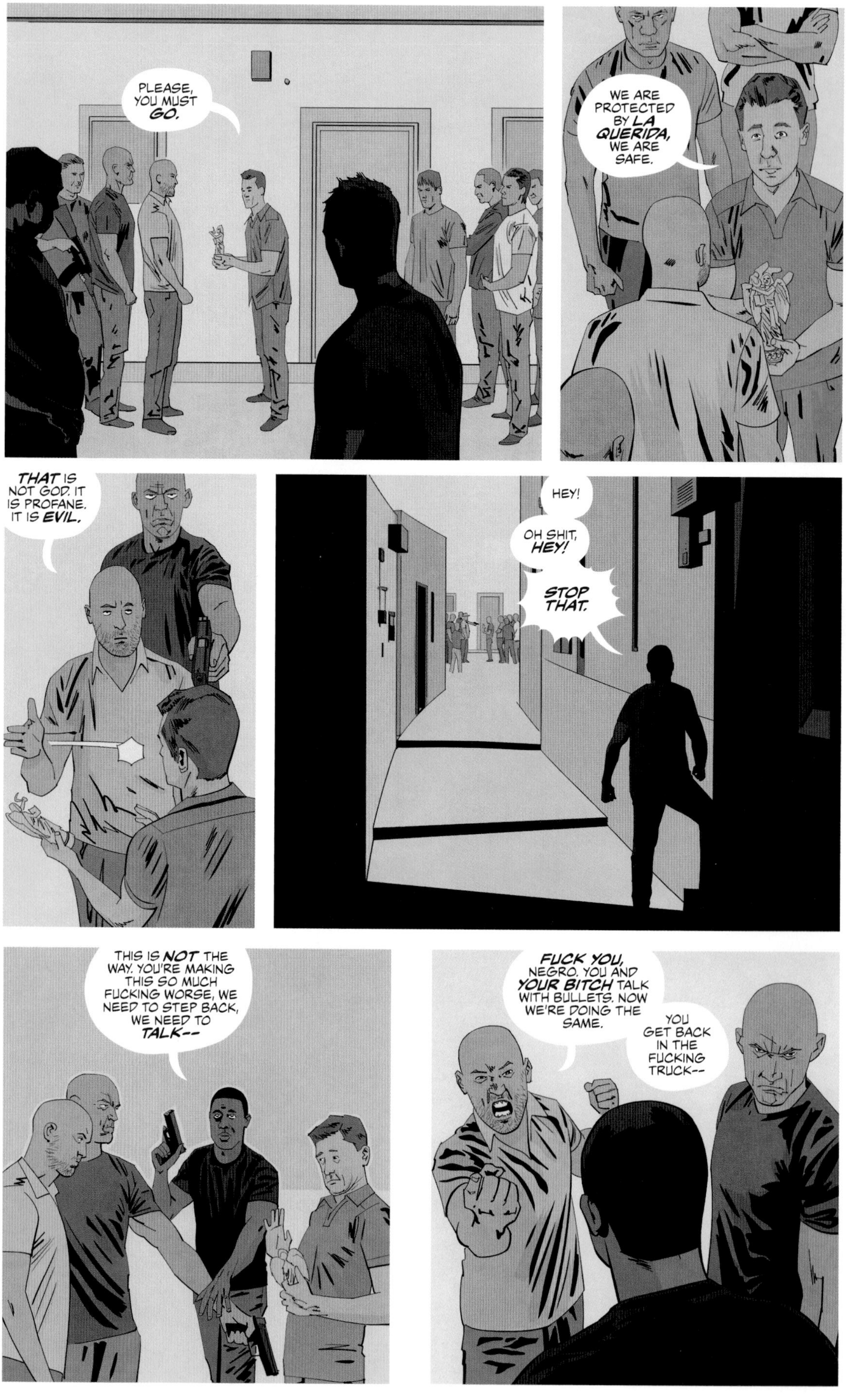
PLEASE, YOU MUST GO.
WE ARE PROTECTED BY LA QUERIDA, WE ARE SAFE.
THAT IS NOT GOD. IT IS PROFANE. IT IS EVIL.
HEY!
OH SHIT, HEY!
STOP THAT.
THIS IS NOT THE WAY. YOU'RE MAKING THIS SO MUCH FUCKING WORSE, WE NEED TO STEP BACK, WE NEED TO TALK--
FUCK YOU, NEGRO. YOU AND YOUR BITCH TALK WITH BULLETS. NOW WE'RE DOING THE SAME.
YOU GET BACK IN THE FUCKING TRUCK--

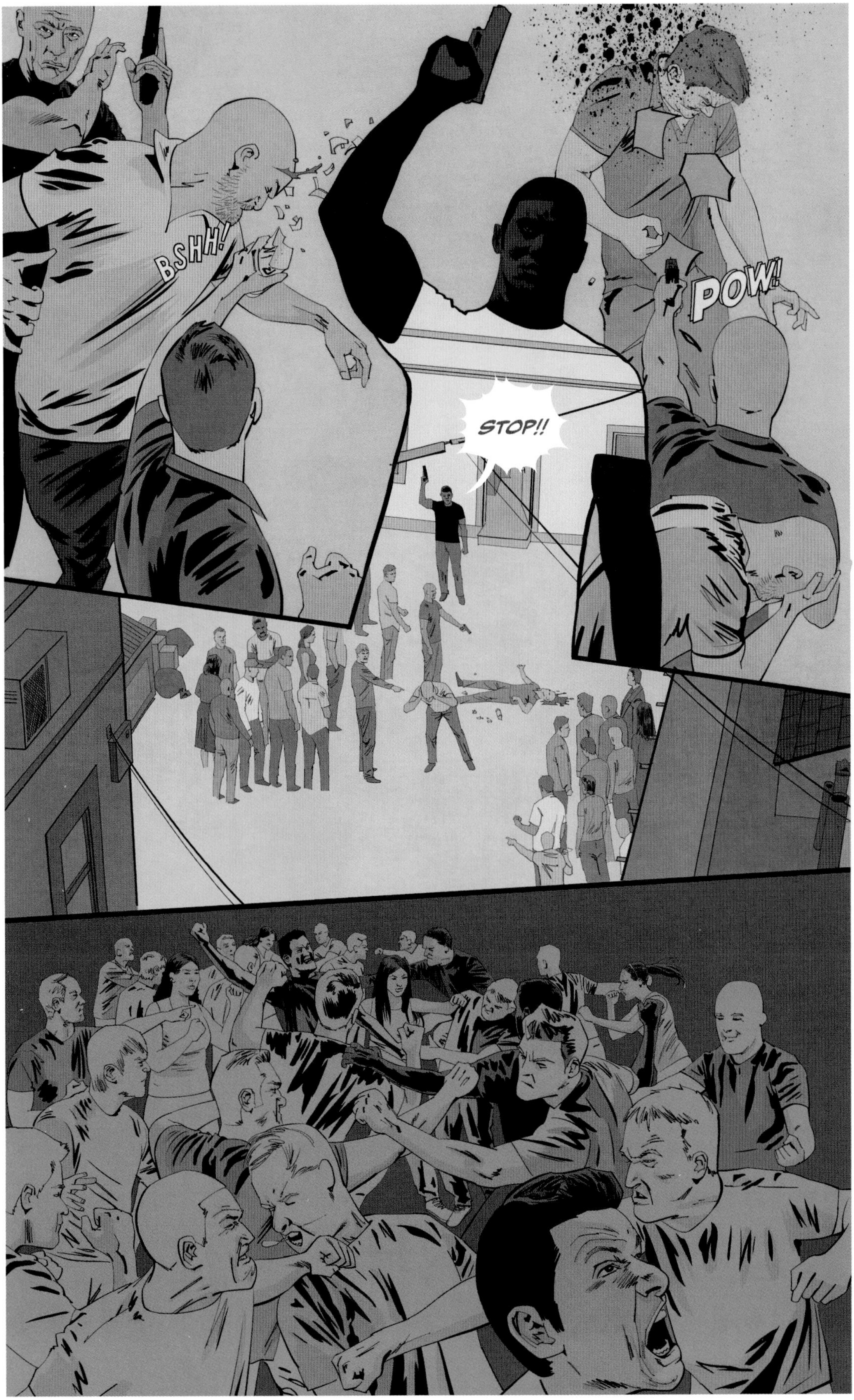
BSHH!
POW!
STOP!!

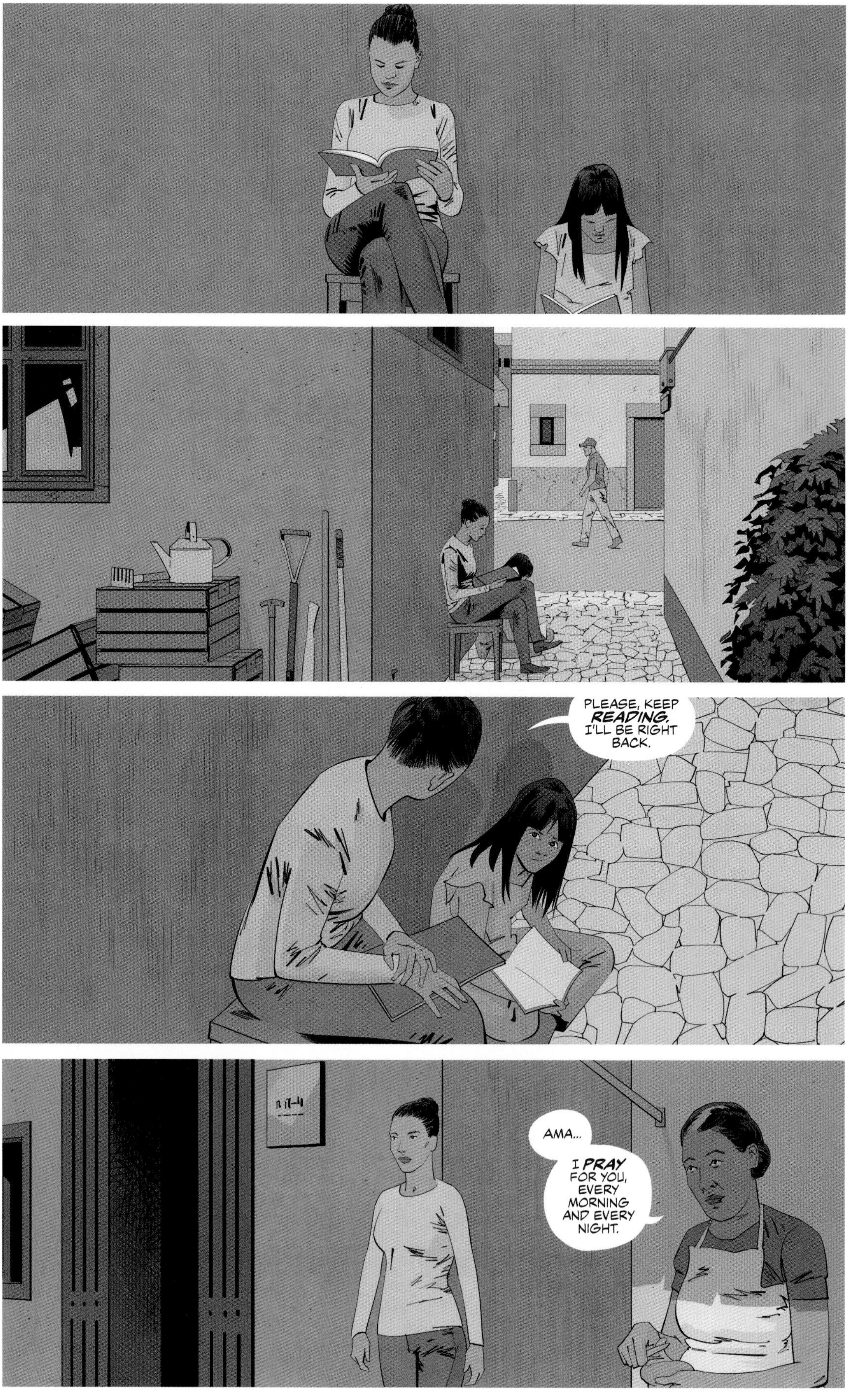
PLEASE, KEEP READING. I'LL BE RIGHT BACK.
AMA...
I PRAY FOR YOU, EVERY MORNING AND EVERY NIGHT.

THANK YOU.

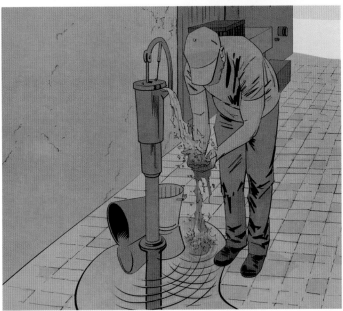

ARE YOU OK?

THAT BASTARD LOST CONSCIOUSNESS FOR A COUPLE MINUTES JUST NOW...

BUT THERE'S *MORE* HE CAN TELL US.

ARE YOU ASKING FOR MY *HELP?*

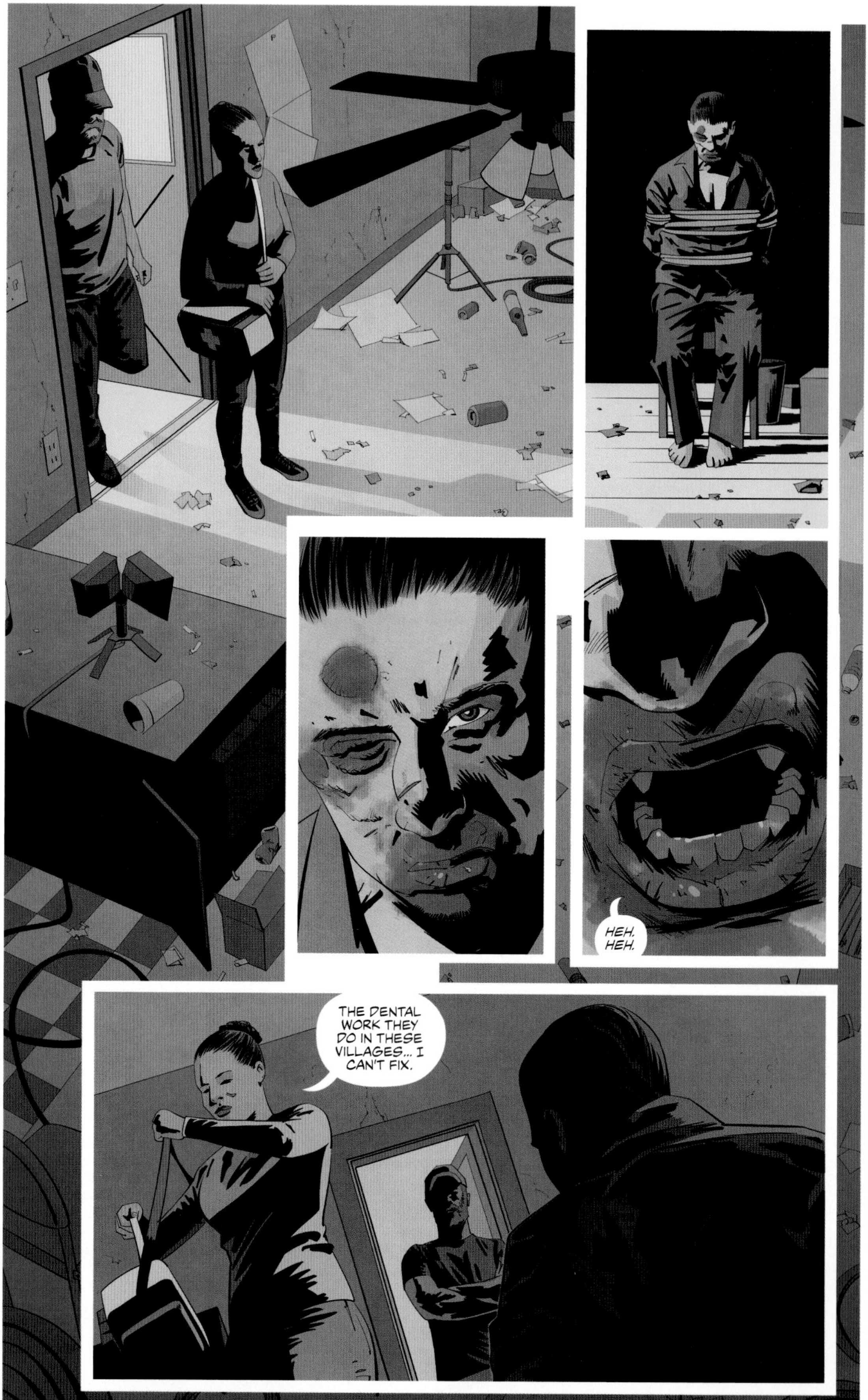
HEH. HEH.
THE DENTAL WORK THEY DO IN THESE VILLAGES... I CAN'T FIX.

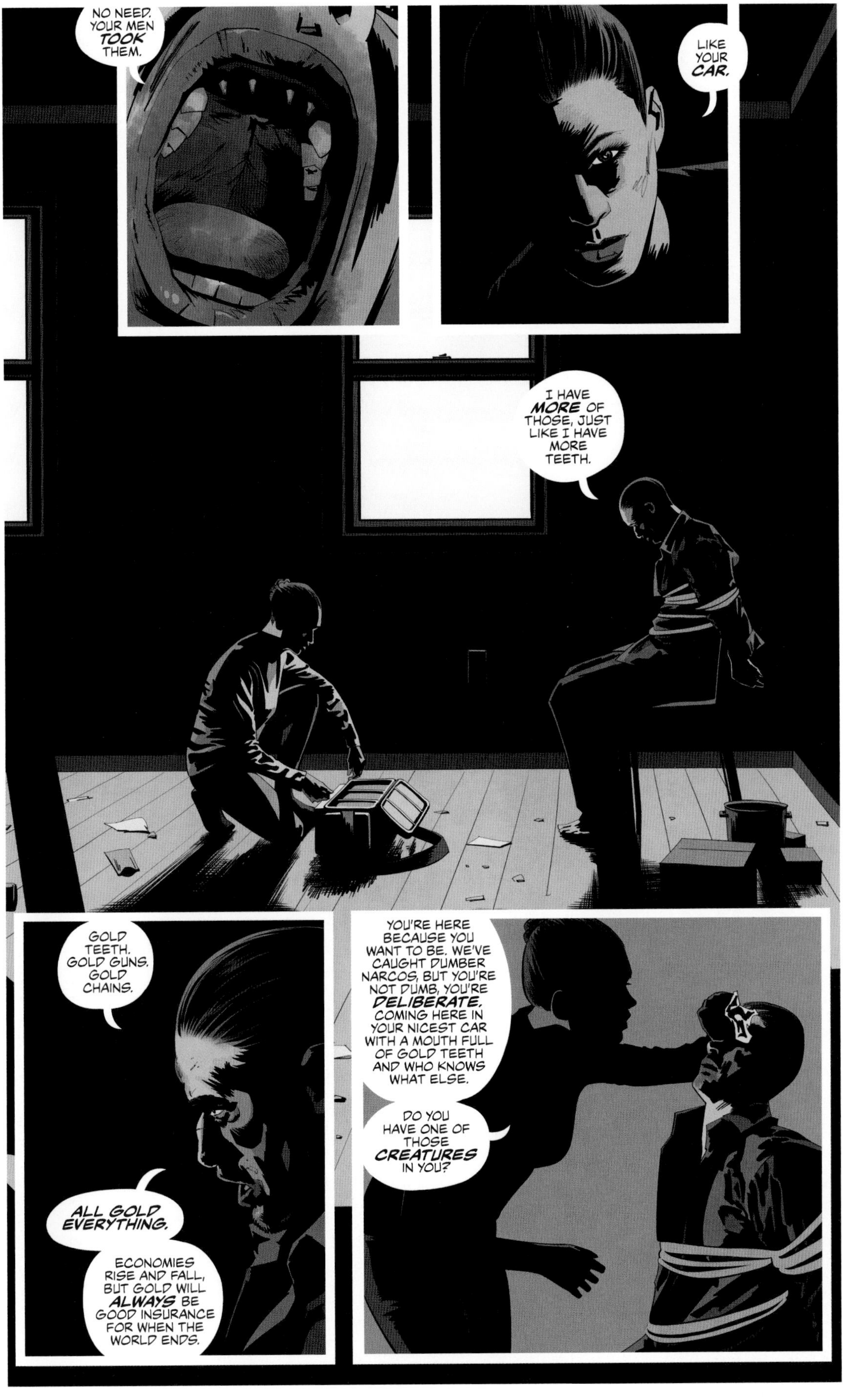
NO NEED. YOUR MEN TOOK THEM.
LIKE YOUR CAR.
I HAVE MORE OF THOSE, JUST LIKE I HAVE MORE TEETH.
GOLD TEETH. GOLD GUNS. GOLD CHAINS.
ALL GOLD EVERYTHING.
ECONOMIES RISE AND FALL, BUT GOLD WILL ALWAYS BE GOOD INSURANCE FOR WHEN THE WORLD ENDS.
YOU'RE HERE BECAUSE YOU WANT TO BE. WE'VE CAUGHT DUMBER NARCOS, BUT YOU'RE NOT DUMB, YOU'RE DELIBERATE, COMING HERE IN YOUR NICEST CAR WITH A MOUTH FULL OF GOLD TEETH AND WHO KNOWS WHAT ELSE.
DO YOU HAVE ONE OF THOSE CREATURES IN YOU?

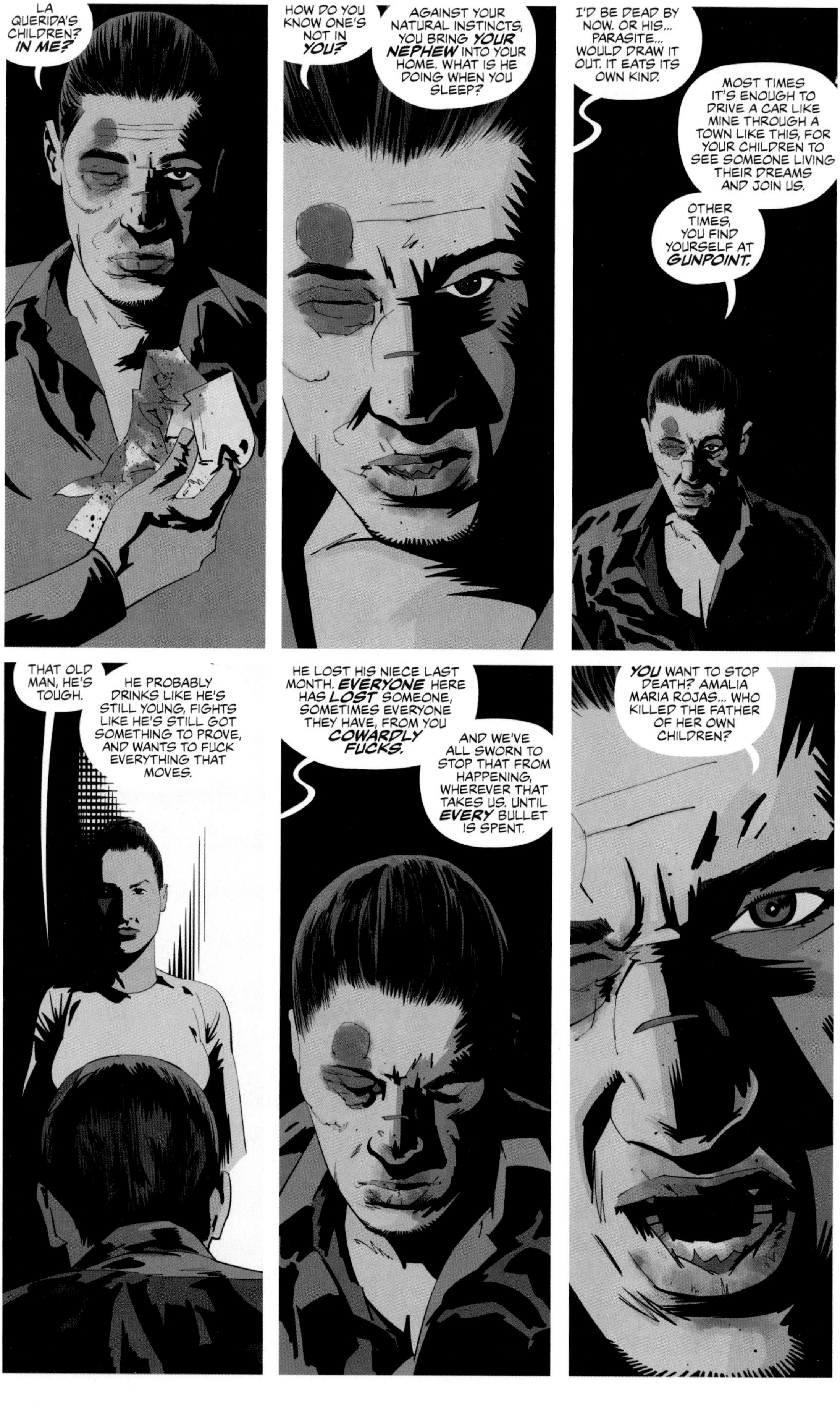
LA QUERIDA'S CHILDREN? IN ME?
HOW DO YOU KNOW ONE'S NOT IN YOU?
AGAINST YOUR NATURAL INSTINCTS, YOU BRING YOUR NEPHEW INTO YOUR HOME. WHAT IS HE DOING WHEN YOU SLEEP?
I'D BE DEAD BY NOW. OR HIS... PARASITE... WOULD DRAW IT OUT. IT EATS ITS OWN KIND.
MOST TIMES IT'S ENOUGH TO DRIVE A CAR LIKE MINE THROUGH A TOWN LIKE THIS, FOR YOUR CHILDREN TO SEE SOMEONE LIVING THEIR DREAMS AND JOIN US.
OTHER TIMES, YOU FIND YOURSELF AT GUNPOINT.
THAT OLD MAN, HE'S TOUGH.
HE PROBABLY DRINKS LIKE HE'S STILL YOUNG, FIGHTS LIKE HE'S STILL GOT SOMETHING TO PROVE, AND WANTS TO FUCK EVERYTHING THAT MOVES.
HE LOST HIS NIECE LAST MONTH. EVERYONE HERE HAS LOST SOMEONE, SOMETIMES EVERYONE THEY HAVE, FROM YOU COWARDLY FUCKS.
AND WE'VE ALL SWORN TO STOP THAT FROM HAPPENING, WHEREVER THAT TAKES US. UNTIL EVERY BULLET IS SPENT.
YOU WANT TO STOP DEATH? AMALIA MARIA ROJAS... WHO KILLED THE FATHER OF HER OWN CHILDREN?

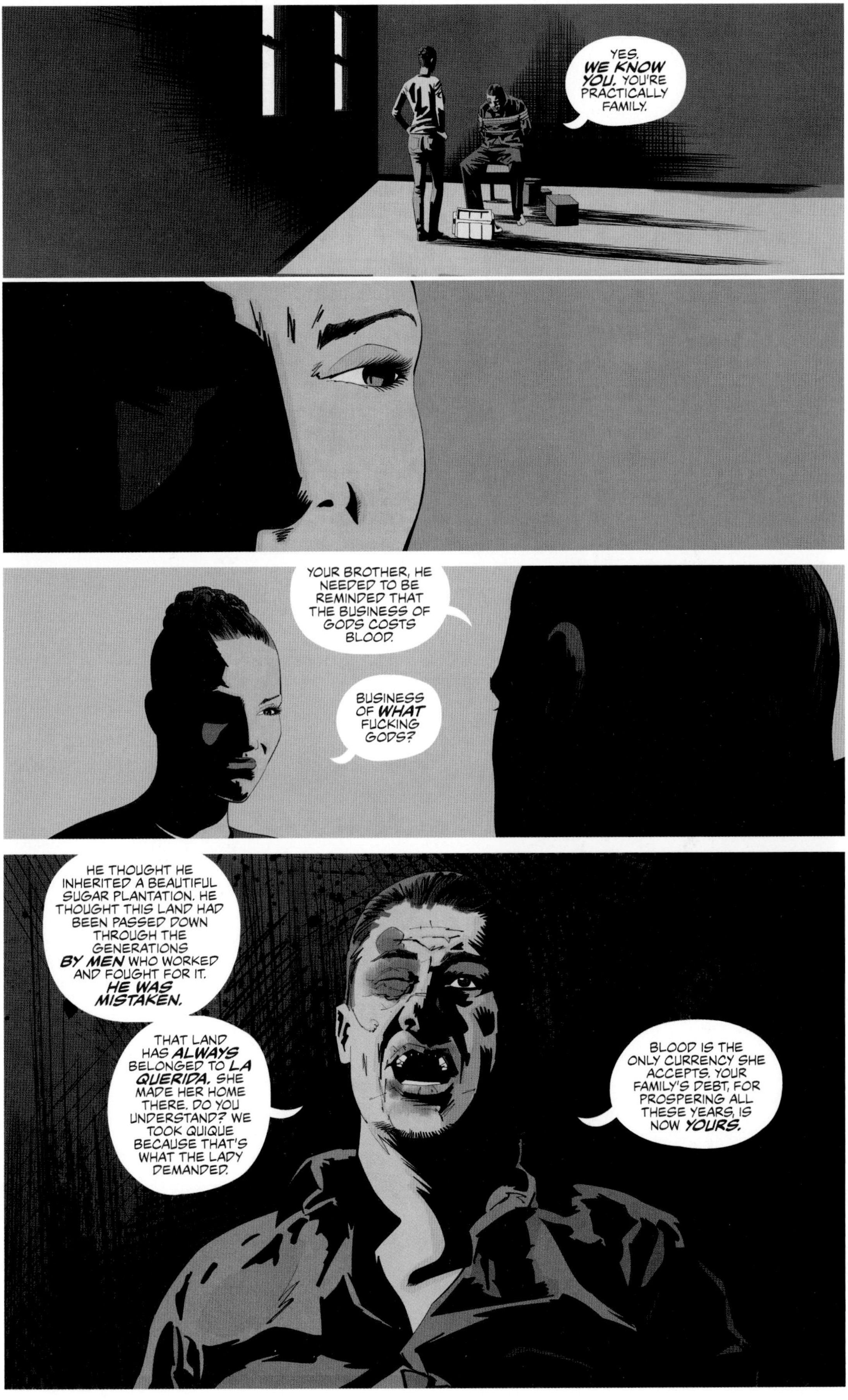

YES. WE KNOW YOU. YOU'RE PRACTICALLY FAMILY.
YOUR BROTHER, HE NEEDED TO BE REMINDED THAT THE BUSINESS OF GODS COSTS BLOOD.
BUSINESS OF WHAT FUCKING GODS?
HE THOUGHT HE INHERITED A BEAUTIFUL SUGAR PLANTATION. HE THOUGHT THIS LAND HAD BEEN PASSED DOWN THROUGH THE GENERATIONS BY MEN WHO WORKED AND FOUGHT FOR IT. HE WAS MISTAKEN.
THAT LAND HAS ALWAYS BELONGED TO LA QUERIDA. SHE MADE HER HOME THERE. DO YOU UNDERSTAND? WE TOOK QUIQUE BECAUSE THAT'S WHAT THE LADY DEMANDED.
BLOOD IS THE ONLY CURRENCY SHE ACCEPTS. YOUR FAMILY'S DEBT, FOR PROSPERING ALL THESE YEARS, IS NOW YOURS.

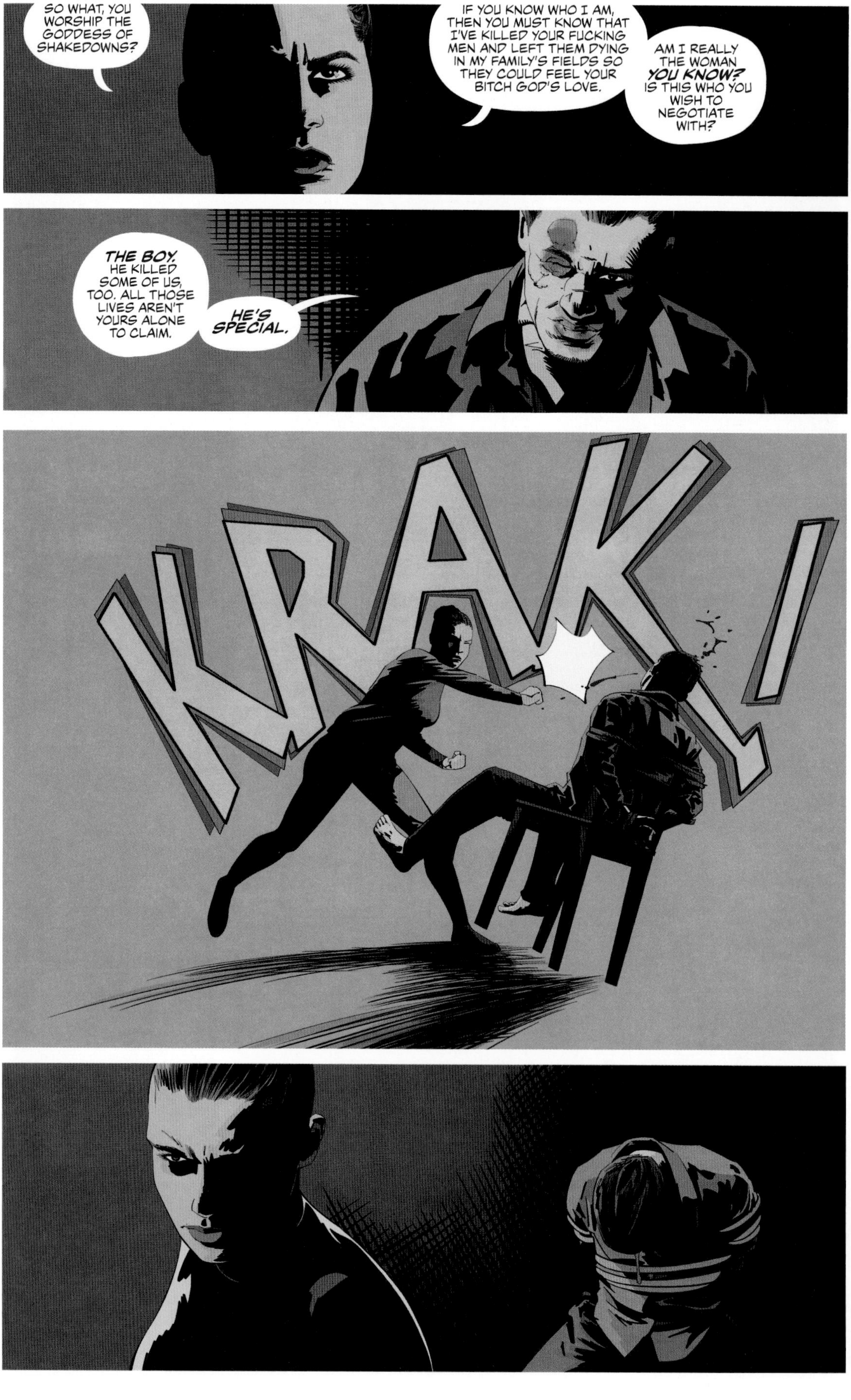
SO WHAT, YOU WORSHIP THE GODDESS OF SHAKEDOWNS?
IF YOU KNOW WHO I AM, THEN YOU MUST KNOW THAT I'VE KILLED YOUR FUCKING MEN AND LEFT THEM DYING IN MY FAMILY'S FIELDS SO THEY COULD FEEL YOUR BITCH GOD'S LOVE.
AM I REALLY THE WOMAN ***YOU KNOW?*** IS THIS WHO YOU WISH TO NEGOTIATE WITH?
THE BOY. HE KILLED SOME OF US, TOO. ALL THOSE LIVES AREN'T YOURS ALONE TO CLAIM.
HE'S SPECIAL.
KRAK!

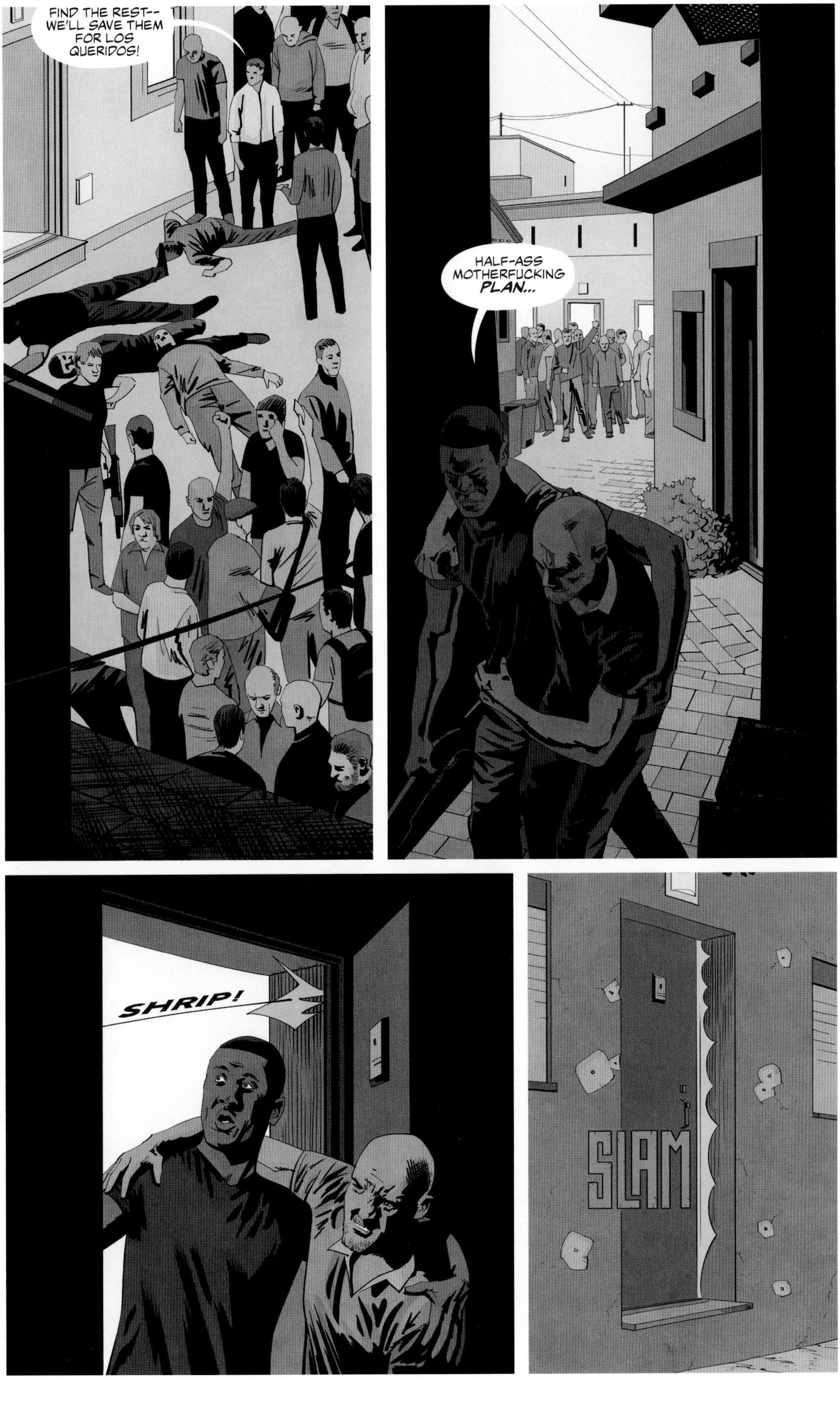

FIND THE REST--
WE'LL SAVE THEM
FOR LOS
QUERIDOS!
HALF-ASS
MOTHERFUCKING
PLAN...
SHRIP!
SLAM

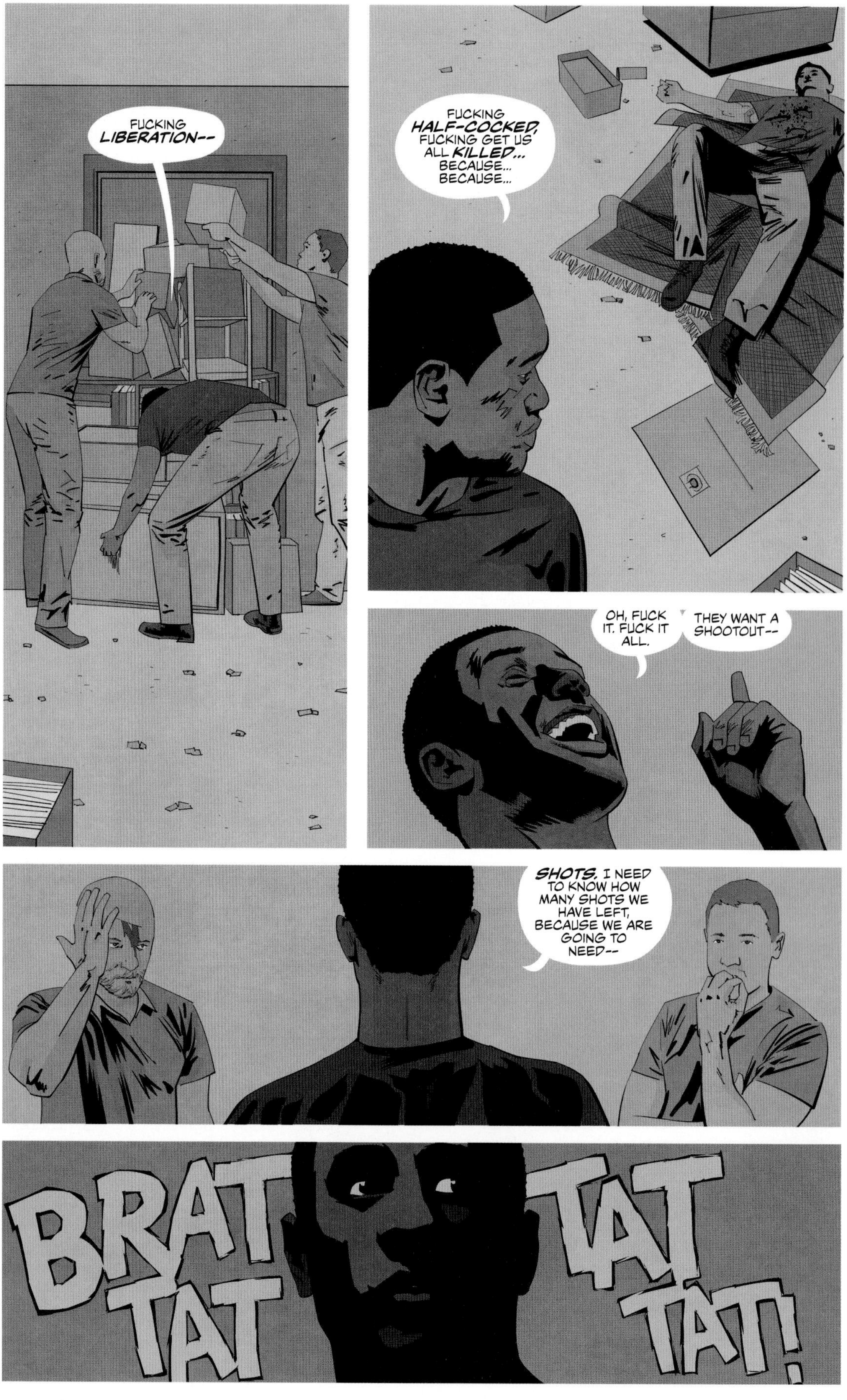
FUCKING LIBERATION--
FUCKING HALF-COCKED, FUCKING GET US ALL KILLED... BECAUSE... BECAUSE...
OH, FUCK IT. FUCK IT ALL.
THEY WANT A SHOOTOUT--
SHOTS. I NEED TO KNOW HOW MANY SHOTS WE HAVE LEFT, BECAUSE WE ARE GOING TO NEED--
BRAT TAT TAT TAT!

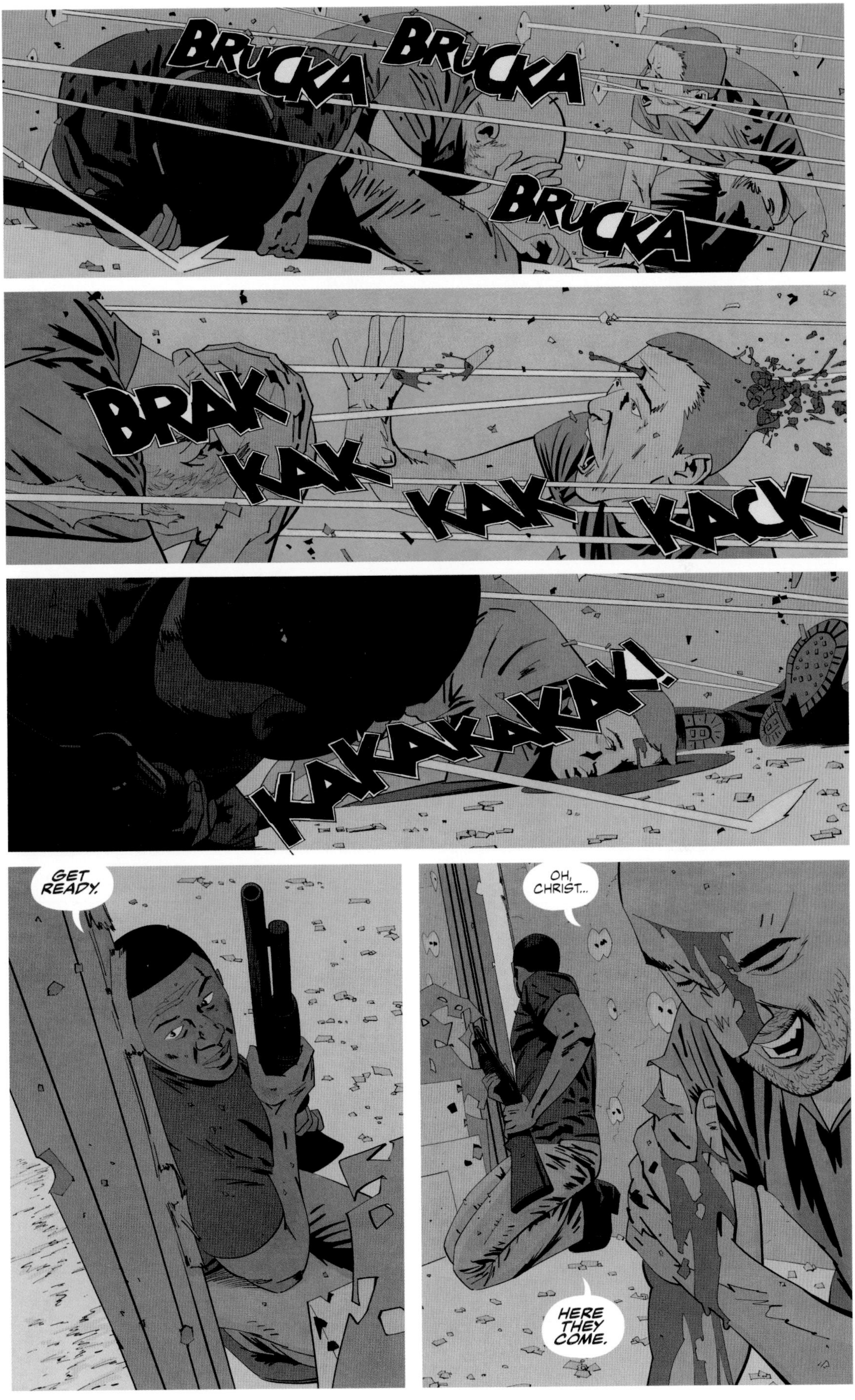
BRUCKA BRUCKA
BRUCKA
BRAK
KAK
KAK
KACK
KAKAKAKAK!
GET READY.
OH, CHRIST...
HERE THEY COME.

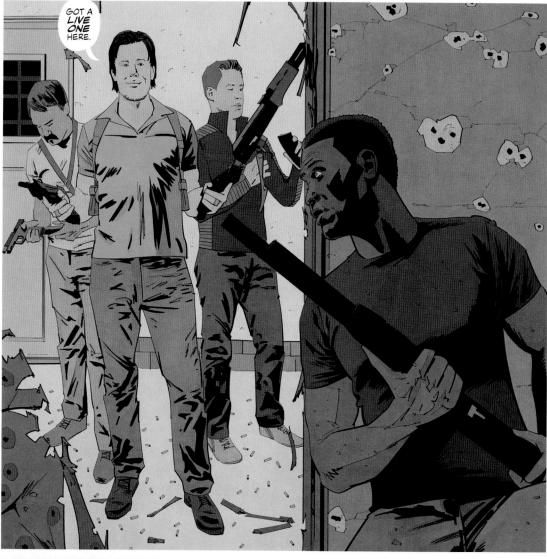

GOT A *LIVE ONE* HERE.

JOVANY.

YOU LOOK LIKE SHIT, RANDY.

SWEET VIRGIN MOTHER OF GOD...

IMAGINE... ME FINDING YOU IN A *FORSAKEN* SPOT LIKE THIS.

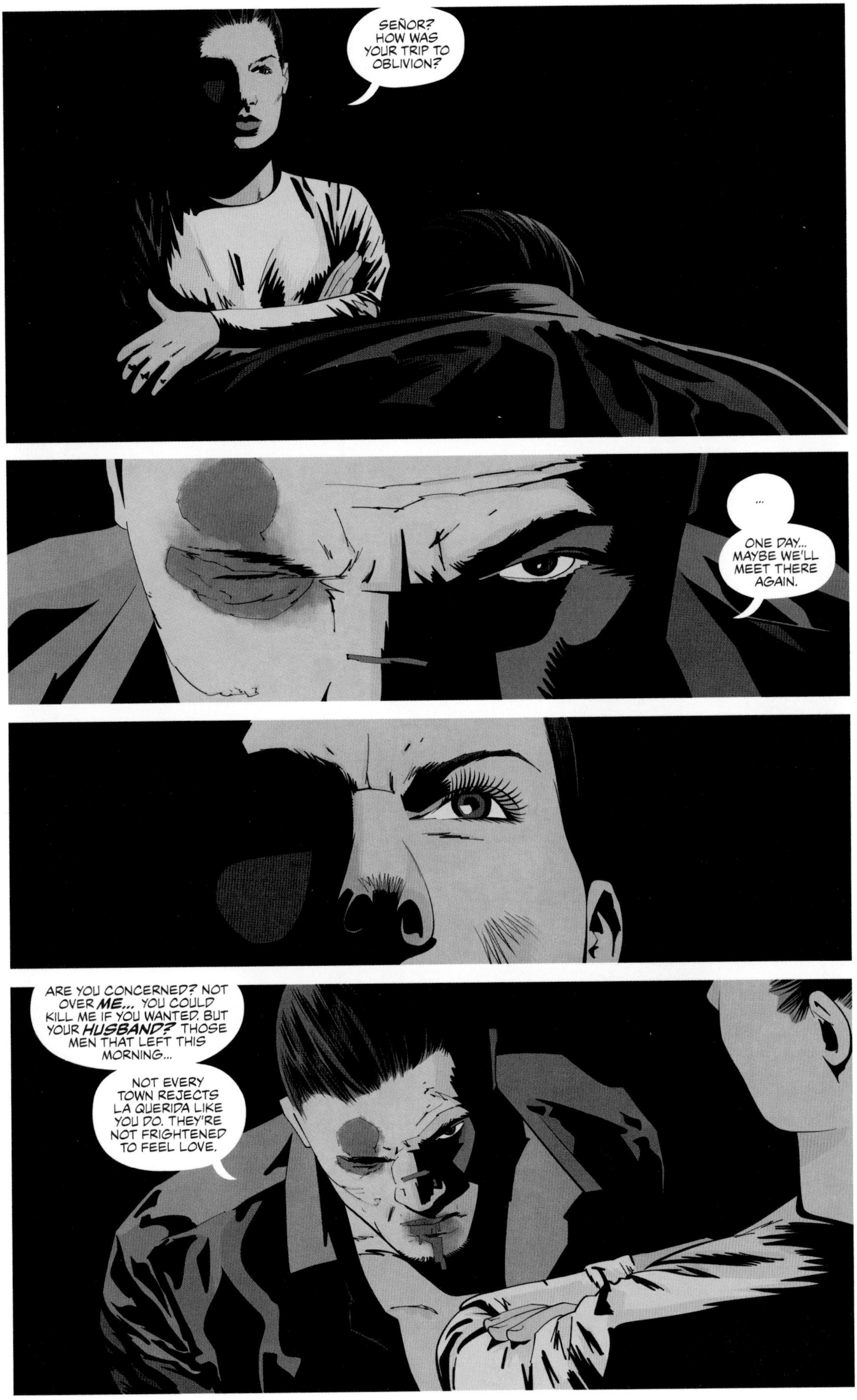
SEÑOR? HOW WAS YOUR TRIP TO OBLIVION?
...
ONE DAY... MAYBE WE'LL MEET THERE AGAIN.
ARE YOU CONCERNED? NOT OVER ***ME...*** YOU COULD KILL ME IF YOU WANTED. BUT YOUR ***HUSBAND?*** THOSE MEN THAT LEFT THIS MORNING...
NOT EVERY TOWN REJECTS LA QUERIDA LIKE YOU DO. THEY'RE NOT FRIGHTENED TO FEEL LOVE.

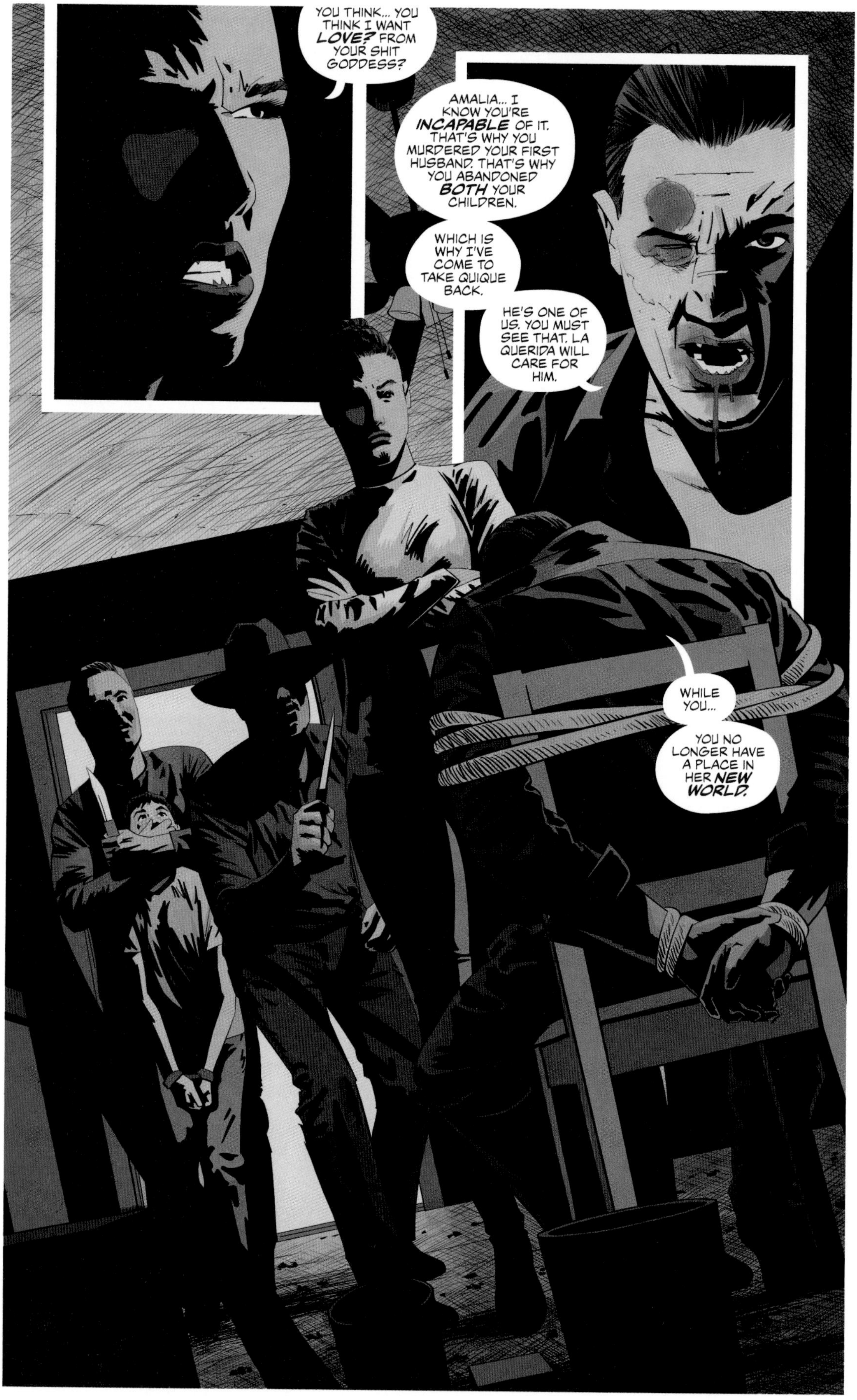

YOU THINK... YOU THINK I WANT LOVE? FROM YOUR SHIT GODDESS?
AMALIA... I KNOW YOU'RE INCAPABLE OF IT. THAT'S WHY YOU MURDERED YOUR FIRST HUSBAND. THAT'S WHY YOU ABANDONED BOTH YOUR CHILDREN.
WHICH IS WHY I'VE COME TO TAKE QUIQUE BACK.
HE'S ONE OF US. YOU MUST SEE THAT. LA QUERIDA WILL CARE FOR HIM.
WHILE YOU...
YOU NO LONGER HAVE A PLACE IN HER NEW WORLD.

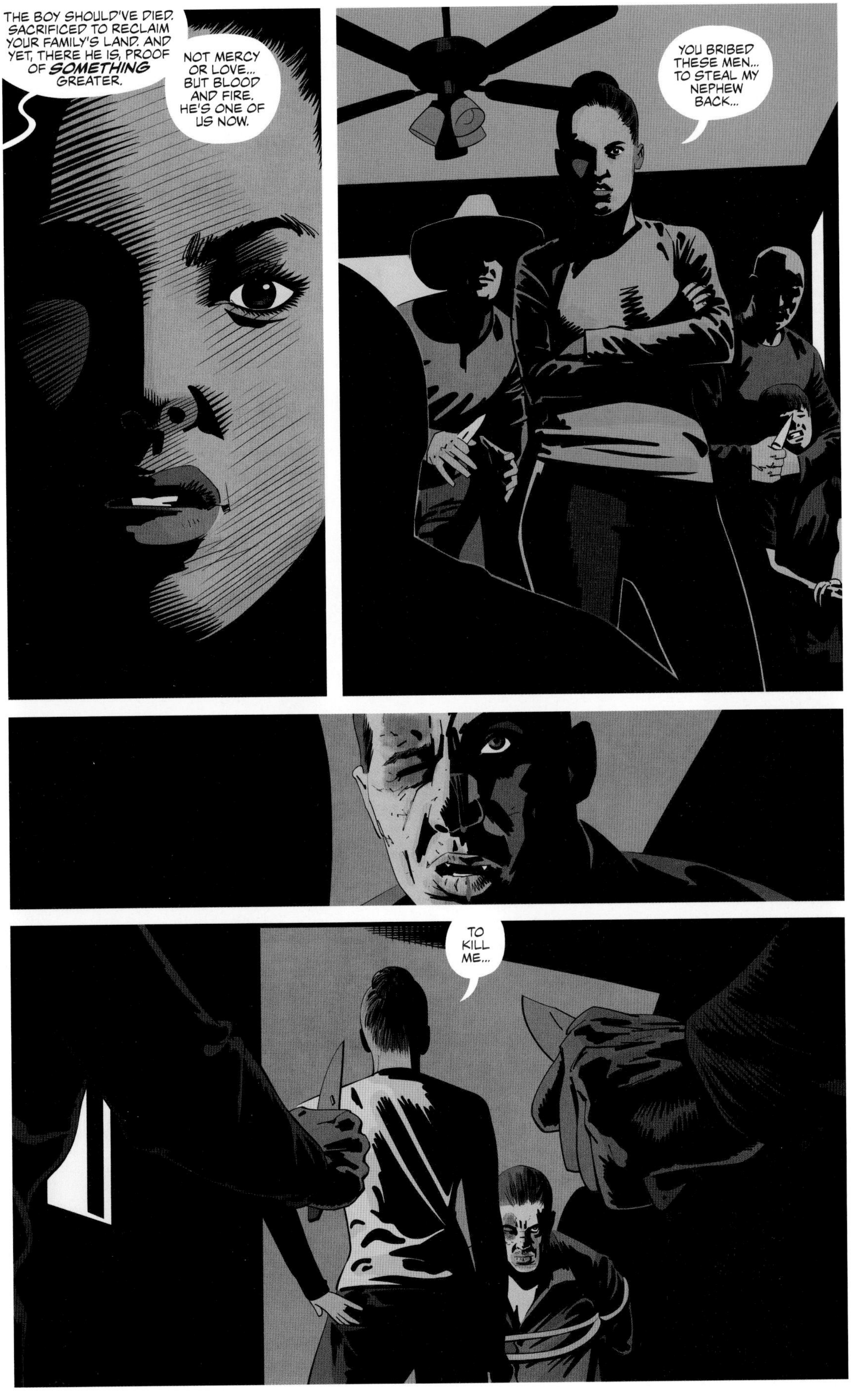
THE BOY SHOULD'VE DIED. SACRIFICED TO RECLAIM YOUR FAMILY'S LAND. AND YET, THERE HE IS, PROOF OF *SOMETHING* GREATER.
NOT MERCY OR LOVE... BUT BLOOD AND FIRE. HE'S ONE OF US NOW.
YOU BRIBED THESE MEN... TO STEAL MY NEPHEW BACK...
TO KILL ME...

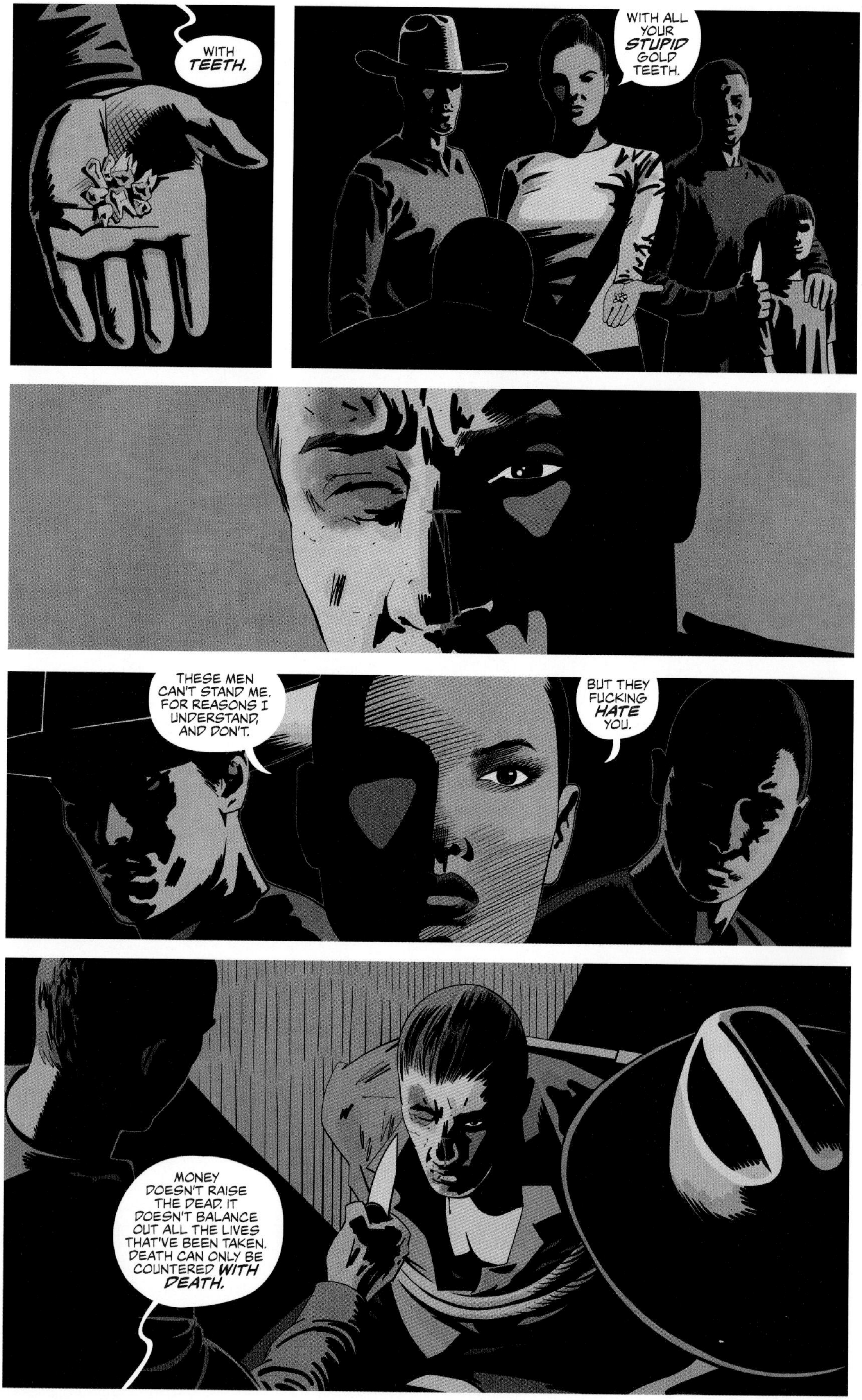
WITH TEETH.
WITH ALL YOUR STUPID GOLD TEETH.
THESE MEN CAN'T STAND ME. FOR REASONS I UNDERSTAND, AND DON'T.
BUT THEY FUCKING HATE YOU.
MONEY DOESN'T RAISE THE DEAD. IT DOESN'T BALANCE OUT ALL THE LIVES THAT'VE BEEN TAKEN. DEATH CAN ONLY BE COUNTERED WITH DEATH.

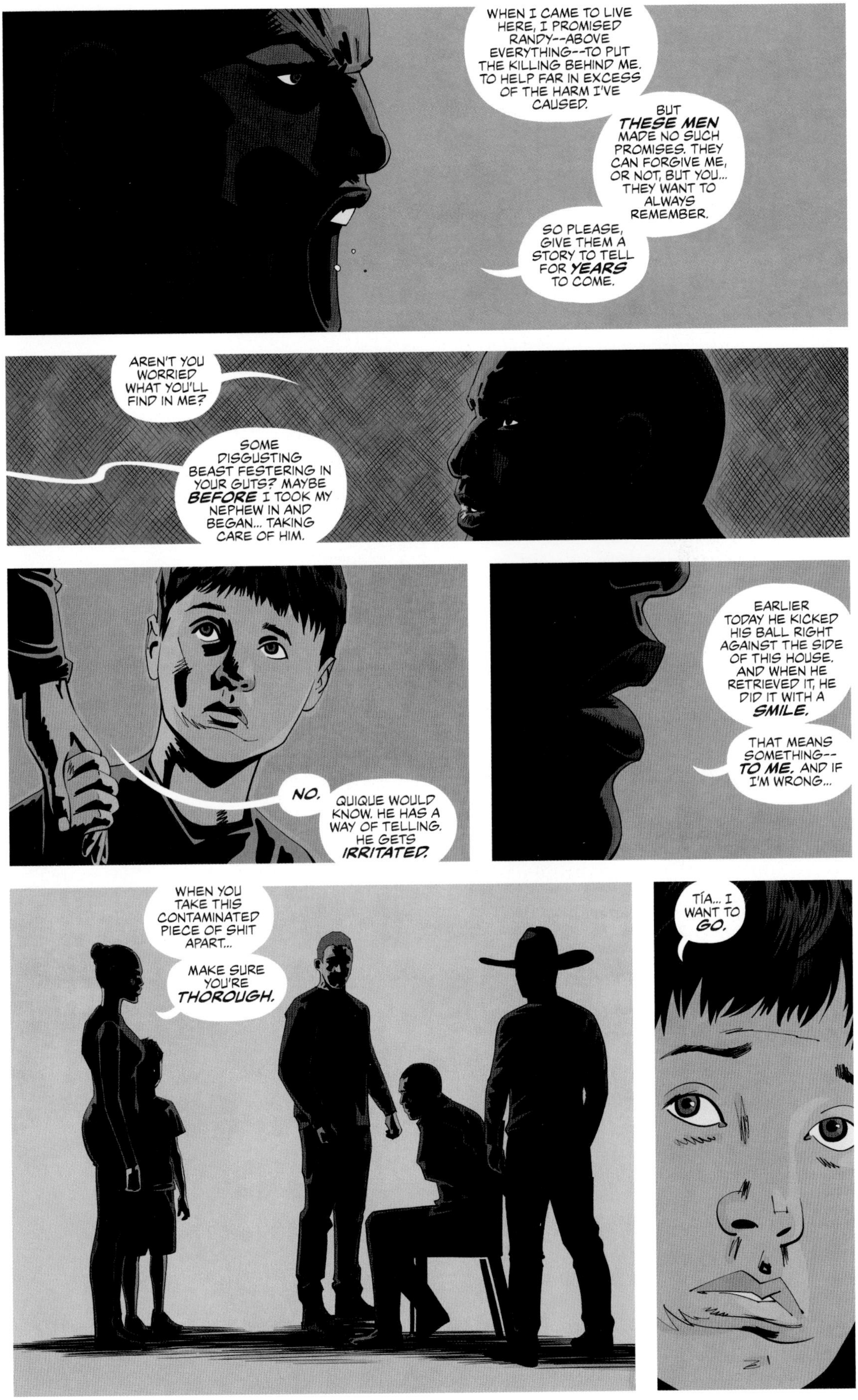
WHEN I CAME TO LIVE HERE, I PROMISED RANDY--ABOVE EVERYTHING--TO PUT THE KILLING BEHIND ME. TO HELP FAR IN EXCESS OF THE HARM I'VE CAUSED.
BUT THESE MEN MADE NO SUCH PROMISES. THEY CAN FORGIVE ME, OR NOT, BUT YOU... THEY WANT TO ALWAYS REMEMBER.
SO PLEASE, GIVE THEM A STORY TO TELL FOR YEARS TO COME.
AREN'T YOU WORRIED WHAT YOU'LL FIND IN ME?
SOME DISGUSTING BEAST FESTERING IN YOUR GUTS? MAYBE BEFORE I TOOK MY NEPHEW IN AND BEGAN... TAKING CARE OF HIM.
NO.
QUIQUE WOULD KNOW. HE HAS A WAY OF TELLING. HE GETS IRRITATED.
EARLIER TODAY HE KICKED HIS BALL RIGHT AGAINST THE SIDE OF THIS HOUSE. AND WHEN HE RETRIEVED IT, HE DID IT WITH A SMILE.
THAT MEANS SOMETHING-- TO ME. AND IF I'M WRONG...
WHEN YOU TAKE THIS CONTAMINATED PIECE OF SHIT APART...
MAKE SURE YOU'RE THOROUGH.
TÍA... I WANT TO GO.

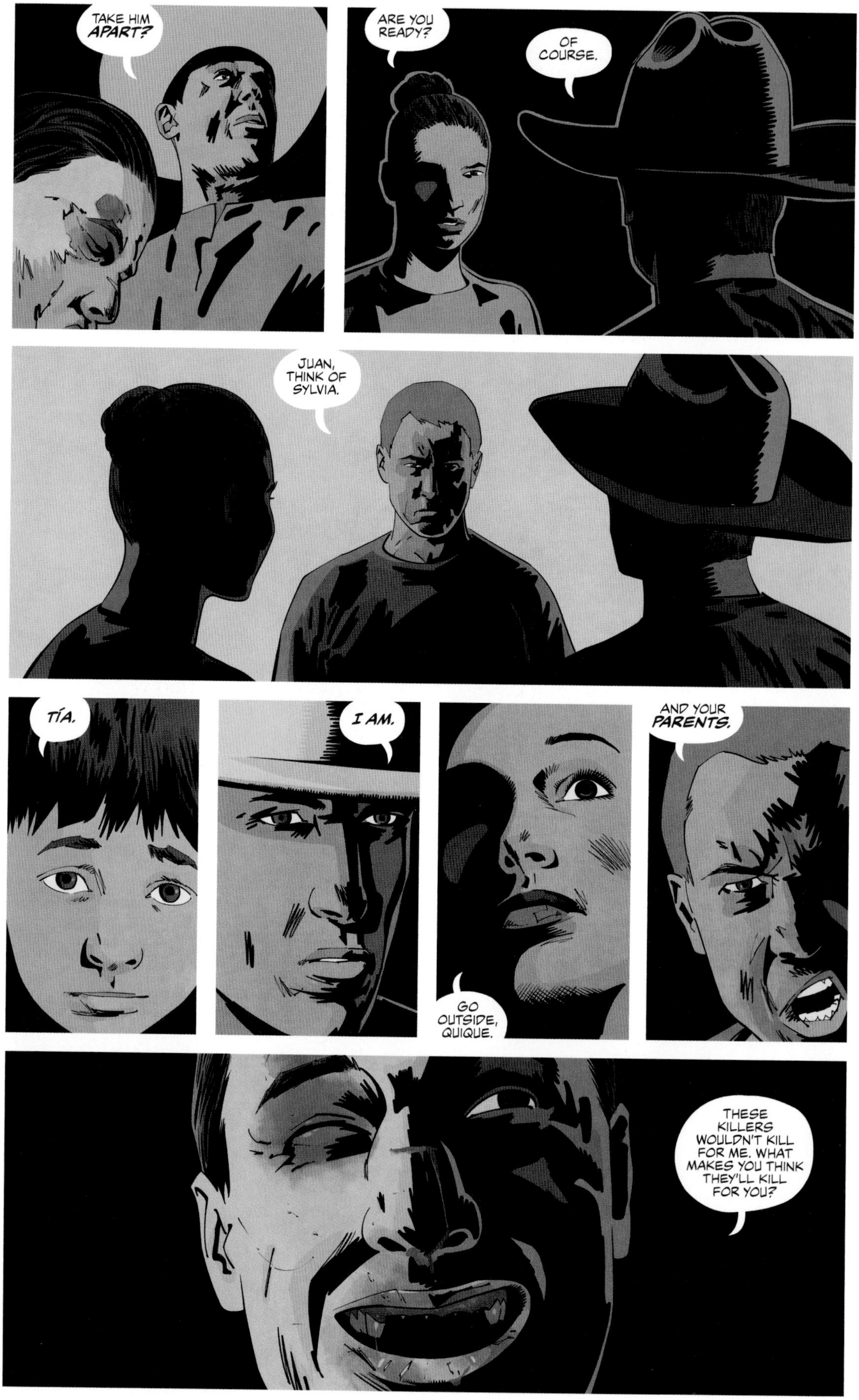
TAKE HIM *APART?*
ARE YOU READY?
OF COURSE.
JUAN, THINK OF SYLVIA.
TÍA.
I AM.
AND YOUR *PARENTS.*
GO OUTSIDE, QUIQUE.
THESE KILLERS WOULDN'T KILL FOR ME. WHAT MAKES YOU THINK THEY'LL KILL FOR YOU?

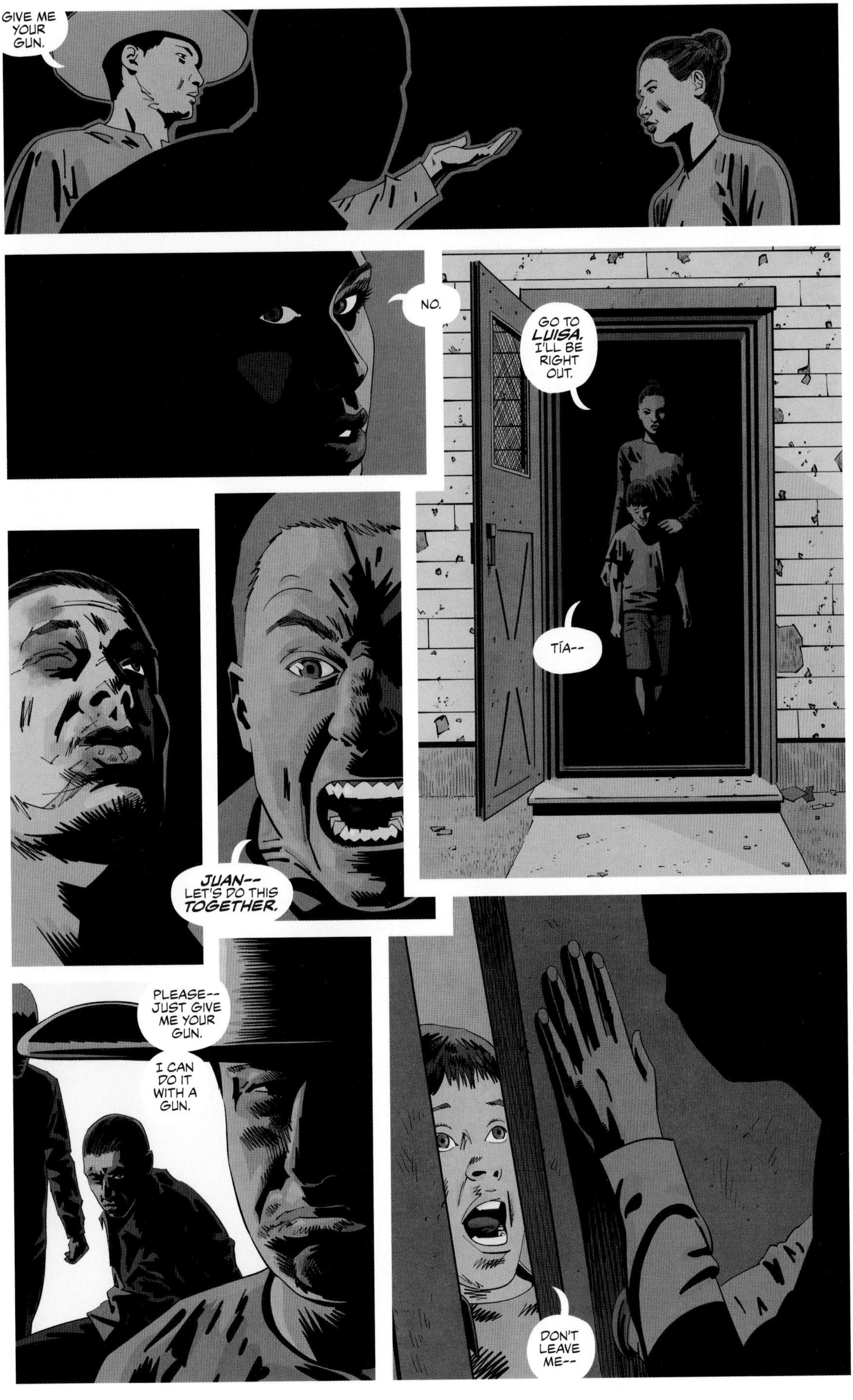
GIVE ME YOUR GUN.
NO.
GO TO LUISA. I'LL BE RIGHT OUT.
TÍA--
JUAN-- LET'S DO THIS TOGETHER.
PLEASE-- JUST GIVE ME YOUR GUN.
I CAN DO IT WITH A GUN.
DON'T LEAVE ME--

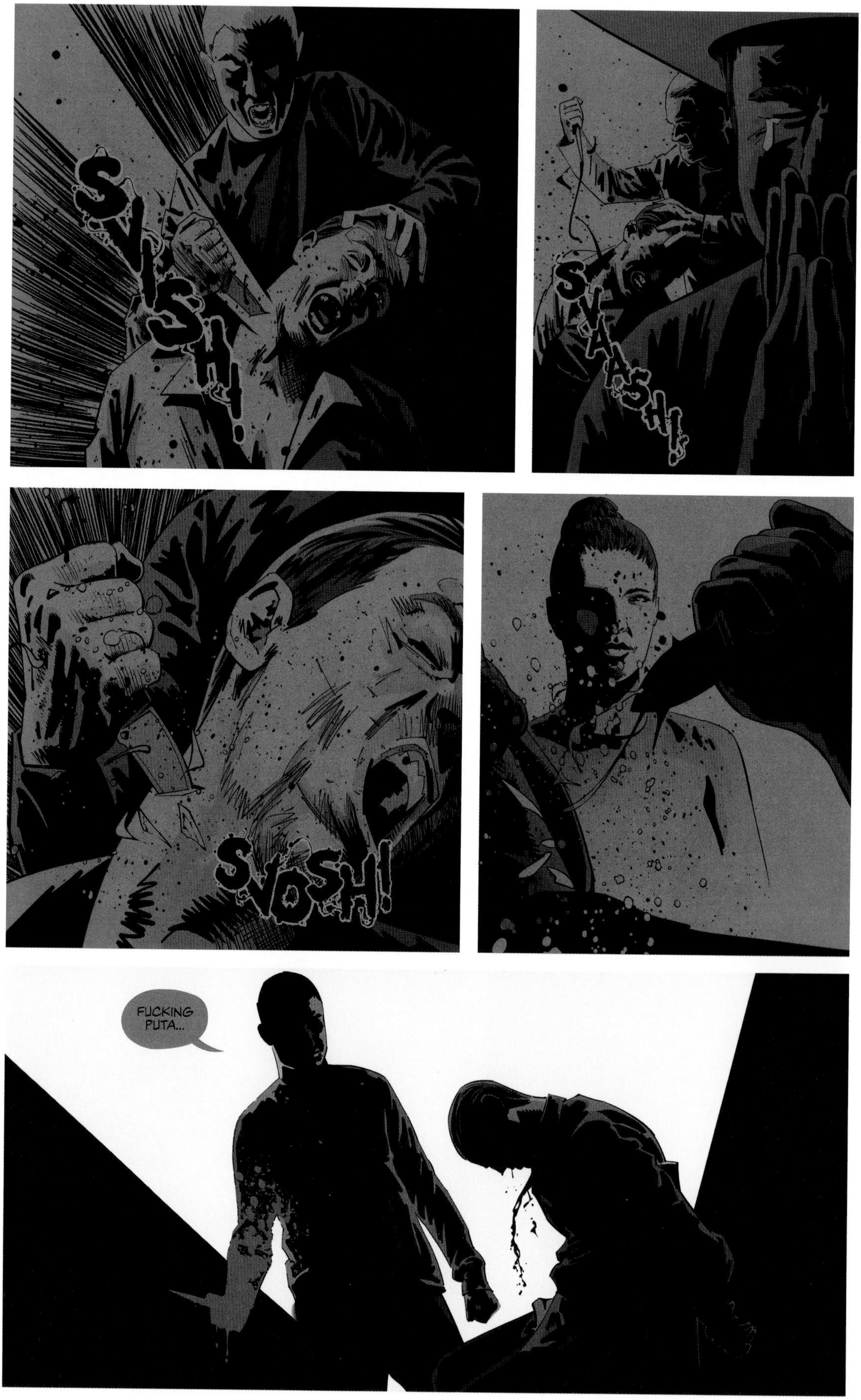
SVISH!
SVAASH!
SVOSH!
FUCKING PUTA...

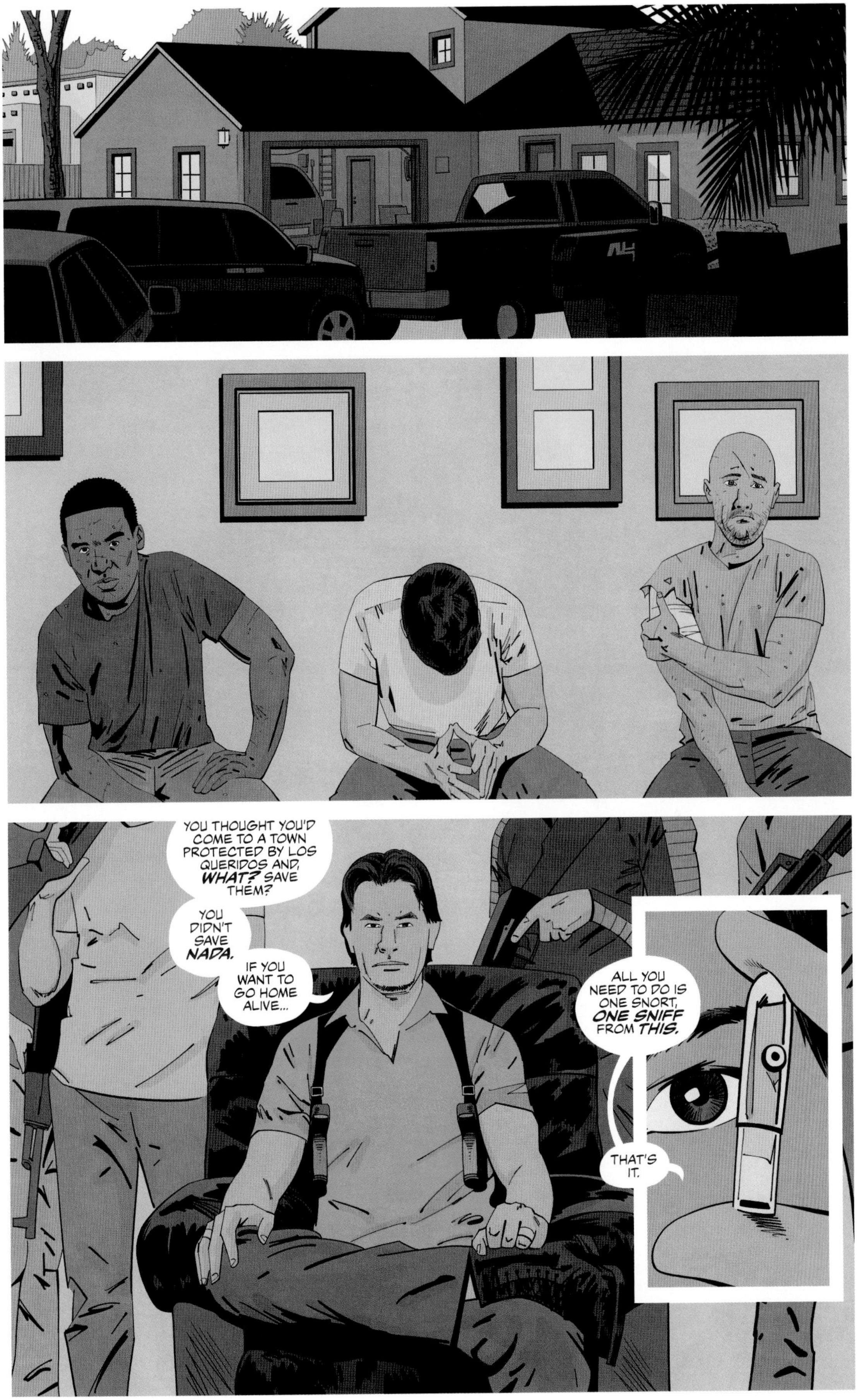
YOU THOUGHT YOU'D COME TO A TOWN PROTECTED BY LOS QUERIDOS AND, WHAT? SAVE THEM?
YOU DIDN'T SAVE NADA.
IF YOU WANT TO GO HOME ALIVE...
ALL YOU NEED TO DO IS ONE SNORT, ONE SNIFF FROM THIS.
THAT'S IT.

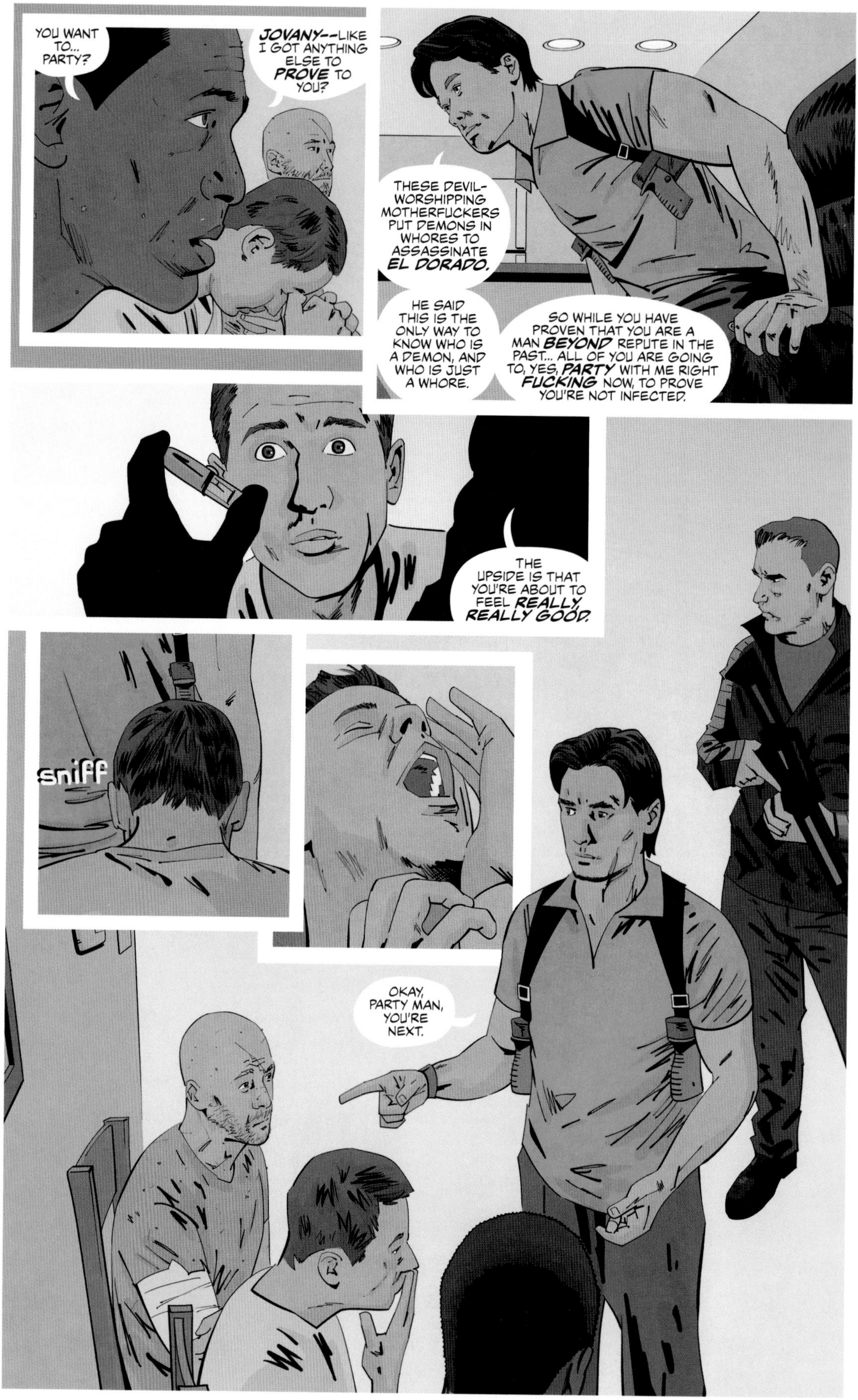
YOU WANT TO... PARTY?
JOVANY--LIKE I GOT ANYTHING ELSE TO PROVE TO YOU?
THESE DEVIL-WORSHIPPING MOTHERFUCKERS PUT DEMONS IN WHORES TO ASSASSINATE EL DORADO.
HE SAID THIS IS THE ONLY WAY TO KNOW WHO IS A DEMON, AND WHO IS JUST A WHORE.
SO WHILE YOU HAVE PROVEN THAT YOU ARE A MAN BEYOND REPUTE IN THE PAST... ALL OF YOU ARE GOING TO, YES, PARTY WITH ME RIGHT FUCKING NOW, TO PROVE YOU'RE NOT INFECTED.
THE UPSIDE IS THAT YOU'RE ABOUT TO FEEL REALLY, REALLY GOOD.
sniff
OKAY, PARTY MAN, YOU'RE NEXT.

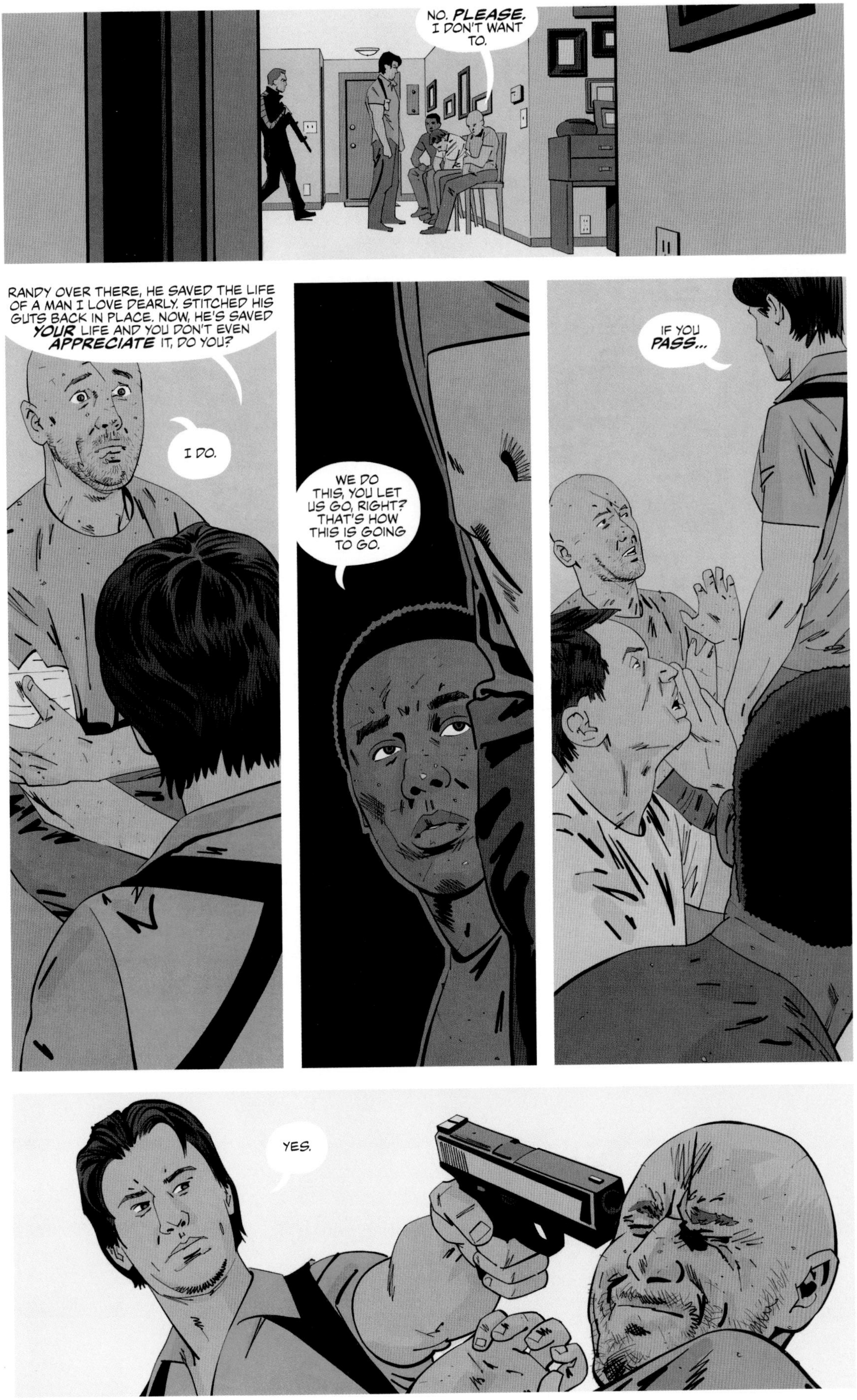

NO. PLEASE. I DON'T WANT TO.
RANDY OVER THERE, HE SAVED THE LIFE OF A MAN I LOVE DEARLY. STITCHED HIS GUTS BACK IN PLACE. NOW, HE'S SAVED YOUR LIFE AND YOU DON'T EVEN APPRECIATE IT, DO YOU?
I DO.
WE DO THIS, YOU LET US GO, RIGHT? THAT'S HOW THIS IS GOING TO GO.
IF YOU PASS...
YES.

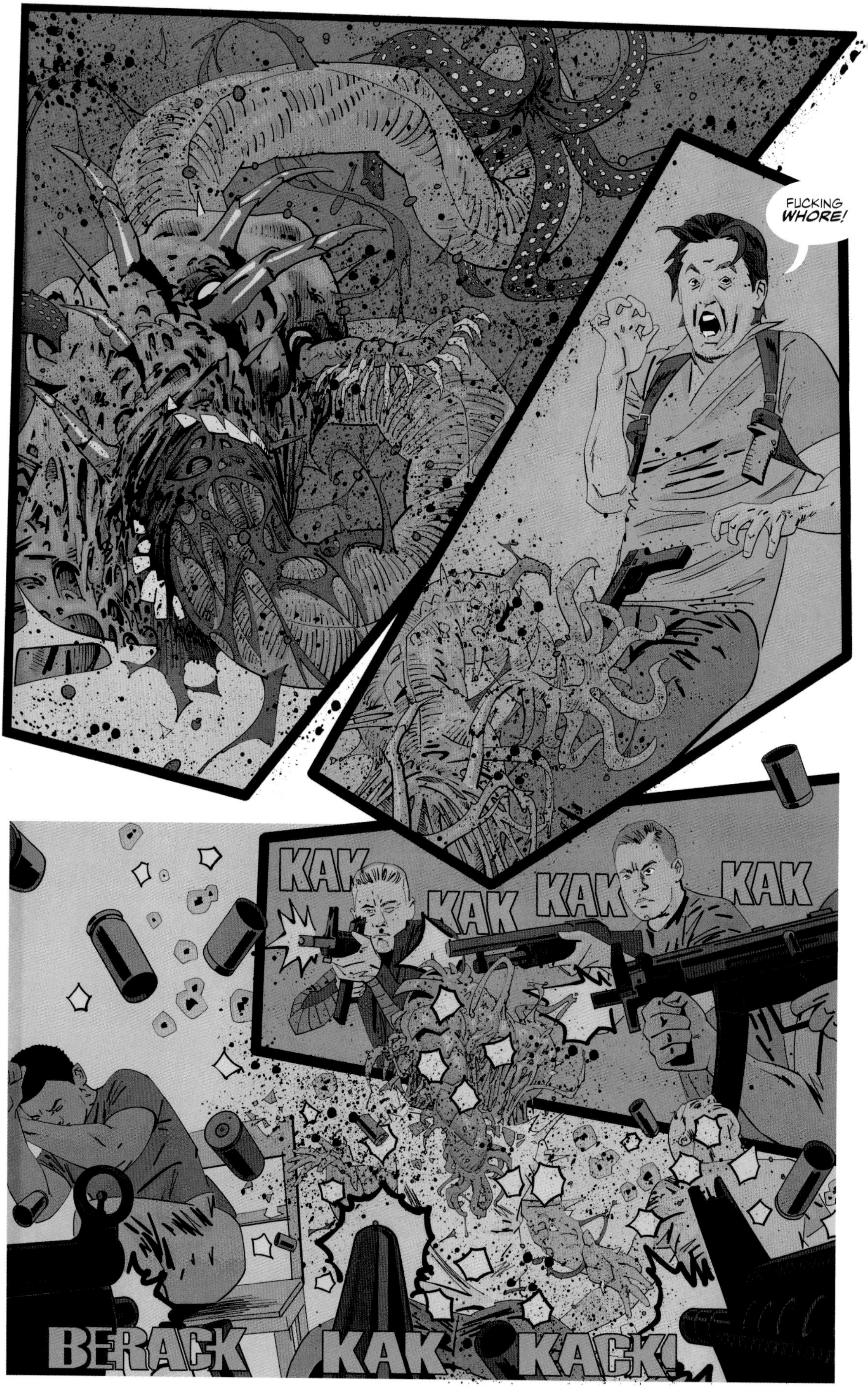
FUCKING WHORE!
KAK
KAK
KAK
KAK
BERACK
KAK
KACK!

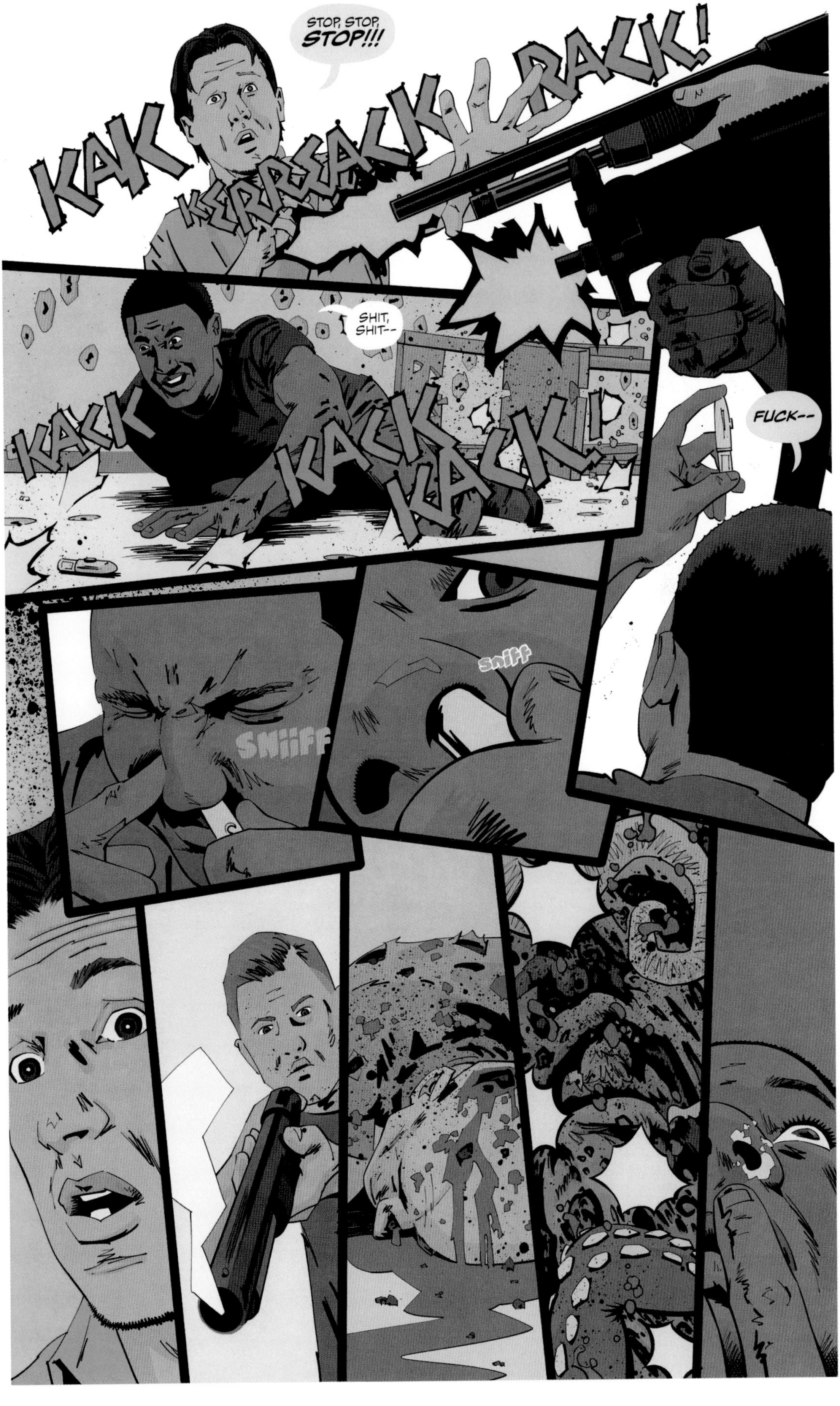
STOP, STOP, STOP!!!
KAK KERREACK KRACK!
SHIT, SHIT--
KACK
KACK KACK KACK!
FUCK--
SNIFF
SNIIFF

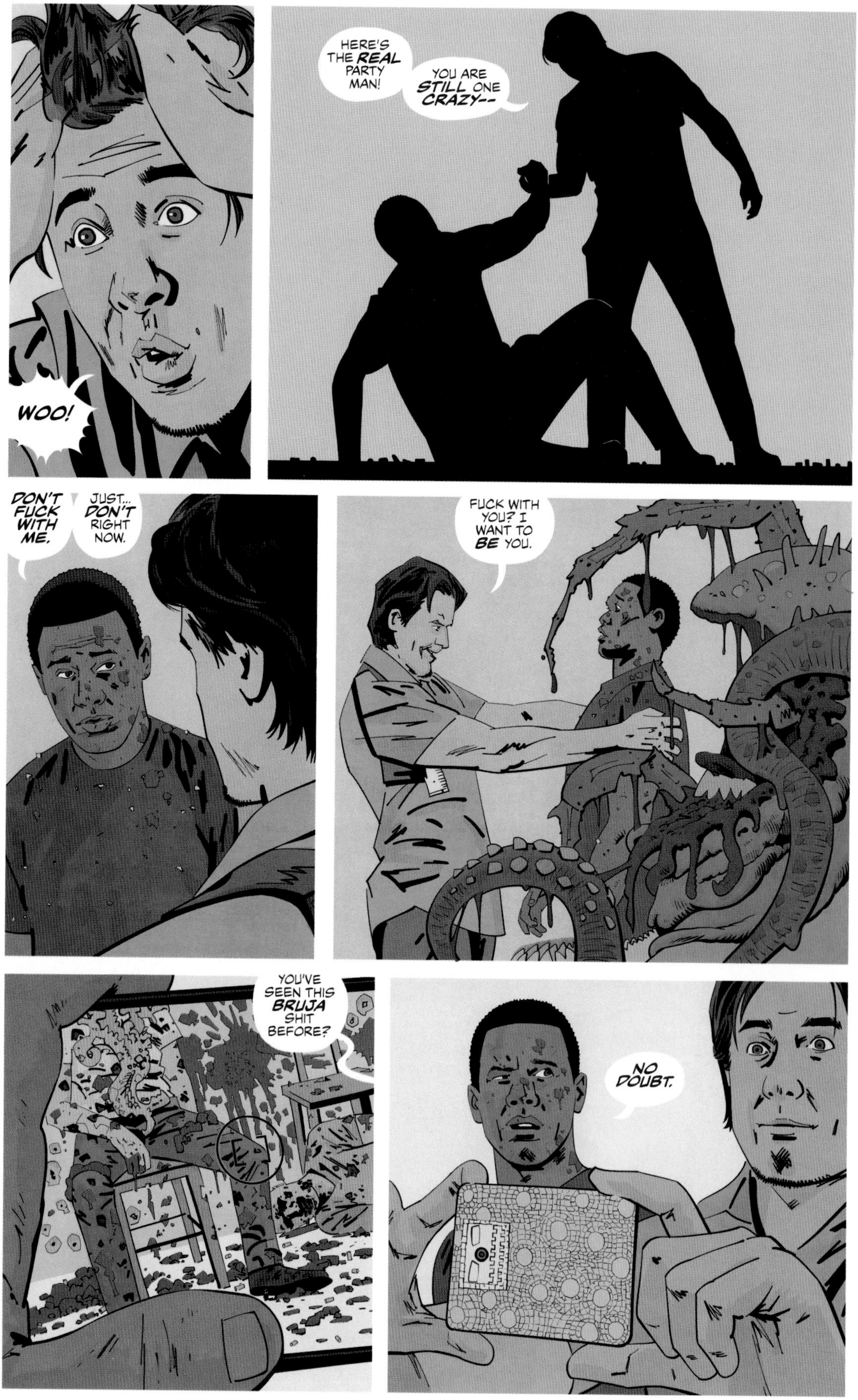
WOO!
HERE'S THE REAL PARTY MAN!
YOU ARE STILL ONE CRAZY--
DON'T FUCK WITH ME.
JUST... DON'T RIGHT NOW.
FUCK WITH YOU? I WANT TO BE YOU.
YOU'VE SEEN THIS BRUJA SHIT BEFORE?
NO DOUBT.

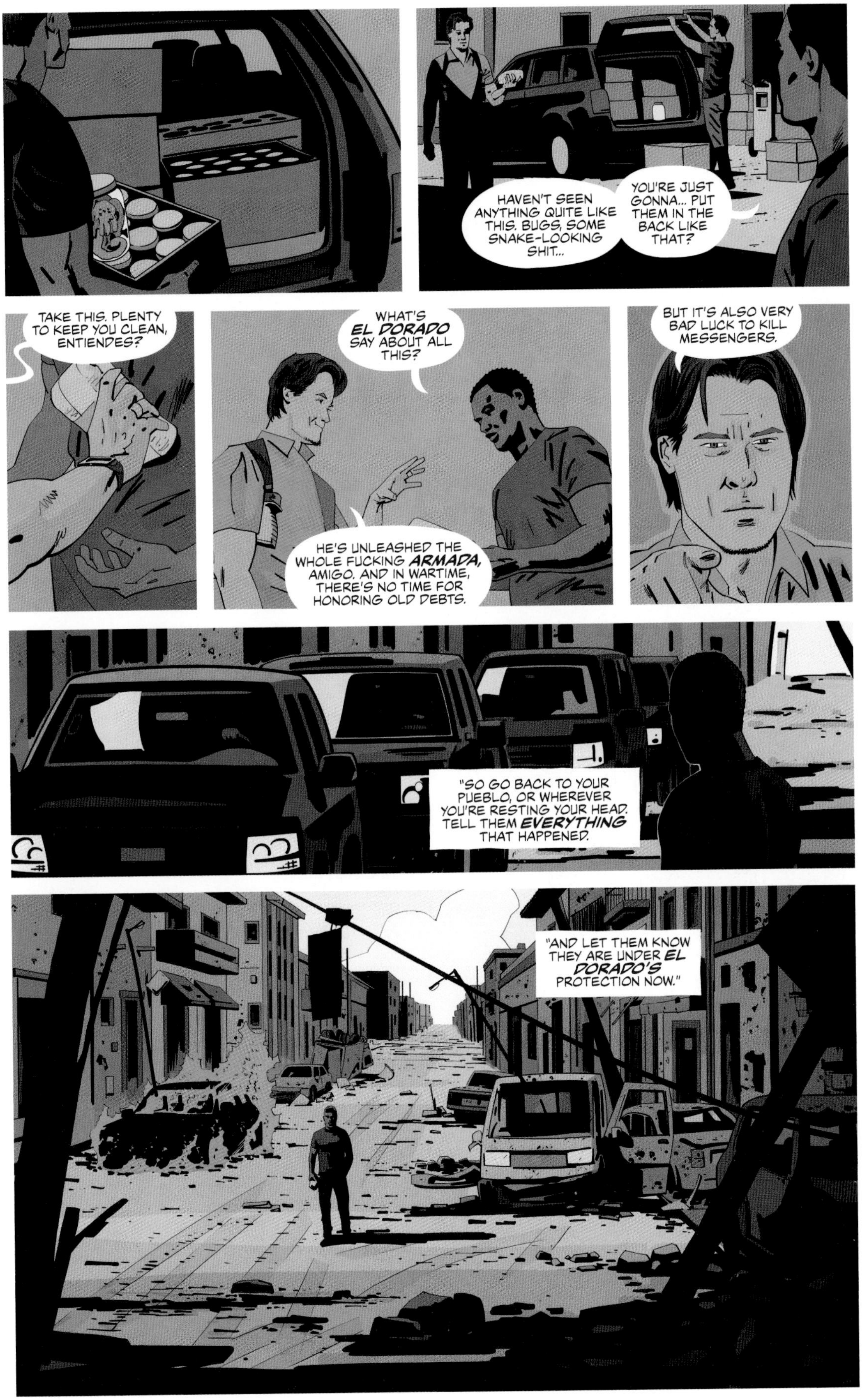
HAVEN'T SEEN ANYTHING QUITE LIKE THIS. BUGS, SOME SNAKE-LOOKING SHIT...
YOU'RE JUST GONNA... PUT THEM IN THE BACK LIKE THAT?
TAKE THIS. PLENTY TO KEEP YOU CLEAN, ENTIENDES?
WHAT'S *EL DORADO* SAY ABOUT ALL THIS?
HE'S UNLEASHED THE WHOLE FUCKING *ARMADA*, AMIGO. AND IN WARTIME, THERE'S NO TIME FOR HONORING OLD DEBTS.
BUT IT'S ALSO VERY BAD LUCK TO KILL MESSENGERS.
"SO GO BACK TO YOUR PUEBLO, OR WHEREVER YOU'RE RESTING YOUR HEAD. TELL THEM *EVERYTHING* THAT HAPPENED.
"AND LET THEM KNOW THEY ARE UNDER *EL DORADO'S* PROTECTION NOW."

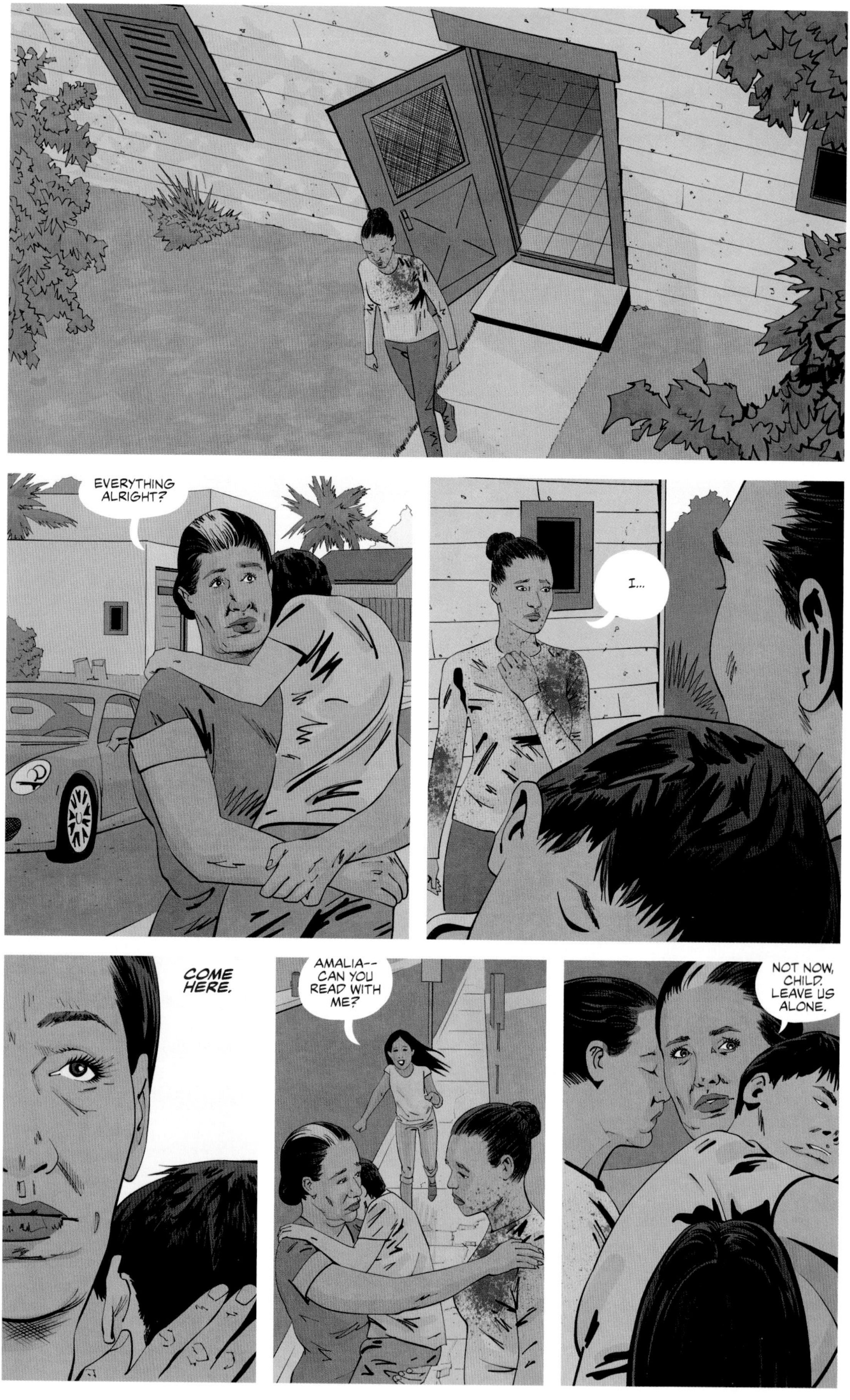
EVERYTHING ALRIGHT?
I...
COME HERE.
AMALIA-- CAN YOU READ WITH ME?
NOT NOW, CHILD. LEAVE US ALONE.

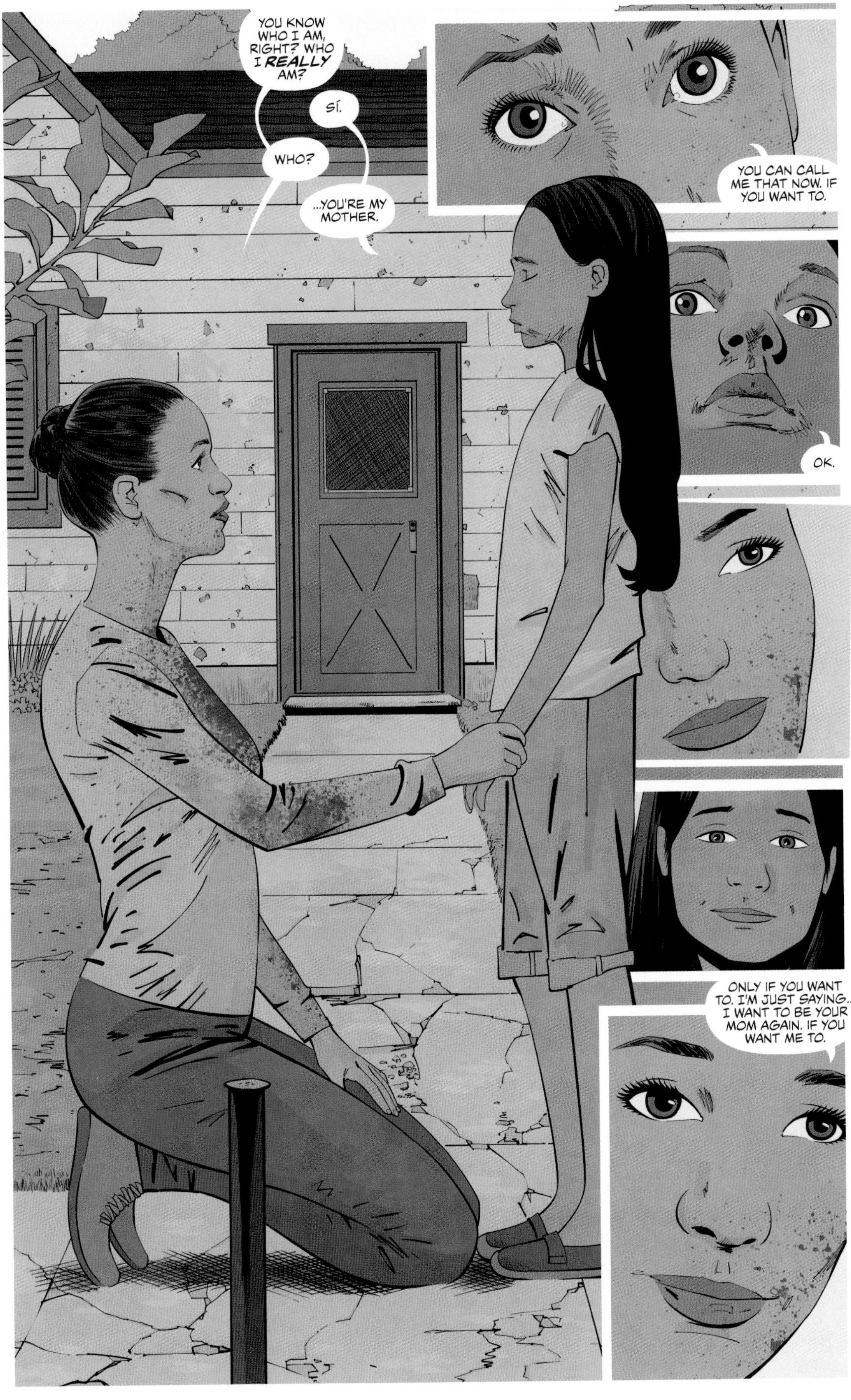
YOU KNOW WHO I AM, RIGHT? WHO I REALLY AM?
SÍ.
WHO?
...YOU'RE MY MOTHER.
YOU CAN CALL ME THAT NOW. IF YOU WANT TO.
OK.
ONLY IF YOU WANT TO. I'M JUST SAYING... I WANT TO BE YOUR MOM AGAIN. IF YOU WANT ME TO.

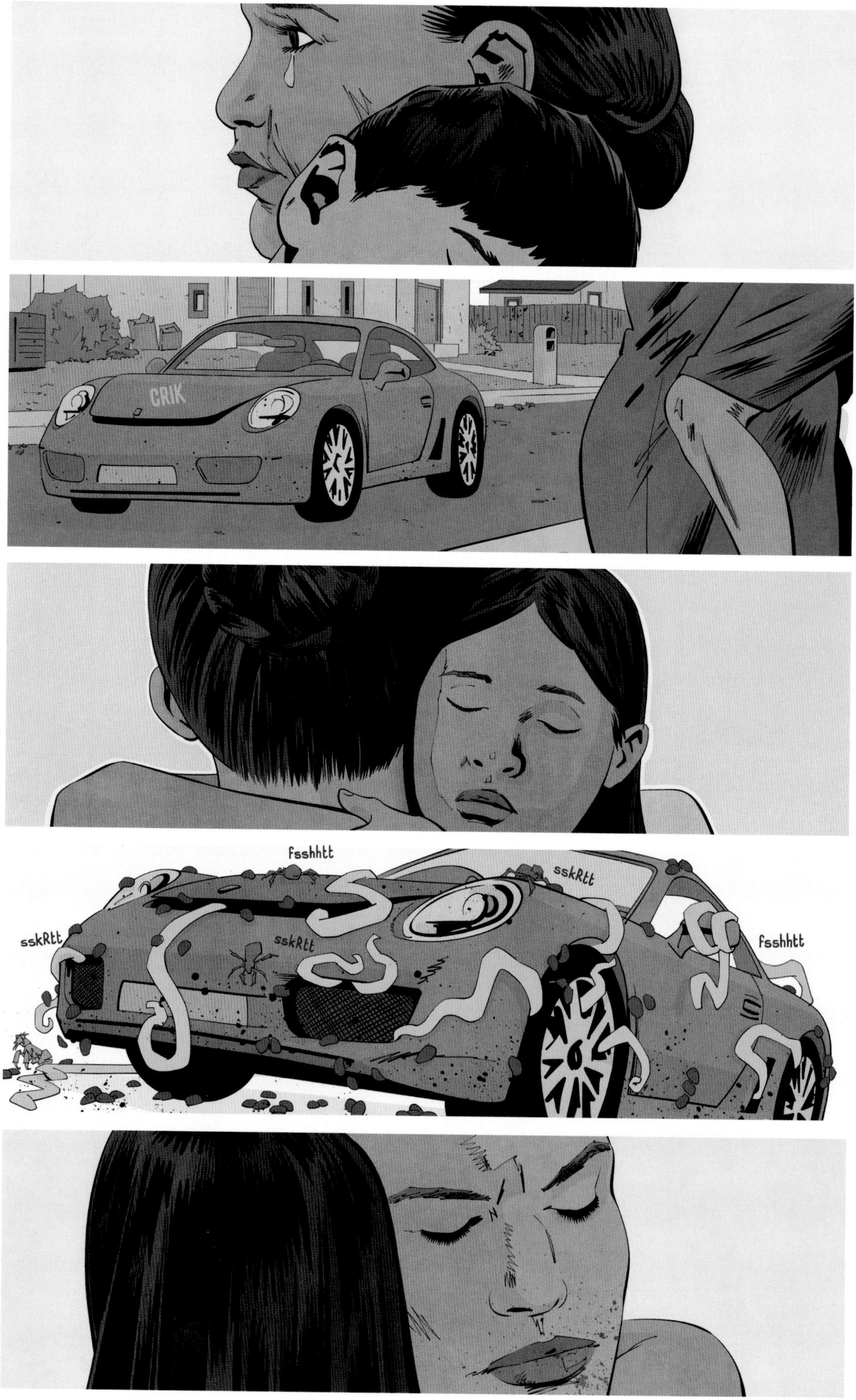
CRIK
fsshhtt
sskRtt
sskRtt
sskRtt
fsshhtt

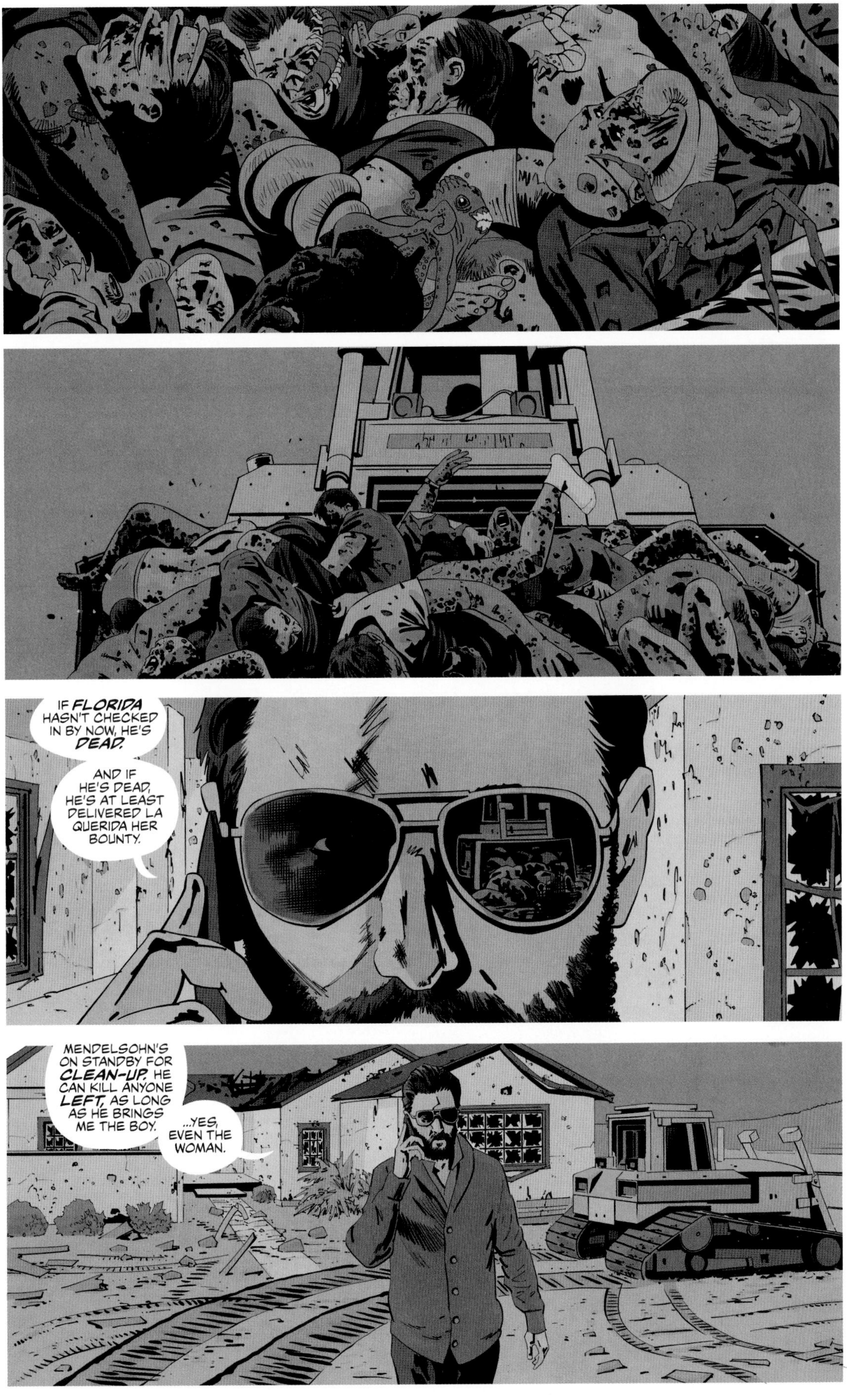
IF FLORIDA HASN'T CHECKED IN BY NOW, HE'S DEAD.
AND IF HE'S DEAD, HE'S AT LEAST DELIVERED LA QUERIDA HER BOUNTY.
MENDELSOHN'S ON STANDBY FOR CLEAN-UP. HE CAN KILL ANYONE LEFT, AS LONG AS HE BRINGS ME THE BOY.
...YES, EVEN THE WOMAN.

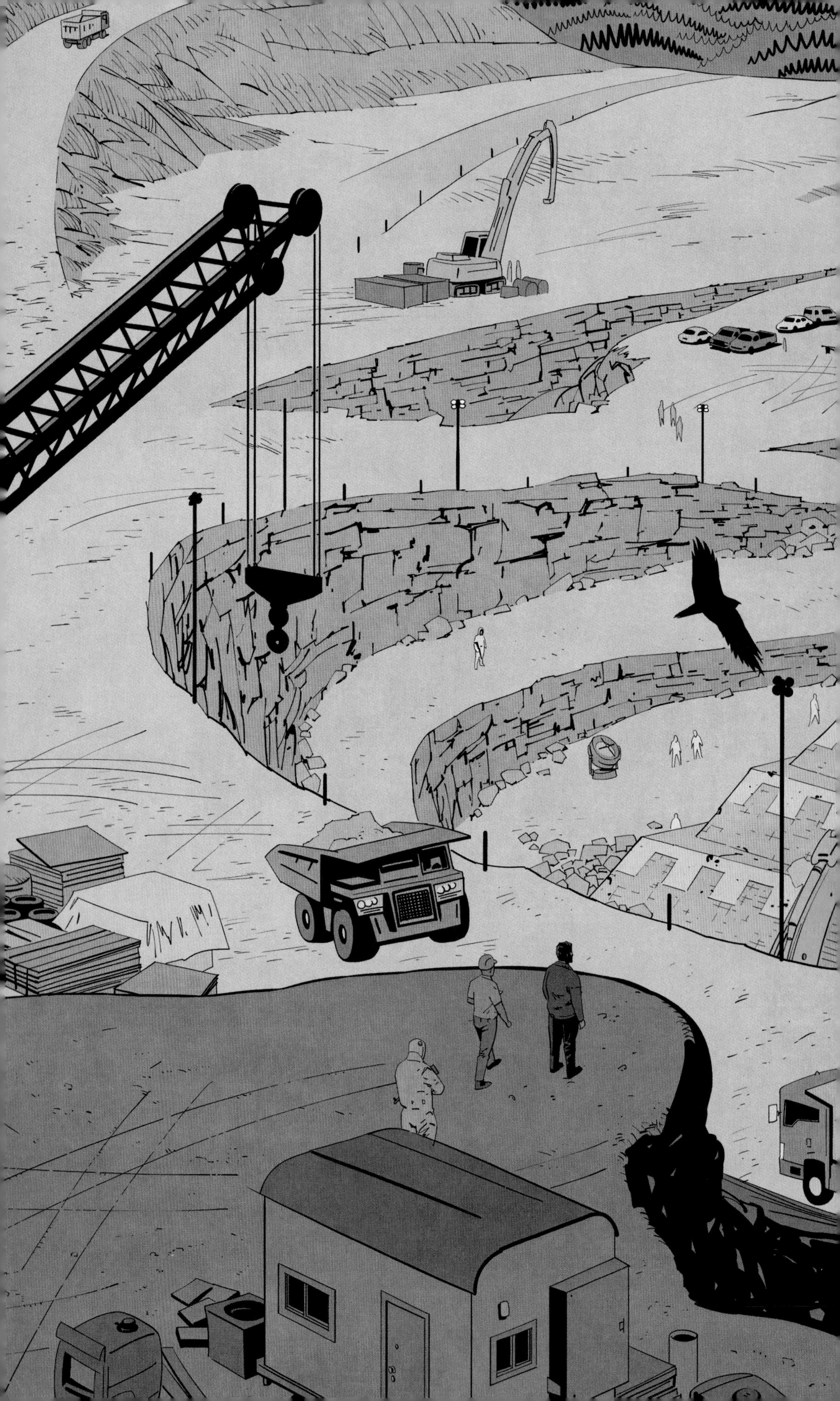

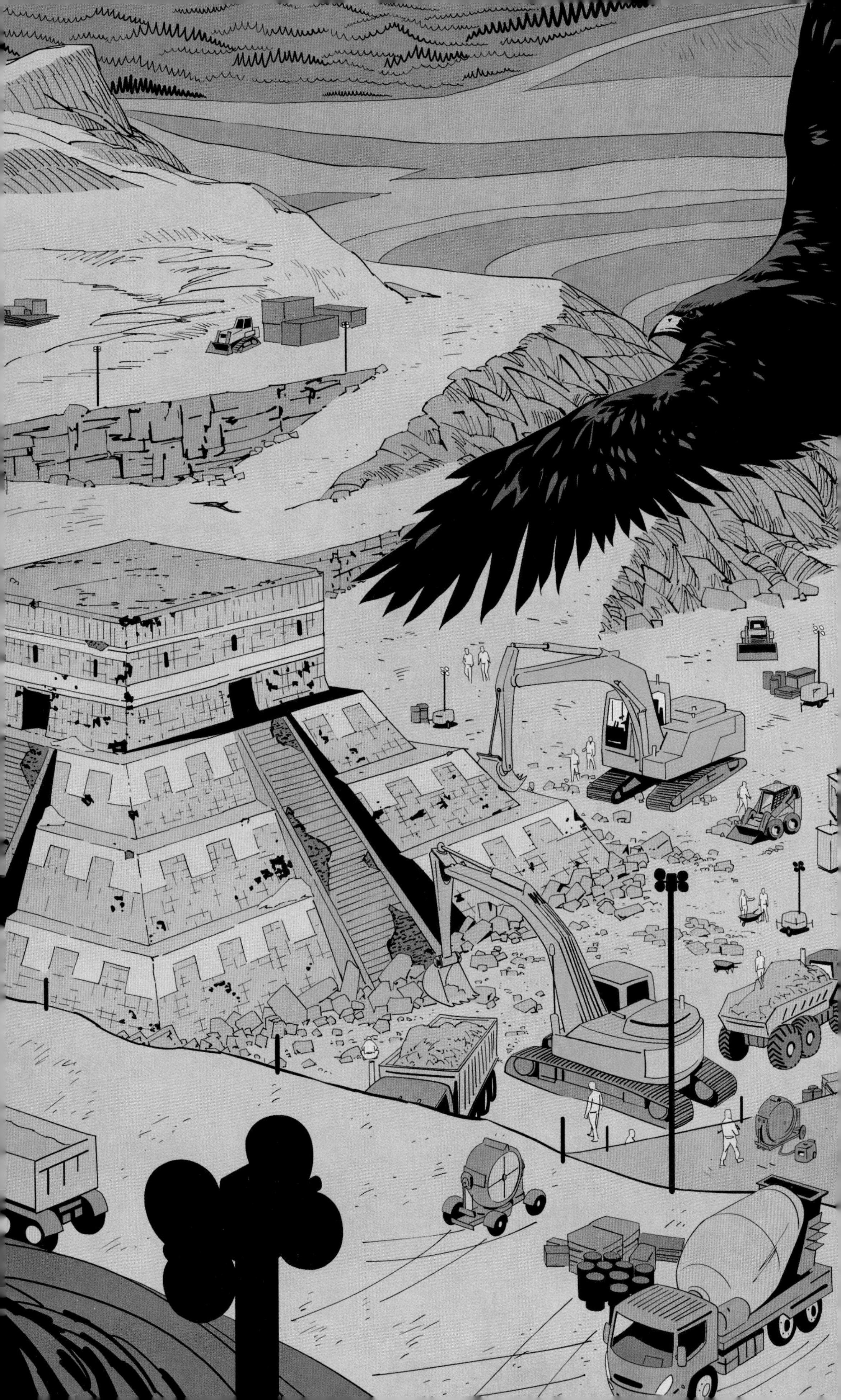

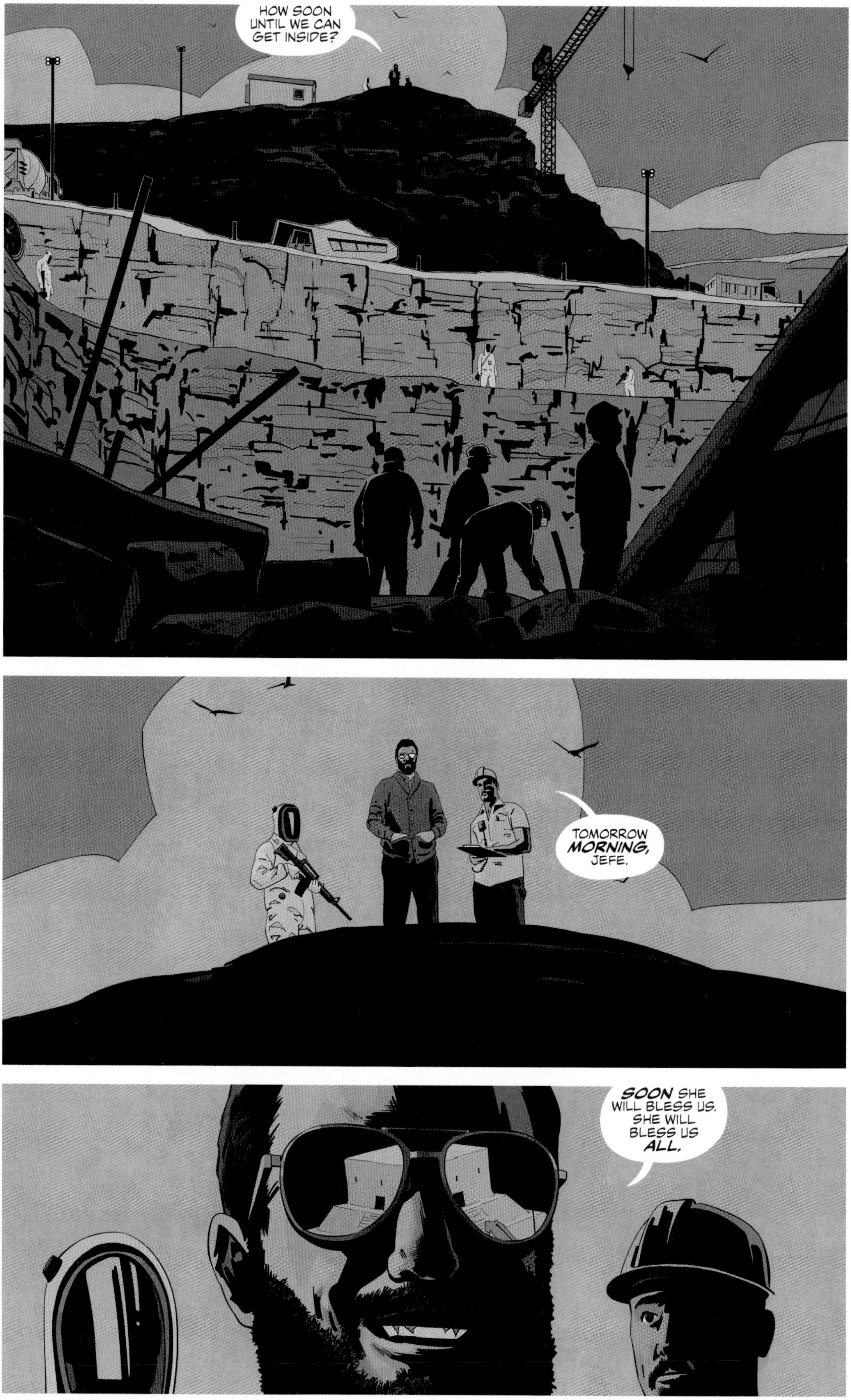
HOW SOON UNTIL WE CAN GET INSIDE?
TOMORROW MORNING, JEFE.
SOON SHE WILL BLESS US. SHE WILL BLESS US ALL.

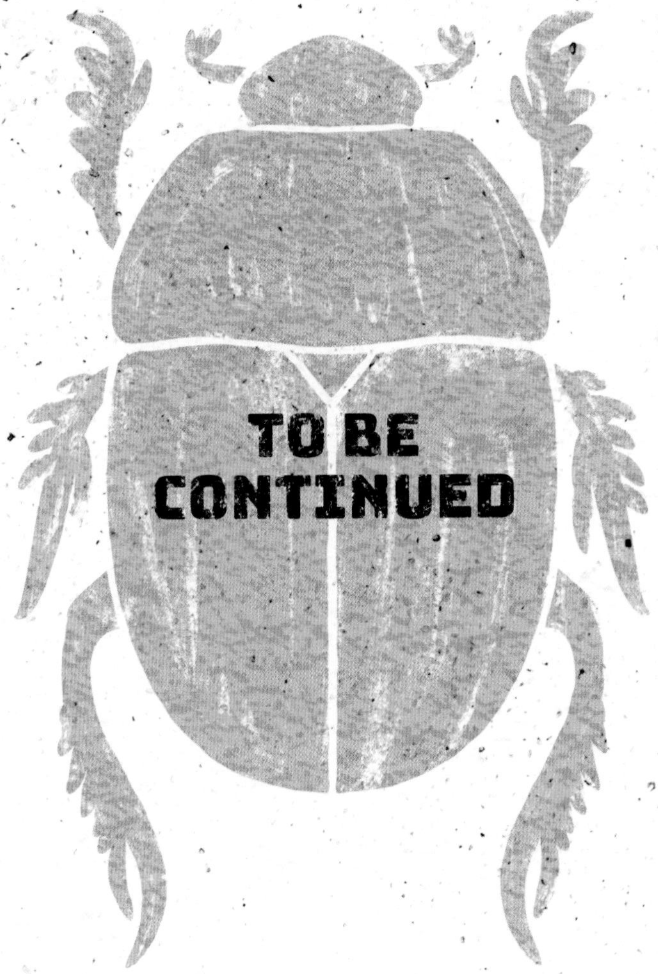
TO BE
CONTINUED

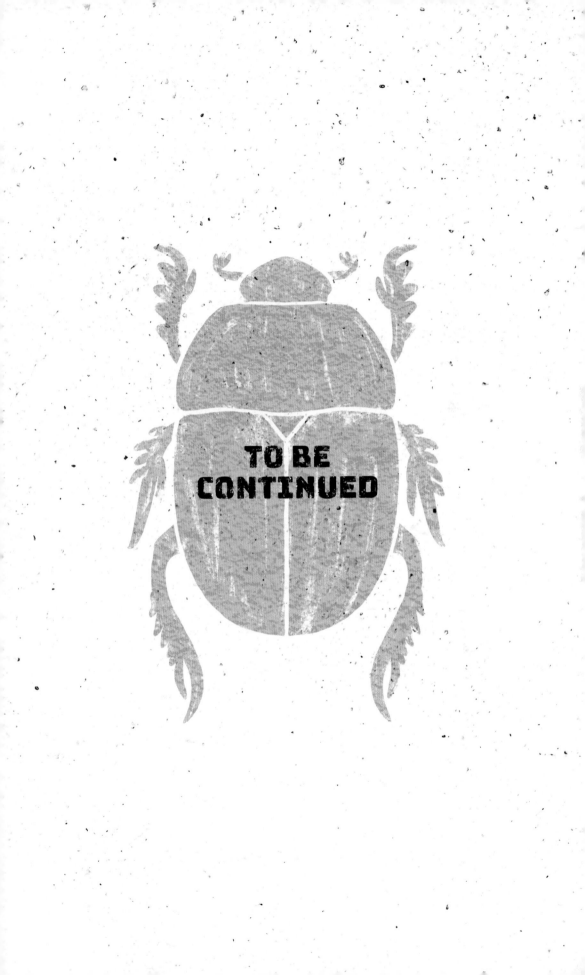

ALL I'M SAYING IS

WEIRD SHIT

BEGETS WEIRD SHIT

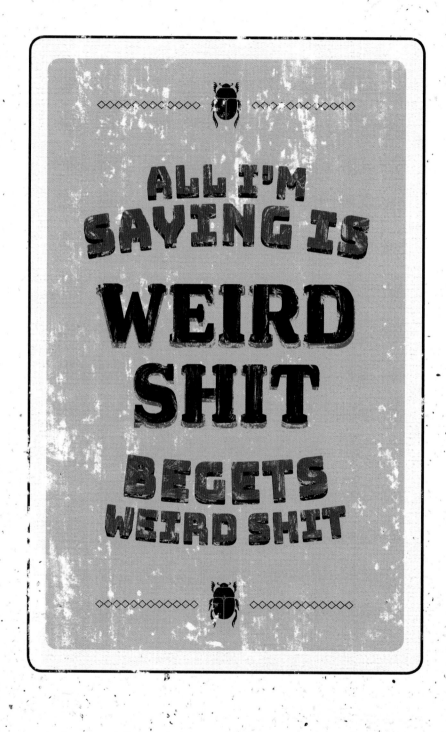

2

EL DIABLITO

For more tales from ROBERT KIRKMAN and SKYBOUND

Daniel Warren Johnson Mike Spicer
EXTREMITY
VOLUME TWO WARRIOR

REDNECK
Donny CATES Lisandro ESTHERREN Dee CUNNIFFE
VOLUME TWO
The Eyes Upon You

VOL. 1: ARTIST TP
ISBN: 978-1-5343-0242-6
$16.99

VOL. 2: WARRIOR TP
ISBN: 978-1-5343-0506-9
$16.99

VOL. 1: DEEP IN THE HEART TP
ISBN: 978-1-5343-0331-7
$16.99

VOL. 2: THE EYES UPON YOU
ISBN: 978-1-5343-0665-3
$16.99

BIRTHRIGHT
FATHERHOOD

VOL. 1: HOMECOMING TP
ISBN: 978-1-63215-231-2
$9.99

VOL. 2: CALL TO ADVENTURE TP
ISBN: 978-1-63215-446-0
$12.99

VOL. 3: ALLIES AND ENEMIES TP
ISBN: 978-1-63215-683-9
$12.99

VOL. 4: FAMILY HISTORY TP
ISBN: 978-1-63215-871-0
$12.99

VOL. 5: BELLY OF THE BEAST TP
ISBN: 978-1-5343-0218-1
$12.99

VOL. 6: FATHERHOOD TP
ISBN: 978-1-53430-498-7
$14.99

MANIFEST DESTINY

VOL. 1: FLORA & FAUNA TP
ISBN: 978-1-60706-982-9
$9.99

VOL. 2: AMPHIBIA & INSECTA TP
ISBN: 978-1-63215-052-3
$14.99

VOL. 3: CHIROPTERA & CARNIFORMAVES TP
ISBN: 978-1-63215-397-5
$14.99

VOL. 4: SASQUATCH TP
ISBN: 978-1-63215-890-1
$14.99

VOL. 5: MNEMOPHOBIA & CHRONOPHOBIA TP
ISBN: 978-1-5343-0230-3
$16.99

VOL. 6: FORTIS & INVISIBILIA TP
ISBN: 978-1-5343-0513-7
$16.99

VOLUME 6: INVASION
BY KIRKMAN & AZACETA
OUTCAST

VOL. 1: A DARKNESS SURROUNDS HIM TP
ISBN: 978-1-63215-053-0
$9.99

VOL. 2: A VAST AND UNENDING RUIN TP
ISBN: 978-1-63215-448-4
$14.99

VOL. 3: THIS LITTLE LIGHT TP
ISBN: 978-1-63215-693-8
$14.99

VOL. 4: UNDER DEVIL'S WING TP
ISBN: 978-1-5343-0050-7
$14.99

VOL. 5: THE NEW PATH TP
ISBN: 978-1-5343-0249-5
$16.99

VOL. 6: INVASION TP
ISBN: 978-1-5343-0751-3
$16.99

THIEF OF THIEVES
VOLUME 6
"GOLD RUSH."

VOL. 1: "I QUIT."
ISBN: 978-1-60706-592-0
$14.99

VOL. 2: "HELP ME."
ISBN: 978-1-60706-676-7
$14.99

VOL. 3: "VENICE."
ISBN: 978-1-60706-844-0
$14.99

VOL. 4: "THE HIT LIST."
ISBN: 978-1-63215-037-0
$14.99

VOL. 5: "TAKE ME."
ISBN: 978-1-63215-401-9
$14.99

VOL. 6: "GOLD RUSH."
ISBN: 978-1-53430-037-8
$14.99

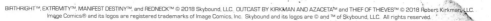